ZOMBIE FALLOUT 11
ETNA STATION

By Mark Tufo

DevilDog Press

SWANVILLE, MAINE

Edited by Sheila Shedd

Cover art by Dane@ebooklaunch

Dedications:

To the missus - we've come so far, this is one more step in our journey.

To my dedicated beta readers - Giles Batchelor, Kristen Beltz, Patti Reilly and Vanessa McCutcheon, I truly appreciate all you do!

To the men and women of the Armed Services and the First Responders - You will always have a place in my heart.

To you my dear reader - Thank you for coming on the journey thus far, hope you enjoy the ride!

Prologue

WHERE DOES ONE begin when the end has already happened? The zombie apocalypse has not been at all what I'd envisioned. I thought I was going to be with a group of my best friends, drinking beer on the roof of some sporting goods superstore, keeping score of the heads we blasted off from hordes of the undead, taking bets on who could kill the most, even playing "take a drink" every time you missed or hit or maybe both. What the hell, wasn't like any of us were going in to work the next day. In this fantasy world, our walls were impregnable, our ammo unlimited, plenty of food, beer, and buxom babes—sorry, hon. There would be a massive underground bunker loaded with all manner of cool, military grade weaponry, and occasionally we would have to fight off some rogue people—all the time swearing and high-fiving each other because we were the good guys. Obviously, I had created this farcical world long before I got married and had a family. It was understandable. Before the z-poc, I was mired in the drudgeries of everyday life: job I could barely stand, paid barely enough to feed us and keep a roof over our heads. Mortgage, credit card debt, expanding waistline…the slow siphoning of my soul through a silly straw as I sat for countless lost days in rush hour traffic. For what?

Gone were the days of reckless partying, sports cars,

perceived freedom, hanging with old friends, and God, I missed that easy time. Then it was about kids going back to school, Christmas shopping, all manner of school events, every season's multiple practices and games, summer vacation going by way too fast. Soak, wash, rinse, repeat; the rut got a little deeper every year. Maybe I had a little wish, just a quietly nagging urge to get out of that rut and take back some of those good times. Then *they* came. Now I can think of little else but that safe, sweet routine of family and wholeness; I want nothing other than that life back. Yeah, the rut. The traffic. The fucking seasonal decorations—the things that I thought were just about the absolute worst that could happen were, in hindsight, that which I missed the most.

It started more or less how I figured it would. One moment normal stuff, next moment dozens of zombies, then hundreds of them, then thousands. Civilization came to a screeching halt; everyone still human went into survival mode. Some wanted to help, stay human, keep sane. Too many others wanted to take advantage, to live out every sick and twisted fantasy that ran through their diseased skulls.

There was the rise of the super-predator, Eliza, an infected vampire that found she could control the hordes and wield them to do her bidding. Through the looking glass of fate and destiny, the Talbot bloodline became ground zero for her revenge. Yes, to a certain extent we pay for the sins of our father, but for how long are we on the hook? How far back does guilt extend? Are the direct descendants of Benedict Arnold still branded traitors? What about Typhoid Mary? Do her children pay restitution for all she sickened? Centuries ago someone at the very roots of the Talbot tree was a sadistic vampire who turned Eliza, and for all those centuries afterward she had sought out every offshoot and branch of that large, gnarled tree, doing her best to hack to pieces the entire lineage.

We won and we lost, but the cost was exorbitant. So many friends, so many family members gone. Homes destroyed, memories buried, the urgency of living moment to moment at the fore. We lived on the edge, only the fittest survived. We did things that only months before would have been unthinkable. We forged, clawed and carved out an existence; but we kept ourselves intact. I and those around me did our absolute fucking damnedest to keep each other safe against insurmountable and increasingly difficult odds. But I knew it, we all knew it. We stood within a sand castle inches away from the rising tide. Our future was in jeopardy; we had doubts, even of seeing another morning. We were a stranded, marooned bunch and eventually, we would all be voted off the island in the most unpleasant way possible. With Deneaux's return and the technology she brought with her, we were able to scope out other settlements, fragmented lifelines at best, but it was something to cling to.

We packed up all that we could carry and left our ghosts behind. It was not an easy decision; there was a comfort and a measure of safety staying at my brother Ron's house. Though oftentimes, the fortress we created took on the feel of a prison; the cost of security is usually freedom. We were as tied to that house as a beached whale, and you know how that goes, no quarter asked for, no quarter received. We struck out, and now we found ourselves on the road with a mean old crow of a woman, one more deadly than an asp and just as likely to strike. A baby that most likely carries the zombie virus; she will be either the key to unlocking a cure or bringing death to those still alive. As if that weren't terrifying enough, there is at least one, possibly two, seriously pissed off vampires on our tail, as well as Knox, a despotic dictator wannabe who is out for blood. Needless to say, we're moving as fast as we can.

We can't imagine what the future holds, nor what lies ahead but strangely enough, we still have hope, though it seems to be in dwindling supply. We have our will, and it stands oak strong, but we've all seen what a really stiff breeze can do to even the mightiest of trees with the deepest of roots. I have family, I have friends, and yeah, even an enemy or two within my ranks, but they're my ranks and I'm going to do everything that I can to make sure we all make it to Etna Station. At this community in Washington state, we may have a chance to rebuild, to plant some roots, to take back control of our lives, to strike some sort of an accord with whatever deity may exist and find our way back to normality; whatever that looks like now, and if such a thing still exists. One thing I know for certain: I fucking hate zombies. I'm sure there are worse things out there, but right now, for the life of me, I can't imagine what that would be.

CHAPTER ONE
MIKE JOURNAL ENTRY 1

"SERIOUSLY, TALBOT. I mean at some point; every person has not given a fuck but to live your life like that? Well that's just unique. A fuck free existence, zero fucks given. Like when fucks were being handed out you went to get a pulled pork sandwich or some shit." BT was walking around the truck, alternating between throwing his hands to the heavens or smacking them against the sides of his head. This was BT's usual reaction to just about everything I did.

One inconvenient thing about traveling on the road with no home base is that there are still the necessary calls of nature. Ever been in a car with even just one kid? You're lucky if you can go more than ten miles without their little bladders needing to be relieved. It's like somehow it shrinks on road trips, and as a parent, I knew this. Regardless of that fact, for some unfathomable reason when we would stop for gas, I would invariably get my kids some giant bottles of Gatorade or jugs of Mountain Dew and then I would get pissed off when five minutes later we were pulling off of the highway to avoid a natural disaster happening in the back seat. I've seen geysers from a safe distance; I had no desire to experience one up-close. I always added an hour to our ETA just for bathroom breaks and that was with three kids. We now had seven, including the two babies, who constantly needed fresh diapers, and that's something *everyone* wants to stop for. Carol's system wasn't what it used to be, and Trip would randomly call for a piss break even immediately after having just gone, almost like he'd forgotten why he'd been out of the truck.

We were making horrible time—could barely get out of our own way. There was no doubt that we were going to need to get a bus or an RV with built-in facilities; pulling over every ten fucking minutes? This was too slow and entirely too dangerous. The kids, Trip included, would damn near drop trousers in the middle of the road, none of them had a modicum of modesty. Well, except for Porkchop who preferred to conceal his business behind a small bush or something, but he always seemed to find one that only covered his middle third, his ass and face sticking out as he squatted. I saw his scrunched-up shit-face more times than I care to remember, yet no one ever said anything to him. It's possible we were all too fascinated; whatever he was eating seemed to be passing like jagged rocks. The adults would usually privy up behind the nearest tree, staying as close to the road as possible. It was Carol that always felt the need to get some fifty feet off the road. It made absolutely no sense; her knees were bad, making the uneven walks painful and slow and even painfully slow. We all dreaded Carol's nature calls.

No matter how many times I told her that it was dangerous and unnecessary to get that far away from our rides, she would completely blow me off. "It's either completely private or it's right here in the car itself." If she hadn't been riding with me I would have told her to just go ahead then. She was endangering all of us: herself, her spotter standing guard, and the rest of us as we just parked on the side of the road with an "old lady pissing in the woods," sign on our bumper. Sometimes I felt like she was doing this on purpose. A fair number of times she would go out, we'd wait, she'd come back and say she had not been able to go. It was like she was a thirteen-year-old girl at her own birthday party not asked to dance; a powerplay for attention, added drama to be noticed.

"Tracy, you need to talk to her," I said as I leaned against the car. It was our fourth stop of the day and she'd been in the woods for over fifteen minutes. "We can't keep sitting out here like this. Eventually someone is going to stumble across us."

"What do you want me to say? She's my mother. If she needs to go she needs to go."

"That's the problem. Half the time she doesn't need to."

"And you know this how?"

I looked at her questioningly. "Ew, no, I don't check. She always feels the need to tell me whether she went or not. It's like she goes out there to read the Sears catalog or something. She's making this harder than she has a right to." I was angry.

"Than she has a right to?" Tracy asked, I could see her building up a little cloud of anger within as well.

"Every time we stop, *every* time, whether she really needs to pee or not, she has to go damn near a quarter mile into the woods. And she needs help because the ground is about as level as a candy bar-loving teenager's face, so that's another person gone into the woods. Then she has to take breaks on the walk out because she gets tired, and it's even worse on the walk back."

"A quarter mile?"

"Alright—however far she can get in fifteen minutes. Don't get hung up on irrelevant details; the rest is completely true and that's why you're fighting the minutiae."

"Look at you and your big words."

"Ha! That is how I know you know I'm right; you're not arguing the point, you big straw-manner. She's going to get herself or someone else killed, Tracy. It's inevitable if she keeps this up, whatever this is."

Tracy's head sagged a bit. Who the hell wants to go and tell their parents they're being childish, or worse yet, that they have to piss too often? We'd had this conversation in the morning; two hours later when we had to stop again, I was the one that pulled guard duty for her.

We stopped, and Deneaux had some choice words. "At some point Michael, you will need to put the welfare of this group above hers," I exited the car. That I didn't immediately tell her to fuck off was all the proof I needed that this little exercise was getting under my skin. I mostly consider myself a low-key individual; BT and my wife would laugh if they knew I said that, but that is how I feel about myself. But shit, I'm still mostly human.

It reminded me of when I was back in cubicle city, working on the other side of a faux wall from Mort. He always talked louder than he needed to, constantly gnawed on hard food and you couldn't help but hear him crunch since he ate with his mouth open. When he wasn't talking or crunching he was whistling disco music from the seventies and tapping his pen off-beat. And, wait…the noise wasn't even the worst of it because when he would finally go silent, it wasn't a reprieve; that's when you knew he was concentrating on trying to release some vile gas into the atmosphere as quietly as possible. You heard the vinyl chair squeak as he tried to pull his ass cheeks apart to clear the release valve. Sometimes he was deadly silent; sometimes there was an ill-timed coughing fit just a moment too late to cover up the sound. The worst part–yeah you already know but whatever–his food of choice was some sort of curried bean paste with crispy fried onions on top. The thick fog, if given the opportunity, could completely clog up the nasal cavity.

You knew the cycle was about to repeat when the whistling resumed. Now, he wasn't my family, so as far as dealing with him, I figured I had three options: quit, (which I couldn't afford to do), beat the tar out of him (and get fired, or possibly some jail time, and as satisfying as it might be to break a few teeth and return the favor of fucking up his nose, I couldn't afford to do that either), or go to human resources. And what the hell was I supposed to tell them? He eats, whistles, and farts? Oh, I know a few of you are like. "Nice move d-bag. Why didn't you just put on your big-boy pants and confront him?"

Well, for your information, judgmental person that wasn't there and didn't suffer through this form of work abuse, I did. I talked to him at least a half a dozen times. When I stood up and asked him if maybe he could go outside before he polluted the air again, he lost it, started swearing at me and HE went to HR and told them I was harassing him. That I had singled him out over all others. When I was on an important phone call and could not hear because he was whistling about staying alive or some shit, I stood and asked him if he could lower the volume. Yeah, that went well, like asking a llama not to spit on you or a rabbit not to bite your finger, it's almost like that's their whole reason to be on Earth, to just shit on it, I mean. He got louder. I had to give him props though, he was dead on pitch.

When I finally went to HR, it took five times before they would even listen to me and not think that I was just belly-aching or pay-backing. Finally, I got this woman, Margo, the HR assistant, to come down to my desk. I told her to sit in my seat for just ten minutes. Of course, Mort was quiet. She was just starting to look at me as if to say I was full of shit, oh, but I knew what was happening. This was the calm before the storm. There were two or three squelches as he got his ass into position. He missed the sweet spot wildly, the quack from the low flying duck was clearly heard halfway across the office. The lung hacking coughing fit immediately followed.

Margo smirked at me. "That's a natural bodily function. I can't reprimand him for that." She was able to say this all the while Mort was coughing.

I held up a finger. "Wait one."

She turned back to my monitor. First, her nose twitched, her head cocked, then her nose crinkled and a grimace pinched her mouth as she turned away, she stood quickly. "I'll talk to Denise." Before she could get far enough away, Mort was whistling the soundtrack to Saturday Night Fever at ear-splitting decibels, maybe figuring that if he overwhelmed the sense of hearing no one would be able to smell the death that issued forth from his ass. She turned back and looked at me. "I'm so sorry."

Want to know the fucked-up part? HR and the company were so fearful about being called out on a civil liberties suit that instead of reprimanding Mort or something along those lines, they just picked him up and moved him to his own fucking office. And, they had to give him some completely made up promotion to justify it. Yep. The fucker farted his way up the corporate ladder; got a raise and everything. It's the Morts that prove the world is truly turned on its ear. The "Mortimer Maneuver" has even made its way into a few HR manuals.

Where the hell was I going with all this? Oh yeah, Deneaux. Damn Deneaux. She was right. Callous and crass, of course, but she was right, it was time to confront the problem.

"I'll say something to her tonight," Tracy said as she came up to my side and touched my shoulder. Carol was already shuffling off to the side of the road.

"Carol, I think this is plenty far enough." I told her, I had my arm up and under her armpit to keep her steady."

"Nonsense, we're hardly off the road."

I turned back, I couldn't even see the road. "This is far as we go." I attempted to extract my arm, she had it gripped.

"Have you no common decency? I'm far too modest to go with that many people around."

"Carol, there is no one around. Can't hear them, can't see them. I barely know the way back. Go here or don't." Yeah, slightly dickish on my part, but I'd heard my last Bee Gees song.

"You're leaving me here?" She had a lost and panicked expression on her face.

"What? No. I'm going to guard our perimeter while you do what you need to." My stomach was unsettled as I began to think that there might be more going on here.

"Thank you, Jacob," she said, looking straight at me then the clouds parted from her eyes. "What are you looking at, Michael?"

"Ah, nothing. Sorry. I'll be right over there."

I was leaning on a tree thinking about what I was going to say to Tracy when I heard movement through the woods. I pushed off and brought my rifle off my back and up, not yet to my shoulder, as I didn't have a clue what was out there. I was taught from a very early age to always identify what you were about to shoot at before you pull the trigger, and there were far too many of us in the general area to just start aiming willy-nilly. It sounded like it was twenty feet away and straight to our back. There shouldn't be anyone else this far out, but it wasn't a certainty. More noise came from our left. I began to move closer to where Carol was.

"What the fuck?" I asked when she wasn't where I had just left her. "Carol," I hissed, unwilling to speak any louder. I did not have a good feeling in my gut about this. More noise—the snap of a branch, the rustle of leaves being stepped on. More noise than one person with limited mobility could be expected to make. There was a line of somethings coming slowly, maybe even stealthily. A dog barked behind me, had to be Riley, it was deep, not the seal-bark of Henry nor the yip of Ben-Ben.

"Talbot!" BT shouted.

"Dammit," I whispered. I shouted back and my location was blown—then it wouldn't be a matter of if something was in here with me, but more a matter of how many. "Where the fuck are you, Carol?" I backed up a few feet into something that was more or less a clearing, although with fields of fire of roughly ten feet around, it wasn't much to hang a hat on, fifty feet would have been better.

"Talbot! Answer me! MJ says we've got company!" BT again shouted.

Something flashed past me on the right. I caught a glint of light off a watch or a bracelet. Safe to say it wasn't a herd of rabid deer finally turning the tables on Man. The first zombie that came into my circle of influence looked just as shocked as I did. I caught him just above his left eyeball, but the storm was just beginning. That shot was an effective dinner bell, and the zombies were going to answer it. I was again, cautiously backing up and continually scanning the area looking for another victim. I could hear people coming in from behind. The jig was up now.

"Straight ahead!" I turned my head slightly, shouting over my shoulder: "Zombies!" I was barely able to turn to my left quick enough to get the speeder that was making a bee line to me right through the vegetation. One in the chest spun him slightly off course, the next in the forehead stopped all advancement. The woods were crawling with them; whatever slow, furtive movements they had been using to get close to us were out the window. They were crashing through the woods at us now. Guns erupted behind me as targets ran past.

"Carol!" I yelled, desperate for some answer. I heard a significant-sized tree snap; the ground vibrated under my feet when it landed. Bulker was the only thing that could do something like that. They were inclined to say "fuck it" and go through rather than around impediments. Two full magazines had seemed a little like overkill for a bathroom break, but I'd had a weird instinct. Next time, assuming there was one, I would bring another couple. I kept backing up, staying aware of anything behind me that could trip me up. Here he came, Paul Bunyan himself, with a trio of speeders hiding behind his bulk like soldiers following a tank. I'd learned my lesson on the bridge standoff; their heads were entirely too fortified. Sure, I could drill through eventually with the 5.56s but I didn't have eventually. I hacked at his knees like a wiry little defensive back would against a mammoth running back. Lord knows I'd been in that spot more than once. What I had lacked in size on the football field I had made up for with tenacity, determination, and a blind willingness to sacrifice myself.

Shooting his knees out from under him was like taking a chainsaw to an oak. It took several seconds but he stumbled then fell to the side.

"Tim-ber, motherfucker," I said as I worked on killing the column of zombies behind him before they could fan out now that their walking wall had been felled. The gunfire was no more than twenty feet behind me and I was not all that keen being ahead of the firing line. Zombies were zipping by on both sides. I was doing my best to keep an eye on the ones to my front and I would have to trust that the people behind me would take care of their fields of fire. The odds Carol had been passed up were slim, her only hope would have been to hide. But if she had another episode, which I was thinking might be early onset Alzheimer's, she was just as likely to ask one of the zombies directions to the bank.

She'd had other lapses before, but I'd just chalked it off to stress or maybe that it was me, that I just had too much going on to pay attention to what she'd said. Thinking back, there had been many small indicators, like when she asked when her sister, who'd been in Wisconsin at the time of the z-poc, was going to be home for dinner. Or the time I found her in Ron's bathroom looking under the sink for her shoes. Or when she'd stood at a light switch for over five minutes flipping it up and down. It had been Tracy that had finally ushered her away. I guess in hindsight, you'd have to group those individual incidents, *then* they didn't seem so small, but still, they were harmless—nothing compared to wandering off in a war zone. I felt guilt for not noticing how bad she'd gotten. I could say that overlook on my part had most likely gotten her killed, not to mention it had indirectly put us all in danger, myself included.

I had a speeder lined up just as that brain splitting shriek blistered through my skull—I fired wide right. Unlike earlier screeches, this continued on like a professional opera singer belting out a glass breaking aria. It warbled after thirty seconds before mercifully stopping. I'd fought through the mind-shredding sound spear to kill the speeder. A few more steps and I found myself abreast of BT.

He looked in pain as he nodded to me. Had a feeling there

were going to be plenty of headaches to go around tonight. Justin and Gary materialized on my other side. We all had grim looks of determination on our faces.

"Where's grandma?" Justin shouted when we had a small break in the action.

I shook my head slightly from side to side. He looked like he was either going to start swearing or crying or a healthy dose of both. Mourning would happen; we didn't have that luxury, if it could be called that, to do it right now. The earth was shaking and that could only mean one thing.

"Bulkers," BT said. "We need to go back." I was in agreement, but there was a chance, albeit an ever-decreasing one, that Carol was still out there. How could I just abandon her? An argument could be made she'd abandoned me, but even I had trouble taking that side of it.

"Where's Carol?" BT asked as if he was just remembering why I was out here.

"I don't know," I told him as I fired.

"You lost her?"

We were backing up. I got the incredulity in his voice, would be like losing the pants that you were currently wearing. We were getting close to the road, I could hear Riley barking like mad, there was more gunfire as our position had been surrounded. Going out to look for Carol was out of the question with the rest of the troop in trouble. An entire line of bulkers formed to our front and they were running. Flight reflex was in full effect; yet we stood our ground.

"Overrun! Get in the cars!" I was screaming as I fired. I don't even know if it was possible I could be heard over the reports. "Let's go!" I told those around me, there was no way we had the firepower to keep them at bay. I had to wrench Justin's shoulder to get him moving. He pulled away hard; it was Gary that finally urged him to give up his spot.

"I go when you go," BT said as we backed up carefully. Heard a roaring growl so unfamiliar I couldn't begin to identify it, but it got me wondering what new nightmare the zombies had prepared for us.

I saw a tuft of brown on an animal so incredibly large, that I thought my eyes were playing tricks on me. My first inclination was to think back to that zombie ape at the Demense Building. BT and I had both moved with a purpose to get to the roadway. It was as I had feared, we were a small group of dog-paddlers surrounded by hungry sharks. Tracy, Deneaux, Gary, Justin, and Travis were firing to keep the zombies off the cars and to give BT and myself a way to get back.

"Come on, BT, Mike, everyone is waiting on you two!" This from Tracy. She was half in the car half out and still firing. I absolutely realize beyond a shadow of a doubt this was not the time, but damn she looked fine. Her long red hair flowing out behind her, she was like a warrior goddess. It was not going to be good when that war face turned its gaze on me and caught me off task. A bulker had broken through the brush to our side, crashed into a car, destroyed the rear quarter panel and spun the car almost ninety degrees, there were screams from inside the vehicle. One of those doing the screaming was Carol. I thought it was a trick of my tortured mind. I got a quick look from Justin questioning what the fuck was going on. I had nothing for him. Another bulker came out close to the other. These were easily six-hundred pound, virally altered beasts, heads as round and big as blue ribbon 4H pumpkins, and I knew from experience they were mostly bone protecting the peanut-brain inside.

Another hit to that car and there was a good chance it would bend the axle or at the very least shove metal into the tire, and a flat right now was as bad as the transmission falling out. I turned my attention to the new threat, never realizing I was up next. I'd fired off two rounds, but before the third could exit the barrel I was blindsided. I've been hit a few times in my life where I figured my brains were going to leak out my nose. Twice in football, I had been so fixated on the person with the ball I hadn't given a thought to the angry lineman downfield doing his blocking. Once, in Afghanistan, we had been sweeping an old building with an army unit we had met up with. I had been watching a fellow Marine's six when he had gone into a room. He'd no sooner stepped in when an IED exploded. The force that propelled him into me drove me head-first into the far wall. If not for the helmet I'd been wearing, I would have left whatever gray matter I had left smeared all over that building. None of it, even all of it combined, didn't add up to the bone-rattling, jaw shifting, teeth-rattling hit I'd just absorbed from that bulker. My ass crushed the door panel and my elbow broke through the passenger-side window; my head whipped down and bounced off the roof of the car with enough force that I was sure I had a concussion, judging by the dent my skull-bone left in the metal. He was crushing me between his weight and the car.

He twitched occasionally–I think that was from the bullets his bulk was absorbing. I was rapidly heading into unconsciousness as the air had been forced from my lungs and I hadn't yet been able to restock the supply. I could feel hands on my back as those inside the car were trying desperately, but hopelessly, to free me. The car was rocking as the bulker was digging his heels in. I don't know if he was trying to make a puree out of me or was trying to move the car; he was effectively doing both. I would have poured to the ground if I'd had any space around me. I had no power to hold my legs up. Black encroached my vision, I was going down for the count, then there was air. Sweet, blessed air was pulled into my lungs as a clawed paw, twice the size of my head, swept past. There was screaming, barking, yelling, a cacophony I could not process as my brain greedily absorbed the necessary oxygen to keep it functioning.

Arms were reaching down to pull me up and through the window, my lack of help was hindering them. I was basically dead weight. Someone inside the car was channeling their inner hulk as I was being yanked up and in; at one point I thought my spine was going to snap as I was halfway in, the small of my back pivoted on the door frame. The beast knocked my legs, and I was ripped away from the grip of those in the car. Can't say I stopped to wonder what it was going to feel like to be ripped apart by a zombie ape. The only thing I could hope was it would be quick. I crumpled to the ground face first, tore up my lips and nose as I bounced off the pavement. I got up on all fours, blood leaking from my face; it was all I could do to lift my head. I was staring at the back haunches of…what the fuck was it? Not an ape, so? It was a bear, an extremely large Brad Pitt *Legends of the Fall* grizzly. My head spun. Grizzly, ape, what did it matter? I wobbled as I tried to get up. My body felt as if I'd had an extended ride in a paint shaker. I was almost mad the bear wasn't hurrying the fuck up, like, don't make me go through all this effort trying to defend myself if, in the end, I was going to be filleted anyway.

I got up on two unsteady stems. A part of me thought that maybe this would bring the size of the bear down, but if anything, it accentuated just how gargantuan it was. My rifle was a few feet away on the ground, laying there about as useful as a Viagra-induced erection in church. The bear had its back to me. Now the question was: could I get my rifle and put enough rounds through to stop this monster before it eviscerated me. I was so fixated on the animal itself I had barely taken notice of what it was doing. Two bulkers had been decimated, puddles of yellowish-red blubber flowed down the slight incline we were on. Ribbons of meat-filled intestines slithered out of their bodies; one had his head nearly completely removed and had been effectively disqualified from playing the crush game anymore. The other still had some semblance of survival mode in it, but even at its best it was nothing compared to the bear. The bulker's arms were out as it tried to pull the bear in for a, yeah, bearhug, but the animal was having none of it. It roared and swung those powerful arms tipped with six-inch claws like a crazed kid surrounded by bullies and nothing left to lose. A block of cheese in a food processor stood a better chance than that over-sized zombie.

Speeders were honing in on our spot. Lord knows that bear could have fed a village and they knew it as well…they'd seen the cave paintings of the tiny humans spearing a mammoth. I bent to grab my weapon and almost pitched over for the effort. I used the car for support, leaned against it and was going to help the enemy of my enemy. I hoped he would consider us even and wasn't fighting off the zombies merely to have me all to himself. I fired off a round just as the second bulker crashed to the ground with a thud somehow louder than the report of the bullet. The bear looked back at me; if it wanted to do me in it wouldn't have taken much more than the flicking of its stumpy tail. It seemed to realize I wasn't aiming for it, but when an eight hundred-pound, all-muscle animal with blood dripping from its claws and mouth looks at you, well, fuck…I couldn't help but swivel my muzzle its way. Riley came from somewhere, she was barking ferociously at me, drool streaming from her snout in runnels. For a hopeful second, I thought man's best friend was going to intercede on my behalf. I'm not the most intelligent being walking the planet, I realize this, but in survival mode, I have instincts that have been honed out of necessity by the events constantly swirling around me. Riley wasn't protecting me; she was protecting the bear. Why? What the fuck for? Didn't matter. Her barking took me out of the picture and the bear went back to doing what it did exceptionally well, and that was killing zombies. The speeders might as well have been mosquitoes crushed between the clapping hands of a human for how easily they were dispatched.

The sound of snapping bones dominated, a brittle forest in the midst of a category-five hurricane would make the same breaking crashing creaking sounds. For the first time in this battle, we were switching from the defensive to the offensive. There was breathing room between us and the enemy. The bear hitched a few times; its massive chest puffed out as it caught its breath. I stepped up and edged past it to keep firing at the dwindling enemy. Riley stayed glued to my hip, in between myself and what was truly the apex predator in this equation. When what was left of the zombies realized they'd been routed, they made an uncharacteristic move: they left. Said it before and will say it again–I fucking hate smart zombies. Now I found myself in the uncomfortable position of having a grizzly bear to my back and at least a half-dozen rifles pointed in our direction.

"Mike?" BT asked nervously.

I was slowly moving to the side, away from the bear. It, she, I think, swiveled that massive head to me.

"Who's a good girl?" I asked, my voice trembling.

"Are you trying to sweet talk that bear?" Tracy asked, she had her rifle to her shoulder and was coming closer, the bear looked over my shoulder and roared, the left side of my face got slathered in a heavy portion of blown spit.

"Got a better idea?" I asked.

There was a delay in responding. "No…no I don't."

"Um, hon, maybe put the gun down." I had bent over and placed mine on the ground and was standing with my hands up by my chest, palms exposed in a "I don't want any trouble here," pose, although holding anything less than a bazooka wasn't going to matter much anyway. Riley rubbed her side up against the bear; she had either lost her mind or knew the bear somehow. Not even remotely sure how that could be possible; it was more likely she just knew a winning side when she saw one.

If I'd been looking down on my body, I'd be wondering if this could get any weirder, but from my position I was just hoping I would end the day with my head still firmly resting on my shoulders. An older man burst through the woods, out of breath and carrying a rifle that looked like a Civil War throwback, a muzzleloader.

"ThornGrip? Riley, is that you, girl?" he asked taking in all that was happening and what had not yet happened. Wouldn't have been tough to realize he was outgunned and out-manned, definitely not out-animaled, though. "You

Talbot?" he asked, looking at me.

Simple as it sounds, that is one loaded question. Not many people that knew my name were looking to shake my hand when the world was normal, certainly there were a lot fewer now.

Deneaux had moved closer to the man, her pistol up and squarely aimed at the side of his head. "Michael?" she asked.

"No," I shook my head slightly.

ThornGrip, I presumed that was her name, roared and charged Deneaux. The cold as ice woman didn't flinch as she pulled the hammer back. The bear knew what that meant and pulled up short. She was snorting and huffing. Safe to say if Deneaux shot the man, she would be ThornGrip's next victim. I warred within myself…how bad would that actually be? Would suck for the man, whom I figured to be an innocent in this, but we'd be rid of Deneaux. And really, that would be a fitting end for her, would it not? This was not a woman that was going to go peaceably in her sleep.

"Everyone take a breath. Weapons down!" came out a little louder than I'd expected. Don't you judge me for the fear and adrenaline pulsing through me.

Deneaux eased the hammer back, I think she did the math as well. Maybe with a little more distance she could have killed the man and placed enough well-aimed shots to stop the bear, but here and now? No way. It was way too close. Even if the animal slammed into her already dead, it would cause her massive impact injuries she could not sustain. She put her hands up, though she still held on to the pistol.

"My name's Harold!" the man shouted, maybe hoping that introductions would keep the bullets from flying.

"Michael, I'm Michael Talbot. You know Riley?"

"Ah, yup," he said in the traditional Mainer way. "She came to me a while back pretty banged up. Her, another dog, a cat, and the biggest damn bear I'd ever seen."

Ben-Ben was yipping like crazy, his face completely smushed up against the window as he desperately sought a way out, his tail wagging fast enough, I wouldn't have been surprised if his ass end lifted up. I'd always thought dogs were a good judge of character, but could you trust your life by their reactions? Could be Ben-Ben just loved him because he'd supplied his belly with bacon. After that, who knew what sadistic things he may have been up to. Dogs are good judges of character, but bacon always wins out over ethics.

"We, that is, my wife, Mabel, and I miss that dog something fierce. She's a special one, but she seemed dead set on getting back to you."

"She was trying to get back to someone."

"Someone?" The man was astute.

"A girl, Jess. She was killed, but her brother, Zach is still alive. Riley sleeps by his side every night. My guess is to make sure the same fate doesn't befall him."

"Big group, here. You all family?"

I looked over my shoulder to BT. "Yup. This one's my younger twin. I pick on him mercilessly."

"You wish," BT said.

Deneaux was putting some distance between herself and ThornGrip, but not much got past that bear.

"Put the gun down, Deneaux."

"Not in this lifetime, Michael."

"It won't be a long one for you, then," I told her.

She reluctantly holstered it, the act was nearly hostile. If I was wrong and lived I'd never hear the end of it. She turned and was walking to one of the cars. Didn't think that would stop the bear if she wanted in. ThornGrip would peel the top off like people do an uncooperative Cracker Jacks box with a prize in it.

Riley whined and then barked a few times and wagged her stubby tail as she headed over to Harold. The man didn't even think twice as he put the war relic down and got on his knees to pet the dog. Could hear the motor of a vehicle approaching.

I didn't say anything, but I was wondering what new wrinkle that sound would add to this situation.

A large, red semi crested over a small rise. Instead of stopping a cautionary distance away, it kept on rolling toward us, though it was slowing down. Who looks at a scene like this ahead, the sheer number of guns, the dead zombies and a massive bear and still keeps coming? Was all I could think. Couldn't imagine it being good, but I was willing to withhold judgment.

"That would be Mabel." Harold stood and was waving his arm back and forth. ThornGrip nearly made my heart stop, she'd come over to me and was sniffing my head, her nose, just the sniffing part, was the size of my fist and it was touching my ear. In a portion of a second, she could snap off my entire head like a Pez dispenser with her jaws.

"Should have let me kill him, Michael," Deneaux said.

"Yeah, this is the time for that," I told her. I turned so I was nose to nose with the animal. "Hi," I told her.

She pulled back so she could look into my eyes and snorted. I tentatively reached out with a hand. She growled low, but did not show her teeth. Truly didn't know if that was a good thing or not, wasn't in the habit of studying grizzly behavior. She bristled as my hand touched her neck and shoulder.

"You are a stupid one," BT said. "Aren't you the one that's petrified of Doberman Pinschers?"

"This look like a dobie?" I asked as I scratched a little more vigorously.

"No man, it looks like a wild fucking grizzly bear that could make you into pudding," he answered.

"I love pudding!" Trip yelled from inside one of the cars.

Mabel, presumably, got out of the truck. "What trouble have you two gotten yourselves into now?" she asked of Harold and ThornGrip, both of whom let their heads droop a bit. No doubt who ruled this roost. I thought it funny that she completely ignored the rest of us. Riley barked and ran toward the woman.

"Oh, my, my," she said as she placed a hand on her throat

and went into a squat. "Oh, it is so good to see that you're alright, girl." She grabbed the dog's head with both her hands. "Don't you ever give me a fright like that." Then she reached into her pocket and gave her a treat, some sort of small, tan cracker thing. ThornGrip spun from me just as Trip opened the car door; they had both seen the same thing and were heading for the woman.

"Cap'n Crunch Peanut Butter Crunchies! Last time I had that was Luxembourg–the Sofitel Hotel room service…silver plates man! Kept the werewolves away." He looked over at me like I knew what the fuck he was talking about.

"Cereal. The bear loves cereal. I think we've cleaned out the entire state of Maine's supply," Harold said.

"Is that why you're in New Hampshire?" I asked, though I had not taken my eyes off the race that was going on for Mabel's pocket goodies. Trip had seen the bear but apparently didn't care; that sugary snack somehow took precedence over being mauled. They were neck and neck for a moment, the bear looking over at Trip like she couldn't believe he was this stupid either. She pulled up ahead of him and with just the slightest hip thrust sent him sprawling.

"Ooooh, you bad girl!" Mabel admonished the animal some six or seven times her size. ThornGrip seemed mortified; she knew she was being dressed down by the woman. "That's no way to treat strangers. No treat for you." Mabel walked past her to check on how Trip was doing. He'd managed to sit up despite the spins. "Are you alright, dear?"

"It's just like the Rice Krispie shortage of 1972, all over again." She reached down to help him up.

She laughed and nodded like she knew what the hell he was talking about. "ThornGrip can be quite a bear when it comes to her sugary tidbits." Mabel laughed at her own quip. "You sure you're okay?"

"I'd be better if I had my own sugary tidbit," Trip told her.

"You…you want some of the cereal in my pocket?" Mabel asked.

"Fool was racing that bear for it," BT told her.

Mabel put a handful of food out to Trip, who, instead of taking it into his own hand, began to eat it out of hers.

"Oh my," Mabel said.

"Talbot, why are you letting him be our representative?!" BT was pissed, like Trip's brand of insanity was my fault.

"Go get him," I told BT.

"Uh-uh. He's on his own." We were all watching as ThornGrip was sidling up to the woman. She roared into the face of Trip, who seemed oblivious as he mowed through the cereal. He had won the snacks and he was going to enjoy them.

"I have a tractor trailer full of cereal! You'll be alright." Mabel reached out with her free hand to stroke the snout of the bear.

Once the treat fiasco was sorted out and ThornGrip was sitting like a circus animal going through a dozen boxes of breakfast food, we were finally able to talk to Harold and Mabel. Found out that they had left Maine for the same reason we had, the giant horde of zombies. ThornGrip had urged them out of the house.

"She must'a caught a scent, beat them by about five minutes," Harold said. "I wanted to go north, farther into the woods, but the missus said we'd never find enough cereal for the eating machine over there. And she was right. Wouldn't want her hungry…you saw how she is in a fight. ThornGrip, I mean, although Mabel is no slouch either. Mabel has a sister in Massachusetts and we're headed down there. Between us," he lowered his voice, "oh, how I hate to go to the land of Massholes."

I couldn't help but smile. "I'm from Mass," I told him.

"You haven't given him reason to doubt his opinion," BT replied.

Tracy had some of the kids over by the bear, I couldn't see how that was a particularly good idea, especially since one of them was bound to have some Twinkie or something still stuck to it.

"She loves kids." Mabel tried to ease my concern.

"To eat, I bet." BT wanted nothing to do with the animal.

Trip had gone through his Cap'n Crunch and was looking to the boxes ThornGrip had.

"Are you insane?" Stephanie asked him.

"Clinically? I think so," he told her.

I was telling them what we were up to when Deneaux came over.

"Is that wise?" she asked.

"Is what wise? I was going to see if they wanted to join us. You afraid you'll lose the Scariest Among the Bunch throne?"

She sneered at me before she lit a cigarette from across the roadway, ThornGrip's head swiveled, she looked at the smoke and snorted before baring her teeth.

"I vote for the bear. Anything that doesn't like Deneaux is alright in my book." BT said.

"I didn't realize I would be traveling with a comedy troupe." She took a long drag and made sure to send a large plume toward the bear.

"Talk about actually poking a bear," BT said.

"Washington state you say? That's a lot of traveling. Took a few thousand zombies just to get me to go to Massachusetts. I'm too old to go cross country, especially these days."

"There's safety in numbers," I replied.

"Seems to me those numbers weren't helping all that much when we stumbled across you."

There it was, the dry truth as delivered by one who had lived in Maine his entire life. I kept my mouth shut, he had me there. If ThornGrip hadn't come along when she had, I'd be working my way through the digestive system of a few dozen zombies. Even more of a reason to see if I could get them to join us.

"I don't mean to be insensitive, but are you even sure her sister is alive?"

"Me and Mabel went round and round on that. We decided at the very least, we had to try."

"And then?"

"Son, do you have it all figured out?" he asked.

BT snorted.

"Don't," I told my friend, he didn't listen.

"Figured out? Mike? Just look at the seat of his pants. You can see how scuffed up they are by how much he travels by them."

"Done?" I asked.

"For now. He seems to get it."

"Zombies coming from the north and the east." MJ had come up to me and was showing me the horde, the purples were a large blotch of storm. For a heart-stopping moment, I thought I saw the black hole that would signify a vampire and then it was washed over. If Payne was among them, she was well camouflaged.

"Mabel, round up the bear. We got to go. That's a nice device you have there."

"Lifesaver, literally. Though it does have gaps in coverage. Listen. We're going to go as far south as Route 495." This was a looping route that, in theory, circumvented the thick Boston traffic, but everyone and their brother used it. So, in reality, it was usually just a very wide, very long parking lot. "Then we're going to pick up the Mass Pike." This bisected the state from east to west. "If you get to your sister in law's and it's not going to work for you, just follow us."

MJ gave him a copy of our route. Everyone had a copy in case for any reason someone got separated from the group. We had proposed stops along the route, theoretically someone could catch us there or wait for us, but those weren't etched in stone—way too many variables. Hell, we'd just hit one. Trip had sat down in front of the bear and grabbed a box that was next to a paw the size of his head. ThornGrip looked down and moved to intercept. She knocked the box out of his hands with a deft movement. Trip got up and posted on the bear. You know, his chest puffed out, his arms stiffened down by his sides, his chin jutting out and up, the universal gesture of "I'm a d-bag and I dare you to take a swing."

"Stephanie!" I shouted. "Could you please get your husband before he causes an inter-species incident?"

She quickly looked around and ran to keep what was left of her husband's head.

"He's a special one," Harold said.

"You have no idea," I told him.

"We got a lot of 'special ones' with us," BT said from the side of his mouth.

Harold nodded at the map. "We were going to take 95 down, but I'll admit it would be nice to have company. I'll stay on 495 with you, then we'll head on further south to Norwood."

"Norwood?" I felt a pang pulse through me. (Not for Norwood–actually couldn't stand the town, but that was due more to the sports rivalry we had while I was in High School.) I did some growing up in Walpole, the next town over.

"You know it?" he asked.

"Been there a few times." I told him where I grew up. "Haven't been back. You got an address? MJ could pull it up real-time give you an idea of what you're driving into."

"You want me to get your wife?" MJ asked as he punched in the coordinates.

"Not just yet."

I could understand that. In the likely event that the house was leveled or surrounded or a hundred other bad things that could have befallen it, he wanted to break it to her himself. The image came up; parts of Norwood looked like you would expect a small city to after the apocalypse–burned out shells of homes, whole blocks reduced to their foundations. The screen showed the scattered skeletons of hundreds of the not-so-lucky. Or the lucky. Who knows? Living through this era was nothing worth overly celebrating.

"That's her house." He pointed to a small Tudor. It looked slightly out of place on the street, which held more one-story businesses than residential homes. Must have been old; the lone hold-out on a street developers had gotten their mitts on. On the plus side, it was still standing, and at the moment, there were no zombies running around it; wasn't any movement at all. That in and of itself is not strange–not many people these days were out running around trying to draw attention to themselves.

"What are you looking at?" Mabel had come up, she was drawn to the screen. "What's…that's Claudia's house!" She was having a hard time figuring out what exactly she was looking at. "How did you get a picture of her house?" She looked to MJ.

"It's a real-time satellite feed," I told her.

I didn't pick it up at first, not something I would typically look for. But Mabel did, she took a deep breath. "She's alive." It came out as a relieved sigh.

I looked over to MJ to ask what she'd seen that I'd missed. "Nothing moved," he told her. "There's a software analyzer that looks for that."

"Look in her backyard." She was pointing at the screen and smiling.

I saw nothing except rows of plant life. Then I got it. "It's a garden," I said.

"A well-tended one," she replied. "No weeds–see there? Claudia always was fastidious on the farm." She stood back, proud of her sister and ready to hit the road.

"Someone say weed?" Trip had to have been fifty feet away. BT flipped him the finger. "That's not the right finger to use for hitchhiking. You know there's going to be a time when people don't recognize that gesture."

"Good thing it's not today," BT told him.

"Well, I guess that's settled," Harold said, though he didn't seem overly pleased about it. "Claudia is a neat freak. Not only do you have to take your shoes off when you enter her house, she gives you these little bootie socks to go over your other socks."

"Cleanliness is next to Godliness," Mabel said.

"He really doesn't care," Trip said as he wiped his dirty hands on his stained shirt and looked up.

"If he does, you have a one-way ticket down." BT backed up a couple of steps as ThornGrip came up to investigate.

"Uh, that's not a very big house," I said to Harold as I glanced over at the bear. "And Norwood isn't exactly rural." There were implications I wasn't saying. ThornGrip could keep a family fed for months, not to mention that nice coat she was wearing. If anybody saw her walking down the street, they were going to do their best to hunt her down both from hunger as well as just plain fear. I'd caught Mabel's attention; she was looking at me like maybe knitting needles were going to shoot from her eyes.

"And this Etna Station would be so much safer?" It was meant as a challenging question.

"I honestly have no idea," I told her. "I'm just throwing my thoughts in, and I'm sorry for that, but you two seem very fond of this bear. I'm having a hard time seeing the upside to bringing her to the suburbs of Boston. More people, more zombies, fewer woods, and what happens when she runs out of Cap'n Crunch?"

Harold looked at his wife. Nicole had come up with Wesley in her hands; she had to reach up to pet the bear's face. There was no part of me that didn't want to scream at her to get away from the wild grizzly. The baby's face led me to believe either he thought he was looking at the world's largest stuffed animal or he was constipated. To me, ThornGrip seemed a little too interested in smelling the baby.

"Uh, Nicole," I said turning her way.

"Relax, dad. They're bonding."

"I used to have that bonding moment when your mom made meatloaf. He's sniffing at your son like he's a Tootsie Roll."

Wesley reached a hand out and grabbed a fistful of bear lip. He pulled away, exposing huge canines.

"So, nobody else thinks this is a bad idea?" I asked.

Wesley thought this was funny as hell and began to bounce his hand up and down, making a motorboat sound and slinging a lot of bear spit around. Justin, upon seeing his nephew having so much fun, thought maybe Avalyn might get a kick out of the bear as well. I've been accused of a rash act or seventeen in my life, but this was seemingly notched up. ThornGrip's demeanor changed swiftly; Avalyn and Justin were about ten feet away when she turned, quickly pulling away from Wesley. She took two large sniffs and bristled. Justin had been so focused on the soft, pink baby he was carrying over to the carnivore, he had not taken note of the bear's change.

"Far enough, Justin." I was moving to intercede, my arm extended out to physically stop him.

"I just want the baby to see her," he said, looking at me like I'd kept him from the balloon twister.

"No closer."

Nicole had backed away as well, sensing the shift. Maybe it was me, but I got the distinct impression that bear was afraid. A scared chipmunk is one thing; they'll scurry off. A scared bear? Well, I'm not sure.

"What's the matter, girl?" Harold asked as he saw what had my attention.

"Justin, back away."

"It's just a baby," he said as if we needed the point reiterated.

Avalyn was staring at that bear, and not in any sort of curious baby way, either. I could just about see the wheels in her head turning as she was thinking. ThornGrip snorted again and stomped her right paw down hard. I, for one, heard: "Stay away." Better yet, "Get away from me or I'm going to crush that baby."

"She's just a baby!" Justin was getting mad like he was offended by the bear's preference to Wesley.

She was a baby, no doubting that, but she was more as well—we just didn't know what yet. Were we like kids running around with sparklers in a dynamite factory? You know, it's all fun and games until shit goes boom.

The scene was getting increasingly tense, Justin had wisely, if not happily, moved away, but ThornGrip had not calmed. If the bear charged we would be hard-pressed to stop her; most likely several of us would die trying, but we'd try nonetheless.

"We should be going," Mabel said.

Riley and Ben Ben said their goodbyes; Patches sat on the roof of one of the cars. Her tail swished back and forth as if she'd like to say goodbye as well, but that was beneath her.

"Zombies are closing." Mad Jack had pulled up our surrounding area again." That was the perfect opportunity to go our separate ways. I wished them luck and thanked them for saving our asses.

"You know where we're at if you need anything," Harold said. I thought Mabel was going to pull out those knitting needle eyes again for even offering. Did she get the same vibe from Avalyn that ThornGrip had or was it merely because ThornGrip had reacted the way she had?

"Same," I told him as I shook his hand.

CHAPTER TWO
MIKE JOURNAL ENTRY 2

WE'D PARTED COMPANY some forty-five minutes previously; our caravan was now nearly halfway across the state of Massachusetts. I'd had to take backtrack and take a detour up route 190 as what looked like a jumbo jet had completely obliterated all of the lanes and left an impassable crater. We were now crossing the state on route 2 which put us close to New Hampshire. Two steps forward and one step backwards and shit.

"We going to talk about what we just saw?" Tracy asked.

I knew where she was going with this but I didn't want to go down that road. "Yeah, that was an awful friendly bear. You think she was a circus animal? Seems strange that she would be that alright around people."

"Mike."

"I don't think it's right, circuses having animals, especially since most treated them pretty bad or were at least neglectful. Big animals need space."

"I can punch pretty hard," she said.

This I knew. We'd played a game or two of Slug Bug and I would lightly tap her on the shoulder when I saw one and she would generally hit back the same way–unless she was losing. Then I got some of the full brunt of her poor sportsmanship.

Like, she was trying to make up for her lack of numbers with force of contact. Travis was even worse when he was playing football in school. He actively looked for Volkswagens and took it as a challenge to deliver as jarring a jolt as he could every time he saw one. Got so that I flinched every time there was oncoming traffic.

"What specifically do you want to talk about?" I asked. I learned this tactic a long time ago. When a woman says she wants to "talk," it is extremely better to let her clearly initiate the discussion. I cannot tell you how many times I stupidly opened with things that weren't relevant and there's no getting those worms back in that can. Once her real agenda had been settled, we would then have to "talk" about my presumed topics.

"The baby! That huge bear was afraid of that baby."

"Her name is Avalyn."

"Don't...don't. Not just yet. I don't want to get attached to it just yet."

"It?" I asked.

"You're avoiding the issue."

"Sure am," I said proud that I was being honest as well as clearly understood.

"An eight-hundred-pound bear was scared of an infant. Don't you think maybe we should be, too?" she asked.

"It's cause for concern, I agree, but what do we do about it? We can't just leave her on the side of the road."

Tracy was quiet. Too quiet.

"Woman!"

"What! That baby is nothing to us! There's something *off* about her. The way she peers at you like she knows what's going on. I don't care if it's selfish or not, Michael, I'm not willing to risk the well-being of my family for what could be a zombie baby."

I wasn't sure what I could say here. I was cautious of the baby; maybe wary is a better word. What if I argued for her and she did end up hurting someone, even inadvertently?

Tracy would never forgive me. But she was still a baby. She cooed, drank milk, formula in this case, fussed…all the things you would expect an infant to do. Did we even try to test her? Did we, I don't know, find some tripe or entrails and see what she thought about that? I mean, if she started digging into some disgusting shit then I might have to reevaluate my stance. As of now, she seemed like a normal, weird-staring, bear-scaring baby.

"I'm not sure what you want me to say here," I told her.

Nicole was in the car with us. "Dad, you know I usually have your back, right?"

"But?"

"She was born after Wesley and she's already bigger."

"What's that mean? It's not like you're a large woman," I weakly argued. "And who is going to tell Justin that we're leaving the baby? He's grown mighty fond of her."

"Too fond," Tracy threw out there.

"I don't even know what that means," I said.

"Somewhere in him he still houses the virus, right?" was what she said. "Wouldn't it make sense he would want to protect her? I'm not saying it's a conscious thing."

"You're saying that instinctually the virus in him is protecting the virus within her?" I hated that I'd said it because it made sense. "I know Justin; you give that argument and you'd better be prepared. We tell him we don't want the baby in the group anymore, he's likely to leave with her."

"What about Deneaux?"

"What about her?"

"She'd take care of it. We force her out with the baby."

"What the….You two are scaring the shit out of me! You'd loose that psychopath on a baby? And what about her makes you think she'd do it? Leave *and* watch the baby?"

"She's not a baby! Wesley is a baby, Zachary is a baby. That thing is an abomination and I wish you'd never brought it back." Well. That was out there.

"We're going to stop this conversation now because I'm

not going to do anything about it today and probably not tomorrow, either. I'm not going to do anything to, with, or about that *baby* until I get a reason to."

"I swear to you, Mike, if you wait until it's too late and she hurts someone it will be a moment you regret forever, on more than one front."

I almost pulled the car over, her response was so visceral and charged with animosity. I had just had those thoughts, but hearing them spoken out loud made me sick. I wanted to put some distance between us before any real damage was done. Even thought about asking her if she wanted to ride in a different car.

"Mike, pick up–this is Mad Jack."

"I'm listening," I told him.

"We've got about a dozen cars and trucks to our six."

"How far back?"

"Five point two miles. They're doing about eighty."

I was doing sixty-five, about as fast as I dared go on a roadway that had no upkeep and had more than one hazard littered across it.

"There's an exit five miles up. Spread the word–we'll take that and let them go on by."

"And if they don't?" he asked.

"Fuck me," I muttered. I was getting asked a lot of questions today, most of which I did not have answers for. "We'll deal with it when the time comes."

"Yeah, Mike. Wouldn't want to plan ahead or anything," Tracy said with a lingering simmer to her voice. What I wouldn't have given to have a VW pass by just then. No pulled punches this time.

"What would you have me do?" I was getting a little pissed myself. "I don't think we can outrun them, and if their vehicles are full they outman us. Would you rather we circled the wagons and prepared for a fight?"

She said nothing.

"Oh, isn't that convenient. Give me crap for making a

decision but then don't offer an alternative." Why I felt the need to push it, I'm not really sure. "It's easy to sit back and fault the choices of others if you're never on the hook yourself. And while we're at it, maybe I'm sick of making all the hard ones."

"Watch where you're going with this, Mike. We do things together; we make decisions together. When you do something it's because I agree with it. Otherwise, we don't."

Hard to argue with that. Now normally, Tracy and I were on the same page so things seemed to flow easily enough; it was when we were reading different books that the waters got murky, choppy, and almost hurricane-like. I wisely said nothing else. Anything out of my mouth now was mired in gasoline, while Tracy held a blow torch.

I pulled off the highway and followed the sign that assured me Wendy's was in a quarter mile. If only. We pulled behind the long, unmanned drive-thru.

"I've got three minutes of feed left," MJ replied.

"And…?" BT prodded.

"It's going to be close if they get to the exit before that," he said.

Deneaux was in her normal pose. Pistol on hood, leaning back against the car, head upturned, smoke billowing around her like a protective cloud. It was going to be a tense few minutes; those that could fight were outside, down behind the cars for just that eventuality. Those that could not were ducked inside for flight, if that became necessary.

"Ten seconds."

"They slowing down?" BT asked.

I had gone to the corner of the building to attempt a visual, should they come this way. I was beginning to hate Deneaux's viewing box. I'd once considered this gadget to be the greatest gift that could be bestowed upon us, our small advantage. But it also caused me massive indecision; it was constantly making me second guess and alter what little plans I'd felt forced to prepare. Our movements were constantly being directed, or at least heavily weighted by what we could see on this viewer, and it cost us the power of spontaneous action. Our intuition was dismissed; now we had to go with what we knew, never again by what we felt. That gut reaction is a powerful Human force; maybe we just weren't supposed to know. It was like those fucking Cyclopes that had traded an eye to divine the future but were tricked into only knowing their deaths; the inevitability of that final drop dictating their lives. Typical Deneaux. She appears as if she's helping with one hand while the other is honing away at a boning knife she is planning on driving into the side of your neck the second you're of no use to her own plans.

I saw BT and Gary coming over; that did not bode well. Deneaux eyed her pistol to make sure it had not moved. Justin and Travis were setting up a perimeter around the kids. Tracy had just pulled her charging handle back, she threw a glower at me, as if this were somehow my fault; partly it was. I'd decided to pull over. All things being equal, I'd rather be here than get into it on the highway with no cover. Car metal is pretty thin and bullets have no problem going through it.

"Here they come," BT said. It was a large tractor-trailer, Allied Moving company actually, though I was pretty sure they weren't delivering furniture to the Hamptons. "How many, you think?" he asked as he rested his barrel on a small cement wall built to hide the trash bin.

"Tough to say. I can't imagine they've got troops riding in the back of that thing, unless it's been retrofitted, so there shouldn't be more than two or three in each truck." The truck was loud, air brakes booming as it came down the exit ramp. "Go right…" I urged. It turned left.

"I don't think they heard you," BT said. "I don't see any others." The truck had made the turn and was coming straight toward us, yet there were no other cars behind it. They weren't here for the lunch menu. If they were, indeed, looking for us and knew where we were, it made no sense to bring the one truck, which had stopped suddenly, halfway between us and the highway ramp.

"They're just sitting there. What are they waiting for?" Gary asked.

And that was a good question. If they got off the highway to take a piss, which also made no sense by the way, why were they just sitting in the truck?

"They looking for a little alone time?" BT asked.

"Shit. Let's go." I tapped BT on the shoulder.

"Where?"

"It's a trap. The rest of them will be coming around from the other exit ramp. These guys are here to delay us, hem us in…keep an eye on us, whatever."

"Hold on a second." BT was thinking.

"Man, we don't have time for that."

"MJ, how far to the next exit?" BT asked across the small parking lot.

"Eleven miles," he answered. That was the beauty of Route 2, the lack of exits.

"That's all great and fine, BT, but there's no guarantee they're going to drive all that way. They could be coming through the woods right across from the highway while we are sitting here."

"They're going to drive. They're overconfident and cocky…add in a little dose of lazy."

"How the hell do you know?" I asked.

"Because I was a cop. Victimizers always think they are one step ahead of their victims. Plus, criminals are just fucking lazy. They'd rather take from others than do for themselves, that's how I know. There's no way they're hiking."

"I'm listening."

"We leave Deneaux here, maybe with Gary, to keep an eye on who is in that truck and so they can report back that we're just waiting them out. Then you, me, Tommy and a few others go out to meet these assholes on our terms."

"Lots of unknowns, buddy. Like what if there are more men in the back of that truck or those two have a grenade launcher. And even if they have more traditional arms and it's only the two of them, we have no idea what the rest of us are going to be running into." I had depended on that real-time view screen long enough to fear the unknown, and BT called me out on it.

"Never seen you afraid of a fight, Mike," BT said.

"I don't like having all these non-combatants in the fold; it changes the dynamic. Gary and Deneaux get overrun, there's not much left to mount a defense."

"So, we doing this?" he asked already knowing I was just spinning my wheels here.

"Of course. I'm leaving one of my boys here too, though. I'd feel better, and I've got a feeling Justin won't want to leave that baby behind."

CHAPTER THREE
MIKE JOURNAL ENTRY 3

WE BACKED AWAY from the wall slowly. I laid out my simple plan and then we took a small side road that cut away from the truck and any possible prying eyes. We were making a good clip and I was doing the math of the other trucks rolling the eleven miles to the next exit and how far they would dare to come back before the noise of their engines gave them away. Figured they would stop a mile and a half, maybe two miles away and then sneak the rest of the way in on foot. We set up our ambush about a mile away from the Wendy's, and we had to really hump it to beat my estimated time of their arrival.

"Holy shit, dad! You been working on your cardio?" Travis asked as he leaned against a tree to catch his breath.

Tommy looked as if he'd gone for a stroll, BT was walking it off, making sure from my angle I couldn't see the heaving in his chest. Meredith may or may not have retched behind a large oak. I would have answered my son, but I had a stitch in my side that was threatening to rip open. And what about those little warnings from the body? Who needs them. About as useless as the nutritional information on a Twinkie. Let's be honest, you know what's in it just by looking at that creamy filling. Maybe reading the label, skipping all the big chemical words, makes you feel like you give a shit, but you're still going to eat the Twinkie. Hell, there's a death warning on the side of cigarettes. They were the first things looted from the shops.

When we were finished breathing like a pack of horned out high-schoolers coupled up under the bleachers, we got into positions with great lines of sight to the roadway. I wasn't overly thrilled with shooting people before the hostilities started; as of yet, they had done nothing to us. But their intention? Well, that was certainly suspect. You don't just randomly come up on somebody's ass, take their exit, then block their retreat with your intimidating vehicle without expecting some sort of preemptive strike, especially now. We didn't have the luxury to ask them what the hell they were up to, nor was there anyone we could call for help if their intentions were nefarious.

We'd clicked off enough time that the pre-jitters of an upcoming conflict began to wear off and as the adrenaline faded, tiredness began to set in. Travis yawned.

"Something's wrong," I said to BT.

"Just lazy, man. They're taking their time."

I thought on his words for a second. "No way, man. If they spent the time and resources to set this up, they wouldn't be so casual about the end game. I think we need to get back." I was looking in the direction of the fast food restaurant, though I could not see it. I was getting the sinking feeling we'd been duped and had left the rest of our people, hung out to dry.

"I see something," Tommy said.

A figure began to appear–still far off–but I could only make out one.

"There's more," Travis said as we all tried to get a better look. I had my four-power scope up to my eye and was still having a hard time figuring it out, when it came to me. That was when the panic set in.

"Rats," I hissed, though I meant to shout. "Rats! Thousands of them."

"What the fuck?" BT asked as he was looking. "Are they attacking that guy?"

"We have to go." I grabbed my stuff and was heading out. "Not being attacked–he's leading them like the fucking Pied Piper."

"Oh…oh no." BT was pretty alarmed. "I hate rats."

"That's two of us, and probably ninety percent of the population."

"That what's in the trucks?" Meredith asked, but it was the answer as well.

"Who does that?" BT asked. It was the last question he would be able to get off as we were once again sprinting at full, back the way we had come.

When the first rat ran out into the roadway ahead of us, I didn't think much of it; figured a small animal by itself would run away as soon as it saw us scary bipeds running its way. But it didn't. It turned and came right at us. All I could think was maybe it had rabies; then I was thinking with growing conviction that it was even somehow more insidious. The ape at the Demense building had the zombie virus; it was not out of the realm of possibilities this rat did as well. What new horror would this be? How could people survive? Here was an animal that could get just about anywhere, one that had proven itself through time to be extremely clever, bold and adaptive. I raised my rifle up, but the odds of hitting the damned thing while we were both running was as likely as a lawyer turning down a frivolous lawsuit, a politician turning down a donation, and if I want to be more relevant, Trip turning down a spliff.

Rats began to pour out of the woods to our right–no one thought twice when I veered left. We heard gunfire up ahead. The trap had been sprung and we had arrogantly and blithely walked right into it–hell, I think we even pulled the lever to spring it while we whistled a catchy tune. I knew rats were fast, at least in bursts, (a Trivial Pursuit question I got wrong). If we could stay ahead of them, theoretically they couldn't catch us. But we weren't really ahead of them if the truck at Wendy's had already let go of its bubonic plague-carrying cargo, and odds were stacked that they had. We were fucked, and there's no way our view screen could have seen this.

"Get in the cars, get out of there," I had told Justin before we left. The plan was if they got into trouble, to get the fuck out and come pick us up, but we had already deviated from the path they were supposed to meet us on. We'd pass like ships in the night. Luckily, I had prepared for Plan C. Plan B, you ask? Well, that was to just use more ammo. Unfortunately, in this case, it wouldn't do any good.

"Tommy, the backpack." I think it was Trip that had come back with a flare gun from a foraging mission. I didn't see the good in it back then; I mean, unless we ended up looking for rescue at sea. As it was, we already had enough shitty things looking for us, didn't need to announce our position by shooting a big, red neon "Open!" sign into the sky. Tommy got in front of me as we ran, fumbling with the thing, just about put a burning canister into his thigh–pretty sure he would have been pissed off about that. The gunfire had tapered off; had to think they were retreating to the cars. I fired the flare, never even wondering if they'd be able to see it from where they were. There was the screeching of tires and then more gunfire. There was a squeal of brakes and then the gut-wrenching sound of metal impacting something unyielding. BT looked over at me and I don't know how we found another gear, but we were racing to the wire.

The flare went unnoticed as a car sped by one street over. Attempting to cut them off was fruitless; they were already past our location and the rats streaming into yards to our side would prevent that anyway. We got to the parking lot just as a dazed and bleeding Gary was being shoved into a car that Deneaux was driving. She looked over at us as soon as the door slammed shut and screamed out of the parking lot. Of all the ones getting screwed, we were first up. There were rats everywhere; I can't blame her for not picking us up, well, I could, but we both knew she wouldn't have made it. I tapped BT's shoulder; off to the side was a two-story home that had been converted into apartments–at least that's what I figured judging by the metal fire escape.

BT didn't even need to jump as he reached up and pulled the ladder down. We about tossed Meredith up there, and Travis was right behind her. BT went next as Tommy and I had to shoot to keep the nasty little fucks from biting us. Mounds of ground were being blown up, taking scores of rats with each strike, but still they came, their beady black eyes locked on; their long, sharp teeth intent on sinking into our flesh. One had jumped onto my leg and was climbing up fast. I grabbed him around the body and squeezed until his lungs burst forth from his mouth–literally. It was just as gross as it sounds. I flung it away and spun to grip the ladder. Tommy cried out as he was bitten on his calf; he reached down and smashed two of them together with enough force to create one disgustingly large and bloody multi-legged rat.

BT was hoisting the ladder that Tommy and I were still on. Travis was smashing away with the butt of his rifle at the animals that had hitched a ride. Took a moment to catch my breath and look out at the sea of swirling vermin. A bunch were looking up at us, figuring how to solve this puzzle. A fair amount already had.

"Inside!" Being out on this metal platform made us perfect targets for any shitstorm.

"Fucking Deneaux saw us, man! She fucking left us here on purpose!" BT was yelling as he was moving furniture to the block the doorway. This must have been a rough part of New Hampshire, if such a thing existed, because the door was metal, not metal all the way through, but enough to stop anything from chewing its way in.

"It was fifty-fifty if she could have got to us. Maybe a little less–she definitely weighed the odds and, without being a clear favorite, we were always going to be left behind." I said.

"We wouldn't have fit." Tommy was checking the window.

"Still, man. I would have ridden on the fucking roof! Now

we have to deal with…with rats, man!" BT was losing his mind.

I had a healthy fear of the animal, that was for sure, but it was obvious to see that this was one of the big man's phobias and he was not coping well. And it didn't get any better as we heard the pitter patter of thousands of feet coming down the wooden hallway. Meredith looked at me.

"Go find some valium in the bathroom," I told her.

"What makes you think they have valium?"

"You're going to find some." I was nodding my head. "Travis go with her, do a quick check of this place." It wasn't large, by any stretch of the imagination. Appeared to be one bedroom in the back, a bathroom, and then the kitchen / living room combo. Although it looked much more spacious now that we had the entertainment center, couch, and kitchen table stacked up against the door.

"They actually had some!" She came out a moment later, already more relieved.

"Really?" I asked.

She looked at me like the idiot who doesn't get his own joke. "You just told me to pretend I found some valium, and now you're thinking I really did?"

"Wishful thinking. Go be that convincing to him."

BT was next to Tommy, though he was not looking out the window. He had his head pressed against the wall.

"Uncle Mike wanted me to give these to you." Meredith opened her hand to reveal two small, reddish pills.

"What are they?" he asked never looking directly at them.

"Valium."

She'd barely said the word when he grabbed them and dry swallowed.

I motioned for her to come over. "Umm, that was good– don't mistake me, but what did you actually just give him?" I'd hoped she'd found some baby aspirin or something useful, but that wasn't what the pills looked like. She handed me the bottle. "Bisacodyl? Oh no."

"Did I just poison him?" Meredith looked scared.

"Nope. Probably the rest of us though. These are laxatives."

"Nothing here worth mentioning," Travis said coming out of the bedroom.

"Dad! Come in dad–where are you? Are you alright?" It was Justin. I could hear his muffled voice coming through the backpack. Tommy tossed me the entire bag, I nearly toppled over when I caught the much heavier than anticipated bag right in the chest. The radio was once again asking where I was when I finally got to it.

"We're fine," I began before looking over to a concerned Tommy. "Fine-ish. How are you guys doing?"

"We're okay. You weren't at the rendezvous point but we saw a thousand reasons as to why–ran over a bunch of 'em. Would have kept doing it but there were also trucks and people with guns. We're at…."

I cut him off. "Don't say it over the radio; it's not secure."

"How are we going to find each other?"

"We're not currently in any shape for travel. Give us a few minutes to figure something out."

"*Few minutes?*" BT asked. "You're going to get us out of here in a few minutes?"

"Valium should just be taking hold about now." I hoped the suggestion would quell the rising panic within him.

"I am feeling a little woozy," he confessed just as his stomach began to gurgle. "Nerves." He grabbed at his waist.

"Keep safe Justin. I'll contact you when we can." This was killing me. We were scattered to the winds at the moment and there wasn't a damn thing I could do about it.

"Uncle," Meredith said. She was by the door. "You need to hear this."

I thought I was going to have to cup my ear and listen intently, blocking out all distractions but I was only halfway across the room when I heard the crunching. "Chewing. I'll be damned. They're chewing through–not the door, though."

53

"The walls," she answered.

"I didn't think of that." I thought about doing the math, but I'd never ran across a word problem that involved the speed at which a hundred rats can chew through two sheets of drywall, framing, and insulation while three humans are swatting and shooting at them. "Any ideas?"

"We could set the place on fire," she replied, and I don't think she was kidding. You didn't need to have what BT suffered from, true musophobia, to not like the fact that you were about to die by a thousand tiny bites.

"This house is old enough it should have lathe and plaster walls," Tommy said.

"That'll slow them down, though I doubt it will stop them," I said thinking about the thin board material and the plaster slathered between them to keep homes insulated. It was a whole might better than the pink stuff, for this application at least. But it was still only a waiting game; the fuckers can chew through brick if they have enough time. Gotta be some asbestos in the walls, right?" I asked.

"I don't think they're going to die from mesothelioma before they get in here, if that's what you're getting at," Meredith said.

"Next time, try not to be so smart."

"The world doesn't need two Talbots like you," she said.

Even in as dire a situation as we were, Travis could not help letting a snort out. "Sorry." He put his hand up when he saw me looking at him.

I was trying to figure out our next move when I noticed that BT was no longer in the room.

"Bathroom," Tommy said.

"Oh lord! What is happening to me?!" BT cried out. Now, I won't swear it on a stack of Bibles, but I think the house shook from the force of his, umm, bathroom volley, if you will. "Is that my liver?" he asked alarmed. "Talbot!" he yelled.

I looked at Meredith. "He's talking about you, Miss Talbot."

"Might not have to worry about the rats now," she shrugged.

We all were inching farther from the bathroom when we heard a high-pitched whistle.

"Yoohoo!" someone shouted from down below. "I fucking said Yoohoo! It's customary to reply!" the voice yelled. "Listen, we know you're in there. The rats have been specifically trained, see? They're like good old hunting dogs–they track down and trap prey so that the hunters can blow your heads off!"

"What do you want?" Tommy asked from the corner of the window.

I wasn't sure if that was the smartest thing, but it was true, they did know we were there.

"What do I want? Why, the world." It was Knox.

"Shit."

"But for now, just you and those with you, specifically. You see I have a few scores to settle; lost a lot of good people to your group. Twenty-seven to be exact."

"Wasn't me," Tommy told him.

Technically that was true, though I didn't think Knox would see it that way or even care.

"Guilty by association, son. The North Korean government was a little strange in how they ruled but I do agree with the fact that the sins of the father are passed down to the next generation. Gauging by your age, I'd say that includes you."

"Can you see him?" I asked. He shook his head.

"Let's get a few things squared up. The rats are highly trained and will kill you if I tell them to. Or I can just set the building on fire. Either way is a pretty gruesome death, don't you agree?"

"So, we should just come out, then?" Tommy asked.

"That would be the smartest choice," he said.

"And you won't hurt us?"

"Oh, I never said that, son," he laughed. "The men are

going to have to go. I think the values your leadership has instilled into you will prevent you from ever being good soldiers in my army. But the women…they're always valuable. We can use them to repopulate our forces or maybe just as entertainment."

"We have children as well," Tommy said.

"Why don't you just give him our social security numbers and password phrases," I told Tommy.

"I don't want them, either," he replied. "I'll tell you what. If we can avoid more bloodshed, I'll let anyone under the age of fifteen go about their merry way."

"So, you're going to kill the men, take our women, and cast the children loose into this murderous world, alone. That about it?" I asked. "Go fuck yourself!" I stepped up to the window.

"Ah, Michael Talbot. I was wondering when you were going to show yourself." Knox stepped from behind a cinderblock privacy fence. "I know you're thinking about raising that rifle up and taking a shot. Just know that I have at least two snipers trained on you and whatever armor you used to stop my bullet the last time will not be effective against the caliber and ammunition they are armed with. It will rip your body to shreds. You do what I ask, and I promise that as much as I would rather prolong and drag out your death, I will be merciful and put a round into your skull, personally."

"Pull me out of the window," I said to Tommy. He'd no sooner wrenched me from my spot when a bullet hole appeared in the floor, halfway across the room.

"Oh man!" Knox shouted. "You would have been a wonderful addition to my army. It's a damn fine shame I'm going to have to kill you." There was another whistle and the rats began their incessant chewing.

BT had finally emerged from the bathroom a much paler version of himself. "I feel better now. Relaxed even."

"That always happens when you drop the kids off at the pool," I told him as I got up off the floor. "I hate to say it this way, but we're trapped like rats. Anybody got anything they think might work? Lay it out."

"Meredith was right, we need fire," Travis said. "I think we need to start our own fire. Those rats might be trained but they're not going to stick around for one. It might create enough confusion to escape."

"Or fry," Meredith said.

"Got a lighter in the pack?" I asked Tommy.

He shook his head. "Better," he said, reaching over to grab it. He came out with a couple of flares.

"The rat wall?" I asked. Seemed the best place to push them away from. I took one from his proffered hand, popped the cap off and struck the flint. Think I shoved a few dozen Our Fathers and Hail Mary's into a quick prayer session as I held the flare up to a wall that took a surprisingly long time to ignite. Once it did, though, it was game on. Now if we didn't die from smoke inhalation, we'd been in decent shape.

BT was moving the furniture away from the door, as it was our only egress. Smoke was beginning to billow.

"Who authorized the fire?" Knox was shouting. "I'll string them up for sedition!"

"Why would anyone follow that man?" I asked as I pulled my shirt up over my mouth and nose in a vain attempt to filter out the worst of it. "Everyone get on your hands and knees," I instructed, the air was somewhat better down there, but our options were becoming limited. We were in a very real danger of succumbing to a smoky end, in a few more seconds we wouldn't be able to find the door either. I reached up and twisted the handle. The rats were almost as surprised as I was. I was staring at hundreds of greedy, beady, hungry eyes. They desperately wanted to reduce me into kibble-sized snacks but they couldn't get at me. Fear of fire is a primal instinct–one not easily trained out. As smoke poured forth from that door, they began to vacate in droves. Those that didn't, I was swinging my rifle at and sometimes I would connect with a satisfying crunch of delicate bones. The problem was they weren't skittering like the ship was sinking, they were only backing up as far as the smoke reached, which was going to make our hasty departure anything but. Tommy tossed his flare down the hallway and again, they scattered.

"Won't they already have this place surrounded?" BT asked as we made it to the stairwell.

That was a safe assumption. "We need to break into another apartment on this floor, and go out another fire escape. It'll give us a couple of seconds; they have to be expecting us to come out on the ground floor," I said.

"You sure about that?"

"No."

"Just checking," he said. As we came back out of the stairwell, he easily shouldered an apartment door open. The stench was unmistakable; we were in zombie-controlled territory. We had our first piece of luck in the fact that the three zombies residing in this apartment were from the beginning— that is, they were slow, mostly uncoordinated, and emaciated. I noticed the carcass of at least one dog and a couple of cats and, I swallowed hard, maybe a baby, though it had been reduced to gnawed-up bones, so it was difficult to identify it definitively. Was going to be hard to dismiss my suspicion, though, as I couldn't pull my eyes from the toy rattle the unidentifiable hand bones had been holding. It was BT that smashed in the skull of the zombie shuffling my way. Cast iron pan, of all things. I think that was a new one for him, but once again, the old ways saved us. The spray of blood on my face got me in motion.

"Thanks," I told him.

He made quick work of the remaining two, spun the pan around as if he were considering keeping this new weapon, but he ended up putting it back on the counter top he'd grabbed it from.

"There's someone on the roof across the street." Tommy was pointing through the slats of the window shade. "I don't see anyone else watching this side."

It was a doable shot, not an easy one, but doable. He was on a terrace with a knee wall, exposing his upper chest and head. Now that I thought about it, there was most likely nothing in that short wall that would stop my round.

"Dumbass," I said, as I rested the barrel of my rifle on the middle of the window frame. Even through the shades, I had him. I was about to shoot when he turned to the side and was looking into the apartment he was outside of. "Fuck."

"What's the matter?" BT asked.

"There's someone with him."

"You sure? I don't see anyone," BT replied.

"Well, unless he's related to Trip and has audible conversations with the people in his head, I'm going to say yeah, I'm sure."

"You could have just said yes, you were sure."

"What fun is that," I told him.

"What part of this is fun to you?"

"Well, none of it, really. BT, you comfortable with that shot?" I asked.

He looked through the window. "I am, but I'm more comfortable with you doing it."

"I'm going to shoot the second one."

How do you know he's going to show?"

"Tommy is going to flush him out," I said, looking over at the boy. We were running out of time. Even with the towel under the door, smoke was beginning to find its way into the apartment. Our avenue of escape was beginning to dwindle.

Tommy went a few feet over to another window and threw it open. BT's mark saw him, yelled something into the apartment, and sighted in. Tommy moved before he could shoot.

"Come on, motherfucker…show yourself. No time for you to be shy." We waited. The sniper kept his rifle up; he was going to shoot the next time anything walked past that window. "Have a zombie peek out the window," I said. "Just make sure you don't expose yourself." Travis was dragging a body over.

"This is so gross," he said as he tried to get a grip on a corpse whose parts were only loosely attached. Meredith grabbed the zombie's other arm and they managed to get it over by the window, leaving a slime trail nearly two feet across in their wake.

"I've got it," Tommy said, getting low to the ground. He hoisted it up. Its head no sooner passed the sill before it was drilled a new hole.

"Guy's a crack shot," I said as Tommy let the zombie fall to the ground. I had thought maybe we could just rush the fire escape; it's amazing how many people are just horrible in a firefight. Adrenaline can make getting off the simplest of shots difficult, but not for this one. Had to think he had some military training in his background, somewhere. The sniper kept looking through his scope, trying to confirm his kill.

"Dad, the door is hot," Travis said. He'd gone back to try and re-stuff the towel to keep more smoke from pouring in. A hot door meant the fire was right outside. If the other guy didn't show soon we were going to have to take the sniper out and hope his partner was less qualified with a firearm. I looked over, the door handle was beginning to glow. We had minutes. Once that fire ate through the wall or the door we were on borrowed time. I snorted. That was rich–as if we weren't merely scrounging on borrowed time from the moment the zombies showed.

Meredith pointed to the wall as it began to blacken, the paint blistering and falling away. Looked like something straight out of a horror movie.

"He's out," BT said.

At first, there was so little of the person showing I couldn't pick him up. Well, the problem might have been that he was a she. Might have let her go if she hadn't been holding a rifle that was nearly as long as she was. Had a feeling she might be the better shot of the two.

"Ready?" I asked.

"Say the word."

"Now." I fired. Almost immediately, BT did as well. My mark had turned slightly just as I'd fired, sending my round into the stock of her rifle. It exploded outward; I don't know how much of my bullet pierced her chest, but she was able to pull herself back into the apartment and out of my view. BT had hit his in a definitive kill shot—somewhere right below the neckline, bursting through the top of the chest plate. The man had at first been pushed backward, but then because of the way he'd been sitting, he'd fallen forward and was draped over the railing.

"She dead?" he asked.

"Don't know," I told him, trying to pick her up in my sights. "We need to go now. If she's still alive she's going to be calling for help."

"I'll go first." Tommy volunteered. He shouldered past us, opening the now broken window. He pulled the shades straight off the wall in his haste to be free. Had a feeling the boy, like the rats, had a deep-seated fear of fire, as is right. In fairness, who amongst us wants to be burned alive? Tommy had no sooner gone through the window and onto the landing when a bullet pinged off the metal to his left.

"I think she's still alive," BT said as we both tried to find her.

"Window," Meredith said as she sent a couple of rounds of covering fire. Our shooter disappeared. The apartment we were in was getting choking thick with smoke and now the temperature was increasing. Fire was licking the inside walls as it seeped through the openings it was creating. Travis was keeping an eye on the fire—transfixed was more like it.

"Come on!" I yelled at him. "You and Meredith, out!" Tommy had gone down a floor and was scanning for targets; as of yet, the only one that was aware of us was a wounded female with a less than serviceable rifle. She stuck the barrel of her weapon out the window and shot a couple of wildly misfired shots that were still entirely too close. Although, if we're being honest, any shot in your general direction is entirely too close.

"Rats!" Tommy said. At first, I thought he was using a less cuss-worthy swear, then I realized he was talking about our four-legged pursuers. Maybe Knox and his men hadn't found us, but his miniature bloodhounds had. The fire was inside our domicile in earnest, when BT and I made our way out the window. The woman I'd shot had either succumbed to her injuries or her weapon had. Either way, she no longer fired at us. Tommy slid the rest of the way down, his feet straddling either side of the ladder. The rodents that had found us converged. He was stomping them out of existence in the grossest game of Whac-A-Mole I'd ever had the displeasure of witnessing. Fire was blowing through most of the windows by the time my feet touched the ground. We were all on the move, the rats included. They were wary, keeping a respectable distance, but not retreating.

BT looked over his shoulder more times than an NFL running back making a break for the goal line with the entire opposing team in hot pursuit. We were heading toward a gas station. I took a hard right away from it; had no desire to be stuck in something that could be made into a mile-high mushroom cloud. Headed toward a strip mall and a Sub Station sandwich shop. Clearly this place was attempting to lure customers from its much larger, more successful competitor, Subway—even had the same color scheme and font for the sign. If you were more than a hundred feet away from it you'd swear it was the National Chain. The window was kicked out; I immediately ran past it. Tommy was pulling open a heavy-looking door to the Chinese food restaurant next to it.

Crystal Ginger, it was called, or something along those lines. The beauty was it had boarded up windows facing the roadway. Not really sure why this is done at most Chinese food restaurants. I mean, is it because they don't want you to know what they're cooking? Honestly, I don't care because it's all delicious, but it should have been something I gave more thought to when I used to frequent these establishments. The smell inside was bad–not zombie bad–old fermented cabbage and long gone chicken bad.

"Tommy, BT, check the kitchen and the back door. Me and the kids will check out the rest." I threw the lock on the door, hoping we wouldn't need to make a hasty exit. For once there was no one and nothing after us. BT came out of the kitchen with a box that looked as if it could be used to ship fifty-gallon drums.

"Fortune cookies," he said happily. "I'm starving."

I wasn't a big fan of the edible message holders that tasted suspiciously like they were made from the same material as the aforementioned message. But even through all my worry, I was hungry as well. I grabbed a fistful; should have known we were playing a game with fate when the first message I cracked open said: "Be wary of those who gnaw at your confidence," and yes, it sure did have a picture of a rat. I put the rest of the cookies down. I'd suddenly lost my appetite. I was listening as Meredith was trying to raise Justin on the radio. What came through was garbled and we missed every third word.

"Mom…Knox…everywhere," was about the gist of it. No matter how much we tried to ask for more information, we were met by radio silence. Now I was about to lose my shit. We were holed up, and being pursued, the worst of it was not knowing how bad of trouble our family was in.

"We have to go," I said.

"Of course, man! But where?" BT asked.

"We'll head out back and hope our furry friends haven't hemmed us in yet."

"Can I bring the cookies?"

"You've been hanging around Trip too much."

He tossed the box across the room. I opened the back door cautiously before poking my head out. I did not see anything that led me to believe we were under surveillance. I had not a clue as to where I needed to go; one way was just as good or bad as another. I needed to get closer to Justin, as we were apparently at the edge of effective communications range, but how could I tell which way that was? All was quiet out on the street. I heard no car engines revving, no squealing tires, and no shots being fired. There were birds and crickets chirping all around us; just another normal day as far as the animal kingdom was concerned.

"Hear anything?" I asked Tommy. He shook his head. I was going to move roughly towards our original rendezvous point, making sure to stay a few streets over. We'd traveled for close to an hour. The sun was beginning its downward journey; Meredith had produced a noticeable limp.

"You alright, kiddo?" I asked, slowing up to let her get astride.

"I found new boots at that outlet mall we checked out a few weeks ago. Don't know why I decided that today was a good day to break them in. I guess I didn't figure we were going to do much running."

I wanted to tell her that you should always expect to do a lot of running at any given moment. But I figured that lesson had been learned on the back of a dozen or so busted blisters. Worry was beginning to weigh on us all, the darkening sky mirrored our moods.

"You think your sister is alright?" BT asked.

I thought it slightly strange that he singled her out above all others, yet I said nothing.

"I hope so," I told him honestly.

"What do you think about that for the night?" Tommy asked, pointing to an auto parts store across the street.

A good part of me wanted to push on, we'd still heard nothing from anyone else and now I was worried I had picked the wrong direction. Did I keep senselessly plodding in the same wrong direction or did I reverse course and backtrack?

"Works for me," I said as I looked up at the flat roof line of the store.

The auto parts store was, thankfully, devoid of all things living and undead and for the most part, it had been left alone.

The cash register was a broken mess on the floor and the oil section had been cleaned out, but after that, it was mostly clean. I think had I raided this place I would have taken all the air fresheners, and would probably grab a handful before we left. I went into the back, the mystical land of auto parts where they seemingly had enough pieces to re-build every car known to man, at a markup. I once owned a Hyundai; decent car, but obviously bargain brand. It was ninety-four hundred to buy one, brand new. At some point, I had needed a special doohickey for the engine and had gone to an auto parts store to get it and was pissed about the price of the thing. How the man behind the counter knew this, I don't know, but he told me that if I were to build that exact car with the parts I could get there, it would cost a hundred and sixty-seven thousand dollars. Talk about getting bent over the counter and being taken advantage of. Oh, screw the political correct shit–that's just getting fucked up the ass without any lube in sight. In hindsight, buying three Hyundais and selling them for parts, running your own scrap yard, so to speak, would pay for you to get a better automobile, or just use them to repair the first car, much cheaper. Wow, I don't even think there's a point there, but not the first time, I suppose. Anyway, I got what I was looking for in the form of tailpipes, exhaust pipes, and even a few mufflers.

"What are you doing, Talbot?" BT asked.

"Making a bong. Come on, grab some."

"Don't go all Trip on me," though he did as I asked. "Talk to me, man," he said as I headed outside with my payload. "Please don't tell me you had some bizarre childhood trauma involving engine piping and now can't stand to be in the same place with it."

"Hey!" I said, much too loudly. "Hameatingaphobia is a real thing!"

"Did you just make that shit up? And don't even get me started on all the things wrong with a person who doesn't love the delicious smell and taste of ham."

I could feel my gag reflex about to work overtime as I listened to him go on and on about the different types of ham and what you could do with it. Part of me felt like we were filming a scene from Forrest Gump 2. At least he was tossing the pipes up to me on the roof. There was a small access ladder that led there. He carried the last few up with him as he was finally finishing up his narrative.

"Oh, now I get it," he said as he saw that I had made a message with the pipes.

In theory, MJ should be scanning the surrounding neighborhoods, attempting to locate us. If he wasn't, it meant he couldn't. I was unsure as of what our next play might be, if that was the case.

"Wait...does that say 'suck it?' Dude, why?"

"I was running out of pipes."

"You've got enough up here to write the Gettysburg address."

"I was shooting for succinct."

"I guess that'll work. Nobody else would have left that message except for you. Now?"

"Now we see if they have any disgusting auto parts store snacks. Like, almost a requirement that they have old, off-brand things you can't get anywhere else."

"What the hell are you talking about?"

"Watch. I didn't look when we came in, but I bet they have one of those old gumball machines, hasn't been cleaned since the moon landing. It will be full of peanuts, cheerios or some such shit, and they expected people to put a quarter in it so it would dispense like, seven pieces of old, dirty, germ-infested, stale food. Who does that? Who gets food from a gumball dispenser? You ever see those things? The tray you place your hand on to get your goodies usually has layers of grease from all the grease monkeys that have gone before. I'm surprised the tidbits don't get stuck in that gel."

"What the fuck is wrong with you? I used to look forward to getting Red Hots when my dad brought me to these places."

"Might be one of the reasons you're so mad all the time. Maybe you're suppressing some anger concerning your father exposing you to all those toxins."

"Look at me. Do I look like I was fed a steady diet of toxins?" he asked, flexing his muscles.

"Fuck yeah it does! I watched Godzilla, like, a hundred times when I was a kid. That was exactly what happened to him."

"You are such an asshole."

"I've been called worse."

"You think we should stand guard?" he asked as I was heading over to the ladder.

"Wouldn't be the worst idea. I hate that there isn't a direct way up here from inside, though."

"Get some sleep. I'll take the first four hours," he offered.

I thanked him and went back in. Travis had busted open the very machine I had been talking about, only instead of peanuts, they were some M&M clones, though by the shape of them, it was clear they did not have the same type of manufacturing. Looked like candy-coated raisins, if I had to describe them. They were so stale they were simultaneously chewy yet dissolved upon hitting the tongue. I had a couple, but only because my son was happy he'd found something food-like and wanted to share. He brought some up to BT. Not sure how long he was up there, but the worry and running had taken its toll on me; I'd found some garage clean-up towels, rolled them into a pillow and dropped right off to sleep on the polished concrete floor. When BT woke me, I was truly surprised my shift was already up.

"Damn. That sure didn't feel like four hours."

"It wasn't. You got a couple of hours. We got activity."

"Shit." I grabbed my gear.

We got onto the roof, could hear more than one engine running.

"Patrols?" I asked.

"Makes the most sense. Don't know what they know, but

67

that they're close means that maybe some of our people are still around."

"Might be better if they're still looking for us. I hope our people got away and that eventually, MJ will stumble upon our message."

"This is killing me, Talbot. I love these people. I mean maybe not Trip and Deneaux but yeah, the rest of them."

"Any one more than another?" I asked, fishing.

"You're pretty low down on the list, if that's what you're getting at."

"Oh, I meant a Talbot, alright? Just not me." He didn't answer; I took that as all the confirmation I needed.

"What the hell is that?" BT pointed up into the sky. We both saw blinking green and red lights.

"That an aircraft of some kind?" I asked.

"You think?"

"Don't give me shit! We haven't seen anything besides birds flying for months. Looks pretty far off."

"Or not." He stood. "Fuck, Mike we need to take the message down."

"Why?"

"It's a lot closer than you think. It's a drone. They see your pipe insult, they'll know where we're at."

"We don't have enough time to bring it all down." I was grabbing pipe and tossing it off the roof, aiming at the overgrowth around us to soften the landings, still sounded like the brass section of a large traveling band had got into a bus accident with a truckload of cymbals.

"Can probably hear this across state lines," BT said as he heaved a handful.

By this time, we had roused everyone in the store. Travis had scaled the ladder and was poking his head up at us.

"Drone coming. Get everyone back in the store. Let's go, BT," I said, making a dash.

"It's not all gone."

"As good as it's going to get," I told him.

Damn near ended up getting done in by BT, as he was faster down the ladder than I was. Felt like he was going to shove my head down into my chest as he hit me with his bulk. I shook it off as he dragged me around and in.

"We should probably leave," Tommy said, looking out the window. I saw what he meant; now there was an arc of galvanized metal piping all around us. We'd torn up the real words and left kind of an open suggestion to come and see what the hell that was all about. Heard the car before we saw or heard the drone; it was close, next street over.

"They're going to see this mess. They'll have the rats back on us," BT whined.

I looked around; we were in no shape for another flight scenario. Meredith would try her best, but no chance she was going to be able to make an escape with any speed.

"We need to take out that car," I said. "BT, let's go. The rest of you–if this goes south you're going to need to get out of here in a hurry. We'll meet back at the gas station. Got it?"

I could tell Travis wasn't all that thrilled with this plan. He'd already lost the majority of his family and now I was heading out. I gave them all a brief hug. We quickly crossed through a few yards and were on the front lawn of a ranch style house, looking over the roadway. A luxury sedan was slowly rolling down the road. I was afraid they were being cautious because we'd already been spotted. When they stopped, I figured my suspicions had been confirmed. Then I heard and caught sight of the drone. The passenger was leaning out the window, constantly looking at the display and controls he held in his hands and the small craft he was piloting.

"Well we got a driver and a pilot, what are the odds they don't have anyone in the backseat?" I asked.

"Slim," BT said.

"Sure do wish you had more of those rockets."

"Me too," he said. "Do you hear that?"

"It's music! Do those dipshits have the radio on? That…wait that's Linda Rondstandt!"

"How the fuck do you know that?" BT asked.

"Ummm…my sister was a fan."

"Uh huh."

"Sounds like 'Baby You're No Good.'"

"It's just 'You're No Good.'"

"How the hell would *you* know that?"

"Good music is just good music, and the woman can sing."

"True that," I said. "I'll take out the driver; you're going to need to take out anyone in the back."

"The pilot?"

"Last. I can't imagine he's operating a radio and holding a firearm as well." I checked to make sure my suppressor was on tight and waited until the car got closer; figured I was going to have to take a shot at a slow-moving target. Not sure if I should have felt guilty when they stopped right across from us. There were two in the back as well. The pilot was sitting with his head buried in his console, making the driver a difficult shot. He was peering at that thing like he'd found gold, or us, I realized, when he looked up and then immediately over to our less than perfect spot. My bullet blazed through the side of his face and lodged deeply into the skull of the driver, whose head, of course, fell immediately on the horn.

The pilot was screaming bloody murder as BT released a volley of shots into the back seat, saw bodies dancing around in a macabre way. The drone had pitched violently to the side and crash-landed in the next yard over. The pilot was leaning over the seat, I imagined going for the radio, when I placed a shot in his spine. He stopped moving, though I could hear him sobbing.

"Let's get the weapons," I told BT.

"Help me." The pilot said when we got to the car.

"I'll help you if you tell me how many of you there are and who sent you," I said.

"Help, please." Blood spewed from his mouth as he coughed and the death rattle in his chest began to vibrate.

"Fucking tell me!" I'd gripped the front of his shirt.

"He's dead, man," BT said as he lightly touched my shoulder.

"Fuck." I had spots of red in my vision, anger was welling in me, that this group was hounding us relentlessly and now I didn't know where most of my family was. If BT hadn't been there I think I would have taken it out on their corpses.

"Lot of weapons here. Let's take them and go."

"You take them back, I need to hide this car so they don't stumble across it."

"Makes sense, man, I just don't like the look in your eyes."

"Grab the drone as well," I said as I handed him the remote control.

"Do I look like a pack mule?"

"Just as ornery, I suppose."

"You're coming right back?" he asked as he fumbled with one of the guns when he bent down to grab the drone.

"Right back, man." I had pushed the dead driver over and was ready to take off. I reached back and grabbed the radio before I did so.

Drove about a mile when the radio came on. "Patrol seven, yo! Hey Haskell, you there man? You missed your fucking check-in again. You can't keep doing that shit, drives Knox fucking nuts."

"Yeah, it's all cool," I said.

"Haskell, you sound funny."

"Eating chicken wings," I said making a slurping noise.

"I'm not even gonna ask where you got them. Has Devon seen anything?"

"Guy couldn't find his dick with a magnifying glass," I said.

"Haskell, that's weird, man, even for you. He is your brother."

"Tell Knox I'm coming for him."

"Who's this?"

I hate that cliché shit. I mean, do I say his "worst nightmare"? Because knowing Knox's twisted up psyche, it's probably something like circus elephants and how am I going to pull that off? "Just let him know it's someone he's met before who will be delighted to watch him bleed out."

"Where's Haskell and Devon and the others?" The voice on the other end demanded.

"Are you really that thick?" I asked. "You think maybe I was a stranded motorist on the side of the road and they offered to let me borrow their radio so I could call for help?"

"Those were my friends, you sick fuck!"

"That's what happens when you cross us. Don't worry, you'll be with them soon enough." I was about to click the radio off when a different voice came on.

"Talbot, is that you?" The voice asked in almost a caring way. I could hear the insanity burning through the airwaves.

"Miss me, Knox?" I asked.

"Seems I did on a couple of occasions, unfortunately. I won't let that happen again though, I promise. Took out one of my patrols, I see. You realize I have dozens just like them out looking; one actually turned up some interesting footage. Looks like one of your cars we've been chasing. They're holed up right now, and I'm personally going to check it out. I'll get back to you with what I find."

"I'm sure an idiot like you, Knox, has done your fair share of dim-witted shit over the span of your life, but you've gone into the big leagues of stupidity this time. And all your little toy soldiers aren't going to mean a thing when I rip your heart from its casing and feed it to them."

"Hey Talbot? Fuck you. I'm going to go and do some stupid shit with some of the people you love. Talk later. Ciao." And that was it, he signed off. I wanted to smash the radio into the head of the dead driver next to me until it was embedded deep into his broken skull. I had turned around and hid behind our building. About ripped the door off its hinges as I walked into the auto parts store.

"You alright, dad? You look like that time Nicole had a party at the house and your baseball card collection got ruined."

"Mike?" BT asked.

"Talked to Knox." I held up the radio. "He says they found one of our cars and are moving to check it out."

"He could be lying," Tommy offered. "Might be trying to get us to show ourselves."

"He's too stupid to lie," I said. "Anyway, he sounded way too smug for this to be a ploy."

"What do we do?" BT's concern level was beginning to match my own.

"What can we do?"

"I've got the drone working."

That was something.

"Effective range is maybe a quarter mile, but we get it high up enough, we could see for a couple of miles, anyway. We would definitely see some lights or something; they're not moving around in the dark."

"Where's Meredith?" I asked, looking around.

"She's on the roof. Didn't you hear her?" Travis asked.

I scowled, so lost in my impending grief, I must have missed her hail. We all went up to the roof, figured it would add some much-needed height.

"You know how to fly that thing?" I asked as BT placed it on the roof and walked away.

"Up, down, side to side. How hard can it be?" he replied.

I was looking at a controller that any true gamer might have been intimidated by; I think the buttons had buttons on them.

"All you," I said shaking my head. I told the kids to keep an eye out for incoming and spread my arms out to move them back.

It was a four-prop drone, though one of the props was noticeably moving much slower than the rest.

"Don't worry, it catches up," BT said. It dipped to the side and came three feet in our direction before shooting straight up into the air.

"Damn," I said, as I struggled to keep it in my field of

vision. We were all peering at the three by four-inch screen, looking for something, anything, as he made the drone spin around. He made a few slow rotations, then a red bar began to flash, signifying the battery was getting low. He brought it down, nearly missed the roof. I walked away; we had nothing. They were close but Knox had military walkie-talkies, they could have a range up to ten miles. We could get a car and drive around, but it was more than likely Knox would be expecting that, waiting for it, even. We neither heard nor saw anything the rest of the night; this I know because I stayed up on the roof the entire time, couldn't have slept for more than an hour, and that in fitful segments. The sun, instead of bringing renewed hope, illuminated a huge storm heading our way.

"We going out there?" BT asked, handing me a beef stick he must have dragged out from some hidden corner.

"I don't know what to do, BT. He's got us separated, isolated, and we have no idea the whereabouts of any of them. Haven't heard from Justin since yesterday." I was hanging on, but just barely.

"We'll find them, Mike. We'll find them all and we'll make him pay for this."

"Dad!" Travis came up the ladder at practically a run. He had the radio in his hand. "It's Deneaux!"

"Fuck, of all the people I want to hear from she's pretty low on the list," I grumbled.

"She's on the list?" BT asked.

"Only because she's with some of our people."

"Hmmph," BT grunted.

"This is Mike," I said.

"Miss me?" Then she cackled.

"Like I'd miss a raging case of herpes," I said, though I had not depressed the send button. "Everyone alright?" I asked.

"Everyone with me is fine," she said.

"And who would that be?"

"I have that nerdy fellow—what's he call himself? Mad

something or other, and your brother and sister."

BT sighed in relief at that.

"Oh, and your sister's son, one of the boys you saved from the gas station, and your daughter and grandson."

It was not lost on me in the least that she did not call any one of them by name.

"This is a bad business, Michael, this feud you have going on with this Knox character."

"What's your point?"

"You know my personal preferences for self-preservation, do you not?"

"I'm well aware…we're all well aware."

"He is very much in a position of power right now. I could secure some much-needed safety from him."

"Really? You're ready to jump ship? You'd use all of those people as a bargaining chip to make sure your own ass is safe?" I asked the question but I already knew the answer, it would be like trying to reason with a lion out on the savannah that he should not eat the injured water buffalo at the cost of some meerkats it had looking out for it.

"I don't want to, I really don't. Your tenacity to survive, to beat seemingly insurmountable odds is the only thing that has kept me from doing it."

"So, only the thought of my likelihood to survive and seek retribution has kept you from doing the unspeakable?"

"It's speakable. For me, at least."

"Get to the point, you didn't call me to hang a threat over my head." I wanted to reach across the airwaves and rip out the cigarette I knew she had in her mouth and bury the cherry deep into her eye.

"I can save them, Michael. I can save them all," her voice came over loud and clear on the radio.

"What do you want, Deneaux?" I adjusted my grip so I didn't crack the radio in my hand.

"Just a promise—just one small promise and they'll all be safe. You can do that Michael, can you not?"

"Tell me what you want." I was doing my best to contain my anger. It wasn't working so well. I was pacing fast loops around the edge of the roof.

"You will bite me."

I understood the implications of this. Deneaux the Immoral wanted to become Deneaux the Immortal. She could make Eliza look like a cartoon character by comparison. Now I had to weigh whether the lives of my friends and family were worth unleashing this creature onto the world, with her own set of twisted rules.

"You're taking an awfully long time to give me an answer. My window of opportunity won't be open forever. Yes or no?"

"You can't possibly understand what you are asking of me, Deneaux. What you are asking of yourself. You realize what happens to your soul, don't you?"

"Soul?" She started laughing. "What am I going to do with that dirty, hole-ridden sheet?"

I heard what I was sure was a distant scream come over the radio. It was someone in a great deal of pain or torment.

"That was your beautiful wife, Michael. Do you want me to save her? Yes or no?"

"FUCK!" I screamed. "Do it! Save her. Save them all!"

"Promise me first."

"I promise! I fucking promise! Just do it!"

"What are you doing?" BT asked. He'd been following and listening.

"You shouldn't have agreed to that," Tommy said. I didn't like that this was his sentiment *after* he had already done it to me.

I knew in my heart any chance of redemption I may have had was squandered. I'd damned myself and I'd damned them all. I thought of a final confrontation with those who would judge my life. There was no amount of good that could balance unleashing the apocalypse that would be Deneaux.

"What have I done?" I held the microphone to my head. Deneaux had left her side on; we could hear her shots and the cries of surprise from the people holding our loved ones captive. My only hope now was that Deneaux would succeed in saving them and then as they retreated to a safer place she would trip and fall onto a land mine. All of my problems solved.

No, I was not going to be able to leave this one up to providence. I would honor this promise and so much more. Deneaux had sealed her fate when she'd forced me to meet her at this crossroads. I knew which road I was going to take. There was no doubt in my mind, Victor Talbot, having presented Eliza to the world, had found a particularly toasty section of hell to spend the rest of eternity in. If I were to be the second Talbot to spread an evil plague called Deneaux, I might get an entire wing named after me down there. There were more tires screeching and more shots fired, then nothing. I looked at the radio as if it had betrayed me.

"Did anybody hear anything, *not* on the radio?" I got a bunch of shaking heads in return.

"What do we do now, dad?" Travis asked.

"We have to wait." Might have been the hardest words I'd ever had to say. I was not great at waiting; just ask my wife about any of our trips to the DMV. I'm ashamed to admit I'd seen spoiled brats at the toy store around Christmastime act better behaved. Tried to raise Deneaux a dozen, two dozen, fuck it, a hundred times on the radio. Nothing. She had either failed or died. I don't think she would have been stupid enough to seek me out if she had not succeeded. There was a chance my family was dead and she was either halfway to California or nestling in nicely with Knox's illusions of dementia. I'd stayed up on the roof even during the worst of the weather that had rolled in. Had made a decent shelter out of those windshield sun block devices the store sold. It was nearly waterproof; not that this mattered, as I continually walked around in a desperate bid to see something.

"Why didn't she ask you to do this?" I asked Tommy as I sat in the store. I was wringing my hands.

"The short, Mr. T? I think she'd be pleased as punch to see the reaction she's getting from you right now."

"This is what I get. I allow a venomous snake into my house and then cry "why me?" when it bites someone. I mean what did I really expect was going to happen? How can I have such a blind eye to her?"

"She's had a lot more experience with being the type of person she is. Your problem, Mr. T, is that your first instinct is to trust. This won't be the last time it will cost you."

I looked at his back as he walked away. I knew he was right. At some point, someone near to me, someone else, was going to burn me something fierce, just wish I knew who it was so I could avoid them.

It was eighteen hours later when we finally heard from her.

"I'm coming to the automotive store," Deneaux said, breathlessly, like she was getting ready to be in the throes of passion. Not a visual I wanted to entertain, just what it sounded like.

"Is everyone alright?" My lips pressed up so tightly against the radio I was in danger of shredding them against the metal screen.

"Everyone that I could save, is safe," she replied.

"That's not really an answer," BT said to me.

"Who exactly?" I asked.

"I can't be expected to remember all their names."

"Fucking try!" I shouted.

She sighed. "Alright, alright, all the flea-infested animals, your son and the weird baby along with the other little girl from the gas station. And whether you like it or not I saved your mother-in-law," she laughed. "How disappointing is that, Michael, that you can't even get rid of your mother-in-law in an apocalyptic event? What wrongs you must have committed in previous lives!"

"She's a good person and I love her. Why would I want to be rid of her?"

"It's just us, Michael you don't have to feed me any lines."

"I'd like to feed her my fist!"

"Oh, is that the big, surly black fellow I hear?" she asked slightly bemused, if her tone was any indicator.

"Who else?" I asked quietly.

"Oh, I almost forgot. I have your wife, as well."

I did not like it at all that she *had* my wife. "She's alright?"

"Of course she is, I held up my end of the agreement; are you prepared to hold up yours?"

"That thing off?" BT asked, I nodded. "Can you even do what she asks?"

"I guess, I mean, I have the virus inside of me. I don't think she'll get what she wants though."

"You can't, you know."

"Don't you think I know that?"

"Do I just kill her when she shows up?" he asked. "And how does she know we're here?"

"This is Deneaux, it's her job to know. And don't you think she knows we'll try to stop her?"

"But what can she do once they're all back here?"

"She said she was alone," I replied.

"Even better."

"Not really, buddy. She's way smarter than we are at setting up things like this. She has a deck of cards in her hand I bet she's willing to play."

"So, she's got them held captive or something? We'll just beat her until she tells us where they're at." BT was getting angry.

"She's thought of that, too."

"No way man. She's not the devil."

I gave him a stink eye.

"Well maybe she is a devil, but she's not *the* devil. You seem mighty sure she's some evil mastermind. Maybe she's just a mean, bitter, old woman. Maybe she doesn't really have it all figured out."

"I like your thought process, man, I really do. I think you're throwing your good copper pennies in a dried-up well, though."

We watched as the demonic driving Deneaux barreled up the roadway, a lit cigarette in a hand hanging out the driver side window. Johnny Cash blaring on the radio, she gave not two shits about who heard her coming.

"She's way too confident," my son said. I was thinking the same thing. What did she know that we didn't? I hadn't personally spoken to any of those she'd supposedly saved. Had she already betrayed us and was now setting us up? The truth was even stranger, at least considering who was involved.

I was at the door about to go out into the parking lot to meet her when she kept on going. Drove right the fuck past. She knew where we were; she tossed a cigarette out the window and held up one finger, and not the middle one, the "wait" one.

"What is she doing?" Meredith asked.

I could only shake my head. She drove past. I waited the allotted fifteen seconds and was heading outside–nearly got spotted by a pickup truck full of assholes. Amazing how many of them you can fit in the back of a full-sized one. That's the thing about assholes, they don't like to do anything on their own; they're pack animals. I pulled myself back in just as they passed.

"Safe to say she's been compromised," Tommy said.

"But she just led them away, right?" BT had a confused look on his face.

"Her cigarette looked funny," Travis said. "Too long."

"What the hell is going on?" I was looking to the spot it had landed. He was right. "Going for it; cover me," I said as I went outside. I did a quick scan, including the sky for another drone, moved fairly quickly, and retrieved a butt that was wrapped in a piece of scratch paper.

It was a note, but I wasn't foolhardy enough to read it out in the open. When I got back we all huddled around when I opened it. The handwriting was atrocious, hastily written, possibly with her left hand-unless she'd been in the midst of a heart attack or stroke, one could only hope.

"Comp…K has wife others, MJ @ 2 Stevens."

"Comp?" Travis asked.

"Compromised?" I threw out there, it seemed to stick. That wasn't the part that hurt though, it was that the K most assuredly stood for Knox, and he had my wife and son. "Let's go."

"Where, man?" BT asked.

"Wherever the hell 2 Stevens Road is," I said, going to grab my things.

"And where exactly is Stevens Road?" he asked.

"I don't know, but we need to go."

"I get it, man! We need to go! But we can't wander around hoping to stumble across it. We need a plan. And I don't know if we should blindly trust this," he said, holding the note up.

"There's a lot of fishy going on here," Meredith said.

"Yeah Mr. T," Tommy said. I was feeling mighty outnumbered. I looked to Travis, he was ready to follow wherever I went to save our family.

"If she's compromised, like she says, isn't she likely to have made a deal?" BT asked.

"She led them away and told us where MJ is, sounds like she's still playing for this team." That logic didn't even sound good to my own ears.

"What if they want to bring us out into the open and she's luring us?" Tommy asked.

"They know where we are," I fought on.

"And what's easier to attack?" BT added. "People in a defendable position or…"

"I get it, I get it. You can't expect me to just sit back and do nothing, though, can you? You heard the screams on the radio."

"There's a chance the whole thing was a set-up, dad," Travis said.

There was some relief in that, that maybe the despot didn't have them. Sure, that would mean Deneaux had flipped sides, but that was always a given.

"If she told them what you are, he's going to want you alive, Mike," BT said. "You as well, Tommy. No reason to think he wouldn't want to be king forever."

"I hate her," I said putting my head against the wall. "What the hell do we do now? She's sufficiently put enough doubt in our heads that she's immobilized us. We don't want to do anything for fear of it being the wrong move."

"Sounds exactly like her," Meredith said.

"I think no matter what, Mike, we should get out of here," BT said. "Got to figure at the minimum they know we're here."

"You're right." I went behind the counter, rummaged on the shelves underneath the register for a minute before I found what I was looking for–a grease-stained, old and ripped phone book. I'd been a fan of new technologies, but was happy to see we hadn't completely forsaken all of the classics. I ripped out the first few pages–they invariably contained a map of the surrounding area printed on them. I folded them up and stuffed them in my pocket. "Let's go."

"Ummm, Uncle, if they know we're here, doesn't it stand to reason that they have this place surrounded or at least under surveillance?" Meredith voiced her concern.

I looked to each of them. Varying degrees of fear, doubt and anxiety warred among their features. "We can play the 'what if' game for all eternity. Inaction is just as dangerous as the wrong action. I've got a hunch that Deneaux might be playing both sides, waiting to see who comes out on top before she hops back on or over to a new bandwagon as the case may be. She's always thought we have an uncanny ability to win; my gut says she may have given us a small window to prove her right again."

"You just said you hated her," BT piped up.

"Yup. Gotta know your enemies. Let's go." I went out first, rifle at the ready. The odds I'd see where the shot came from were minimal if we were being watched. I turned my head when I heard a dog barking off in the distance, maybe a few streets over; there was more barking, nothing for a few seconds, then those high-pitched yelps as something or some things got a hold of it. My guess was rats; they were going to hem us in again with the little vermin, then we began to hear the chittering, tiny squeakings of them.

"That what I think it is?" BT asked. Though he already knew, he began to run in the exact opposite direction, which was easily the best and most natural option, given the circumstances. We'd gone about fifty yards and Meredith was already twenty behind us, she looked like she was running in uneven heels or had one mother of a rock in her shoe.

"They got worse," she said as I went back. She was leaning heavily against me as I half carried, half dragged her. More times than not, the toes of her boots were scraping across the ground.

"Were you going to say something?" I looked down and her boots were wet, it was either burst blisters or blood.

"I don't think so," she said, giving me a weak smile.

We'd gone a half mile and I was starting to lose sight of BT, who was seemingly running in a blind panic. Tommy and Travis had held back somewhat, as an intermediary so we could see them and they could see him. When they stopped, I could not immediately tell why until I looked past and BT was on his knees, hands up in the air, rifle on the ground next to him. I saw two camo-clad men approaching him with what looked like M-16s.

I made Meredith take a hard right with me. No way Tommy and Travis weren't spotted. I needed to get around the men and get us free. I deposited my niece on a small porch completely enclosed by the privacy of a few strategically placed oaks.

"I'll be right back," I told her as she gingerly sat down. I went through a small gate, then hopped a fence. I was going through the backyards before I cut back to get to BT. When I was across from where I needed to be, I slowly worked my way to the front. BT was face down on the ground, his hands had been zip-tied behind him. One of the men had his rifle trained on him as the other was now directing Travis and Tommy to drop their weapons and come forward. I saw the barrel of the rifle before I saw the person wielding it. No doubt he'd known I was coming. I grabbed it and forcibly wrenched it from his hands even as the word "stop" was coming out of his mouth. He hit me in the jaw hard enough with his fist that the marbles in my head would be spinning for a good long while. I took a few steps to the side, he had pulled out his Ka-Bar. I brought my rifle up.

"Put it down." The words hurt to say. I was slowly moving my jaw, it wasn't busted, but I was going to want my food soft for a couple of days, I mean, provided I made it to my next meal. "You look like you know what you're doing with that…trained, even, but so am I. With the rifle I mean. I'm not fucking around, Major," I sneered when I saw the insignia on his collars. "If you want to play soldier in Knox's psychotic little fuck-fest that's one thing, but don't you dare desecrate my beloved Corps uniform. I should shoot you just for that, but I just want my friends back unharmed."

He put the knife down, way too willingly. "You're not with that idiot then?" he asked. His hands up by his side.

"You telling me you're not either?"

"Son, I am wearing this uniform because I am a Marine, not some para-military mercenary wannabe."

"I'm thinking we might be close to the same age; you calling me son weirds me out a little. This isn't the South. And listen, I've had my fill of potential mind-fuckery today, seems like a pretty good time to denounce your affiliation, considering you know…this." I said as I jiggled my gun.

"Winters–let the man up!" The major yelled across the yard.

Winters turned. "You think that's–" He stopped when he saw me holding a rifle on his commander. He moved fast, bringing his rifle to bear on me. "Put it down now!" he screamed as he advanced. "Biddie! Got a problem!" He never took his eyes off of me.

"Stand down!" I was sparing glances to the man that had me dead to rights on my side. I moved in closer, slowly putting the major between me and that rifle while pointing my muzzle straight at the Major's head. "I'll take his head off!" I told him. "Sanders," I saw the man's name on his camouflage blouse, or at least it was the name of the person he'd taken it from, "Sanders, tell him to stop. I'm getting mighty nervous." I had my finger on the trigger. At this point even if Winters shot me, odds were good I was going to plug one into Sanders' cranium.

"Whoa, everyone, just take a step back!" Sanders ordered. Had to admit the man had that officer authority about him and that's hard to fake. Couldn't stand it too much when I was in the Corps, but out here someone takes charge well enough for others to follow, you have to admire that. And now that it got Winters to stop moving, I was alright with Sanders having it. It kept others less powerful from becoming the slaves of those that wielded power indiscriminately. "Winters stop, it's me he has that gun pointed at, son."

"I've got a shot, sir," Winters answered. Biddeford came running up, I now had two rifles pointed at me, although he seemed torn between spending time on me and following up on Travis and Tommy who, I would imagine, would be coming up to investigate any second now.

"Someone better get me up off the motherfucking pavement!" BT yelled. "Fuck it, I'll do it myself." He strained and I watched two sets of heavy zip ties break in half and fly off into the air like string.

"Major Sanders, if that is who you are, I have you, no two ways about it. They kill me, I'll still kill you. And those boys coming up the road right now are excellent shots; those two with you are going to get hurt or maybe die if there's a firefight. Plus, well, that gigantic black man is coming over here now and you'll notice he's so pissed he didn't even grab his weapon. He's just going to knock heads together like coconuts. Not sure who will be dead when it all shakes out, but we'll both take some losses and I'm not really up for that, at least not on my side."

It was a standoff at the moment, a lot of guns pointing in a lot of different directions and we were just one itchy finger from a bloodbath. Tommy and Travis were up here now and had fanned out to the side of Winters and Biddeford, giving us superior position. BT had finally gone back and retrieved his rifle when he realized that neither man was going to let him get in close enough to play head bongos. He seemed genuinely put out about it as he reached down and snatched the weapon off the ground.

"Mike," he said, gesturing with but not actually pointing his rifle. "What are we going to do with them? We let these douche bags go they'll head straight for Knox."

"Let's make one thing clear, now. We might be strangers to you but we are not with that jackass Knox. My name is Major Sanders. I am a Marine and was attached to the First Marine Expeditionary Brigade, although I don't think they exist anymore. Over there is Sergeant Winters and Corporal Biddeford. They were with me when the dead shit-birds began to take over."

"Don't know of any Marine Corps bases in New Hampshire," I said to him.

"There are no organized Marine Corps bases anywhere. I came up here to find my family."

"And did you?"

"Mike! You taking that man out on a date?" BT asked. "If you haven't noticed we've got some issues to take care of first."

I lowered my rifle. "Semper Fi, Major."

"What's he doing?" BT asked Travis.

"You served?" the major asked.

"As hard as it may be to believe, I did five years."

"Thought I might have seen something in the eyes, though you could use a shave," he said as he pointed to my goatee.

"Swore I was never going to shave again once I got out."

"I can get behind that sentiment," Winters said. "Sir?" he asked, raising his rifle slightly. The major motioned for him to put it down.

"Dad?"

"Looks like no one is shooting anyone here today," I said.

"Today?" the major asked.

"I like to keep my options open," I told him.

"Want to give me the short story?" he asked.

I was about to tell him to go first, instead, I answered. "We found a settlement we're trying to get to, it's been a hard road. We had the unfortunate luck of running into one that would consider himself king. We've been separated from our main group and there's a good chance this lunatic has some of our people."

"This Knox fellow?" he asked, though it sounded like he already knew.

"One and the same. You know him?"

"Know of him. We've been monitoring the radio bands. We were actually on our way to the parts store to see what kind of people were holed up there."

"That would have been us. Have you seen the rats?"

"Rats?" Biddeford asked.

"He's got truckloads of them. Trained little assassins." BT shuddered.

"He sends the rats in to either flush out or do the wet work," I said.

"How many men?" the major asked.

"Tough to tell; he gathers stragglers. We had a run-in up in Maine, did a fair amount of damage to his kingdom, but there's no lack of stupidity. I'd say maybe a hundred, though I don't think he brought all of that with him."

I noticed Biddeford handing Tommy a granola bar, which he gratefully accepted.

"Where's this settlement?" the major asked.

"So far, major, I've given all the information."

"Came for my wife and kid, sent them up here to my

sister's when it looked like things were going from bad to shithole."

"And?"

"They're all doing fine. The not-so-good news is I might have to consider Winters an in-law soon, the way I've seen him and my sister making eyes at each other."

Winters turned. His mouth opened wide and he had a flush of red up his neck. "We've been discreet, sir."

"Discreet? I think you'd better look up the definition of that word."

"I told you he knew." Biddeford shouldered his friend.

"You knew and didn't tell me?" Sanders asked.

"I, um…I just found out." Biddeford set up a weak defense.

"Relax, Winters. I still need you," Sanders said. "For now."

"And if you didn't?" Winters gulped.

"You'd be spending a lot of time on point." Winters blanched at that. "How confident are you about this settlement?" Sanders turned back to me.

I looked over at BT. He gave me that "you stepped in it" look of his. "What are you looking at me for? You're going to do whatever you want to anyway."

"We have, or had, depending on circumstances, access to a spy satellite with a live feed."

Sanders sucked in his breath. "That's a pretty powerful tool to have in your grip. You should have done more to protect it."

"I don't need shit from you, Major. My wife, son, and others may be in danger. We are a fairly large group, spread thin with fighters, doing our best to survive–just against zombies. You throw in a douche renegade group that has listed us as their enemy number one, and right now we're lucky to be alive, much less keep our gadgets secure. You say you're active? What the fuck have your trio been doing to preserve the American way of life?"

Don't think the major was all that used to a dressing down,

especially from someone that had only been a Corporal and barely held on to that rank. "Fair enough," he said after a moment of reflection. "What can we do to help?"

"Um, well…" He kind of…nope. He caught me *completely* off-guard.

"You'll have to excuse my friend, Major. He's not much into the planning phase," BT said coming over. But before he did so he got up in Winters' face, well, chest to face, but you get the idea. "You ever put zip ties on me again and I'll squish your head like a stress ball," he said as he squeezed his massive hands into fists. Winters the man was beginning to resemble winter the season. Pale. He was pale, if that wasn't clear.

I told him mostly what was going on and where we were headed and that there were still rats on our tale, actual rats, not tattletales. We had since moved out of the open and into one of the abandoned houses—the one that I had come through the yard of and sent Travis back to gather up my niece.

"This Deneaux, I'm not understanding why you've let her in amongst you if you are so distrustful of her," the major said. "She sounds like a real piece of work."

"Necessary evil, I'm afraid. Not that many of us are fighters." I looked up as Travis returned with Meredith.

"Uncle, I might be in a little trouble," she said as she down heavily on one of the kitchen chairs. She winced as she reached down to undo her boot laces.

I went over and helped her; had to completely remove the laces to give her swelling feet enough room as I quickly pulled her boots off. For a moment, I mistakenly thought she had on red socks, until some of the coloring dripped to the floor.

"Holy shit, Mer. When were you going to say something?" I was doing my best to peel her socks off without taking skin.

"Damn," Biddeford said. "Don't touch it. I've got supplies here."

I was just thinking that was mighty convenient when Sanders spoke up.

"We have a bunch of safe houses in the neighborhood in

case we have to bug out from our primary; this is one of them."

"Smart. Wish I'd thought of that," I said.

Biddeford came back with a basin, some Epsom salts, water and a few medical supplies.

"Whatever you two come up with, this one is out of the equation," he said as he cut the other sock off with some medical scissors. Her left foot was even worse than the right.

Her feet turned the concoction that Biddeford had made in the basin to a frothy pink, she winced then sighed.

"That should help," he told her.

Now I was a little fucked. I trusted these three men to a point, but I wasn't ready to leave my hobbled niece with them. Yet whatever was happening at 2 Stevens Road, needed to be checked out, and soon.

"She'll be fine here." The major saw my concern. "I can get my wife over here to watch her, and short of a chainsaw and maybe some explosives nobody is getting in here."

"What about rats?" I asked.

He didn't answer. Every man who's ever lived in a house knows that if a rat wants in your home there isn't much you can do about it.

"Alright, let's work on something we may be able to fix," he said. I know where Stevens is and remember the general layout. It's a corner lot. If they are setting you up it's a perfect place—great views all around the house, no stealthy way to approach. We got a few tricks up our sleeves we can use to cancel that out. Winters, head back to base, bring a car. We're going to need all the smoke you can muster, and grab a couple of the SAWs as well."

"The SAWs? Really? You know how long it took me to hand-fill those linked rounds? And who was the brainiac that called the M249 a 'light machine gun'? Weighs over twenty damn pounds!"

"Sergeant!"

"Yes sir. I'm on it, sir."

"I don't know who is in there yet, Major. I don't really

want to go in with guns blazing, and I definitely don't want my family shooting at me. I mean, I'm sure there are times when my wife wants to, I mean, at some point, but that isn't now."

"Just going to have to do some recon," he said. "Let's go over some of the details."

"Got to admit, Talbot, it's kind of nice to actually have an idea of what we're going to do. Instills confidence," BT said, smiling.

"Fuck off."

He smiled wider. I don't know exactly where their base of operations was, but it was close because Winters was back in under fifteen minutes.

"This is my wife," Sanders said as he got up from the table. "Kylie, this is Michael, BT, Travis, Tommy, and the person you'll be keeping an eye on, Meredith."

She was a slight woman, early forties, blond hair, very pretty and very dignified looking, even with a pistol on each hip. She shook my hand. "I truly hope your family is okay," she said to me.

If I still had any reservations about this group they dissolved in her deep blue eyes and the look of concern on her face.

"Oh, honey! Where did you get these boots?" She picked them up and admired the cut and leather before discarding them to the side. "If there can be happiness found in an apocalyptic event it's that I have raided every couture shop up and down the coast."

"I can attest to that," Sanders laughed.

"I'll get you some new, better fitting ones—just as pretty. I have some in your size," Kylie said. "You be safe out there," she said to her husband, to his two charges, to us all, really.

CHAPTER FOUR
MIKE JOURNAL ENTRY 4

"BIDDEFORD MUST BE a quarter Cherokee and maybe three-quarter Japanese because he is damn near a ninja. We'll send him to get right up close to the house; see if he can let us know what's going on. We have a safe house the street over from Stevens. We can sit tight there while he goes out."

"So, if it's just them, I'll be looking at a bunch of animals and kids, one young adult male, older woman and your wife?" Biddeford asked.

"That's our best guess," I said.

"His wife is the fiery red-head," BT said. "Don't piss her off—it'd be a bad day for you."

"I'll keep that in mind," Biddeford said as he ratcheted down anything that might come loose and make noise on his approach. "Testing," he said into his small radio. "Why the hell didn't the Corps have these?" he asked. "Had to walk around with radios bigger than my head; looked like a punk with a boombox."

"Tough to find something bigger than that head," Winters jibed his friend.

"You know what they say don't you?" Biddie asked him.

"No, but I'm sure you'll tell me," Winters responded.

"Big head, big head." He thrust out his pelvis.

"Get the hell out of here," Sanders told him. "And be careful."

"It's a Marines thing; you wouldn't understand," I told BT as he shook his head in confusion at the exchange.

"Do you all have to pass the socially dysfunctional test before they'll let you in?" BT asked.

"Who needs to be social? We shoot things," I explained.

As twenty minutes passed, we grew tense. We'd heard nothing from Biddie, and just sitting there while we waited was excruciating.

"Kentucky, this is nugget. We have at least two home fries at the desired location. Possibly a dozen foreign bodies in the fryer."

"What's with the fast food references?" I asked Winters.

"The major was up for promotion right before the zees came," he whispered.

"Oh." I got it quick enough, especially for me.

"Biddie loves the jargon and the major seems alright with it."

To me, it looked like Sanders wanted to take bites from the radio but I held my opinion to myself.

"Pulling back. Foreign bodies suspicious. I think they may have a transmitter detector." We heard gunfire just as the radio cut out.

If I thought the previous twenty minutes had been tense, they paled in comparison to the next five.

"Nugget A-Ok," he panted. "Back in five."

He came in the door breathless; he'd run the entire time. "Shut off everything that transmits. Got a couple on my ass." He took a deep breath. Wasn't a half a minute later a drone flew across the yard.

"These guys aren't playing around," Sanders said as he stepped away from the window. "You must have really pissed them off."

"To be fair, it was BT." I pointed. "He destroyed their toilet."

"Feel all safe and warm next to your Marine Corps buddies, do you?" BT asked threateningly.

"Well, I did right up until now."

"Done?" Sanders asked me. I nodded.

Winters had given Biddie a drink; he took a couple of seconds to get his wind back. "Pretty sure I saw your wife and son. Couldn't get close enough to see any others. I didn't get the feeling that they were aware anyone was out there–they were alert but not alarmed. The ones watching the place though, they were all business. A fair amount of them, Major, are definitely prior military. A couple could even be special forces–they were on me pretty quick."

"Night vision?" Sanders asked.

"I couldn't stick around to ascertain, but it stands to reason."

"So, they have the numbers, at least one eye in the sky, and a defensive perimeter."

"Sir, Major," I began. "I can't believe I'm going to say this, but I wouldn't feel right if I didn't. This isn't your fight, sir. I want my family back more than you can know, but I can't ask you to sacrifice your own."

"You're a jarhead, right?" Winters asked with a lopsided smile. "You know we can't leave anyone behind." He clapped me on my shoulder. If I could have cried from relief and gotten away with it, I would have done so; I'd save the tears for when I had Tracy next to me.

"Let's go through some plans," Sanders said as he began to draw a map on the table.

"A man after my own heart," BT said as he grabbed a chair.

"I could plan if I wanted to," I said.

"Right. Keep telling yourself that."

"Alright. Tonight, is a three-quarter moon, plenty of light. My guess is not everyone that has the night vision will wear it, but let's say half. If they've got a dozen, we have to assume they're evenly spaced at the intersections, keeping every approach in sight. We have enough here to easily overwhelm each position, but we'll need to be quick. They'll have radio contact with each other, so our unknown factor is how often they keep in touch; that's our window to move from one team to the next. I think our best bet is going to be to spread thin. Teams of two will take out two intersections at the same time, and meanwhile we send three people in for extraction; I'm thinking Winters, myself, and you. What's your name?"

"Tommy."

"Tommy, you alright with a knife?" I think he had his doubts, looked like he was thinking the kid might be a liability and wanted to keep him under his wing.

"I've been known to use one from time to time," he answered.

"Good. You're with us. Biddie, you, Talbot, his son, and the range here, take on this area."

"The range?" BT asked.

"As in mountain," Sanders said without looking up from his map.

"Oh, I can live with that." BT was smiling.

"More like a volcano, always ready to erupt...but range works too," I said quickly as BT frowned at me.

"What about me?" Meredith hobbled over.

"I have no doubt you're good in a fight, but right now you're a liability. If we have to move fast I'm not sure you can keep up." I think Sanders saw something in her eyes that she was going to prove him different. "Listen, Meredith, there's no shame in sitting this one out. I know you could put those boots back on and suck it up, but you'll undo all the work Biddie did to keep your feet clean and infection free. You can't risk further trouble; his expertise only goes so far, you end up needing a doctor and you could lose either of those feet."

"Uncle?" Meredith pleaded.

"There is no part of me that doubts you as a warrior, kid. You're a skilled survivor, but he's right, we can't risk you getting worse. Please do this for me," I asked.

She nodded reluctantly.

"You realize that means not sneaking out after us, right?" She nodded reluctantly again.

"I'll keep an eye on her," Kylie said. "We'll make a batch of brownies, do some needlepoint…" everyone was staring at her like she was sprouting a tail. "I'm kidding!" she yelled just as Meredith was going for her boots. "We're going to defend the homestead until they come back. Just because we're not in the action now doesn't mean we won't be."

"Once we get into the thick of it we're not going to be able to communicate," Sanders said. "I'll click one time on each squad's radio once we've dispatched them; you do the same on your end. I think it would be best if you, Mike, and either your son or Range went in to retrieve your family. There will be fewer chances of mistaken identity and someone getting needlessly shot."

"His wife might shoot him just out of principle," BT said.

"Got movement." Winters was looking out the window. "Drone operator and two armed escorts walking straight down the roadway like they own the place. Look like they're mighty interested in this spot. They're pointing."

"I think I know why." Meredith hobbled over to the back door. "Ninja over there left a trail." She was looking into the backyard at the bent-over tall grass Biddeford had compressed.

"I hear an engine," Kylie said.

Wasn't a few seconds later we all heard it, or more accurately, them.

"I'm sorry about this," I said to Sanders.

"Not your fault. Now, Biddie could shoulder a little bit." He looked over at the corporal.

"Must be getting rusty. The zees are easy to evade compared to the living."

"Shit," BT and I said together when a tractor-trailer pulled up and parked down the road a bit.

"There's another truck coming," Travis said. He was

upstairs. "This one is different, dad. It's a cattle car."

"Cattle car? Now they have trained pigs?" I asked aloud.

"I think it's *people*." Winters had a set of field glasses.

"Zombies?" Sanders asked.

"I don't think so, Major."

"Combatants," BT observed.

"I'm more inclined to think fodder. They look malnourished and beat to shit but they have weapons, melee ones, anyway. Bats, sickles, pitchforks, that kind of thing." Winters replied.

"What the hell?" Sanders said as he borrowed the binoculars. "Forced conscripts? This guy is one sick fuck."

"Sir, what do we do?" Biddeford asked, but we were all feeling it. They were slaves. Killing those that were forced into doing the sick bidding of a megalomaniac was not something any of us were comfortable with.

"They probably don't want to fight and are most likely being compelled to do so for a variety of reasons. But make no mistake, people, they will kill you. Killing us is still better than whatever alternative there is for them. That makes it an 'us or them' scenario. We cannot be swayed by our moral compass or get mired in why they are doing what they are doing," Sanders said.

"They're opening up the other truck," Meredith said.

"They must have really liked that toilet," Winters said, looking over at BT.

"Just my luck to get stuck in a house full of crazy Marines." BT shook his head.

"So, the rats come in to drive us out into their suicide army. Alright. Time to evacuate," Sanders said. Winter, Biddeford, and Kylie began to move.

"What's the plan?" I asked. BT had a point–it was kind of nice to have one in place.

"Like you give a shit." BT was going over to help Meredith. I frowned at him.

"All of our safe houses have an alternate means of escape.

The person that lived here supplied most of New Hampshire with weed; he converted an old Cold War bunker into a grow room for his plants. Only took us a couple of days to dig out a small passage from there to the neighbor's house, went right through the foundation."

"I like these guys, BT, they know what they're doing, unlike you," I said as I grabbed Meredith's free shoulder. "Shouldn't we be going downstairs?" I asked, thinking that the entrance would be through the basement somewhere, but Winters was halfway upstairs and telling Travis to turn around.

"The entrance is through the fireplace in the master bedroom," Sanders told me as he brought up the rear.

"Gonna be a bit tight for you, big fella. Hope you're not claustrophobic," he said to BT.

"How…um, I mean, how tight is it going to be for me?" I was nearly in a panic thinking about being surrounded on all sides by brick. I'd read more than one horror story about some over-zealous dad disappearing around Christmas, wanting to surprise his kids as Santa Clause. Then, instead he gets fished out weeks later when his rotting corpse begins to foul up the house.

"Everything but your mouth should fit down nicely," Sanders said.

"Well, good to see he knows your type," BT said.

"We should make sure he goes last. He can plug it up like a wine cork, that way nobody else will be able to get to us," I said.

"I realize you're nervous and that makes you say things you might not normally, but you're still an asshole," BT said.

Winters got down on his knees in front of a small fireplace. Whoever put this chimney in was definitely not looking to impress anyone. Winters pulled on a small catch and the entire floor of the fireplace, including the wood and the grate the wood was on rose up into the chimney above.

"You need to be quiet in here," Winters said to us. Kylie

sat down on her rear and slid forward, her left foot going in first. Her back just reached the edge when her feet must have hit a foothold; she bent up a little and then lowered herself more, she ducked her head down and then popped it back up into the chimney top, then she descended out of sight. Seemed like there was plenty of room for small, agile women.

"You next," Sanders said to Meredith. A light shone up the tunnel; Kylie illuminated our way down once she got to the bottom. I poked my head down the hole; there was a series of ladders—well, rungs cemented into the brick, but the opening didn't magically get any bigger like I'd hoped.

"Uncle, could you maybe get out of the way?" Meredith asked as she scooted over to the edge. I came face to face with her bandaged feet. She went down with no problem, Travis went next, then Tommy. I went to the window in the flying-against-the face of reality-hopes that they'd decided there was nothing here to investigate and I wouldn't have to go down the chimney, or as I thought of it, Satan's asshole. Knowing him, Satan, that is, there'd be some carnivorous tapeworms in there waiting for some unsuspecting body parts to enter so they could grab a meal.

Biddeford went just as we heard the explosion of a window from the first floor, then the loud hissing of a gas canister, releasing tear gas, most likely. I convinced BT to go next—not out of any heightened altruistic reasons—but rather, if he got stuck I wouldn't have to. Go, that is. Much easier to fight men rather than the rapidly growing legion of demons that infected my mind. I watched as BT placed a leg inside the opening; that alone seemed to take up most of the room. When he got his other leg in they were definitely scraping the outer edges of the chimney. He was going to have to do some contortionist shit if he was ever going to get his chest and shoulders through. Even Sanders had taken note of his descent—I could see him doing the math in his head as his expression changed from mildly concerned to truly doubtful. He went over and shut the bedroom door just as the gas was nefariously climbing the stairs like a slivering serpent, cascading over each riser, making its way up step by step until it could finally choke off our airways.

Then I wondered. With all the equipment that Knox had been using, was it possible he'd just popped a nerve gas canister into the house? Because in that case, we were going to die a horrible death. That shit would seep through the cracks around our magical trapdoor and come after us brick by brick until it hit our air. Then we would bleed out through every orifice and eventually even our skin. I'd seen firsthand the effects of this particular way of dying. There was a reason most nations, even the crazy ones, had banned its use (even though everyone stockpiled it.) I'd been so fixated on watching the insidious gas work its way under the door I had not even realized BT was no longer in sight.

"He made it?" I asked no one in particular.

"You're up." Winters clapped my shoulder.

"Rats are on the way," Sanders said helpfully, stepping back from his view of outside.

"Nerve gas, death by rabid incisors, or Satan's asshole. I really wish there was a door number four."

"Huh?" Winters asked.

"Fuck, I hate when I talk out loud when I don't mean to." I went for the asshole. Figured if there was anything in there that could have got me, BT would have been like the world's biggest colon brush and just scraped it all clean. The panic didn't hit me until I dipped my head down, under, and into the fireplace proper. Things got real small real fast.

"Get your ass in there, Marine," Sanders said with enough authority I became that kid again with a flat top and a rifle.

"Yes, sir," I mumbled as my dangling foot finally found purchase and I put weight on it. In my perfect, updated, vision of the zombie apocalypse, I would be with my family, friends, and a brigade of Marines as we defended a wide mote surrounded castle in the English countryside. The moat would be stocked with bass; there would be fruits and vegetables in the courtyard, hell, my grandkids would climb stunted apple trees. We would only shoot game. We'd have more food and ammunition than we could ever hope for. Clear fields of vision for a quarter mile and not an enemy in sight because we had done such a thorough job of eradicating them, or at least we'd been able to stay under their radar. Instead, we were being chased relentlessly and I was currently in a vertical fucking tomb. BT reached up to grab my leg, at first, I thought maybe it was to pull me down because I was going too slow, but it was actually for reassurance. It worked; I was thankful for it and it brought my mind back to the business at hand. By the time I made the two-story drop, I was coated with a thick layer of sweat, and according to Kylie, I was the pasty gray color of old Elmer's glue. She pointed down a corridor that was about the width of my shoulders, and said Biddeford was waiting.

I felt better by the time we were all in the shelter slash grow-room. It was decent sized, twenty by twenty with an eight-foot ceiling. The fact that it had no windows and was underground was beginning to unravel my psyche at the edges and I could only hold that off for so long. As much as I would have liked to hang out there and regroup, I knew resting comfortably was out of the question. The walls would begin their slow press inwards and the ceiling would invariably begin to shrink down. It would be slow at first, almost imperceptible, but quarter inch by quarter inch it would come until I woke from a slumber to find it pressed up against my nose and I would not be able to do much more than wiggle my toes.

"Talbot, you listening to me?" It was BT. I was busy looking at the ceiling. I knew that if I kept doing that it would not be able to move. Sort of like a game of red light, green light.

"I'm with you, man," I told him.

"Not what I asked, but okay. We're leaving now. There's a tunnel up ahead; you're going to have to low crawl through it. I'm told it's bigger than the chimney."

Deer in the headlights, kid lost in Walmart, parent looking

for his lost kid in Walmart. I had all of that accumulated paralytic anxiety surging through me. Trip's spelunking adventure was still vividly fresh in my mind. I looked around and did not see any vats of lard, so that was a good sign, right?

"Mike. Winters is going to go first and secure the other house. You're going in right after him. That clear?" Sanders asked right in my face.

I nodded because that was the appropriate thing to do. Really wasn't feeling it, though.

"Autopilot, Talbot, don't think, just do. That should be second nature to you." BT was doing his best to assuage my fear.

I found it amazing. When I should have been thinking, I often just acted, but now that I needed to just act, I was thinking. When the day came I met my maker, I was going to ask for a refund, or at least leniency because of all the head maladies that I'd been given or had been afflicted with.

There were two blinks of a light from Winters when he made it through to let me know it was safe to go.

"You got this, dad," Travis told me.

"It's barely twenty feet across. Close your eyes and low crawl like you mean it. You'll be through in ten seconds," Sanders said.

"Could you order me through please?"

"Talbot! Get your fucking ass through that opening or I'm going to have you cleaning latrines with your tongue," Sanders said.

"Yes, sir." I took his advice—kept my eyes closed and moved with a mission. I may possibly have broken a land speed record. Didn't hurt that when I was halfway through I heard gunfire; it was muffled but distinguishable. There are certain sounds that trump even the voices in your head.

"Not coming this way," Winters whispered when I got through. "I think they're just randomly shooting at the house—or maybe some of their people aren't so willing to go in."

"Can't imagine why," I said as I checked my rifle. We'd

come in through a panel behind the wall-mounted water heater. "Neat trick," I said as I saw how tightly it fit together when it was swung back in place. The relief I was feeling was palpable.

"Do you mind?" It was Meredith who was trying to come out.

"Sorry." I helped her out.

Winters held his hand out and down at me. "Have everyone be quiet. Someone is in the house," he whispered and pointed up. We could hear the sound of footfalls above us. He pulled out a large knife and sidestepped out of the utility room we were in. I followed him to the doorway, watching as he moved to the stairs.

BT sounded like a freight train rolling through a tunnel. I think he was cutting his own wider path through. I wasn't so far off the mark. When he popped out of the wall his shirt was dirty and ripped up around the shoulders.

"Shh." I put my finger to my lips, effectively diffusing the swear bomb he was ready to let go as he climbed out.

"Bassly! I'm going to check out the basement. Go on and check upstairs," we heard the man that was going to try and expose us shout out to the person he was with. There was a response—though it was difficult to tell whether he'd said, "can do" or "fuck off." Winters was under the open framed wooden staircase. I had my rifle trained on the upper steps. When the door opened, sunlight streamed through. I pulled back, fearful that he would see me. He paused at the top. Not sure if maybe he sensed something, but more likely he was waiting to see if any zombies sprang out. He placed a foot one step down, then another before pausing again. He bent over, leaning into the darkness so that he could look around the nearly barren space. I was too far in the shadows for him to see me.

Winters was pressed up against the wall, doing his best to impersonate concrete. I'd know what it was later because I would pry it from the intruder's mostly cold, dead fingers. A Heckler and Koch 123 machine gun. Wasn't sure what it was when I was looking at it, other than it looked wicked and extremely dangerous. Made my AR look slightly anemic, like maybe it should eat a little more red meat. He came down another step, slow and cautious. He knew something was up, could probably feel it in his bones. Then it dawned on him. The most vulnerable place for him was the stairs. He turned and his rifle was pointed down, pretty much where Winters was; not much chance of avoiding a hail of bullets, should he decide to pull that trigger.

Back to not thinking, I put my rifle down and stood with my hands up in the air. "I'm here, unarmed. Don't shoot!"

He turned quickly. I was staring straight down that barrel topped by a smug smile. "I knew you were here. Could smell your fear…"

Not sure if he would have continued his victory speech because this was when Winters stabbed him through his calf. Must have severed everything that kept him standing because he collapsed faster than a teenage girl on the Ed Sullivan show the day the Beatles played. His head struck six steps down at terminal velocity. Either the wood cracked or his skull did. Either way, he was out cold. I ran over and dragged his body away and into the shadows, though how anyone was going to miss that blood trail was beyond me—had to have been a foot wide. He was going to bleed out long before he ever regained consciousness. On a scale of ways to go, this was one of the better. We had everyone through by the time Bassly finally decided to see if his friend found anything.

"Yo, Craigs. You find anything?"

"Yeah, check it out!" I mumble-yelled into the utility room, hoping that the diffusion of my voice would lead him to believe it was his friend, or at least, associate.

"Better be some fucking food. I'm starving." We could hear Bassly trudging through the house. "Craigs!"

Winters ran up the stairs just as Bassly shouted out. I watched as the Marine brought the near-sword knife over his head and chopped down—not going to lie—I was pretty happy

I didn't see it connect, heard it though. That wet, sickly sound as it sliced through the side of Bassly's face and lodged into his shoulder produced all the visual I needed. There was a keening, hitching sound, as the hungry Bassly was fed something I'm sure he had no desire to eat. Winters yanked the blade free from the neck and drove it through his rib cage and into his lungs in an effort to keep the man from alerting anyone else who might be nearby. I was going up the stairs just as he was easing the petrified, dying man to the ground. I felt for the guy, as I stepped over him and out into the hallway to cover Winters, but when you set out to harm others it shouldn't be all that big a surprise when they strike back. We used to call it Karma.

The hallway was clear, as was the rest of the house. The rats had already stormed the beach of Normandy; that is, the house we vacated was surrounded and rats were streaming through a half-dozen different weak spots they had found or made. The conscripted that were being forced to fight had taken spots all around the house to intercept us when we attempted to escape from the rodents; I wondered if the rats would consider them when they didn't find us. There were three bedraggled people standing pretty much right over the bomb shelter. We'd put some space between us and our pursuer, but it wasn't much and they still had a drone up in the sky. There was a high probability we would be spotted if we made a run for it.

"We can't stay here," Tommy said to me as I kept a look out from the kitchen window. It afforded me a decent view of what was going on.

I knew this: Bassly and Craigs were going to be missed soon and it wouldn't take much effort to redirect the animals or the humans. I supposed wrongly we could bounce back and forth between the homes, I shuddered at the thought of going back through that claustrophobic deathtrap, plus the rats, yeah, they'd find us soon enough. Running in the great wide-open sounded way better.

"Charge set?" Sanders asked Biddeford.

"Charge?" I asked. Hard to miss the conversation, considering we were in the same area.

"That house is wired to blow," Sanders said, matter-of-factly.

"When did he do that?" BT asked.

"It's been wired since we set up shop there," Sanders said. "Blow it in two." He was talking to Biddeford.

"We were in a house wired to explode instantly?" I wasn't a fan of that at all. In fact, this group's whole MO was starting to worry me.

"Just like you are now." Winters was smiling. I think my distress amused him.

"You sure you're going to blow the right one?" I asked.

"Don't worry, I'm a Marine," he told me. "I know my ABCs. That's house A," he pointed at one button, "and this one is B." Biddeford was smiling, pointing at an identical button a fingernail apart from the first.

"Fuck me, Biddie! This is house A," Winters said.

"Oh, that's right!" Biddie exclaimed.

"They're just pulling our leg, right?" BT asked.

"Fuck if I know," I answered.

"Guess we're about to find out," BT shook his head.

"Be ready to run when that goes off–it's an incendiary device. That house is going to burn hot and fast; should give us the cover we need to get away from here, though. Oh, and you might want to step away from the window."

I moved like the house was already going up.

"These guys are hardcore, man," BT whispered to me, I didn't know if he meant it as a compliment or a warning.

"Got a couple of those people looking over here," Travis said, he was peeking through the window.

"More like heading over here, now." Tommy went to look as well.

"Everyone ready?" Sanders asked. When no one dissented, he ordered Biddeford to blow it early. I was still squinting out the window, but from a much safer distance. There was a flash in the kitchen, not much bigger than a lighter, then there was a loud whooshing sound like a huge dragon with an incredible wingspan had landed in the yard. Then to top it off, this dragon breathed fire; there was a flaming explosion large enough to blow holes all around the structure.

"Incendiary device my ass," I said as I hustled to keep up with the rapidly vacating tenants. I had caught glimpses of dozens, if not hundreds of burning rats being jettisoned into the air like rodent loaded Roman candles. Anyone within ten feet of the house had been obliterated by glass, plastic and wooden shrapnel or set completely ablaze as fire clouds the size of pick-up trucks blew out the windows and vaporized everything in their path. Flaming debris was raining down on us and we were at least a hundred feet away.

"Might have overdone it," Biddeford said as we continued on. Couldn't wait to see what he'd come up with for the Fourth of July.

"What now?" I asked Sanders as we entered into a home a good mile from where we'd been. We were all winded and BT looked exhausted, considering he'd carried Meredith the entire way.

"This Knox guy isn't an idiot, unfortunately. When no one runs out screaming, he's going to realize that we weren't in there. He'll figure we're going for the hostages," Sanders said. "What else could we possibly be doing?"

We had to get there and quick, he'd either kill them or they would be used to play parts in his fuck festival of a fantasy.

"How far are we?" I asked.

"Another mile. I figure we have a maximum fifteen-minute window, starting now. There's a car; I'd rather not use it, but time dictates otherwise."

"Let's go," I told him. We were all ready.

"Just you," he said to me.

"What?" I think it was BT–his voice was just louder than mine.

"Listen. It's a small car, but that's not the only reason. Us three have been fighting together for a long time; we know what the other is going to do almost before they do it. Now no disrespect to your group, you obviously know what you're doing as well, or you wouldn't be here, but we don't know how you react to situations and I will not unnecessarily risk the lives of my men. That half-second delay in coordinated effort could mean a death. The only reason I'm bringing Talbot is that he's a Marine, so we already know he has some reactions built in. Also, I need him to identify us to his family so they don't take a shot at us." I was getting the stink eye from everyone in my group, like I had made that declaration.

"We'll be right back," I told them, following Winters out to the garage.

"Kylie, when we leave, head back to base. We'll follow when it's safe," Sanders told his wife.

CHAPTER FIVE
MIKE JOURNAL ENTRY 5

DON'T GET ME wrong. I was all about going to save my wife, but I wasn't overly thrilled about the three guys I was with. I'm sure they were more capable than any three of us, it was just that I didn't know them like they didn't know me. If I got into trouble, would I just be collateral damage to them? I was relatively sure they weren't bad guys. They most definitely weren't working with Knox, not unless this was some super elaborate trap to catch us. We'd already wasted a number of them and a truckload of rats. If they had been with him, they would have just been waiting for us when we exited the other end of the bomb shelter. The car was a Prius, which I found slightly absurd, that was until Winters told me how little noise they made. Sanders was right; BT couldn't have fit in this thing with a tub of Vaseline and a crowbar.

The drive was only a couple of minutes; Sanders pulled up to a tidy, ranch style home. Winters hopped out and pulled the garage door open as Sanders pulled in.

"It's the next street over. I'd like to have more time to recon but I think this is going to be a hot zone soon. The idea here is a smash and grab. You alright with that, Talbot?" Sanders asked.

"That's fairly normal for me," I told him. Winters smiled

at that. "Do you have this entire neighborhood scoped out?" I asked, not believing this home had been picked at random in the hopes that it was empty.

"It's how we have ensured our survival. It's basic, well, it's imperative that we know our surroundings. Don't you?"

"I, ummm, yeah, sure. Not much of a neighborhood where we were," I offered in defense. Although I realized we had not really even checked out the houses nearby. I had figured the risk too high; if people were keeping to themselves, I had been perfectly willing to leave them alone. Now I wasn't so sure as I watched the ease at which this group melted into their different locations. They were as adept as the Viet Cong, striking out from their hidden caves and disappearing before an offensive could be mounted against them. Any village could be full of them or not; they owned the home-field advantage. I realized I wouldn't have known how exposed I would be attempting to save my own family if not for this commando squad. What's worse was Deneaux surely would.

"The house we want is the next street over. I've got to believe we are going to encounter unfriendlies the moment we leave this yard. As always, I expect extreme prejudice when encountering them."

"Locate, close with and destroy the enemy by fire, and maneuver," Biddeford said the mission of the Marine Corps rifle squad verbatim. Back in my active duty days I had heard it a dozen times just before we were sent on missions. Gave me chills.

"You any good with a pistol?" Sanders asked, as he handed me a suppressed Ruger 22/45.

"I'm better with a rifle, but I'm no slouch." I took the weapon. The 22 wasn't my preferred caliber, but with a suppressor on it, dropping change would be louder than the firing of a bullet. If you weren't within fifteen feet of the person on the business end, odds were you weren't going to hear it; that buys you a lot of time. I released the clip. I looked up to Sanders when I saw that it had no bullets in it. He had a smile that I figured signified the time when Biddie would place a neat hole in the back of my head. He had circled around, I presumed to get into position. I clenched my rifle; if he somehow missed, I was going to make them pay.

"Just checking your situational awareness," Sanders said as he pulled out a small box of fifty rounds and tossed it my way. I released my rifle with one hand and let the sling hold it up as I caught the box even over the throbbing of my heart, which I know was making my hands shake from the sheer pressure of the high pumping blood. I filled the magazine and chambered a round.

"Big chance you just took, Major. Would anyone have told me I didn't have rounds, had I not checked?" I asked.

"You would have figured it out soon enough. Let's move out."

Can't say I was a big fan of that type of thinking. We were going to get my family; I was going to thank them profusely and then put a shitload of miles between us. We quietly made our way across the yard. The house on the other side of the fence was a two-story job; if anyone decided to look through the window, we were there for all to observe.

"Oh, come on," we heard just from the other side of the fence. I moved cautiously to the privacy divider, as did the rest of the group. There was an older man, maybe in his sixties. Had his junk out and was beating it mercilessly. Wait, hold on…not in the way you might *think* a male alone would. I mean he was whacking his flaccid dick back and forth like they were in a bar fight with each other because his penis had called the man's sister a whore. I couldn't for the life of me figure out what the hell he was doing until he spoke again.

"Fucking prostate! I just want to piss!" He was almost crying.

The guy's prostate must have been the size of a watermelon because there was absolutely nothing coming out. Whatever biological problems he had ended with the insertion of a bullet into his head, probably could be classified as a mercy killing. His eyes crossed, he grabbed his dick so hard I thought he was going to yank it off. I turned away to see Winters wincing at the sight. It's a fucked-up world when you can't even piss in peace, I thought.

Sanders moved a couple of the fence slats to the side so we could go through rather than over. These guys didn't miss much when it came to planning. Biddeford grabbed his handiwork and pulled him into the yard we'd just vacated. I wish I'd missed it, but the man's beleaguered bladder was now flowing like a fountain at a Vegas casino. Had to admit, finally relieved and dick in hand is not the worst way to go, but there was one of those sights you cannot unsee.

"Talbot, Winters, you two inside. Biddie and I are going to check the perimeter."

I followed Winters in through the open sliding glass door that Peeing Man most likely had exited from.

"Hey, Tresser, you get your dry well to pump?" A voice laughed from upstairs. In typical guy fashion it was laced with crude humor designed to discomfort the other. "Answer me, man! You know I get spooked when you do that shit." We were about to head upstairs and give him some answers, maybe none he wanted to hear, but answers, nonetheless. That was until another came around the corner. He had a turkey drumstick in one hand and an old car magazine in his other.

"Hey what are you doing here?" he asked, spitting out a mouthful of food. This guy wasn't going to join Mensa anytime soon, but he still managed to drop what he was holding and run for his rifle, which was across the room. He'd probably left it right where he was going to eat some lunch and read. My first shot missed completely; my second ripped into his shoulder, skidded up off the ball joint, and lodged into his neck. He reached up to swat it away, blood began to pour through his fingers.

"What did you do?" he asked. "Feeling a little light headed." He went to sit but misjudged where exactly in the room he was, went down hard on his ass. We just stood there watching him catch up with the situation.

"What the fu…" The upstairs man yelled from the top of the stairs just as Winters placed two rounds in his chest throwing him backwards into a wall. Winters motioned to me that he was going upstairs; he proceeded slowly with his pistol out in front of him. I did a quick check of the main floor, making sure there were no more surprises. I looked at the door that led to the basement but I didn't want to check it until I was sure of Winters' status. He was down in less than a minute.

"Clear." he said. "You ready?" He was pointing to the basement. I nodded. He pulled the door open and I did a quick head in to see. There was nothing there, so I started down the stairs. I was thankful this basement was finished, as I did not want to get a knife to the back of my leg. Two things I noticed quick enough: the first was the blood, the other was an open window on the far side of the room. Someone had been in here but had left when the festivities started upstairs. I turned the corner just enough to see what I had to imagine was a murdered family. Father, mother and two kids; bludgeoned to death. A heavy mallet lay next to the bodies. This had been recent, few hours at the most, as the blood had not had the opportunity to tack up yet.

"Oh man, that's the McKenzies," Winters said, taking it in before turning away. I pointed to the window. There was gunfire. Out there, the fight was on in earnest. I raced back upstairs. I didn't see the need to vacate the house like Winters did. We had a strategic position and we'd fought to earn it. I could not see Biddeford or Sanders. The gunfire was to our right—the sound of heavy AK rounds. I didn't hear return fire, but I watched the machine gun wielder go down in a heap.

"They're all around us!" someone shouted. More gunfire, though I don't think this was directed at anyone in particular; more of a spray-and-pray type of approach. I saw a couple of people run through a yard across the street. They were going the wrong way if they wanted to engage us. I put the pistol down and switched to my rifle. The two that had been running stopped and dove down under a row of hedges. They would have been invisible had I not known exactly where to look. I lined up the shot; I was shooting at something the size of a dinner plate, basically, just the top of the man's skull. Was using iron sights, but it was only a fifty-yard shot. The trick was going to be getting his partner. I blew one well-placed round through the heavy bone plating, even watched as pieces of it peppered the shrubs around him. I moved my barrel an inch, estimating where the other man had been, and pulled the trigger five times in succession. I could not confirm the kill, but the shots had been dead on and he'd not had enough time to clear the area. If he wasn't dead outright, he would be soon. I looked up just in time to see someone taking a look from our target house. Pretty sure it was Justin, though he did not stay long enough for confirmation.

"Looks clear," Winters said.

"Maybe you should go and check it out," I told him.

"I said *looks.*"

"My guess is they won't abandon their post so easily—not because they're disciplined soldiers, but rather they're afraid of what Knox will do to them if he finds out they ran."

"Winters, this is Sanders. Come in."

"I hear you, sir," Winters replied.

"I don't see anybody and there is the sound of engines coming. Our window is shrinking. Tell Talbot it's go time."

Winters looked over at me.

"I heard. Shit." Vesuvius looked like a mountain, the Titanic looked like an unsinkable ship, and that street looked devoid of enemies. "Justin! It's me!"

I saw my son poke his head up.

"We need to move!" I yelled to him.

"There's more of them on the side of the house!"

"Which side?" I asked.

"Both."

"We don't have time to clear the perimeter," Sanders said over the radio. "We need to pull back." The sound of the engines were nearly on top of us.

"I have to go in, Winters," I said. If I left now there would be nothing to come back to. Knox wasn't afraid of going into that house; he could burn it, send rats in or his slave army. Made no difference to him. This whole thing was a plan to get me and BT out into the open, teach us a lesson and show his people he was the brute in control, always. I don't know how they could think that, though. He'd brought his entire shit show on the road to catch two guys. Seems like right there he'd already lost it.

"Talbot, you heard the major," Winters said, though he knew how this was going to go.

"It's my family, Winters. I can't leave them."

"Negative, sir," he said into the radio. "Talbot is not leaving."

To his credit, Sanders didn't lose it and start calling me every colorful name he could think of, and believe me, I'd heard a bunch. "Biddie and I will take on the newcomers. You two get those people out of there. Good luck, out."

Justin was looking out the window at us, I held up Winters radio, wondering why Justin hadn't been using the one he had. He put his fists together and then twisted them in the "broke" signal.

"How many?" I yelled across the street.

He held up three fingers and pointed to the right, held up two fingers and pointed to the left, and held up four and pointed to the rear. Now, obviously, this was a fluid equation and any or all of those people could move around the house easily enough. We had nine on two, and they were in somewhat defensive positions. I was not a fan of our odds.

"Open the front door!" I yelled.

"You realize you're telling them what you're about to do, right?" Winters said as somewhat of a question.

"Exactly. I need them out in the open waiting for me. If I try to run across the street now they'll cut me down."

"You're pretty smart for a Marine."

"You're a Marine, too."

"I just did it to pay for college. Should have already been out by now, working," he responded.

"What did you go to school for?"

"Business administration. What's that got to do with anything?"

"What's a more practical skill these days?" I asked. "Running a company or shooting?"

He grunted.

I saw movement to the left; someone was on the move. Someone in the house must have seen it as well because the person running got lit up. A three-round burst sent them immediately into whatever afterlife awaited them. Figured it had to be Tracy doing the shooting because Justin was still visible from where I was. Multiple vehicles were heading to our position. After the shots were fired that was the sound that dominated. Of course, that was right up until Sanders and Biddie unleashed their surprise. I felt my fillings move around inside my head from the explosion.

"What the fuck was that?" I yelled over the ringing in my ears.

"Claymore," Winters replied.

There was a secondary explosion and then multiple guns firing.

"Winters, we can hold them for a couple of minutes but there's at least twenty of them. You two had better make your move now!" Biddie shouted over the radio.

"We're up," Winters said.

"This is my family; you don't need to do this," I told him one more time.

"What kind of jarhead would I be if I ran?"

"A live one, running a business one day," I mumbled, but we were already leaving the house by a side exit.

I crossed the street at a full sprint, making a straight line for the hedges. In hindsight, I wished I'd picked a different spot. I did a stealing-second base-slide feet first into enough viscera to coat a truck bed, I mean, if you for some reason wanted to do something like that. The second man, whom I had assumed was dead, was not quite gone. He was flat on his back looking up at the bottom of the bush taking shallow breaths, gasping really. There was panic in his eyes as he struggled to get oxygen into his system. I'd put at least two rounds through his shoulder and one in his abdomen; from the sound he was making, one of the shoulder shots had traveled down and ruptured a lung. Blood colored bubbles were forming around his mouth and running down his cheeks, some mixing with the tears that flowed from his eyes.

There was a part of me that felt bad; he was basically a kid, maybe mid-twenties. Maybe in his next life he'd choose a better path, maybe not. Either way, I could not spare him any more of my thoughts. A man and a woman were running from the back right toward me, though I don't think they knew I was there. I turned my head to see what they were looking at— it was Winters. He was coming, but in a much more methodical, tactical approach, which was usually all great and fine, but this time it was going to get him killed.

I wasn't quite ready, but death waits for no one. I spun and barely got the pair's lower legs into my sights before I started firing. I don't give a fuck how long I live, I am always going to have a problem with female combatants. I don't know if it's sexist or misogynistic, it's certainly not meant to be and it's certainly not because I believe them any less capable or deadly. There is no part of me that doesn't believe them to be the stronger of the sexes and perhaps even more adept at fighting. They certainly can be more vicious; just think about the animal kingdom. I think it's the chivalry in me that finds harming a woman so fucking distasteful. In a world gone to shit, I hold it in my heart, for right or wrong, that women are the ones that will nurture it back, and here I am killing them. My first round hit her square in the shin, severed the bone so that when she tried to come down with her foot it ended up being her splintered bone that cut through her muscle and stuck into the soft earth. She fell over screaming, must admit, I winced at that. My next round hit her in the thigh; the final one traveled up into her chest and silenced her.

For the briefest of seconds, I thought I had disturbed a hornet's nest as the pests whizzed by me, then I realized it was suppressed rounds. I was pinned down and did not know where the shooter was. The man with the woman had dived for cover. I may not have seen it, but Winters sure did. He was advancing and firing on the man's position.

"Clear!" he shouted. He was near to the low front porch as I emerged from my spot. There were now shots coming from the house as Tracy and Justin were covering our flanks. "We have got to get them out of there."

"Let's go!" I shouted up.

"Can't, dad," Justin responded.

Could see the first of the cars making it through Sanders' improvised roadblock. Had seconds. I retreated or I advanced. It was a no-brainer; I ran for the door.

I heard Winters say this was a bad idea as he came in after me. I spun and took a couple of hasty shots at the lead car; fucked up the hood and I think I winged the front seat passenger. The driver veered hard to their right and across the street. Five people poured out of it but we got the door shut before their return fire found us. By the time they were done shooting the door it had been completely blown from its hinges and the holey hunk was laying on the ground.

"Now what?" Winters asked as we saw another car pull up.

"I'm thinking we should head upstairs. Anybody starts poking their heads in the windows on this first floor we could be in some trouble," I said to him. The only problem was that the stairway was in complete view of the outside considering that the door was now a floor mat.

"There's like ten guns pointing at this house," Winters said, having poked his head high enough to see out. You won't make it up three steps."

"Who's up there, Justin?" I asked

"Me, mom, grandma, Angel, Avalyn, and all the animals."

In terms of being the fastest, most nimble and ready to fight, I had been dealt a bad hand. I let my head rest on the ground for a moment.

"That bad?" Winters whispered.

"One bad-kneed senior citizen, a little girl, a baby, a surly cat, one slowpoke English Bullie and a hyper little dog, my wife, son and one of the dogs can take care of themselves; we'll have to carry everyone else."

"Leaves shit little for firepower if we're busy playing delivery men," he replied.

"Winters—more coming your way. We've had to pull back before we got overrun, we won't leave you out to dry. Out," Sanders said.

"He'll be back," Winters told me.

"Better be soon," I said as I saw a large group coming toward the house. They were indeed going to surround us. We were popup targets in a shooting gallery.

"Downstairs." I pointed behind us.

"I like that idea less," he said, though he followed me as we low-crawled around and to the door that led down. A few bullets ricocheted in the house; as of yet I didn't think we were targeted. I reached up and twisted the handle to the door, never even stopped for a second to think about what I would do if there was a zombie or an enemy on the stairs. I suppose I could have slammed the door shut, but I was in a pretty compromising position. I crawled down two steps until I felt confident enough to pull my legs in and get my feet up under me. Winters was right behind me, he pulled the door shut quietly.

"I've spent an inordinate amount of my time with you in basements; this a normal thing with you?"

"Not really. You've just been extraordinarily lucky."

"I don't feel lucky," he said as he went down a few more stairs.

"Seems like I've heard that before." We quickly went into

the basement where we saw shadows moving past some of the windows. I froze when a face pressed up against the glass, the man was peering intently—and overconfidently. Must have had something to do with how dingy the lighting was in here because he never registered the fact that he was staring straight at me. I was slowly raising my rifle; suck place to get shot, the face, I mean.

"Don't," Winters whispered. "We'll lose our element of surprise."

"Yeah, we wouldn't want to lose that," I said, doing my best impression of a statue. The face finally stood. I took a deep breath and we moved away from the staircase and to a shelf stacked high with paint cans and motor oil. "Any chance there's a bunker in this house, too?"

He shook his head. "Help me move this away from the wall."

I saw what he doing: we could hide behind it, use it as cover and concealment. "It's the only thing in the basement. Don't you think it will be pretty obvious where we're hiding?"

"Like you said, it's the only thing in the basement. I mean, unless you want to hide behind the stanchion poles."

The loaded down shelves were heavier than they looked and the metal framing was flimsier than it appeared. Was more than half convinced the whole thing was either going to tip or collapse as we slid it about a foot away from the wall.

"Yeah, that doesn't look suspicious," I said when I looked at our handiwork.

"Well let's see. Since your actions have directly led us into this predicament, I'm all ears if you've got something better."

And I didn't. I looked around, but it was one giant square of concrete with hardly any light coming in. I was staying close to the walls, hoping for some sort of crawl space or box of grenades. Didn't find either. The grayish light was blocked out as someone once again came up to the window. That could only mean they weren't satisfied no one was in here. I couldn't tell from my angle if it was the same person. I stayed close to the wall and made my way to the window. I could just see Winters over by the shelves; hard to say, but I don't think he was all that thrilled with what I was doing. The light was completely gone and then there was a muffled crack as the man had put something up against the glass and then broke it. He was coming in. As soon as he poked his head in I was as good as caught. I reached down and grabbed my Ka-Bar, not at all happy with what was about to go down.

He took his sweet ass time about it; he must have thought he would just sneak in down here and make his way up to where the people were. Winters was shaking his head back and forth with his face pulled in like he was four and I was trying to give him an extra heaping of gross cough syrup. The muzzle of a rifle came through first, then a hand, an arm, finally the crowning of a head, like the world's largest baby being birthed, gun first, which would be a handy mutation for our next generation. I was in motion the second his head showed; he never even had the chance to register my presence as I drove my knife into his temple. His body went rigid then limp as I pulled it through and dropped him to the ground. His muscles convulsed as I pulled the blade free. I hoped that the action looked as if he had come in on his own. So far, so good; no alarm had been sounded, and no one else was following. Either he'd come in solo as part of a plan to sneak up on us, or there was indeed suspicion and he was the guinea pig. I grabbed his rifle. It was tough to tell without proper lighting, but I think it was an Uzi, and he had a couple of extended mags on him. Well, that was mine now, at least.

"We can't stay here." Winters had come over.

I couldn't have agreed with him more. We were in a shit spot. Just then, the light in the basement went to nearly zero as four of the five windows were blocked.

"Down." I grabbed him just as all the windows broke out. Dozens, hundreds of rounds were blown through as they shot at every conceivable angle they could, hoping to kill us. I thought my ears were going to bleed with how loud it was in there. Chunks of concrete were raining down on us, dust and smoke threatened to choke our airways. It was so thick I could not see my hand in front of my face. When it mercifully stopped, I was not grateful to be alive, I was angry, like pissed-off hornet-swarming angry. I stood up and pointed toward one of the murky fingers of light filtering in through the window and fired. There was a surprised cry and then a thud as I'd shot whoever had been there. I was able to take out one more in this manner before they realized they had not killed their targets and now they were on the docket.

"Now let's go," I told Winters, reaching down and tapping him on the shoulder.

I ran up the stairs and into two men that had the misfortune of being the vanguard. I didn't even bother aiming, anything that can shoot six hundred rounds a minute doesn't need much in the way of that. In half a magazine I had riddled them each with half a dozen rounds, more than enough to do the job.

"Up the stairs–go!" I told Winters who didn't need any more prompting as I switched out magazines. I unloaded the entire new clip out the front door in two, maybe three seconds; didn't really count. It was enough time for Winters to make it up and gave me a window as those outside had dived for cover as I made my suicide covering fire. I was already on the upstairs landing by the time return fire made it into the house.

Tracy was standing in the hallway, when I got my wind back I gave her a hug that threatened to meld us.

"Took you long enough." She was kidding. I could see the strain in her features from the ordeal.

"You…you're fucking crazy. What the fuck is wrong with you?" Winters asked as Justin helped him up off the floor.

"Marines," I answered calmly. "The Marines did that to me."

"Bullshit. You can maybe tell that to those around you that have never served but I am a Marine and I can tell you right now you're fucking certifiable." He was genuinely upset.

"You get used to him," Justin said in my defense.

"Or dead," Winters added.

"Everyone alright?" I asked.

I got nods all around. Henry was wagging his stumpy little tail, his ass shaking he was so happy to see me. If it wouldn't have cost me some funny looks I would have wagged my ass too in like greeting.

"Good to see you, too." I got down on my haunches and grabbed his massive head and hugged it tightly and then scratched behind his ears.

Justin got Winters a bottle of water and I hoped a valium—he was still looking pretty stupefied. Carol was looking a little rough; this "on the road shit" was hard on us all, but these circumstances brought it to a whole other level.

"How you holding up?" I asked quietly.

"I've been better. I sure could use a drink."

"You and me both," I told her. "We'll get out of this and I'll raid a liquor store for you."

She grabbed my hand before I could leave. "Michael, I don't know how much more of this I can handle." The look in her eye is one I'd seen before, it was of a person giving up, and for reasonable cause. There comes a point in a lot of people's lives where the accumulated weight of all things lost begins to bow and then break the spirit, few ever recover. Once you start down that spiral the inertia is too great to overcome, especially when you don't have anyone else depending on you to go on.

"We'll get out of this Carol. We will get to Etna Station; it will almost be normal."

"I just want to go home. To be buried on the farm."

"Nobody is getting buried," I told her forcibly. It was one thing if she wanted to cash in her chips, but that kind of mood could and would spill over, crushing all morale as it went.

"Talbot, I am getting so fucking sick of you!" This was shouted over a speaker.

"Great, Knox is here," I said as I tried to get a peek out the window.

"I haven't quite figured out why you won't just die. It would make my life a whole lot simpler if you did."

"Mine, too," Winters said quietly.

"I heard that," I told him. He shrugged.

"I've lost a lot of good people since coming across your sorry ass. That doesn't even bring into account all of my wasted resources. Do you have any fucking concept of how difficult and how long it takes to round up that many fighters and zombies? And the rats! I can't stand rats! But one of my people has this *affinity* for them; knows how to make them do things. It's weird, I'll grant you, but I let him do it because, well, everyone hates rats, disgusting little creatures. If you could just let them peel your face off and maybe chew through your jugular I'd seriously owe you one."

"This guy might be more off his rocker than you," Winters said.

"I think he was Army," I told him. Winters made an "Ah." face.

"You come out right now, Talbot, hands held high. I'll put one in your head and that will be it. Your people will be decently cared for. Not going to say great, not for a while, anyway; they'll start at the bottom of the hierarchy ladder just like all new recruits. You can't just force a former Soviet bloc country to come over to NATO and then hand them the nuclear sequence. They'll have to prove themselves in a variety of ways. Won't be easy, but everyone will have their place. Well, except for you, because you'll be rotting out on the front stoop. But dammit man, those you care for will be alive."

"He's serious?" Winters asked.

"You wouldn't think so, but yeah," I replied.

"Deneaux said you wouldn't capitulate."

I heard the words and this was on me. There was never a part of me that didn't figure she would cross me, cross us; it was always just a matter of when. Why I hadn't simply ripped her throat out when she was in my grasp eludes me.

"Time's up." Sounded like a battalion's worth of tanks

were driving up on us.

"Zombies." Justin was in one of the bedrooms as he called out.

"I hope I don't see you on the other side, Talbot. Not sure why I would, as I'm the one doing God's work, lifting the helpless up and bringing them along with me. I once read that the meek will inherit the earth; what a load of horseshit that was. It's the ones willing to take chances, to force others to see their vision. Those will be the ones to own the world and that is what I intend on doing. Going to leave you a few hundred presents; take my advice–just let it happen. Oh, and I got this for you too!" He started laughing.

"No!" Mad Jack yelled.

I ran to the window, heedless of a sniper's bullet. Mad Jack had been pushed out of the cab of a large pickup. His hands were handcuffed behind him and his face had been beaten badly.

"This loser one of yours, Talbot?" Knox laughed again.

"Run," I said barely above a whisper. Mad Jack was just standing there. The dozens of zombies in the general vicinity had not noticed him yet but it was only a matter of seconds. "Run!" I yelled, he looked up, his eyes pleading for help. I turned and was heading for the stairs. Winters and Justin were right behind me. By the time I got to the front door, MJ had only moved enough to try and get back into the truck.

"This is happening because of you, Talbot!" Knox said. "And, oh yeah, I have your cool toy now!" Mad Jack fell over into the street as the truck sped away. He'd most definitely attracted the attention of the zombies now. He was sobbing on the ground.

I didn't have time to ask why he wasn't running. All I could do now was try and kill all the zombies near him and see if we could attempt a rescue. Time and distance were not on our side. Even as we were killing them, more were taking their place. And as we moved forward, we realized that zombies were taking flanks to us; soon they would envelop us and cut us off from our only avenue of escape. Then I noticed something; they were within striking distance of Mad Jack, could have taken him a few times by now, yet they didn't. That struck me as extremely fortunate...until I figured why that was. As long as he was still alive, we would keep trying to get to him and that would give the other zombies enough time to blanket us, not to mention more flesh for all. If he were to be bitten and die, there would be no sense in a rescue attempt and we'd proceed with defensive maneuvers. We were being fished and Mad Jack was the lure. I don't know why one of the zombies jumped the gun, but he probably saved our lives—well, some of them. He bit into Mad Jack's head, ripping away a chunk of scalp the size of a hand. Mad Jack's scream was savage, blood poured down his face and flew from his mouth as it hit the expelling air. I shot that zombie, but the spilling of blood was too much for those around him, they dove in like sharks to chum. A lump the size of a fist formed in my throat as I watched the man be torn apart.

I ran when Justin urged me to go, but I felt like I was in a tunnel; everything was all echo-y and surreal. He wasn't supposed to die. He was one of the good guys, one of the people that was going to find a way to fix this world, to set it back to something approaching normal. I heard one final gurgle for life as we just made it into the house—the speeders fast on our heels.

Tracy leaned over the railing to take out a couple of the closer ones. I pushed everyone into the master bedroom and shut the door; we could barricade for a while, at least. As expected, the door was getting slammed up against and it was not of the extra strength variety, just a common, hollow-core door. I reached for Tracy, I wanted to sob into her shoulder for a month, maybe more.

"He was a good man," she said to me as she gently pushed me away.

"He was," I said. I knew what she'd meant with those words and that action. He was indeed a good man and we would mourn for him later, but right now, there were still all the rest of us in this room that needed my utmost consideration. The problem was, I didn't have any clue of what we needed to do or even what we could do.

Winters went over to the window. "What about the roof?" he asked.

"What about it?" I asked, though I already knew what he was asking. I poked my head out. It would be a stretch, but it would be possible to reach the low-hanging eave. "Look around Winters, how many of us are going to make that?"

"What about going through the ceiling?" Justin asked as we all looked up at the drywall.

"No access in the closet?" I asked.

He shook his head. "Hallway."

"Through the ceiling it is, then."

The door was being punished – we heard more than one crack. The only thing holding it in place was the dresser we had shoved up against it and which we were now going to have to stand on so we could rip down some drywall and make good our escape. I jabbed my knife up and through, not thrilled to be using it like this but desperate times and all, so here went the desperate measures. The dresser was rocking back and forth as the zombies kept slamming into the door. Winters and Justin were leaning in on our side attempting to keep me from being knocked off. I dropped a fist-sized chunk on top of Winters' head. He didn't say anything as I sawed away. Fine particles drifted down at first, and then fell away in clumps.

"Is that vermiculite?" Winters asked.

I didn't say anything as I was making the hole big enough to fit us through, breathing in more dust than air just then.

"It is!" He said, alarmed. "That could contain asbestos!"

Right then a zombie arm blew through the door and was brushing up against my leg.

"Time to think short-term, kid," I told him as I shifted to avoid the dirty, scabbed over hand and arm from clenching my ankle. When the owner of that arm pulled back and decided to get a view of what he was seeking, that was when the activity out in the hallway picked up. He must have communicated to those around him that there were some live ones inside. I grabbed on to a couple of the two-by-eight joist beams that crossed the house and pulled myself up to get a better look at the attic. Couldn't see much past the hole I'd cut out. This place made the basement look like downtown Tokyo on New Year's.

Justin tapped my leg with a small flashlight. I dropped down to grab it before going back up. It was as barren as the basement had been, a seven-foot wide section the entire length of the house, had some plywood down on it, at least we wouldn't have to do a balancing act on the joists as we thought out our next plan.

I dropped back down onto the dresser, not at all happy to see face sized holes behind it. Zombies were tearing at the door with their hands and their mouths.

"Tracy, let's go."

"The kids? The animals?" she asked.

"I'll need to hand them up to you."

She looked over at Henry.

"I'll send Justin up to help you when we get to him," I told her.

Got her through easy enough. Next was Angel, who was still crying about Mad Jack and would be for a good long time; they had developed a relationship, those two. When he wasn't trying to figure out ways to make cold fusion bombs they could generally be found playing board games. It took Tracy longer than I'd wanted for her to walk the child over to a safe area and do her best to calm her down. I could hear her talking.

"I'm going to bring Avalyn over to you real soon, honey. Will you be able to watch her while I get the animals up here?"

There was now officially less of the upper half of the door still in place.

"Tracy, no time!" I shouted up.

She came back just as Justin handed me the baby. I was

doing my best to shield her from the zombies, but she peeked around anyway. She let out a blood-curdling scream that turned into a wracked cry. But, strangely enough, I think she'd confused the hell out of the zombies because they stopped what they were doing for a moment to watch her. I took full advantage of the lull in activity. By "lull" I mean a solid minute; they just stared through the holes in the door. Could be useful; could be the beginning of the end of our friendly relationship with Avalyn, or could be something more. I would have to think on this later; maybe run it past some of the group.

"Get the animals up first," Carol told Winters as he helped her up.

"That's not really my preferred order," I told her.

She gave me a look and then I realized just exactly where Tracy had got her signature steely gaze. I couldn't refuse her. Patches was easy enough, she was already on the dresser, arrogantly waiting for me to grab her. For once she didn't hiss at me, though I think it took every bit of self-control she had. Henry was by the dresser with Riley. My dog was easier going than Trip at his calmest. He looked perfectly content to go up into the attic whenever we could get him up there and maybe catch up on a little shut-eye. Riley, on the other hand, appeared as if she was ready for a fight. I could see her saying "I'd eat those zombies, I would, Michael. But I can't get at them from here, so let's move." Ben-Ben, well he was just running around in room-sized circles, God knows, thinking what. He stopped every turn or so and sniffed, probably hoping he was going to find bacon. He was going to be sorely disappointed.

"Justin, you need to go up now. Mom can't handle Henry by herself."

I don't think Winters was all that thrilled with my need to get the animals up, but wisely said nothing.

"Why are they just staring at us?" he asked.

"Don't know, don't care." Avalyn was no one's business but ours.

He grunted as he hefted Henry's considerably bulk up as did I. We'd all trimmed the fat since the zombies came, getting supplies, stress, little food and the constant running had honed our bodies into the machines they were supposed to be and not the sedentary dumps they'd become late in the twentieth century. Not Henry, though. He seemed to be stubbornly holding onto the past, he wore his girth like a badge of honor in the face of all things apocalyptic, and I loved him even more for it. But I also thought maybe he could help a little by lifting or at least thinking light thoughts. I was grunting like a Sumo wrestler as I shoved him up through the hole like a sack of loose ground chuck. There was a brief moment where Justin teetered on the edge of being able to hoist the weight or come tumbling down.

"I told you, Talbot, we should have got a Border Collie. But oh no you had to have the Marine Corps mascot, which makes no sense, since Marines are lean and mean and Henry is neither of those things," Tracy said, breathing heavy from the exertion as she helped pull on Justin.

"He can hear you!" I said, pushing his ass up.

"Good! Maybe he'll lay off the doughnuts." They had finally got him up, and judging by a long throaty grunt, I don't think he was all that thrilled by the handling. Justin walked him over to the platform.

"Carol, you ready yet?" I asked.

"I will not have you pushing on my backside. It is very undignified."

"None of this is the highlight of my life either, Carol, but getting eaten is a whole lot worse," I told her. Yeah, that went over real fucking good. I was now caught in a cross beam of death stares. Add to that, the zombies were coming out of their stupor. Winters had to pull me away from the grip of a zombie that had gone shoulder deep through the door.

"Grab the rat dog!" I told Winters as I did a balancing act on the edge of the dresser as far from prying hands as possible. I was thinking that the animals were in tune with us more than they ever had been because I'm telling you right now, Ben-Ben understood me. He stopped on a dime, spun toward me and growled. "Shit, sorry about that," I told him, as Winters ran and picked him up while he was still. The dog barked happily at Winters, even gave him a little kiss, which Winters wiped off across his shoulder. But Ben-Ben growled at me as I took him in my hands. "I didn't mean it," I said as I handed him up. I was staring straight at his ass when he let go an eye-watering bubble of gas.

"I don't think he's accepted your apology," Justin said.

"Like that needed to be voiced," I told him as I wiped my face, there wasn't actually anything there, but the smell was so cloying that it felt like there was. "Let's go Riley."

Winters hoisted her up and I had her through the hole; my arms were still up over my head and I only had my heels on the dresser when it was rocked from behind. My ass landed hard on the wooden top, my neck and head swung back, dangerously close to the door as multiple hands reached out to entangle themselves with me before I unceremoniously slid forward and thumped to the floor, thoroughly battered. I'm sure most of you, at some point in your life, have fallen on to your ass and whacked yourself on the way down. It's disorienting and sure can be painful, but there are times where it travels to whole new realms of agony.

There was this one time–not at band camp–I was working construction. We were pulling a new phone cable through an underground conduit. One guy was feeding it and it was my job to pull it through. It sounds easy enough, but when you're talking a few hundred feet of underground pipe, things tend to get difficult. So, there I am, I've got the feed cord wrapped around both of my hands, I'm leaning back at about a forty-five-degree angle using all of my muscle and mass to pull this fucking thing back. Shouldn't be too hard to figure out what happened next. The cable snapped. All of my weight, coupled with all of my force, and then not even being able to use my hands and arms as braces meant that I impacted the cold, indifferent concrete at what felt like crotch breaking speeds. Two words: tail fucking bone.

I wanted to get up and walk it off, but I was in serious distress, it was one of the most uniquely painful sensations I had thus far encountered in my life, and momentum was the only weapon involved. I'd never, nor have I since, had my asshole hurt like that. If I had to give words to the description, it was like someone had shoved a street pole up my ass while two someone else's had gripped each side of my pelvis and cracked it in half like you might a crab at Red Lobster. Took fifteen minutes before I was finally able to get over the notion of an ambulance ride and further explanation to the doctors and nurses on why I had a street pole up my ass. So, yeah, I was reliving all of that as I sat on the floor wondering if this time my age might have finally shown itself and I did, indeed, break something.

"You alright?" Winters asked, seeing my obvious distress.

"I'm hoping I only hurt my pride," I told him."

"If nothing is broke, we need to move fast; not much between us and them anymore."

"Carol," I grunted. "It's time. There's no one else to hide behind." I stood and then immediately hunched over, the pain wasn't quite done with me.

"Dad, you need me to come down?" I shot out a hand without standing up just yet.

"I don't want to," she said.

"Mom!" Tracy yelled. "Get your ass up here!"

"I had a little bit of an accident a few days ago," she said in defense, as if that explained everything.

"What?" Tracy asked.

"I threw them out," Carol responded.

"What are you talking about, mom?"

"I don't have any panties on! There, I said it. Are you happy now?!"

"I'm definitely not happy," I told her just beginning to tentatively stand completely up.

"I have a dress on and no panties!"

"Alright, we get it," I told her. "Let's get this done."

Winters expended a few bullets. The zombies were getting more bloodthirsty as they stripped the door away. "Talbot…we don't have long."

"Carol, I don't care about your bare ass. Let's go!" Yeah, I was surly. Zombies were breaking in, my entire nether region felt like it had been Mike Tysoned, plus my mother in law was making this exponentially more dangerous. At this rate, I was unlikely to make it up there myself.

Winters had enough. He wrapped his arms around her and hefted her onto the dresser, he joined her immediately, then got her under the hips, trapping her skirt between them and put her straight up in the air, Justin and Tracy were leaning down to pull her in, but she would not raise her arms.

"My shoulders hurt," was all she offered.

I loved my mother in law, but she was pushing the boundaries of becoming a major burden. Right this very second, four people's lives were in danger because she was being petulant. Winters was struggling to hold her up; she was exerting almost none of her own energy. I climbed up to join him.

"Raise your fucking arms Carol or so help me God I will leave you down here," I said almost in her ear. She must have seen something in my eyes that this wasn't a veiled threat. Oh, she winced and moaned as she raised her arms up, making a great show of the pain she was in, but at least she did it. I know Tracy was raining down some hate stares at me, but for the love of all things holy, right this very moment I was not looking up. I was getting grabbed repeatedly and the dresser was being pushed away from the door; the latch had finally fallen out of it and now it was just a weight game and the zombies had more of it.

Winters and myself were more forced off than anything, as we jumped down. I bit my tongue nearly in half in the hopes that it would keep me from feeling the pain lodged deep in my rectum. Yeah, it might be hard for you to read that, it isn't particularly easy writing about it. I checked the magazine on my Uzi, told Winters to step back and unloaded that whole thing into the zombies. Blood, gore, brains, clothing, wall, wood, dust, hair, and maybe a unicorn or two were all splashed and splattered in a circle around the opening. Chunks of things I could not identify were raining down and slathering the top of the dresser and coating everything else.

"You enjoy that?" Winters asked.

"How the hell could you not?" I told him, putting it down. I had used up all the ammunition and I didn't think Knox would be decent enough to reload me. There's something inherently fun about shooting a shitload of bullets all at once. Not sure what it is, and I realize not everyone shares this sentiment, but for those of you that do, you know what I'm talking about. Those of you that don't; don't knock it till you've tried it. The only thing that might be better (outside of the bedroom) is watching things explode. Oh, I might have done a double entendre there; should probably just leave it alone.

"Go." I tapped him on the shoulder. The zombies were in disarray. I had blown back the initial few rows and the rest had not yet clambered their way to the front. He made it up with no problem. Just as I put my feet on what was left of the dresser, the door was blasted inward, the dresser toppled over, and me with it. I was able to turn enough that I didn't land once again on my bruised behind, but where I landed was the least of my problems. Zombies were streaming in over the debris they'd created. I was pushing back with my legs, attempting to get as much traction as I could. Going for the hole in the ceiling was out of the question; going out of the room the traditional way was also a big fat No. The window was my only out. I grabbed the windowsill and pulled myself up and out in one smooth move; I stretched until I was rewarded with the lip of the gutter.

I heard and felt the screws start to give the moment I put some serious weight on it. I did not have the opportunity to pull myself up or swing a leg onto the roof, because the entire gutter system on this side of the house pulled away, taking me with it. I'd like to say my landing was cushioned by a bulker's abdomen, but that wasn't the case. I came straight down on my legs, rolled my left ankle to the point where something definitely snapped—tendon or bone—tough to tell. I cried out as I collapsed. Pain was now searing into me from ankle to groin.

Before the zombies came, I would have just stayed there and cried and screamed until someone came to help me, maybe brought me a cold cloth, cradled my head, and waited with me another five to seven minutes for an ambulance to show up. Then I would be rushed to a hospital where I would wait for three hours while they filled out a great number of forms regarding my medical insurance. Then there would be the obligatory hour-long wait at x-ray while the technician does whatever x-ray technicians do, probably shining up those lead sheets, or wiping his lunch off of one.

Then he or she would put me into positions that would cause more pain, but only for a few seconds. When they were done confirming what everyone and their brother could tell just by looking at me, I'd be wheeled back behind my privacy screen where I would wait another two hours. Invariably, a drunk asshole or a desperate junkie would be put in the curtained off area right next to me. They would yell, swear, sometimes shit themselves and generally be among the biggest douches known to mankind. Sounds pretty awful, doesn't it? I would have taken that particular scenario in a heartbeat over the one I was in now. Instead of lying in a gown in a safe, clean environment waiting that seven hours on pain medication, tended to by clean, polite healthcare professionals, I had to get up and drag my useless leg behind me, which was right up there with placing my balls into the loving embrace of a cold steel vise and turning the handle until they ruptured. Or I guess I could just get eaten where I lay. Believe me, I considered that an option.

So far, I'd avoided that particular door prize, but as soon

as I saw a zombie poke its head out the window and look down at me, I realized I was about to be a winner if I didn't act. The zombies were adapting, getting smarter, as all predators do, but that didn't mean they actually *were* smart. With a considerable amount of fucking pain, I had to roll out of the way as the zombie that had seen me quite literally pitched head first out the window in its haste to get to me. I'd like to say he crushed his skull; instead, he merely snapped his neck, maybe spine. Normally this would be enough to take out your enemy. Not this one. He couldn't move anything below his shoulders, but that chomping mouth was entirely too close to my side. More zombies were coming to have a look; I had to move now.

I got up on my good foot and leg, the pain rocketed up my bad leg like it had been shot through a super-collider. Bursts of agony began to ignite within my skull. I had to hop, as that is the fastest form of locomotion one leg can make. Each hop up meant a violent collision back down to the earth, and just those few inches were enough to jolt my entire being in fresh, ripping torment. Stupid zombies were piling out of the window, most breaking something; less stupid zombies were making their way back downstairs and out the door to find me. It was over. I couldn't run, there was nowhere to hide; I had some ammo but certainly not enough. I did a quick scan of the fence-enclosed backyard; even if I made it to the barrier I didn't think I'd be able to climb over it. There was a swing set with a small clubhouse to the side and a decent sized above ground pool. Did I make that clubhouse into my fort, like the kids that lived here before me had done? Didn't seem like it had worked out too well for them. Anyway, it was too small. I wouldn't be able to stand or turn very effectively and it was only about six feet off the ground. I'd have zombies tearing at me in seconds.

It was the pool I was subconsciously moving toward. It was a little more than halfway full, completely green and covered with enough growth as to seem like it had its own hard-pack surface. I was thinking the buoyancy would help take the weight off my ankle and the water would hinder the zombies' ability to get to me. My traitorous imagination attacked immediately, producing all kinds of nasty things hiding just under that layer of slimy vegetation, but I was fairly certain it wouldn't be an alligator or anything quite that carnivorous. I was two feet from the ladder and the nearest zombie twenty feet; it was anyone's guess who would make it to the pool first. The ladder was a piece of shit, the thing wouldn't have passed quality control in a Chinese sweatshop.

"Must be French," I said as I grabbed the rail. The entire thing swung around like it was being buffeted by hurricane force winds. I was hop-jumping up each wrung convinced the thing would collapse somewhere between the three steps I needed to ascend. By the time I got to the top platform, the nearest zombie had run, arms outstretched, right into the ladder, I pitched over to the side and right into the drink. It wouldn't have been cosmically correct if my bad ankle hadn't got caught up in one of the rails on the way over the side. My scream was muffled by the scum covered water-like substance as I went down, but it was still very much audible. I was hanging upside down, dangling by a cracked leg and in danger of drowning in three feet of water. Who fucking dies that way in a zombie apocalypse? Pretty un-fucking-dignified, if I'm being honest, and not even close to heroic. Where I was getting so much air to expel my screams was beyond me. But when I took in that first chunk-laced bit of water, I knew my time was growing short.

I wriggled my leg back and forth violently in an attempt to free myself, maybe it was the lack of oxygen getting to my head or that I was so distracted by the taste of the green algae, but the pain seemed muted, like it was happening to someone else, or possibly to me—but from a distance. Or who knows? Maybe it was because I was too far gone to even care anymore. When the piece of shit ladder finally decided to let go of me, I almost didn't care anymore, content to lay on the green vinyl bottom of the thick-slime covered pool, the disgusting liquid a couple of feet above my head. I'd swallowed enough of that so-called water that I figured I'd die from some waterborne illness anyway. It was when I felt something with many legs walk across my face that I decided maybe I should get up and face the zombies. I was wondering what effect the slimy liquid I'd splashed into was going to have on my rifle. This particular rifle was not known for its ability to keep shooting while gunked up.

I came up out of the water, spewing all manner of organic and inorganic material. I coughed up things that looked like half-eaten green-brown moldy tuna fish sandwiches with pickles and maybe some teeth. I was on my knees; it gave me the ability to keep my head above water and also not put pressure on my ankle. Figured it was all for naught anyway, that a couple of dozen zombies were about to join me and like it was free-for-all Saturday at the city pool during the hottest summer in recorded history. I don't know if you've ever had the displeasure of this fine social activity, but it's not all that fun being in a pool with two hundred other people, packed so tight you can't touch bottom, you can't move around – it's like being the styrofoam popcorn packing in a shipping container. Can't splash because your arms are locked to your sides, though someone is invariably able to splash obnoxiously near you. Obviously, you can't swim around. You are not beating the heat because of the press of flesh and the highly unsanitary quality of water filled with people that feel a pool is nothing more than a giant urinal or who are too wedged in to get to a bathroom. Only your feet are cooled by the water, but that's no good because the concrete bottom is shredding your soaked-through soles. When I was able to pull the vegetation from my eyes and face, I realized I was still very much alone in the pool, as bipeds go, anyway. I found it more than strange that the forty-inch-high, four-millimeter-thick, vinyl pool wall had been enough of a barrier to confound the beasts.

There were zombies afoot, of that, there was no doubt, but they weren't paying any attention to me. I was like that weird kid in class that constantly keeps sticking a hand down the back of his pants every time he farts so he could catch a whiff of what he was delivering unto the world. What? You didn't have that kid? Lucky you. Because the wet gas our kid pressed from his bowels smelled something like old road kill blended with garlic and mildew. He was a strange one. I think I remember hearing that he'd become an IRS agent; seemed to suit his particular talent. Of all the pencils and pens I'd borrowed during my high school career, I made absolutely sure not to use one of his. Even got a zero on a surprise quiz rather than use the infected writing instrument he had attempted to hand me. I swear it walked off my desk under its own power.

Weird, the gopher holes the mind travels down at any given time. I spun slowly, taking stock of my situation. The zombies were everywhere, yet none were looking directly at me, they were much more interested in the house, where I could now hear multiple people screaming my name. How in the hell did I respond, without giving myself away? I realized I was in a delicate predicament. If I responded and the zombies discovered me, I wasn't going to get too far with this busted ankle. But if I didn't say something, it was good odds someone was going to risk a rescue, and I could not afford for that to happen. Luckily, I was spared from having to do anything at all on my own. Winters and Justin emerged onto the roof; they were frantically looking around. I wanted to shout "here I am," to wave, something that would garner their attention and allay, at least, my son's fear. I'm sure Winters would have been just fine if I'd disappeared off the face of the earth.

"Dad-is that you!?" Justin yelled. He was shielding his eyes and looking directly at me. He couldn't have seen much in the murk of the pool; my head and shoulders were covered in the floating filth and gave me a pretty good camouflage effect. He was moving closer, coming down sideways along the dangerous slope of the roof. I slowly raised a hand to the halt position.

"You alright?!" he yelled.

I couldn't say anything but the zombies were sure getting

interested in his voice, and also in the fact that he was pointing at something–that something being me. Unlike most dogs, zombies seemed to understand the concept of spotting something with a finger. It was Winters who, thankfully, put all of this together and pushed Justin's hand down when he saw the zombies looking around to see what the food on the roof was looking at. Winters turned about ninety degrees so he wasn't even peering my way.

"Going to assume you're more or less okay, Talbot, and that somehow that cesspool you are hiding in is masking you from the zees. Hopefully, they'll leave your area, but you can't stay in there all night. It's going to be cold–you could die from exposure. If you want to fight it out, shoot two quick rounds and we will do our best to give you the hole you need to run."

I silently thanked him.

Justin turned in the same direction as Winters, though he was having a much more difficult time not looking back at me. "Everyone here is fine, dad. We…I love you."

"I love you too," I said, no more than a hush of air escaping my lips.

They came out and checked on me periodically. I was still there, and still couldn't do much of anything, although my ankle had begun to knit itself together. That hurt like hell, but what was really becoming troublesome was the cold. It was a decent autumn day out, somewhere in the mid-sixties, if I had to take a guess, actually a beautiful day as far as that goes, but not exactly what we up here call swimming weather. And with night approaching, I had to think it was going to drop at least into the forties. Survivable outside, even without a jacket. But when every part of me was exposed to the cold, no way to get dry, so completely miserable, and injured, I would be in very real danger of dying from hypothermia. The zombies weren't attacking; in fact, they weren't even actively looking for me. I might as well have dropped off a cliff. Unfortunately, they also weren't leaving, like they had some legacy memory that something good used to be here and they wanted to bask in the remembrance. The sun had just begun to set when the first of a violent series of shivers wracked my entire body. I did not know that toes could be made to shake, but I knew they could cramp. Had to add that to my list of complaints.

There was a good chance by tomorrow morning my vampire virus-infused body would be able to repair the break. The problem was the human casing I was in being able to make it through the night. It might be a faster healing process if I wasn't also attempting to fend off freezing to death. I had to clamp a hand over my mouth when my teeth chattered loudly from a body twisting spasm. I needed to send my mind away and let my body deal as best it could, so I found a gopher hole. I was ten the first time I saw a ghost; not the last time, not by a long shot, but definitely the first—and you know what they say about your first: it's terrifying and you never forget it. Yeah…I was more relaxed already. That's the way you start a side story, a way to distract you from what is actually happening; you remember the first time you were truly terrified.

We had just moved from Boston proper to a sleepy little suburb called Walpole. I knew no one; I hung out with no one, and maybe that is who came to hang out with me. I was feeling pretty pissed off at life when I left the house, well, actually pissed off that my parents had put me in this *position* in life. My mother had tasked me with a list of chores longer than my arm. I walked into the garage, past the stack of boxes she wanted me to bring into the house. I walked past her car, loaded down with all manner of cleaning supplies, down the driveway, onto the roadway and hooked a left.

I had no idea where I was going, but anything beat what my day was going to entail if I stayed home. Sure, there was a piper that was going to need to be paid for my transgression, but for good or bad, I never really gave a shit about that future piper; he was always kind of a bitch. Well, that's sort of a lie, and even if I'm relating a story just to keep from freezing to death, I should, at least, attempt a truthful telling. I didn't dismiss Future Piper because he was a little bitch; I didn't give a shit about Future Piper because he literally did not exist in my present tense mind. He was not born yet, I couldn't see him standing in front of me, so therefore he had absolutely no bearing on my life whatsoever. In my broken head, there was no room to entertain thoughts of consequences. Wait…that makes me sound like a sociopath. Was it apathy, then? Was I apathetic to ramifications? Maybe even back then I knew I could easily be dead before they or any form of Karma caught up with me, but I'm pretty sure it was just a case of "who gives a fuck," the textbook definition of apathy. I'm sure there's a fifteen-hundred-page psychiatric book that discusses this in depth; no need for me to go through it.

I hooked another left when I got to the end of the next street, I think I heard my mother call out for me a couple of times as I increased my pace. I didn't know it then, but I was heading toward Indian Hill–not the hill proper, but the far-left side, which was dominated by streams, bogs, and heavy woods–pretty much the ideal setting for all things creepy. I was on a side street in Walpole, which basically means I was alone. In Boston, a "side street" was where you got your tattoos and really good pizza. Here, it was empty. So, I took a hard turn into the woods. No reason why I chose to verge at this particular spot; it was visually the same as the entire wood-lined roadway. There was no path, no break in the fauna, no blazed trail to let me believe walking through here would be easier than any other place–this was just where it was decided that I should turn in. Sometimes there is not an explanation. Remember those words; I'll be using that exact same phrase a little later in this narrative, but the next time, they will be a lot chillier. Whether it was in my mind or was an actual phenomenon, the temperature was much cooler when I went into the woods. Had to have been a balmy 85-ish on the road, and I realized the canopy the trees made and the nearness to water would have a cooling effect, but I could see my breath. That seemed excessive. The niggling in the back of my skull didn't start for a few hundred yards. The pines had given way to white birch, which always make a normal woodland seem ethereal or at least strange. They have a subtle glow to them that makes everything around them appear blanched. Even as chills ran up and down my forearms I walked forward like I wore blinders, lost in my own thoughts, not taking in the scenario around me.

An icy finger scratched its way from my lower back up my spine and circled the top of my head. I had to stop right where I was and look around. I no longer felt as if I were alone, and not in a good way. It was that overwhelming feeling that I was being watched. I did a slow spin and scanned those trees, peering hard at all of them. I didn't see anything, but the feeling intensified so much so that I was thinking now might be a good time to vacate the area and maybe go to a less creepy place. The problem was, the automated guidance system I had employed to get here had suddenly gone on the fritz. I'd turned myself around. Now, I wasn't in any true danger of being lost in the woods of Walpole, but when you want to leave somewhere quick and don't know which way to go, well that can be terrifying; it's easy to succumb to panic. Everywhere I looked was the same, an endless line of trees, no path, no vista, no big rocks I could have used to mark the land. I walked a little longer hoping I was heading in a direction out, and I did my best not to constantly keep looking over my shoulder to see if I was being followed. I didn't want whoever it was to know I knew, or that I was lost.

For a while I was watching where my feet were going, doing my best to avoid rocks and branches. To this day I wonder why I looked up when I did, and I permanently regret that decision. There she was, ten feet up in the air, her head hanging askew. If I'd dared to approach, I could have reached up and touched the bottom of her dangling, bare feet–though I had no such desire. She was not some wisp of smoke, an ethereal mist; no, she appeared as real and solid as the tree she was hanging from, though I could not see the rope that kept her tethered there. She seemed a few years older than me, fifteen, maybe sixteen, blonde hair. She might have been pretty were it not for her bulging eyes, swollen, protruding tongue, and blue face. She was dead, and had been for a while.

"Help," barely escaped my mouth. But she heard it; oh yeah, she heard it. That tiny cry for aid was a catalyst. Her eyes turned to me, her head, which rested completely sideways on her cracked and broken neck, straightened itself out. Sounded like dry, brittle branches breaking under the weight of a nightmare. She floated down toward the ground, though she never really touched it, hovering a few inches above. I would have pissed my pants if I'd not been stone cold paralyzed from the crown of my head to the soles of my feet. She raised her arm up and extended a finger toward me.

"You did this to me," she said in a tortured voice, the rope having twisted the ligature of her vocal cords, making it sound like she was whispering through razor blades. I involuntarily backed up a step; she floated two steps' worth closer. Again, she hissed:

"You did this to me!" Now these words had some force to them; this threat seemed to overcome my stupor.

"Please...I don't know you." As if a case of mistaken identity would offer up some defense to the specter before me.

Her head cracked loudly to the side as if she had maybe forgotten her neck was broken. Her eyes took me in, *really* took me in. "No, not yet you don't, but you will."

Might have only been ten, but I knew where this was going. The vengeful demon was going to make me pay for a transgression she believed me responsible for, and ummm...yeah, fuck that. There may have been maniacal laughter, difficult to say as I was running as fast as I ever had– my heartbeat was like a bass drum and the air was rushing past my ears. Somehow, I popped out at the exact point I had entered. I didn't stop running until I got all the way home. You'd think this would be the strangest part of the story, maybe even the ending, but you'd be wrong. When I ran back through the garage, grabbing a box to bring back into the kitchen where my mother was, she smiled and told me: "That was quick." Sometimes there is not an explanation, and in this case, I don't think I wanted one.

I never told anybody about that ghost; even spent a few days at the library trying to find some story about a local girl committing suicide or being murdered–didn't turn up anything. In hindsight, retelling that story from decades ago was most likely not the best avenue of retreat for my mind. I was already freezing to death; thinking of that chilling encounter had done little to warm me up. Night had settled in for the long haul; I could feel nothing below my shoulders, I had been making tiny tsunamis on the pool surface with my uncontrollable shaking, now even that had stopped. I was pretty sure I had read somewhere that this was not a good development. The moon had not yet started its journey up, but the sky was clear and there was some visibility with the light the stars offered. The zombies were still fucking afoot; like a stubborn wart, they would not go away. Not that I could have done anything about it anyway, I wasn't even sure how I was going to get out of the pool. It seemed beyond my capability to move any part of me.

"Dad, you still alright?" Justin asked.

His voice brought me back to the present; I was still alive and that was something. It wasn't pitch dark, but I couldn't see him; I had to think he could not see me either. Not sure how he thought I was going to answer without ringing the dinner bell. This was when I ran into a whole new and deadly situation. My body was failing me, or more aptly, I was failing it. I was teetering like a bombed out building that had lost three of its four support columns. It was a slow process, but the direction my body was going was taking my head with it, and I was powerless to stop it. I commanded, demanded, ordered, then finally begged my arms to move and brace me so that I would not be submerged within the oily confines of the polluted pool. Didn't work. My head drifted down and bounced off the bottom where my lips made contact with what I hoped was only a small tree branch. I don't know if I have ever been more powerless during a life-threatening event in my entire life, at least, I mean, when I knew it was happening.

I was holding my breath; I think that probably happens automatically, but I knew my limits. Best of circumstances, I wasn't going to go much more than forty-five seconds. Like the vast majority of humans, I liked to breathe. I didn't see the benefit of knowing how long I could go without air. I felt the same way about the other three necessities in life; I ate and I drank and I returned the finished product, never having any desire to find out how long I could push my body to go without. I used to watch this show, *Naked and Afraid*, where they would send a male and a female to some remote, inhospitable armpit of the world, usually only supplied with a flint and a knife, and they had to survive for twenty-eight days. Sometimes they both made it, usually one did, sometimes neither did. They suffered hardships like thirst, hunger, plague-proportion bugs, heat, cold or constant rain. The question I always asked myself was, *why*? Why the fuck would someone send their resume in for this? Is it important to have the skills necessary to survive in extreme circumstances? Of course, it is! Very important! But testing them out under useless conditions just seemed like an arrogant waste of time, and could possibly even lead to harm. Who knows? Maybe harm that could prevent you from actually using those skills to survive for real one day. I would never even consider what they were doing. Hell man, they didn't even get any sort of financial compensation for what they did. Did the fifteen minutes of fame have such an allure that they could not resist? Pretty fucking elaborately useless pain-threshold game.

Where was I? Oh yeah, I was dying by at least three different ways and if I managed to pull myself from the jaws of death, zombies awaited. I tilted my head to raise my mouth a few inches off the pool floor, not enough to make a difference, but being able to make my body do anything at this point was a victory. Next was a savage demand to my shoulder to do something besides connect my arm to my torso. It flinched at the request, but yielded to me and I was able to gain another inch toward salvation. The command then went down an arm that was much less willing to begrudge me, like I was an affront to everything it stood for. At this pace, it was a foregone conclusion that my loved ones were going to find me in the morning with leaf-choked lungs. I think it was my middle finger that finally relented and figured we were on the same team, no doubt remembering the good times. Amazing what your "fuck you" finger can accomplish when it sets its mind to it. As it pushed up, I made another inch or two toward my climb for safety, but it was a "fuck you, death" couple of inches. My hand, forearm, elbow and upper arm began to work, not in concert, mind you, more like a hipster jazz band, each doing their own thing, but at least they were fucking moving. My elbow collapsed once, sending me back to the dreaded slime covered bottom, before rebounding and giving me some thrust. I was stuck in no man's land, halfway up, but still vastly short of my goal. My internal clock was crunching the numbers. Yep, I would need to breathe real soon. My heart was in over-exertion mode, it was thumping so loudly in my chest it was hurting my eardrums with its percussions. My lungs were beginning to constrict on themselves, a fire burned within them like I'd inhaled habanero infused smoke. How's that for a descriptor? That's the searing sacks of pain that were my lungs.

My torso thought now might be a good time to get into the game. My stomach muscles convulsed as they clenched and released in brutally painful contractions. Can't say that I'd ever had a charley-horse in my gut, and right now didn't seem like the optimum time to dwell on the new sensation. In between painful eruptions, I would force it upwards, ever upwards. I felt the cold night air brush across my head, so close, so achingly close. I dipped down grudgingly, knowing I was a second from taking in a deadly mix of water and all manner of microbes and parasites. One final surge; it was now or death, simple as that. I tilted my head above the surface and sucked in a combination of sweet, sweet air and salty, tainted water. I coughed vigorously for a minute before I was able to expel the worst of it and also get enough air into my oxygen-starved brain and extremities. The zombies were shuffling around from the noise but still, the water was acting as some sort of crazy alien cloaking technology.

Drowning throws up an instinctive red flag for mammals, and certain systems kick in, and the panic in me had not settled down. I had fought hard for this victory, but I would not be this lucky next time. A fair portion of my life, even before the z-poc, had been me rolling the dice—you won some and you lost some, it's the nature of the game. But when the stakes are your life you play with loaded dice—fuck the rules, and fuck all if it's considered cheating. If you want to bet your friend a twelve pack on the outcome of a football game that's one thing. Right now, these were stakes I was not willing to pay on and this was not a debt you could run from. I'm not proud of some of the defaulted lines of credit I left in my wake during my so-called "normal" life, especially that Best Buy one when they sold me a piece of shit laptop that died after three months and they wouldn't honor the warranty because it was a discontinued model. Didn't stop them from selling it to me though, did it? Fucking pimply-faced sales puke still got his commission. Maybe a little guilt there, but none of that mattered now.

"Priorities, Talbot." I managed to say in a small, shaky voice as I slowly made my way to the edge of the pool. I didn't want to be any closer to the enemy than I needed, but if I pitched over again, it was my hope that I would fall against the lining and could prop myself up, stay above the casualty line. My teeth started to chatter; this time I thought that might actually be a good thing. I leaned against the vinyl, the body tremors started again. I could not control them—I certainly could not stop them. Water was splashing and my body thumping up against the pool wall was making a hollow, bonging noise. The zombies were most definitely interested. I think my ankle was on the mend, but just because I couldn't feel it didn't necessarily mean good news, more than likely it meant the circulation was sluggish or gone. I could not ride the night out in the water. I didn't think it was much past midnight, still long hours away from the warming rays of the sun, and if it was a cloudy, rainy day, what then?

I reached a weakened arm up and grabbed the lip of the pool while also tentatively placing weight on what I hoped was a freshly knitted ankle. The pop it made was audible through the water. The pain was sharp and sudden. Yup, it was safe to say my ankle was still there, now the question was could I do anything with it? I put as much weight as I could on it, knowing the answers that yielded would mean the difference between escape and becoming a midnight snack. I stood to my full height. If I thought I'd been cold before, it was nothing compared to what I felt as the wind blew past my soaked clothes. My skin was stretching due to the oversizing of my goosebumps. I wanted to make a grim joke about how my junk had retreated inside looking for heat, but I was pretty sure that might actually be the case and that even if I did somehow make it out, it might not ever come back down. That's shit you just don't kid about.

I took a minute to look around me. For the most part, the zombies were doing traditional zombie things: smelling up the area, rotting some flesh, chewing on some human remains, you know, normal shit. But there was this one zombie, one with a little more brains than he had a right to, who was looking my way. He knew something was up and he was going to spoil my little planned get away. My rifle was at the bottom of the pool somewhere, and not only was I in no hurry to go back down there, I wasn't even sure if I could trust its effectiveness just now. M-16s and their civilian counterparts, the AR-15s, aren't particularly known for their ability to fire predictably when fouled. And the wet gloop it had been submerged in for hours, can't have done it any favors. If the barrel was in any way clogged up, I could make an already bad situation fatal. I'd seen barrels blow up before, some on the battlefield as they were overused, and others at ranges when dipshits failed to do even the most basic of maintenance. Most had escaped with minor injuries; even those in battle had others around them to pick up the slack, but if my weapon blew, I only had me to count on.

Yes, I would grab it because I had to, but I didn't think I dared to use it, even to signal Justin and Winters. If I caught blowback in the face and eyes it could be enough to disable me and allow the zombies their treat. I felt better for moving; my ankle was holding up reasonably well, but the true test was coming when I put it under stress. I slogged around until I struck the rifle with the toe of my boot. Now I had to do a little gut check and reach back into the water. For some reason, it felt like barb-laced ice cubes. There was a slight panic as my mouth dipped down and I almost went in face forward. I snagged it and jerked quickly up, happy for the weight of it in my hands, even if it was no more useful than a club.

So, there I was, standing in the middle of the stinking pool, pondering how in the fuck I was going to get out of there. Climbing the inner ladder seemed tantamount to Everest about now. Then I still had to get down and somehow make haste. Any maneuver with quickness seemed as elusive as a minotaur or a yeti, or more like a yeti riding a minotaur, or the other way around, if you want that visual. Wasn't going to see it. I once had a fight with my wife, can't remember what the hell it was about, something inane, I'm sure, didn't matter. The point is she had me so twisted up in my own words, instead of telling her "not to fuck my shit up," I said "Stop being a shit fucker." Instead of getting pissed off, she got a confused look on her face and proceeded to bust out laughing. So, there I am, being all pissed off, having spoken a potentially horrible and rude insult, and she's laughing her ass off, I mean to the point where she bent over and was grabbing her gut.

"I don't want to ever be a shit fucker, Talbot, and I would hope the same for you, and I'm not sure if I should thank you for that visual or not." She left me alone so she could go and enjoy the rest of her laugh and maybe ponder the question she'd raised. Not sure the reason for the tangent, I guess I was just trying to show the importance of visuals and why you might want to be careful with what you use to display your thoughts; remember, an idiotic picture will haunt you much longer than a dumb sentence. Right. Back to reality. I was looking to the ladder while also keeping watch on the zombie that was ever so slowly making his way over to the pool. Yeah, that one was definitely giving me the old stink eye. He wasn't completely sure what was going on, but the pieces of that puzzle were beginning to fall into place. If he got close enough and I could make everything work right, I was going to shove a knife blade through his temple.

We were approaching each other like two lovers might across a smoke-hazed dance floor, a slow, sweet song serenading in the background. We would finally meet up, look deeply into each other's eyes, kiss, and then a slow clap would ensue. Again, man, I don't know why my mind diverges like it does. I'd like to say it's a defense mechanism; keeps me from going insane from the reality I was actually living, because really, a broken and decaying undead cannibal was ass dragging what was left of his jaw over to bite into my face, and I was freezing my ass off, hobbling broken-ankled through thick green sewer slime, carrying an inactive gun, to kill him up close and personal, obviously you can't kill what is not alive, but you get my meaning. The only music we had was the percussion of my teeth and the hollow moan of the cold wind through his missing flesh. We both halted with the sound of a car engine approaching, I turned to the street, which had been to my back.

"What now?" I asked. If Knox and / or his henchmen were coming back, what was I going to do? Odds were, I'd be overlooked in the pool; it would be the house he would be

153

going for. I wondered idly whether rats could climb the aluminum siding and swim at me.

"Talbot!" It was BT shouting. Like a dumbass, I tried to shout back. As luck would have it, I sounded more like Rose Dewitt of Titanic movie fame after she'd been in the Atlantic for an hour; a cricket farting would have carried more sound. By this point, the self-preservation part of my brain had kicked in and I realized how bad of an idea that might be.

"BT!" It was Justin.

"Justin? Are you guys alright? Where's your dad?" I could hear the concern in my friend's voice.

"We're fine…well, dad might be busted up. He's in a pool in the backyard."

"Talbot, answer me!" BT demanded.

"He's frozen and surrounded by zombies," Justin clarified.

"Right. Hold on, pal. I'm so going to get you the fuck out of there."

"Thank you," I whispered.

The car was idling on the street. BT didn't even need to climb the privacy fence to look over it. A flashlight that could potentially burn out retinas illuminated the area.

"Whoa, you look like shit," BT said as the light found me. "You a zombie?" he asked.

I managed to unfurl one finger, obviously the most useful one I had in any given situation.

"Good to see you too, man," he said. The zombies made a go for the fence. "Can you run?" he asked as he realized he was pulling them all away from the pool. I gave him a thumbs-down. "You really do look like shit. Got the Marines. We'll come up with something and get you soon. Hold on." With that, he took the light and was gone.

Not going to lie, there was a dip in my morale as he vanished. I wanted to be gone now too. I've been in some armpits of the world; I've seen the horrors that one man can do unto another. Killing in war, while not necessarily the best way to go about getting something accomplished, is still leagues better than torture. There were times we came across whole villages that were tied up in a certain way; a rope bound their hands and legs behind their back then noosed around their neck. So, if they relaxed their extremities they would begin to be choked by their own body pressure. There is only so long the human body can be forced to hold out like that. Knees and shoulders began to burn as if they are on fire; eventually, ligaments will tear, yet this is still worlds better than when you try to take pressure off your screaming joints and the ligature in your neck is compressed and your airway is pinched off. Waves of panic, surge though your brain, forcing you to struggle and press even more against the bindings, producing a whole fresh wave of pain that you can barely tolerate before you start the whole process over again. It's criminal how strong our will to survive is—the horror we will endure to keep breathing.

By the time we got to the village, it had been two days since the insurgents had worked their nightmare. Men, women, children—didn't matter. Every single one of them had been bound up and positioned so that they could watch neighbors and loved ones die next to them. Only one woman, one, eighty-five-year-old woman had survived. For forty-eight hours she had fought to stay alive so she could tell someone, anyone, what had happened there. I heard she died three days after we'd freed her; her injuries too great. More likely she died of a broken heart; she'd only kept living to accomplish what she'd set out to do—to carry her people's pain to an ear that might give a shit. Why'd I relate that...? Because right now, being in the pool was a form of torture, and I wanted out of it in the worst way possible. Not in an hour, not in ten minutes, but right fucking now.

BT's voice came back over the fence, swear to God just the sound of it brought me back. "Going to do a smash and grab, Mike! Get to the far end of the pool!" he shouted.

I was already there, so that wasn't a problem. I wasn't keen on this idea, as my brain slowly processed what he'd said. I heard the revving of what sounded like a diesel truck, I hadn't realized there was still some adrenaline in there, but I got nervous. If they misjudged their approach, I was certain I would not be able to jump out of the way, and it nearly went down like that. The Ram truck burst through the wooden fence sending a fence slat nearly three feet long right at me. It missed impaling me by inches, and that it missed had nothing to do with my cat-like reflexes. The flying stake had been coming in so fast I hadn't even had the time to shield my face; I just closed my eyes. It was sharp enough and had enough force that it went through the vinyl siding like a skewer through the skin of an orange; I would definitely have been kabobbed good. The Ram symbol on the front of the truck was looming larger and I had nowhere to go. The first zombie that impacted the front end was sent spinning wildly off to the side, as was the next. The bumper was taking some punishment, but Dodge's advertising claim seemed to be holding strong–built Ram Tough. Gunfire was coming out from both sides in sustained bursts and still, that grill grew larger.

"Close enough, man," was what I said as the truck obliterated the far side of the pool. As seems to be the case when the action starts, multiple things happened simultaneously. Sparky, the zombie who had a sense that I was there and trapped, so named for his spark of intelligence, grabbed the back of my head and a fistful of hair. As he was wrenching my skull backward, the truck plowed through the pool wall before coming to a skidding halt. Water did what water does–it rushed for the low ground. I was sucked out toward that opening like a turd in a previously clogged toilet. So, flushed with a vengeance, if that wasn't clear.

Sparky had such a good handhold, he decided to come for the ride. My ankle, which was still throbbing in pain, was nothing compared to the fresh feeling of being scalped. I was heading straight for the front end of the truck and was in danger of splitting the tires and going completely underneath. My guess is I wouldn't stop until I made the curb and finally the storm drain, and by the way things were going this fine fucking evening, odds were there would be a red balloon tied on the cover. All of this action was Broadway show-illuminated by the high beams of the truck. I was literally traveling toward the light, though I didn't think this was the way that scene was supposed to play out. My head was mostly underwater, Sparky had yet to let go, I was choking on slime again. Then the light dimmed and was nearly extinguished, I figured I was at the end. But, unbeknownst to me, BT had exited the vehicle and was, mitt out, going to play first baseman with me as the baseball that dribbled down the first base line.

If you don't realize where I'm going with this, you aren't a baseball fan or don't know that I bleed red not because that is the color of blood but rather that of my beloved Red Sox, and that runs deep. If you're following, let's just say I hoped he didn't Billy Buckner me. A leg and a foot hovered above my head, I felt like a prehistoric rodent attempting to dodge the footfalls of a Titanosaur. There was a sickening crunch behind me as Sparky had first his arm crushed, then his skull. BT wrapped an arm around my side and hefted me up into his arms. I'm not sure if I should be ashamed to admit this, but I felt sort of like the damsel in distress being saved by the dashing hero as he swept me up. That ended quick enough when he threw me over his shoulder like a sack of potatoes. If the world ever got its head screwed back on I was *so* going to make an action figure of him. There I was, waterlogged and broken draped over his shoulder like an unneeded coat on a warm night, while with the other arm he is firing a machine gun. I mean that shit is just iconic, right? He tossed me into the bed of the pickup truck before hopping in himself. Two slaps on the truck top and we were thrown into reverse and with a screech of tires, I was whisked away into the night. Wasn't a few seconds later I passed out from exhaustion.

CHAPTER SIX
MIKE JOURNAL ENTRY 6

I AWOKE WITH a start. I was under five blankets. At first it was comforting, and then I realized I was baking hot and started throwing covers off me.

"Hold on man!" BT said, shielding his eyes. "You don't have anything on under there."

I wisely threw only four of the blankets off and was left with a light one that made it much more comfortable. We were in a small house and I was on a couch, settled fairly close to a roaring fire.

"What's going on?" I repositioned myself so I was sitting up.

"Here. Eat this and I'll give you an update. Pork belly," he said as he handed it over.

"Not ham, right?" I asked, looking at the meat.

"You'd turn down food right now?" he asked.

"If I'd found you in the same situation and you were laying here just barely holding on and I handed you a plate with your mac and cheese mixed in with your meatloaf would you eat it?"

"Of course I wouldn't. Now you're just talking crazy. Who the hell mixes up foods that have no right to be mixed together? We're not animals!"

"That's how I feel about ham."

"It's not ham, man. You want me to tell you what's going on or you want to talk about pork products?"

The pork belly was a little on the salty side but still delicious. I tore into that thing. I nodded at him to go on.

"All the social graces of a turkey vulture."

I stopped eating. "What the fuck does that even mean?"

"They'll vomit on their food to keep others from eating it."

"Really man? You're comparing me to that?"

He shrugged.

"Just tell me what's going on and I won't talk about dipping my bacon in maple syrup." It was funny to watch the big man gag. "Or pour milk over my collard greens. Hmmm, sugar frosted collard green cereal!"

"When are you not a dick? Since that is a rhetorical question, I'll just start talking while you think on it. Tracy, Justin, and the rest are fine. Tommy and Travis are keeping surveillance–don't worry, it is from a safe distance. They are using lasers and Morse code to talk."

"Not too surprised Tommy would know Morse, but Justin?"

"Freeze off a few brain cells? Winters is with them."

"Right, sorry. Wait where'd they get lasers?"

"Dude, they just fucking have them! Are you going to hit me up with the finer points throughout this whole thing? They all have their bootlaces tied, their rifles are locked and loaded, everyone has had a bathroom break."

"Who's being the dick now?" I asked.

"Sorry man. I'm so worried about your sister." He looked straight at me as if daring me to say something inflammatory.

"I already consider you a brother. Nothing would make me feel better than to say you were actually family."

"Still a dick by not being a dick! How do you do it? How do you make me feel like shit for yelling at you even when you deserve it?"

"It's a tactic I developed with my mother. I could infuriate and confuse her all at the same time. Kept her off balance."

"You pull that shit with Tracy?"

"Oh hell no. She wouldn't put up with it."

"What makes you think I will?" he asked.

I could only smile.

"We're in a world of shit," I told BT. "Knox has the satellite system."

"I was going to wait until maybe you felt a little better, but Sanders believes he knows where Deneaux is."

I knew what was going to happen if I sat up too fast; did it anyway. Very nearly swooned.

"Why aren't we on our way?"

"Well, the only reason Sanders knows where they are is because he stumbled into a pretty secure stronghold of Knox's."

"I hate that woman and I would risk just about everything to get rid of her."

"He says he's not sure if Deneaux is being held or is there of her own volition."

"Fuck. Maybe we let her stay there, then she'll be Knox's problem and eventually she'll do the same to him as she's done to a good long line of people; maybe she's our infectious plant, take them down from the inside. What about the rest of the people that were with her?" It hurt to ask this question. My sister, nephew, brother, daughter, and grandson had been among the people in that car. Already knew the fate of Mad Jack; it was not a stretch at all to believe that had or would happen to every one of them.

"We're going to get everyone back, Mike. We'll take care of Knox and we'll do what we've set out to do."

"Any news on Trip?"

"Nothing. But we're talking about Trip; good chance they're holed up in a snack cake factory."

I smiled at that. "When are we going to get Tracy?"

"As soon as you are able to move. Another thing though, Mike...Kylie is a nurse. She looked at your ankle; she knew it was broken and she knew it was healing at an incredible pace. She's suspicious."

"I don't have time to worry about that."

"Any chance you have enough time to worry about getting dressed?" he said. I grabbed a blanket quickly as Kylie spoke from the other room.

"Your clothes are almost dry; you may want to put them on," she said.

"Are they clean?" I asked BT.

"This look like a laundromat? I mean, sure, we wiped off some of the bigger globs but you still smell like low tide in New Jersey."

"Like dead fish and washed up gangsters? Is that what you're implying?"

"Along those lines. I'm going to get out of here while you put some clothes on. I've seen enough pasty Talbot ass for a good long while."

"Have you? Have you seen enough 'Talbot ass'?"

BT turned; he did not look like a happy camper. A big meaty finger came up. "That's your sister you're talking about."

"She'd laugh if she were here."

"That's the problem though, isn't it?" BT let his head dip as he walked out.

"How are you doing?" Kylie had waited a minute while I got my clothes on. I wasn't in the mood for answering questions, but at least it distracted me from the disgusting feel of my slightly damp and definitely moldy clothes.

I looked up from the magazine I was loading. "Great." I plastered on as fake a smile as I could.

"What are you?" she asked. Without any type of warning she was going to dive right into the deeper end of the pool.

"A husband, father, brother, and marine that very desperately wants to get his family back together."

"Near as I can tell you had a bimalleolar ankle fracture less than twelve hours ago. With a proper set, splinting, good diet, and positive outlook it would take a minimum of six weeks to heal, yet you seem nearly whole."

"Must be wrong about your diagnosis. I mean, how would I be able to step down on it?" Which I did, with maybe a bit too much vigor. Might have been able to throw a little more shade on her inquisition if I hadn't winced as I did so.

"Hold your leg up and rotate your ankle."

"I hurt it, ok? There's no doubt about that. Right now, I'm not going to do anything to further aggravate it, not when I still have so much to do."

"What would I see if I took a sample of your blood?"

"Red, I would imagine," I told her.

"Marines are tough, Talbot, I get that, but they don't shrug-off broken ankles," she said as I squeezed past her at the door, making sure she got a good old whiff of the essence I was cloaked in.

Sanders and Biddeford were out in the garage going over a fairly decent mock-up of the house Tracy was in.

"You're up?" Sanders asked.

"Yeah, ready to go," I told him.

"My wife said you have a broken ankle."

"Must be wrong."

He looked at me. "Good enough. We can always use the help, although I'm not going to be the one that tells her she was wrong. Good news is most of the zombies left with the pool maneuver." He pointed to a smashed-up water bottle. "While you were sleeping, Biddeford and myself mounted some reinforced plywood walls in the truck bed. Now we just have to get the truck into position, extend the twenty-four-foot ladder, and get everyone out."

"Wouldn't a bucket truck or a fire truck be better?" I asked.

"The bucket truck is slow; remember how long it took just to get them into the attic? Getting them into a cherry picker would take an inordinate amount of time and we just don't have it. The fire truck is unwieldy; if we found ourselves in a chase it would be highly unlikely we would be able to shake our pursuers. Besides, there's not much room for passengers in either vehicle."

"Pickup truck it is," I said.

We took a stealthy approach to where they had left the truck, and in ten minutes we had arrived. Biddeford spun the wheel and was going in reverse nearly as fast as he had been going forward. He did his best to avoid the zombies, though he still hit two. A decent spray of misted viscera came up and over our impromptu wall and splashed across my chest.

"For once I'm glad I'm not clean," I said as I plucked something that looked a lot like an optic nerve from my pants. There weren't many zombies around, but let's be honest—one is too many. We were dealing with twenty times that number. Sanders was adamant that we were not to use firearms as Knox's patrols were running all through the city, and our earlier shots had drawn them closer. The truck was taking some dings as zombies were running into it. Biddeford was working on the ladder. I was trying to slam zombie heads with my buttstock, but I didn't have the heft or the angle to do it well. And, let's be real. It wasn't like I was swinging an M1 Garand around, the wood on that thing was designed to become a headbanger when ammo became an issue. But the lighter 5.56s had composite stocks designed to be lightweight. It was more likely I'd break the stock than a zombie's head. BT reached down into the truck bed and picked up an aluminum bat. He stood tall, rolled his shoulders and his head a couple of times, took a breath, admired the bat before turning to absolutely destroy the zombie I could barely shoo away. The classics; am I right?

He brought the weapon over his head again, moved slightly to the side, and caved in a zombie's skull so deeply the rest of the head appeared to fall into its neck. I did what was prudent and just stepped back and into a squat as he swung another ten times; each time a kill was visually confirmed—it was up there vying for a spot on the most disgusting things I'd witnessed award, not to mention Hall of Fame RBI stats. By the time he was done, he was breathing heavy, the bat had some serious dents in it, and he'd spilled enough brain matter he could have painted an elephant with it.

"You look like you enjoyed that," I said to him, breaking through the haunted look he was wearing. "You alright, BT?" I asked when he didn't respond.

"I will be," he said, looking for something else to annihilate.

I turned my attention to where I could help. Biddeford had the ladder against the roof and the evacuation was happening. Justin had brought Avalyn down and went back up to grab Angel from Tracy. Once he was down with her, I had to go up and get Henry–first because he was a big dog and unwieldy and if anyone was going to take a tumble saving him it would be me, and secondly, he wouldn't budge for anyone else. He was having none of that ladder. I had to promise him a box full of cookies, even though I could not deliver on that just yet. The look I got from him when I put him down on the truck bed and didn't give the four-legged stomach anything to eat was priceless. Then I remembered that bulldogs had perhaps one of the strongest bites in the dog world and thought better of my smile. I scowled and solemnly promised he would get the first goodie I found.

Justin was coming down again with the other dogs when I saw Carol got a bit of vertigo; it was touch and go there for a few seconds as Tracy did her best to keep her mother on the roof. I moved Justin out of the way; if there had been a ladder racing event I'm pretty sure I would have taken home a medal as I went up to make sure she was staying put, along with my wife. The zombies that were still in the house, once they realized that their guests were leaving were coming outside to see them off.

"I can't go down that," Carol said as she tried to squeeze my hand off.

"Not much of a choice," I told her.

"The zombies are gone now. I'll just go down the stairs."

This was my mother in law and I loved her, but I was starting to see why some married couples moved away from their families.

"We don't have time, Carol. We could be spotted at any moment, and we'd still have to get you out of the attic. You forgetting how difficult it was to get you up there?"

"I understand, Allan, I do. But I left the oven on."

Tracy looked at me. "Stress sometimes forces the issue."

Alzheimers or dementia or maybe a little bit of both was rearing its oh-so-ugly fucking head. None of us were taught to deal with this in a battlefield scenario; someone said something crazy you just shoved them on forward. I rubbed my head before I spoke.

"We'll go down this ladder and shut the oven off," I told her.

"You always were a sweet talker, Allan." Carol's hand lingered on my face. I think it's times like this you want to start creating new words because "uncomfortable" didn't even scratch the surface. I felt more like "zrardreth"–as prickly off the tongue as my insides were feeling.

"Yeah, Allan, come on! Help her get to the oven." My wife wasn't playing with me; she was playing along with her mom to get them the hell off the roof.

"We should pick a better hotel, Allan. The staff here is very rude," she said, just loud enough to me so Tracy would know she was talking about her.

"Biddie! Get them the fuck down! I'm hearing engines." Sanders was leaning out the driver's side window.

"You heard that, right?" Biddeford called up.

"Carol."

"Yes, dear?" she asked with eyes that were reserved for lovers only.

"Zrardreth. Tracy, come on–help me. We have to move."

"Unhand me!" she said to Tracy. "This is assault and I will not stand for it."

BT had finished his killing spree and handed the bat off to

Justin as he came up to help. He didn't even fuck around. He pushed past me, grabbed Carol and draped her over his shoulder much like he had me, maybe a little more gently. She was ineffectually beating against his back. Tracy went next and I was last. We'd no sooner pulled the ladder down when headlights swept onto the street.

Sanders shut the engine down. The zombies were grumbling and groaning, making a fair amount of noise as they slapped and slammed up against the truck. A spotlight shined on the roof of the house; from their angle on the street they would not have been able to see the impromptu exit. The light was tracking down, but was blocked by the fence before it could see us.

"They're looking for us. Why aren't they using the satellite?" BT asked.

"Might be a blackout time," I told him.

"I hate Deneaux," he said.

"Yeah, we all feel the same way," Tracy replied.

The truck was slowly retreating down the roadway, now gathering its own zombie following. I was letting out a sigh of relief when Carol began to scream.

I looked around wildly for the zombie that had to have been eating her before she clarified.

"My broach! Who stole my broach!" This followed by a mournful wailing. I didn't know what to do. My first inclination was to wrap my hand around her mouth but it was my mother in law. Biddeford had no such reservations as he dragged her down. Lucky thing he had gloves on because she was gnawing on his palm. Of course, the truck stopped, idled for a moment, then began backing up. This was when the screechers made their debut—a blessing and a curse. My guess was they had been called up from the bullpen when they were informed that a clutch of humans had been corralled and they were coming to force them out. Even through the brain-splitting sound the screechers made, it was easy enough to figure out that the bulkers would be next. What the screechers tried for in subtlety, the bulkers would make up for in gentle passivity.

Sanders started the truck back up. Either Knox's men didn't feel we were worth battling a horde to get to or thought we were already about to become chow. In any case, they took off. We pulled out of the lawn, through a few zombies, and into the night. I looked up, knowing that at some point we were going to be on camera. We needed that device, otherwise they could follow us to the ends of the earth. Maybe Etna Station could help, but maybe they wouldn't want to. Who the fuck were we to them? Entirely too much trouble, that's who. I could not justify bringing destruction to another base. I realize there was no way I could have known Eliza would do what she'd done, but Knox was fucking nuts and Payne was still out there, and this fuckfest was on me. These things needed to be dealt with before we asked for sanctuary. When you think "zombie apocalypse," this running from human madmen is not what immediately springs to mind.

I went back to that Perfect Post-apocalyptic World. You are holed up in a well-stocked Sam's club that has been made into an impregnable fortress. You have enough guns, ammo, and video games to make North Korea salivate. All of your friends and family are with you. It's like a big fucking party; you go up to the roof in the morning, play some betting games to see who can thin the zombie horde out the most, you drink some beer and eat some beef jerky before wrapping up your day by going downstairs to have some roast chicken and potatoes, kept nice by solar powered generators. You revel in the fact that April 14th just passed and you don't have any taxes to pay, or a boss to give you shit…no commute to stoke your ire, no rude fuck at the movie theater talking or texting during the movie. None of it. It's like a fantasy world; all the shit of society vanishes and you're there, alive and safe, on your own little island. But in reality, you're always covered in muck and slime and loss. Everything else is just a fantasy, and the joke's on us. The z-poc, in a couple of words, sucked balls. I'd watched as friends and family died all around me, unable to save them. We were always on high alert, always under threat, and seemingly always running. There was no such thing as "safe." I figured there would be desperate people looking to take what was ours, but I guess I imagined just bringing them into the fold. Never in my wildest dreams did I consider that every evil, low life, crazy motherfucker would band together and become an army of asshats. The meek couldn't inherit the earth because the jerks kept trying to take it from them.

We met Tommy and Travis at a safe house. I did my best to not cry—from joy—as most of my family members were reunited—and from worry—as some were still in danger. Sanders had Biddeford and Winters guarding different sides of the house as he continually paced around.

"I'm sorry about this, and thankful," I told him. "I didn't mean to bring this kind of shitstorm into your life."

"You're a Marine, right?" he asked.

"I am."

"Marines never leave one of their own behind," he repeated. I knew that, but I guess I kept thinking as circumstances got worse they would eventually run out on us.

"What if you find out Knox was in?" I asked.

"Oh, not that shitbird. No way he was in my beloved Corps. I would have made personally sure he washed out. Plus, he's too stupid to have been a Marine."

"Don't think I've heard that one before," I told him.

"Yeah. Anyone that crosses me is too stupid."

I gave him a much-needed laugh, on my part anyway. He was deadly serious about it.

"What now?" I asked.

"We need to get that sat-track device back. We can't scratch our ass without them knowing it, and you seem like a decent guy, Talbot, but I'd rather spend my nights with my wife and I can't do that if they know where we're going—and don't apologize. I take this as a personal challenge. We needed this exercise; I think we were getting a little lackadaisical."

I could see Winters out of the corner of my eye shaking his head. I would have laughed again, but it might have got the sergeant in trouble.

Sanders was thinking. "It stands to reason they will attack this house; they will know we're here. The question is, how can we set something up to where we surprise them? Going to need to snatch one so we can find out where Knox is."

"The device only has fifteen minutes every hour; we have a seventy-five percent chance of moving without them seeing us," I said.

"You're okay with those odds?" he asked.

"Shit, sir, those are the best odds I've been afforded in a good long time. And we could increase that by sending out teams at fifteen-minute intervals. One will be seen the rest won't."

"You weren't an officer?"

Now it was BT's turn to laugh. "Of latrine duty, maybe," he said.

"I finally come up with a plan and you're going to give me shit about it?"

BT merely shrugged. It was a decent plan and it wasn't. If Knox and his men saw me moving and came for us, that was great; if it was Tommy and Travis they spotted, that was bad. It would depend on what kind of response they sent and how fast the rest of us could make it there to close the loop of the trap off. And to make it more difficult, we had to have a plan of attack for four locations. Logistically, it was a nightmare. Luckily, Knox was playing it much more cautiously since we'd been bleeding him continuously. We settled on a cul-de-sac that had been reserved for doctors and lawyers. Each and every house was a McMansion, close to five thousand square feet, and I'm sure had price tags over a million each. I couldn't even begin to comprehend what the nut on that was each month. The basis was my idea; sure, Sanders cleaned up the rough edges, but this one was my responsibility, so BT and I were the first out.

We headed out on foot as fast as we could, knowing that if the timing was fucked up it could potentially give Knox enough time to watch where we went and then see another team leaving our headquarters. We just had to hope that luck was more on our side than his, considering I was using my family as bait. Yeah, that was sitting wonderfully in my gut, wriggling around like a fat, wet mass of live maggots. Once all the fire teams got into position, it was Tracy's job to pretend to take her sweet ass time loading up the animals, the kids and Carol, and bring them to a central house, a nice easy trail of breadcrumbs. It was an hour and a half later when we were all in position, and still nothing happened.

"He's not biting," I said to BT as I looked out the window.

"He will; he can't not do it."

"How are you so sure?" I turned to look at him.

"He's insane. He can't not do it."

"Have a lot of experience with insanity, do you?" I asked.

He just kept looking at me. "Oh, by now you could say I was an expert."

"Fuck you." I turned back to the window when I heard the high whine of props. "Drone."

"Like I was saying."

I gave him the finger off to the side, not taking my gaze from the window as I tried to find the small flying machine.

"That's helpful," I said as I moved back.

"What's going on?" BT didn't want to come over and potentially get caught looking.

"It's literally in the middle of the road, doing a slow spin, surveying the area. So, they know we're here, we know they know we're here, but they're not really telling us which house they suspect we're in."

"Do you think they got our little ploy figured out?" he asked.

Sanders must have been thinking the same thing because a single shot was fired from his location. The drone spun wildly as one of the props was sheared off. I'd like to say it crashed hard and there was a concussive fireball, but it more or less came down gently. Whoever was at the controls wasn't quite ready to let their toy go, as they tried to make it rise with three props. It struggled to lift, but did not have the proper thrust. Finally, it stopped. Either the battery gave out, or the operator realized the futility. After ten minutes of no trucks driving up with dozens of men spilling out, I was feeling worse for it. I know, strange reaction. Who actually wants to get into a firefight? But that was what we'd been planning for; when the enemy does something different, that's when you have to start watching your ass. The unexpected is always a bitch because by definition, you're not ready for it.

We'd come to the decision to pick these particular houses for a variety of reasons: proximity to where we'd been and how close to each other were the most obvious. Also, that the approach from behind was impractical. However, it wasn't impassable. Let's face it, the super rich don't really like rubbing elbows with the masses; maybe they're afraid they'll catch middle-class syndrome or a poor people virus. So, these houses had a small patch of woods behind them with a thick ribbon of swampy wetlands, a kind of moat, you might say. Not much more than a shallow bog, but it would keep most casual walkers or hikers, their dogs, and maybe even thieves from coming that way. I mean, not even us poor folk want to walk around in wet shoes. Sure, the mosquitoes must be brutal during the summer, but it's better than dealing with "those" people.

"They're coming from the back," I said, heading for the door that led out to the yard. I knew it without having one shred of factual intel.

"Mike, you, of all people, should know we can't leave our post."

I stopped for a handful of heartbeats. "I'm thinking you've been around Sanders for a little too long, buddy. I was in the Marines and then I left because I have a serious hang-up regarding authority. And that's our family in that house across the street. What if I'm right and we're waiting here manning our post?"

"But Mike, you never see the other side of the coin. What if you're wrong?"

"There's another side?" I was already halfway through the door.

As I was running, I glanced at the house on our left; Winters was at the window. He was pointing vigorously and must have been asking Sanders what the fuck I was doing. I pointed to the back, he was trying to figure out what I was looking at, but I couldn't see anything wrong, so it was safe to say he couldn't either. The yard was decent sized, but not Texas ranch-sized. There was only about an acre of overgrown lawn before we crossed into a small patch of woods. According to Sanders, it was another hundred yards to the protected wetlands. I got us in deep enough we were covered from the rear by some trees before I stopped and sought total cover.

"Mike, what the fuck are we doing out here? If you had to take a piss you should have just used the toilet," BT said.

"You fucking nuts? How long you think it's been since that thing was cleaned? I'm not lifting that lid to see an eight-month-old turd growing all sorts of fungal spores."

"Fungal spores?"

"Nature channel. Watch it sometime; it's a little more informative than Australian Rules football."

"Don't go there, man."

I placed my finger near my mouth then pointed. Three heavily armed and camouflaged men were off to our side, cautiously approaching.

"Fuck. I hate when you're right. Makes you damn near insufferable," he'd said so close to my ear I thought he might just come in all the way and blow me a kiss. I mean, what was I going to be able to do to stop him? Instead, he low-crawled to a tree next to mine, but we're talking BT, so it was almost like he was standing upright, like us normal-sized humans.

"Want a strobe light?" I asked caustically, meaning he'd

have a harder time being less inconspicuous.

We each had suppressors on our weapons, thanks to Sanders, but a shot would still sound like two pieces of wood slapping together. Might not be heard from too far out thanks to all the brush where we were, but these three guys would most definitely hear it. That wasn't a huge problem because two of them would either be incapacitated or dead. Disarming the third and hoping there weren't more behind them was the problem. We would be forced to fire soon as they were abreast of us, and unless they were wearing blinders, we'd be seen. I had a chest shot all lined up, had a few pounds of pressure on the trigger, when BT quietly said: "Mike."

I knew what that meant. We had company. "How many," I said, not taking my sights off my target, though I had eased up on the trigger.

"Four," was his reply.

It was seven on two, and we could make it five on two soon enough, but then our element of surprise was shot, so to speak, and they had bigger, faster weapons.

"Pick a target," I told him.

"We're going for this?" He wasn't a fan.

"No choice now." Probably liked that answer less, though he said nothing. What was happening was right in front of us, couldn't ignore it; couldn't just pay it no attention and hope it would go away. We were deep in it now. "Concentrate on the right." My reasoning here was that if we took those three out, we'd have an avenue to run if we needed to.

"I have the one farthest away," I told him. Wasn't more than twenty-five yards; at this point, could have thrown a rock and hit them. BT's rifle cracked a fraction of a second before mine; it was so nearly simultaneous that my victim hadn't even had a chance to react to seeing the man he was with go down. The third one was winged by one of us. He went down fast, but not because of a fatal shot–that was something he was trying to avoid. It was only another moment before BT and I were hugging the ground. The trees around us were catching hellacious and sustained machine gun fire. Even if we weren't directly hit, we would soon be in danger of the falling trees.

Ever watch the movie *Predator*, with Arnold? There's a scene in the beginning when they know they're being hunted and all of these mercenaries line up with this incredible weaponry and they are just blasting the living shit out of all the fauna–trees are exploding, branches are falling, leaves are disintegrating. As a guy, it is truly a monumental movie scene to watch. When you're living it on the receiving end, well it sucks, and it sucks big time.

"Brilliant fucking idea, Talbot!" BT shouted. I could barely hear him over the expulsion of so many high-speed projectiles. The lone man on our right wasn't firing and he wasn't moving; there was no way yet to know if he was out of the fight, could be just lying low until we walked into his sight of fire. Not like we could get there, anyway. The four on the other side were keeping us pinned with superior firepower, and not only that; they were tactically leap-frogging closer to us and there wasn't a fucking thing we could do about it for fear of having our heads riddled with bullets.

I had to think at some point they would run low on ammo, but this was not something we could count on. They'd be on us in a minute or two at best.

"I'm sorry," I told BT.

"Not yet man, not yet." He pointed behind us and to the left, the Marines were coming–well, one marine, anyway. Winters must have followed us. He was low-crawling into position, making sure that every shot he fired counted. I'll take one Marine over four mercs, any day. Even through the blistering sounds of the heavy 7.62 rounds obliterating everything in their path, we heard Winters, who had a Barrett M99 fifty caliber. I'd never shot one, personally. Seemed too much like overkill. Yeah, that was until I felt, not just heard, the percussion as he sent that monster bullet down range. His target didn't just fall down, it was lifted and blown backward. If it hadn't been for a tree behind him, he may still have been going, like a leaf taken hold by a gale.

I could have driven my fist straight through that unfortunate bastard and not touched any human material. That was not a bullet designed for mere flesh to catch. Winters got another round off before the two remaining started spreading their suppressive fire around. The second man that Winters hit had been in the midst of diving for cover, and in a series of disastrous circumstances, ducked right into the path of the oncoming projectile. The devastation was immediate and profound. Let me see if I can paint the scene right. So, you take some random bad guy's head, you neatly remove it from his body, you puree the thing in an industrial food processor. When it is nothing more than a heavy concentration of reddish gray pulp, you pour the contents into a large spray bottle. When you're ready, pull the pump repeatedly and watch as the contents mist all over everything you are pointing it at, almost like an anti-Windex. That's what I saw when the bullet pulverized that man. My guess was his soul was still wandering around trying to figure out why he couldn't fire a gun anymore and why no one was paying him any attention because there was no way he knew he was dead. The transition had been too sudden and traumatic.

Two to our left, one to our right. Winters had caught the group unawares, but now that they knew where he was, he was actually in a pretty bad spot, mostly wide open. I didn't think the hydrangea bush he was behind was going to stop much. Only one man was firing at him; I'm thinking the other guys had seen what a fifty cal could do and were having none of it. The one still in the battle was lining up on Winters, more or less forgetting about BT and myself. I stood up to get a better shot—nearly cost me my life as he turned and sprayed a half dozen rounds my way. Want to know what saved me? The size of his magazine. He ran out of rounds an inch or two from riddling me. I took that as a personal affront and put four or five rounds into him. He stutter-stepped backward; his rifle fell from his hands a moment before he himself toppled over.

"I surrender! I surrender!" the fourth man said. That was all great and fine, but we still had at least one off to our right.

"Stand up!" I shouted, "And if I see a gun, I will kill you!"

He did as I said, his hands high up in the air. BT stood as well. "Interlock your fingers and place them over your head!" he shouted. I had turned to make sure we weren't blindsided by the other guy. Winters was now up, and had the Barrett pointed at our prisoner; looked somewhat like he had a Howitzer. Could have driven a fucking VW down that barrel.

"I've got zip ties," Winters said. "You cover him, I'll get him handcuffed."

"I've got you," BT responded.

"Be right back," I told BT.

"Just wait a minute." BT looked over his shoulder.

"I saw movement."

"Even more of a reason," he replied, although I was already moving away. I took note of the two men that would be lying right where they were until they became one with the earth again, but it was the blood of the one missing that had me transfixed. The part of me I did my best to ignore was completely enraptured with the fluid that was pouring from the wounded man, there was enough of it that I wondered how he had even managed to move. He was leaving a thick trail of blood globs, and I was following it like a fat kid might a luring route of gummy bears. The man was no more than fifty feet ahead of me. He was hunched over, one hand on a tree for support and the other, I would imagine, was attempting to stem the tide that had sprung forth from him. He half turned when he heard me approach.

"Please," he groaned. He didn't have the strength to beg for his life or for me to finish him. I came up warily as he slumped to the ground. His eyes were locked on mine, I alternated between his gaze and the blood that issued from his splayed hand. I should have shot him and been done with it. I couldn't. Ripping into his neck and feeding the monster inside of me was fast approaching the fore, if not for BT trampling through the woods to make sure I was alright I think I would have succumbed right there and then. The man's eyes were glazed over and he was reflexively gasping for air as his body had not quite caught on that his mind had given it up.

"Mike?" BT said as he approached cautiously. I had not moved; almost didn't hear his words. He shook my shoulder gently. He never said anything, but he knew I'd been having an internal struggle. "We've got a prisoner. Come on, let's go."

I turned to look at him and he stepped back.

"Your…your teeth, man–your eyes; get your shit together."

I had to shake my head several times before I was able to shake the demons away.

"I'm, I'm good." But I didn't feel good. Like a man lost in the desert, I'd been shown a jug of water only to have it removed before I could bring the life-giving fluid to my lips. I was thirsty; oh, so fucking thirsty. I would regretfully come back to that moment for a few days before I was able to submerge it down with the other vile things that sometimes pass across my thoughts; those things that by my will, thankfully, never see the light of day.

CHAPTER SEVEN
MIKE JOURNAL ENTRY 7

IF KNOX WAS planning something else for us, it was in the long game. We got our prisoner, a one Barry Smintner. Sounded like someone that should be playing tennis at the country club with Mimzy, but he was as far from money as a monkey is driving a car. Let me take that back, with enough training and under the right circumstances, I'm pretty sure a monkey could drive a car.

"You killed me friends." He glowered in the small room. We'd left the cul-de-sac and went a street over. Odds were that the five minutes we had been exposed were not on Knox's screen.

"Me friends?" BT asked me. We were off to the side. "You think he might be slow?"

"Knox is going to come here and kill you, kill you all." There was a sinister sneer on his face.

"Slow or not, he's a piece of shit," I said, wanting to beat that upward tilting lip right off his face.

"You ready?" Sanders asked Biddeford. The other man nodded.

"Hey! What are you doing? I'm part of the Knox army. You can't do anything to me, I'm untouchable."

Biddeford punched the man hard enough it hurt me.

"You tell us what we want to know, and we won't do anything to you. Much. How's that?" Sanders asked.

"I ain't telling you shit." There was still a sneer, but it had dropped a little of its pop.

"As part of my officer's training," Sanders enlightened our prisoner, "I was part of an exercise called SERE: Survival, Evasion, Resistance, and Escape. It was one of the hardest things I have ever done in my life, and that is including active hot zones. That being said, when we were captured, which was inevitable, by the way, part of the process was being waterboarded,"

Sanders continued in almost a fatherly way—certainly as a good teacher might, "In my head, I was thinking, 'How bad can it be? Sure, I was captured, but we were still all on the same team, right? They weren't going to seriously injure or maim me.' So, you're lying down and restrained, an old shirt is stretched tight over your face and head so you can't move, and then water is poured over your head. Sounds fairly pedestrian really. But Barry, I'm going to tell you something, when that water starts splashing up your nose and into your mouth, some primitive instinct kicks in. Between the darkness and the drowning…well, I don't know if I have been more scared in my life. And it wasn't a rational fear, not something I could control. I knew where I was and who I was with, but the sheer panic in my body and brain completely took over."

"You can't do that shit. There's some sort of rules of engorgement!" he shouted.

Listen, I realize I have the mentality of a five-year-old, but if this hadn't been such a serious scene, I would have busted out laughing. I turned my head and coughed.

Sanders nodded to Biddeford as he and Winters pulled the zip-tied man down to his knees.

"I'd rather not do this. You ready to do a little talking?" Sanders asked. They picked the man up and placed him on a table. "How about now?"

"How about fuck you?" Barry said.

"Fair enough." Again, Sanders nodded. Winters pulled a towel over Barry's face. He was struggling, shaking his head back and forth, at least, as much as the pulled taut towel would allow. Biddeford started pouring water over his head from an orange, Home Depot five-gallon bucket. The sputtering and choking was followed immediately by whimpers to stop.

"Again," Sanders said to Biddeford.

It was a strange sensation to watch a man get tortured; not something I was completely on board with, but this man could hold the key to me getting the rest of my family back, so basically fuck him. By the time Biddeford had emptied that second pail the man was sobbing; he had absolutely been broken. I honestly didn't want to know how much torture I could endure, but fuck, I hope it would be more than ten gallons of water that did me in.

"Stop, stop!" he sputtered. "I'll tell you whatever you want to know. Please, just stop."

Probably a good thing he was done, because Biddeford didn't have any more water. Talk about an economy of tribulation.

"Pretty unique sensation, isn't it?" Sanders seemed bemused. "Alright. Let's start with where Knox is."

Barry spewed forth more information than a breached server from a fortune 500 company. Even started talking about how he missed his Miyaku, which some guy had taken from him; we felt bad until we found out that was not his girlfriend in the normal sense but just his anime pillow. When he began to talk about the people of mine they had captured, I thought my heart was going to break through my chest; felt like I was the one drowning.

When we were all done and had gotten more information than we ever wanted, we went upstairs to figure out a game plan.

"What...what about me?" Barry begged.

"You're staying here, Barry," Sanders said. "I mean, unless you want to fight on our side."

Silence from the table, and then he spoke just as the door was closing. "You can't leave me here. I'll die! And it's dark! I don't want to die in the dark!"

"Biddeford, put a gag on him, please," Sanders said.

I looked to BT. I didn't disagree with what the Major was doing, but holy fuck if it wasn't hardcore.

We went to the dining room. Sanders pulled out a map of the area and spread it out; Knox was about a mile away in a small office building.

"I know that place," Winters said. "Mostly brick. Got a couple of windows on street level. Fairly secure—especially against a small assault. It's two stories and has clear lines of sight in these three directions." He traced his finger on the map.

"It stands to reason if Knox has any sort of military mind, he will have patrols out, especially for this blind spot," Sanders said. "We don't really have the numbers or the equipment to do this," Sanders was looking at me.

"Listen, Major, you've already done more than I could have ever hoped for. My own life is in your debt, but my family is in there. I can't walk away from this, but I understand if you do."

"No part of that was me walking away from it; I'm just saying it's long odds for success."

"Long odds?" BT laughed. "Shit, man, we haven't had any odds for so long that even long ones are welcome." I fist bumped the man. Winters and Biddeford got a kick out of that. Sanders, not so much.

With Tommy and Travis, we were seven strong heading into the teeth of Knox's army. I would have brought Justin and Tracy, but someone needed to stay and watch that group and I didn't think two more guns were going to change anything. We got close enough to the building to get some visuals. Looked like a party on the roof; had to have been a dozen people patrolling up there. The street was much more modest, six men with guns that we could see; had to guess more than a dozen we couldn't. Creeping up was out of the question. Brute force, which was my preferred method, also seemed unrealistic. Sanders was just beginning to direct us to the only approach that had some merit when Knox showed himself.

"Talbot!" he shouted. "Just come out. We have some things we need to discuss!"

I looked up and flipped the techno-bird in the sky, aptly enough, the bird.

"Come, come. There's no reason to be rude. Don't make me compel you to come out into the open." Before I could do anything, he nodded to someone off to the side, then my daughter appeared with a rather large revolver held to her head.

"What are you doing?" Sanders asked when I got up.

"He knows we're here, and that's my daughter. What do you expect me to do?" I stood my ground.

"It's nice to know you're reasonable." Knox was smiling, which was further unsettling. "Just a couple more things, though. Really going to need you to put the rifle down and the rest of your little Girl Scout troop is going to have to come out as well. I don't want any accidents to happen."

I undid the strap holding my rifle and placed it on the ground. "I'm here—let's trade. Me for my daughter," I yelled.

"Ah, not that simple, really. There are some things we need to discuss first. This is an all or nothing scenario, and trust me, I'm not trying to be dramatic when I tell you the clock is ticking."

BT came out.

"What the fuck are you doing?" I asked.

"We stand together, brothers forever."

"I appreciate the sentiment, but if you're dating my sister that's going to get real awkward."

"You know?"

I turned to him. "Well, I didn't know for sure. Not until now."

"Shit," BT muttered.

"You two done? Everyone, Talbot, or I'll kill them all and do what I can on my own."

"What the hell does that mean?" I whispered.

"He's insane. How the fuck do I know?" BT responded.

"You two idiots ever hear of a directional microphone?" Knox asked. "Listen, I'm going to make this easy–even something a Marine can understand. Phillips, get the screen. Going to do an audiovisual presentation for you. Pretty sure you'll figure it out quick enough."

Heard a generator kick on and then a large screen television was brought onto the roof; two of Knox's men were holding it up.

"In for a dime." I started walking closer.

"You're pretty cheap with your life." BT was matching my strides.

"I'll say. Now I have to split it. Can't buy much with a nickel."

The screen powered on. I was actually watching myself walk toward Knox. Hated this show, got bad reviews and had horrible plot lines. Who willingly gives themselves up to a madman?

"Only have another two minutes of view time; you might want to get closer," Knox warned. "Not sure if we'll be able to keep up this cease-fire agreement for another forty-five minutes."

The guards at the building entrance let us in. We walked by at least fifty soldiers and they watched us pass with murderous intent in their eyes. Can't say I was a fan of that gauntlet. My heart soared when I saw my daughter.

"I'm here. Put that gun down or I'm going to shove it up your ass," I told the man. He sniffed, shrugged a little and then lowered the gun, putting it back in its holster. Nicole came to me and hugged me tightly."

"We're alright. Just hear him out, dad," she said. I didn't like that at all. I'd read about Stockholm Syndrome, but never understood it. Who in the hell starts to identify with the crazy people holding you hostage? I always thought that excuse was a pile of shit.

I kept watching the screen as Knox fiddled with the controls on the device and panned out. Wasn't a few seconds later when I think my stomach dropped out through my anus. Too much? Because fuck if that isn't what it felt like.

"So, which is it?" Knox asked. "Like a kick to the teeth or to the balls?"

"Both," I told him honestly.

"How many?" BT asked. I was too transfixed by the sight to say anything.

"Software started to freeze up somewhere around ninety-five thousand, figure that might be a little light, but what's a couple tens of thousands among friends?"

"You didn't do this?" I finally managed to ask.

"If I had this much power, the world would already be mine," he said. "This is why I haven't put a bullet in your head. I'm not sure what, if anything, your group can do, but it looks like we're going to need each other's help to get out of this."

I didn't even know where to begin. The small town we were in was surrounded by zombies, and not just a few scattered around, but one, giant, thick unbroken circle around the whole town and we were in the middle, like a bullseye. "How...I mean, how could this happen? Where could so many zombies come from...and why gather like this?"

"I was more than hoping you might have an answer," he said.

"How many men do you have?" I asked.

He didn't hesitate. "A hundred and twenty, and I've radioed for the rest to come down here; total's about five hundred."

Never had I thought we were so outmanned by Knox. Figured he had forty at the most, sure, still pretty bad, but not "pulling dried rat shit flakes from your cereal" fucked. Oh, and just in case you didn't know, there used to be an acceptable level of rat feces allowed by the government to be in your cereal. Bon appétit.

"Talbot, what is going on up there?" Sanders asked.

I'd been so taken back by the pictures on the screen I almost forgot what we were here to do.

"Things have changed," I yelled down to him. "You can probably only see a blob from down there but this entire town is surrounded by zombies. A hundred thousand, maybe more."

"Not doctored?" Sanders asked.

"Do I look like I know how to use photoshop?" Knox said to me.

"Definitely not!" I told Sanders.

"I'm coming up."

"No weapons," Knox said.

"Horse shit." Sanders holstered his weapon and was with us in a few minutes. I noticed him looking pretty intently at a certain area of the map without trying to make it too obvious. I had a good idea where Kylie and Tracy were, and it didn't look good, as the house was right in the heavy band of the undead. "So, what does this shitbird want us to do about it?" Sanders asked me.

I didn't think poking the psychopath was such a good idea. Knox laughed it off like they were friends and this was an old routine.

"Alright, I'm good," he said to his men. All of them left, like, each and every fucking one of them. "Yes, I realize there are three of you and just little old me up here, but remember, I still have members of your family, and if I were to, say, make a two-story leap from here, they would suffer some harm as well."

I wanted to tell him I'd take my chances, but I wasn't interested, not at all. "Go on," I told him.

"Listen. Your group has been kicking my ass since we came across you. I chased you down because I wanted to make an example of those that would stand against my rise to power."

Sanders scoffed; Knox continued.

"I had hoped for a quick kill and an absorption of some of your people, double win for me. When that didn't happen, it was becoming difficult trying to justify this detour with my followers. I was trying to find a way to pull the plug on the entire operation, take who I had with me, and go back."

"But the zombies changed that," I said. "So now, what? We're just going to be one, big, cohesive, happy unit and work together for the greater good?"

"I still want you and him dead," he pointed to BT, "in the worst way possible, like, so much I can feel it in my toes." It was not lost on me that he jabbed a finger into his head when he said toes. "But, you're leaving the East Coast completely; that much I got from your man. I can live with that. I can spin it that I forced you out. You go live on your coast and I'll live on mine. Someday, I will have power over all of this land and we will meet again, but that's in the future. We have to deal with the present, with today. If we don't make it out of here, how can we continue our legendary conflict?"

This guy was certifiable, but I could play the nuts game. I'd walked that fence long enough to speak the same language.

"Like Ali, Frasier, Tyson, Holyfield, North and South Korea, shit, even like North and South Carolina!" I said.

"He gets it." BT stopped me.

"I do get it," Knox said excitedly, that old familiar slant of insanity burning heavily through his eyes. "I don't want to die here, this isn't my destiny. I'm meant for much greater things; I've been told that."

I left it alone that it was only the voices in his head that had told him anything of the sort. We were playing nice, and he still had possession of my toys, so to speak, and I wanted them back all in one piece.

"I get my people back, and then we talk in earnest," I told him. "Hey, it's not like I can go anywhere."

"I don't like that. What's to stop you from going it alone?" Knox asked.

"Listen, man, I'm nucking futs, I get it. But it seems to me that you're bringing much more to the party than I am. Not really thrilled to say it, but we need you more than you need us," I told him.

"Just hand him the keys to the city," BT said. It was easy enough to tell from Sanders stance he was thinking the same thing.

"I like the insurance of having them around; you're very pliable this way," Knox said.

"Talbot, right now I've been assured that Knox's head is in the sights of my unit's best sniper. You say the word, I have him taken out, and we launch a rescue attempt for your family." Sanders lifted his uniform to reveal three pistols in his waistband.

"See? This is what I'm talking about. None of you ever give up. Why you don't want to join me is beyond my understanding." Knox lifted a small radio to his mouth. "Phillips, release our guests."

BT and I looked over the lip of the building as my sister, her son, Gary, Ryan, Nicole, and Wesley exited the building. Sanders had kept his eye on Knox the entire time.

"What about Deneaux?" I asked, once I saw that Biddeford had met and then moved my loved ones away.

Knox smiled at that. "Oh no, you can't have that one. She's very important to me now." He pointed to the device. She made it perfectly clear that killing her will end this thing's usefulness, and now that I have it, I can't imagine how I ever survived without it. You should have been more careful. Plus, she made it abundantly clear that if I exposed her, you would more than likely put a bullet in her head."

"Trust me, I'd be doing you a favor. Since we're friends and all now, I'll let you in on a little secret. That woman isn't a fox in a henhouse—she's a wolf."

"Her? She's a frail old woman."

"Yeah, you keep telling yourself that while she smokes a cigarette over your body," BT said.

"There was another car," I said.

"We found the wreck. Some blood, but no one was in it," Knox said.

I wasn't so sure I believed him. It was more likely he was lying and was going to use them against me if I tried anything, or even if I didn't.

"How long until your reinforcements get here?" Sanders asked.

"They're on their way, should only be a couple of hours."

"What kind of weaponry do they have?" he asked.

"So, we're buddy-buddy?" BT asked me while Sanders and Knox talked about their arsenals.

"You saw what I saw, right?"

"He'll kill us as soon as he thinks he's safe."

"Naw, man, look. He's had a change of heart."

"You're crazier than him if you think that," BT said.

"Not really sure what to do here. If we somehow get by this horde we'll have to deal with his whole army. He actually might think of letting us go now, but the moment he realizes he can have it all, there definitely isn't a voice of reason that's going to rein him in," I said.

"If you two Sallys are done with your little bromance, wouldn't mind having you over here so we can discuss this," Sanders said.

"Sallys. Oh, how I miss the Marines and their political correctness," I said.

"Did he just call us women?" BT asked.

"The Marines somehow feel it is a negative motivator to call you a woman. Now, the misogynistic person might believe that this is because women are perceived as inferior, so the Marines in question need to step up their game. But you and I both know who holds the real power; I'll take it as a compliment to be called a Sally."

"You would," Sanders said.

"Should I repeat your stance to some other people?" I asked, referring to his wife.

"No, we'll just let this be between us," he replied. "As far as our problem right now, I see that we have two options. We bluntly try to force our way through, which, even with Knox's substantial armament is destined for failure, or we have the approaching men create a massive distraction that will draw enough zombies away that our force here will be able to weave through the opening."

"I'm all for the diversion, I'm just not sure it will do much. Sure, it will create a shift, but these numbers; they'll never all go for it. They're smart and getting smarter. They'll send what they need to deal with the attack, but they've set up shop around us for a reason. They won't so easily yield their position."

"You're giving a mighty amount of credit to the deaders," Sanders said, clearly not giving any stock to my concerns.

"Well, near as I can tell, they have encamped a huge horde around the entire town, effectively trapping us. They're not moving off or through; seems pretty intelligent to me," I said.

"Yeah, it does," BT echoed.

"What about burning them…burning them all." I could see the licks of flames in Knox's eyes as he said this.

"Not a good idea," BT piped in. "It's been tried. They don't disperse, but rather converge. This entire town would be a forest of flames in a couple of hours."

Knox still looked like this was an acceptable outcome.

"We'd be in the blaze zone," I said, trying to get him back.

"Is that like being in the danger zone?" BT asked.

"You did not just pull out a Kenny Loggins reference. Listen, I realize you're happy that some of our people are free, but really, man?" I asked.

"Fuck you, Talbot."

"There's the surly beast I know."

"And love" he added. "You're supposed to say 'and love.'"

"Am I?"

"Dick."

"Sally."

"You two!" Sanders shouted. "We're in some serious

trouble here. Could really use you shitbricks in this conversation."

"Shitbrick?" BT asked.

"It's a Marine Corps thing. Pretty much believes we're incompetent," I explained.

"Well, he is," BT said.

"And you wonder why I didn't add the last part to my statement. I'm sorry," I said to Sanders, who looked like he wanted to punch me in the head. "It's how I deal with adversity. I would imagine it's going to get worse before it gets better."

"You don't think if I had my men get some trucks that they'd be able to force their way through?" Knox asked.

"A few tanks, those huge mining trucks, maybe. I don't think a semi or dump truck could do it, even fitted with a plow. It would bog down." I'd had enough experience with trucks to know they could crush through a few cars, but not a sea of the inhumanity.

"We might be able to find a tank or two; there are National Guard posts all along the coast," Knox said. "Will take longer, though."

"For some reason, the zombies aren't moving. I'm in favor of tanks," I said. "Plus, it will give us some time to look for our missing people." I was keeping an eye on Knox to see if he gave away a tell that he might be lying about their whereabouts. If he was holding them, I saw nothing that made me believe that was the case.

"I wish it was just Trip," BT said. "I'd be more inclined to leave him here."

Knox was warring within himself like he'd just remembered we were the enemy and he wanted us dead. "I don't think I like you running around all that much," he said.

"You have the device; you can monitor where we go. I still need to get those of us here on board. And you're forgetting, we're hoping you can get us out of here," I told him, letting him believe he was the absolute power in this equation, and he would be, at least right up until I leaked his twisted brains all over the ground. I had to. There was no way I would be able to sleep at night knowing I'd stepped aside and let him bring his own version of what the world should be like to any unsuspecting souls.

I let the thought linger of grabbing a pistol from Sanders and killing Knox or maybe giving a nod to the sniper to do so. I could hope the house of cards he had built would come crashing down if the crazy glue was gone. But really, we were going to need him or at least his leadership to get out of here. Maybe that's selfish; I was putting the lives of those with me and myself over the lives of countless, nameless others. But shouldn't I be?

"Holy fuck," I said aloud, shaking my head, trying to erase that line of logic.

"You alright, man?" BT asked.

"I think I had a mind convergence with Deneaux for a second."

I got "the look." You'd think BT would be used to me by now.

"Could you show me where you saw that car?" I asked.

He did so, it was so friggin' weird, him being helpful, like maybe his rabies was in remission, if such a thing were possible.

"Remember, when this is all over, you said you were keeping Deneaux," I told Knox as I headed to go downstairs.

"You'll want to take this." He handed me a radio. "I'll let you know when my men are in position or if anything changes. Don't make me regret that I reached across the river; I can still drown you."

"I'll keep that in mind." And then I went down. Still a bunch of murderous intent staring at me; maybe their boss was cool with it, but these guys had suffered the loss of friends and family at our hands. They would want payback. The thing about Knox was he was a sociopath, on top of the other dozen ailments he possessed, and for the most part, he could not bond with another, so felt no great loss when he lost one. Right now, that was working to our advantage—as long as he kept the rest of his goons in line.

"Winters still has a shot," Sanders said to me just as we cleared the entrance.

"It's like he's daring us to," BT said.

"Make the call, Talbot."

"No, he could be lying about where Trip and the others are. Maybe Knox's world domination plans are knocked loose when he goes, but those men back there want us dead and the only thing holding them back is the crazy man. And if that isn't bad enough, we're dealing with a small city's worth of zombies that have decided to play ring around the rosy. We need him, if you can believe that."

CHAPTER EIGHT
MIKE JOURNAL ENTRY 8

"ARE YOU GUYS alright?" I was so happy to see them, I was nearly reduced to tears. Relief flooded through me at seeing them all. I gave each one of them a hug and was reassured that Knox had, for the most part, been a decent captor. This guy made about as much sense as those people that used to go on the Jerry Springer show. Like, literally. I once saw an episode where they had a woman that confessed to eating four rolls of toilet paper a week. A lot of fiber, I'm supposing, but umm…well, you get it.

BT gave my sister a hug that I thought was going to swallow her up completely–definitely weird from my perspective. Not many times that a best friend dating a sister works out too well. But these times were all about unprecedented precedence.

"What are you doing?" my sister asked him quietly.

"Don't worry, I told him," BT said.

"Wait 'til I tell mom you're dating a giant. You know how she feels about interspecies romance," I told her. My sister flipped me off, but she looked happy enough. Jesse, on the other hand, looked like he might have swallowed a whole lemon.

"Talbot, our safe house is right smack dab in the middle of

that zombie ring, and I can't pick my wife up on the radio. That can be good and bad news," Sanders said.

"I'm listening."

"I know my wife. She saw those zombies coming a mile away, and they're all in the bunker."

"The bad...?" I prodded.

It was Biddeford that was looking a little sheepish. "I was working on the receiver in the bunker; one of the boards went down and I didn't finish fixing it."

"Don't they have one of these?" I asked, holding up the handheld.

"I'm sure. It just won't penetrate the concrete." Winters finished.

"They'll be fine inside," Sanders said. "Plenty of air, water, and food, but no comms. I don't know how we can possibly get to them."

"We don't, we just leave them there," I said.

"There are easier ways to get a divorce," Gary said.

"Funny. No, the zombies are here for someone in the city, don't know who, but once we all leave, we wait until they vacate, and then double back," I said.

"And if they don't move?" Sanders asked.

"You're a Marine; don't over think it," I told him. "Right now, we need to use the time afforded us to finding Trip and the rest. Knox is either going to rethink his position or the zombies are. Either way, it's bad news for us."

We made it to the crash zone just as a soft breeze picked up, bringing with it all manner of ill tidings. Maybe ill-smellings is a better way to describe it. The inside of the car was indeed bathed in a fair amount of dried, red liquid, but it was not blood.

"Hot sauce," I said, dipping a finger into it and smelling before wiping it away on a seat.

"You hear that?" Winters had his head cocked to the side. I watched as others began to swivel around, looking.

"Fucking concerts," I said. I, as of yet, had not picked up

the sound.

"Choppers," Sanders said. "Military."

"CH forty-seven F, Chinook." It was a familiar voice directly behind me, his breath smelled suspiciously like weed and cheese. Not a pleasant combination.

"Trip!" I turned quickly. "Are you alright?"

"Ponch? What are you doing at the State Fair?"

I didn't have to ask if everyone else was fine as they were all walking toward us. My relief was palpable. Stephanie had Zach in her arms, with Tiffany, Porkchop, Sty, Melissa, and Mark following closely.

By now we could see the machines as they flew past us on our left, heading to where Knox was.

"What the hell?" I may have asked it, but everyone was thinking it. Two of the three choppers had landed, we could no longer see them.

"He's offering cover," Sanders said as we watched.

"What is going on?" Some part of me knew, though I didn't want to believe it.

"Looks like our new ally found a ride out of here. Son of a bitch," Sanders said.

"He had those in his pocket the entire time. So why the spectacle, then?" BT asked. "I mean, I'm glad we got our people back, but why would he bother?"

"Because he's a sick fuck and he's going to watch all of us get buried together with his eye in the sky," I said.

"At least we know the sat schedule now," BT said, pulling a watch from his pocket.

I wanted to ask him why he had a watch, like, what was he going to be late for? But in this particular case, it worked out.

"Great. We can make sure we know when to flip him off," I said, and you know what? Every fucking hour we knew that thing was overhead and I was available to, I did just that. And I would do so until I no longer could.

The choppers made sure to steer clear of us, flying even farther away from us on their return journey. We could see them hovering where we figured the ring was and could just barely see something being dropped, at first, we couldn't tell what. In another hour, we realized he was bombing the horde with Molotov cocktails, whipping them up into a burning frenzy. He was not going to leave anything to Providence; it made no sense. Why not kill the hostages? Why not kill me, after all his hunting and tormenting, when I was right there in his clutches. Unless you are insane yourself, it is impossible to understand the inner workings of a madman. So, maybe there was hope for me yet, because Knox had me completely befuddled.

He'd left us alive, but we were defeated, and we'd yet to fire a shot. We went back to one of the safe houses, unsure as to what we should do next. We were surrounded by enemies with vastly superior numbers, both live and undead, and out of the reach of our loved ones. And to top it off, if we did somehow pull an orangutan out of our ass and make it, Knox was still watching, and he had visual and battle control of the sky. He could be upon us at any point that suited him. So much for living the dream of a zombie apocalypse in the comfort of my den, making love to my wife, eating fresh game, and catching up on all the reading I would ever want to do.

I had my elbows on the kitchen table and had my palms pressed against my eyes as I held up my head, which was getting exceedingly heavy as I weighed the few options we still had left to us. Biddeford was upstairs keeping a lookout when he shouted he had spotted a fire. Sanders and BT joined me as I went up. Thick, black roiling smoke was billowing into the sky, three miles distant at the most.

"Safe to say what Knox was dropping out of the helicopters." It was BT that caught on first. "Hey, it could be worse," he said when he saw my face.

"Yeah? How's that?" I asked.

"He could have given us Deneaux back."

I let out a small laugh. He was right, it could always be worse.

"You think she'll ever get what she deserves?" he asked.

"You can only die once, so I'm going to say no." Then I thought about it; maybe she could get her just desserts.

"There have been very few instances in life when I have even thought about hitting a woman and all of them revolved around self-defense, but I'll tell you what," I said, "I would gleefully haul off and punch her square in that cigarette clad mouth. Maybe she'd choke on all that tobacco, or better still, the lit cherry would burn all that dry, crinkly mess that she is inside."

They were staring at me open mouthed now, so I followed through. "Or, possibly, I would have enough of an upward angle to my punch that I shattered the cartilage in her nose and pierced her fucking brain, making her an instant vegetable so that I would be able to get in a few more savage licks before she collapsed to the ground and even then I might tie her corpse to a tree so I could use it as a punching bag for a few weeks, I mean, at least until the stink really started to settle in. Then at the very end, maybe fill her bloated carcass up with a few pounds of tannerite and blow what remained of her all over a cow pasture."

"I take it you're angry with her," Sanders said.

"I feel like you've given this too much thought," BT said.

"Yeah? Look at me with a straight face and tell me you aren't thinking the same thing now that I've spelled it out."

"No offense, man, but if I punched her, it would be a one-and-done. I'm thinking I'd rather twist her up like a pretzel. The satisfaction of hearing her bones snap would be beyond reproach." He was wringing his hands as he said this. "But I wouldn't spend a lot of time on her corpse."

"Alright, so we've decided we all want this old bat dead, but that isn't our immediate problem," Sanders said. "If everyone's favorite psychopath did indeed set the zombies ablaze and they are now running around like flaming chickens without heads, this town could be swept up in a wildfire, and us with it." We nodded, grudgingly. "Now, that being said, maybe they are dispersing. That merits us taking a look."

"You're right about that, Sanders, taking a look is as good an idea as any, but things could spiral pretty fast; we'd need to move as a group," I said.

I could see the Marine in Sanders having a tough time with this new equation, and I got that. Things worked a whole lot easier with able-bodied men and women not only willing to fight but trained to do so very effectively and cohesively. We had a bunch of kids, assorted "others," and Trip. If we left here to check then got overrun and had to make a mad dash to safety, who was here to defend the homestead, so to speak? Every time we split up our chances of getting everyone back together in one place got smaller. The other side of this coin was also a blast to think about. What if we had to move fast and we couldn't?

"Pogo sticks!" Trip shouted. "Man, we could just jump over their heads. Went to a dead show back in the seventies…this guy must have been eleven feet tall in front of me, or maybe it was a big hat, but I had a pogo stick and I just kept jumping up over him so I could see the show, that was until I realized he was behind me." He started scratching his head.

Stephanie grabbed his hand and pulled him away, I heard her saying something about coming with her so that the grown-ups could talk. I watched as Sanders wrestled with his thoughts; he dragged a hand across his face, something I had done a lot of since the z-poc, surprised I hadn't worn my nose off this way.

"Are there any other bunkers we could lie low in?" I asked. "Something fireproof?"

"There are, but we usually only put enough supplies in them for a few days and for many fewer people. Not really prepared for anything of this magnitude. We get stuck in there for more than a couple of days, we would be in a world of hurt. Could be a last resort," Sanders said.

"Mr. T, what about putting all the kids in there?" Tommy

asked.

"We'd have to leave Stephanie with Trip to keep him from eating everything in the first hour."

"Five days max with rationed water–shitty living conditions; you're talking about that many people basically living in a shoe box. Gonna have a hard time being able to lie down comfortably," he said.

"Beats being dead," BT said, I nodded in agreement.

"You are not going to believe this shit!" Biddeford said from atop a telephone pole. Sanders had explained that they had put footholds in a bunch of them so they could survey from a high point if necessary, this was one of those. Biddeford was there with a pair of binoculars seeing something he was having a hard time relating, judging by the shaking of his head.

"You realize, Corporal, we can't see what you can, right?" Sanders asked, looking up, shielding his eyes from the sun.

"Sorry, sir. The zombies–the burning zombies–they're heading by droves into Miller's pond."

"That solves one problem," I said. *And added a hundred more,* I thought.

We quickly made our way to a bunker house, which was more of a safe room...well, safe closet is a more apt description.

"Gonna have to split them up, Talbot, you can't put everyone in here," Sanders told me as an aside. "There's another, bigger bunker up ahead. It will fit the rest."

"How far?"

"Little under a mile," he replied.

It didn't sound far, but in hostile territory, it could take us an hour or more to safely traverse that span, and I didn't trust Trip not to double that. Add to that Zach looked sick; he needed rest and whatever nutrition there was.

"Trip, you cool with staying here?" I asked. "Keep an eye out on some of the kids."

"You're a good dude, Ponch. You're doing the best you can," he said.

"Umm, thanks, man," I told him.

"We'll be alright," Stephanie replied.

I did not like the look in Trip's eyes as we closed the door to the room. He looked very much like he knew something about this but had been doing his best to keep the truth even from himself. I had to let that nagging feeling go; it could just as well have been that he had some murderous gas built up in him and was fearful of what it would do to those poor souls locked up with him.

We had most of those that needed safekeeping, safely placed. Now we just needed to get the rest to shelter. To get them there was myself, BT, Tiffany, Sanders, Winters, Biddeford, Gary, Travis, Tommy, Meredith, and my sister. Eleven skilled shooters against a hundred thousand zombies. It sounded fair. The idea was to stay off to the side of the fire, hoping for a clear avenue through. If we found a way out, we'd circle back around, once, hopefully, we had pulled enough zombies away or they'd lost interest in following. We'd gone a mile, no more, when we saw our first zombies. There were seven of them, and they were on patrol; couldn't really call it anything else but that. They were actively looking for something or someone; their heads were on a constant swivel. We watched them pass on the street through knot holes in a privacy fence. I wasn't thrilled that they appeared to be heading the same way we had come.

When they stopped fifty feet past us, I was thinking that maybe they had caught wind of us. Then they showed just how serious they were when one of them did their version of flushing the prey out with that mind fucking screeching sound. I gritted my teeth in pain as I kept that particular one in my sights. Him, I wanted to kill personally. At that point, six would have been easy enough to deal with. But this was a patrol, the vanguard. The main force was still waiting to get in on the action. We did almost nothing as we waited for them to be out of range. Came across three similar patrols, though luckily none had a screecher with them. Whatever aberration those fuck-nuts must be, they were in short supply. We were being so cautious, I think Henry could have kept this pace up. By the time we got to the inner edges of the horde, night was fast approaching.

We were creeping around houses like thieves looking for an easy target when the nightmare began. As if they were on cue, the zombies started moving as one cohesive unit. I'm sure if we had an aerial view, it would look something like those schools of fish or birds that all turn on a dime in unison; just change directions all at once and swoop in. I'd not known that people, I guess you could call them people, moving could be so loud; if we dared to talk we would have had to speak like we were in a concert pit to get a message across, even though the zombies were still quite a ways away. With that many pressing to maneuver down constricted avenues, they were going through fences, tearing down covered parking spots, beams on porches and decks…the press of them alone was shifting houses on their foundations and as far as I could tell there weren't any bulkers, at least, not on the front lines. It was like a herd of buffalo that decided to shift from the plains straight through Dodge.

"We're in a little bit of a fuckery," Sanders said.

That was obvious enough; then it really dawned on me why we were in the fuckery. We had wandered directly into tornado alley, or for those of you unfamiliar with the term, straight into a mobile home community–a location where, seemingly, every natural disaster known to man ultimately befalls. Why is that? Does nature possess some vulnerability awareness? Does wind and water seek out places where it can cause the most catastrophic and graphic videos to be played out on the news? Maybe nature has a flair for the dramatic; it wants us all to know abundantly who is in fucking charge. No one can look away when that home goes twisting into the air or sliding down the side of a mountain or as it collapses under the weight of a four-foot snowfall. You should have to sign a disclosure when you buy one of those death traps, those hurricane flood beacons. Sign here that you realize at some point in your residence, your lovely double wide with the built-on porch will end up washing down the Mississippi, even if you live in Oregon. It's just a foregone conclusion. I actually shook my head as Sanders ripped through the lock and started ushering us inside the doomed aluminum Twinkie.

"This is about as good an idea as landing the Hindenburg on the Titanic," I said as I walked up the flimsy, two-step steel stairway with the rickety railing. Sure, you're not going to die if you fall a foot and a half, but it doesn't bode well for the rest of the construction if the steps up swayed like a funhouse attraction. The thin aluminum walls of the single-wide did little to muffle the march of the damned. Then there was nothing. They'd once again acted in unison; they came to a full stop. I could not help thinking they were merely tightening the noose they had secured firmly around our necks.

"Mike, do we make a run for it?" Gary asked.

"Stuck now, brother. Good chance they'll see us, and even if we make it away from this group, we'd have a decent chance of running into one of their patrols."

Gary pressed the kitchen wall and we all heard the small pop as it gave under the minimal pressure he had exerted.

BT groaned. "Sort of wishing we were in a high rise right now."

Personally, that didn't sound much better, especially if the zombies were inside the building. There were only so many ways out that didn't include plummeting to your death. Fighting in a stairwell, while standard in survival tales, was not a fun proposition. Usually not factored in is the echoing percussion of shots fired, it was murder on the eardrums and thus the equilibrium, which, I learned, have some causal linkage to each other. Then there's the ricochet; if you're not shot directly or by accident or devoured by your enemies, you still emerge deaf and disoriented.

"Why'd they stop?" Biddeford asked. It was a question we were all wondering. I had to remember he was a young kid and a Marine. He was used to his superiors telling him what was going on, so when Sanders did not respond, he turned to Winters, then, really, each of us in turn. But everyone either shook their heads or shrugged at him. How could any of us truly know what the hell zombies were thinking? It was definitely tactical, whatever it was. These weren't just brainless brain-eaters, nope, not these fucks. Our particular kind were apparently well-versed in the Art of War. I jumped when I heard the splintering of wood. Now I think everyone did, but I had gone to the back bedroom to peek out a small window to make sure we didn't have any company sneaking up on us while all else was quiet.

"Ignorance is bliss," they say, and I would have been much happier had I not witnessed two bulkers blowing completely through a storage shed. Books, dolls, old toys, brewing equipment, along with sheet metal, tools, and wood exploded up into the air as if a detonation had occurred. I'd not initially seen the two bodies; they'd been wrapped in blankets. Not sure if it had been a murderer hiding his victims or a couple of innocents that had found an easy way out, hidden among their treasures, not wanting to deal with the difficulties this world presented. Whatever they had once been, they were long dead and the ripeness must have attracted some attention. They may have been rotting, but that did not prevent the zombies from descending on them. I didn't like watching people eating popcorn; there was no way I was hanging around to watch zombies rip through putrid people meat. I'd seen enough humans eaten that I would never need to refresh the visual. I could basically pull up the rolling reel in my head whenever I needed to lose a few hours of sleep.

"Bulkers," I said as I came back into the main living room.

"They'll cut right through this tin can," BT said. I'm thinking he immediately regretted saying the words aloud.

"You been hanging with Justin a little too much?" I asked him, quietly trying to lighten a pretty tense situation. (For those who may have stumbled on to my later journals, my son has a proclivity for stating the obvious and was very early on nicknamed Captain Obvious, which he thoroughly dislikes.)

"Running sounds pretty good now," Gary said, once again popping the kitchen wall as he stood away from it.

"Stop that," I told him after the third time.

It wasn't long afterward, I would imagine the time it took to eat a couple of corpses, for the zombies to start their march again. Was this their new tactic? Surround an entire community and flush out the prizes? Wring the final drops of humanity from the fabric of life? It was safe to assume that some people had just stayed put where they had lived. That they had eked out a quiet existence so far. The possibility that the zombies knew this and were capitalizing on it, well, that just sucked. How long would it be until they had sufficient numbers to encircle someplace the size of Boston or New York? There might still be thousands of people holed up in there. People were even more fucked, if that was possible. How could we possibly counteract what they were doing? Even if we somehow pulled off a heroic stand like the Spartans against the Persians, we'd never kill enough of them to make a difference. They wouldn't lose the appetite to fight like the Persians had; they had nothing to lose, nothing to live for. They would just keep coming, keep eating, their resolve was insurmountable— basically because they didn't have any. They did what they did because they just did it. Would the fucking aphids that invaded your garden give two shits if you killed a million of their brethren in an attempt to save your crop?

Nope, not at all. They would keep coming, happily munching away at your corn, cabbage, and cucumbers. "More for us!" their tiny brains would say. Individuals don't matter to them, only their continued survival as a group. The zombies had a sort of hive mentality, at least they were developing one. As of yet, I'm not even sure they understood the concept of "survival." They were like a pillbug rolling down a mountain; it did what it did, then it stopped and unrolled to eat. Zombies were approaching and exhibiting higher brain functions, and maybe someday they would wrestle with existential questions. Right now, though, all that mattered was for us to not become mobile home soufflé.

"I'm terrified." I thought my sister was talking to me, but she was moving in closer to BT; this was seriously going to take some getting used to. The army was advancing and their stench with them. It was not easing my trepidation about the robustness of the house with so much of the stink pouring in.

We were all at corners of windows, trying to get the best view for the oncoming disaster. It's one thing to watch an accident or gawk at the aftermath, but waiting for it to hit you? Well, that just sucks. Can't tell you how many times I looked to the door and wondered if Gary might have had it right; maybe we should have taken our chances running. Might as well have been in a beer can, and I'd seen enough brainless idiots crush a shitload of those on their foreheads to know what the zees outside could do to this thing. They got in here…there was no upstairs, no basement crawl space, no roof we could climb to for safety. We were in a dinghy; they were the tsunami.

Tiffany had sidled up next to me. "When Payne killed Pappy, I had a chance to leave it all. The rest of the world had left me to rot, but he picked me up and dusted me off, sent me on towards life. I owed him some revenge; though, knowing him, he would have never thought that. I think he would have been happier, me just turning around, but I stayed the course. I followed that bitch and her sisters," she said.

I wasn't entirely sure why she was telling me this; she'd recounted this story before and right now…well, it didn't seem relevant–until it was.

"I'm thankful you did follow. We would have been in a world of hurt, had you not," I told her.

"Me too. And not only because I got to take that shot, but because I met all you folks. I never knew that I could care for so many people, simultaneously. I never had a real family, and in my most vivid imagination, I would not have believed it could be this good. Yes, what we are going through is terrible, but I am so glad I have you people to go through it with. Even…" she hitched, "even if this is the end, I wanted to say thank you."

"You're welcome, kiddo," I told her, "but this is far from the end. You going to tell *that* guy it's over?" I asked, pointing to BT, "or that guy, or her? It's not over until it's over, and then you don't really give a shit. You'll be too busy adjusting your halo and getting fitted for your robe."

She smiled, but she was scared. We all were. Could try to cover it under a thick veneer of bravado, but, oh what I wouldn't do for some Viking mushrooms right about now. A little parboiled fly agaric to make us go berserk might just be the antidote to what ailed us. Hell, it wasn't like I hadn't been dosed before, during an attack. There's nothing wrong with accessing the secret door to your subconscious fight mechanism; after all, the flight part was pretty much on the surface, but we couldn't run from this. There had been some ambient light leaking into the small house from the moon and stars, but the zombies seemed preternatural at this exact moment; or at least I credited them for the dramatic lighting that came with the horde. A thick fog was rolling in; it had at first been behind the horde, but had now completely enveloped them and with it half the house. It was getting darker by the second. It had been relatively easy to see each other's facial expressions, now I could barely make out my own hand in front of my face. Anxiety was heightened as dark settled in. Fear of the dark is a basic, innate fear, something we're born with, a legacy gift from our ancestors. When your eyes can't assure you of safety, your imagination panics. And with good reason; scary things do run around in the night, things that don't come out in the light. Maybe in the 20th century we started to feel better about the dark, though the makers of night lights would tell you differently. Of course, there is a big difference between being afraid of the nocturnal roaming of the real saber tooth tiger and fearing the legendary boogie man that somehow lurked under every child's bed, which would make him more prolific than Santa, cause that fucker was in every room, every night. Now, in the 21st century, we had a right and need to address and discredit that "don't fear the dark" adage. Now, what you couldn't see would definitely kill you and eat you. Turning on a light would not save us.

It wasn't long after I waved my hand in front of my face and could no longer see it that we heard our first thump. There was a small squeal; I'd like to blame on Tiffany, but honestly, I think it was Gary. Shit–it could have been me. This initial thump was followed by another and then another to the point it sounded like golfball hail popping onto a tin roof. It rolled in, just like a storm, sprinkling, then raining, then suddenly there was a shift, and it was a fucking torrent. We had been expectant, maybe nervous, but now fear became a tangible, palpable entity within that enclosure, now we could not just choose to stay inside; we were trapped. And that fear wrapped its cold, callous, uncaring hands right around our hearts, minds, and throats. But this shift was more than psychological. The trailer-home we were in had been sitting on a cement slab, maybe lifted by a few cinder blocks and some six by six pressure treated lumber, but certainly not sufficiently anchored. The ass end of the house, which was facing the enemy, slid counterclockwise about a foot at first, then was forcibly broached until we were offering a broadside to the zombies flowing around us. We've all been at those concerts; you're standing peacefully in your little spot in the lawn seating when some asshat starts to dance and the field becomes a writhing, flinging, drug induced clusterfuck and you are shoved right along with the fleet. More times than not, I was that asshat and I sincerely apologize if you were caught up. Oh, how I wish we were a pirate ship of old and could have opened some cannon ports and sent some chained together steel balls hurtling into that mass. Instead, we were more like the doomed Poseidon presenting ourselves ahull into the oncoming tidal surge.

I could hear the rustle of the group moving, from standing or kneeling positions to most likely sitting or prone. The house began to rock, an inch or two at first, and then it became more violent as the press increased. Don't know what everyone else was thinking but there was no way we weren't pitching over. I started reaching around and tapping people.

"Move to the far wall." I was whispering. "Cover your head." Seemed like common sense instructions, because we were about to flip and be pelted by tumbling furniture, lamps, mirrors, décor, dishes, and plates. Something funny happens to common sense when you're terrified; it basically goes out the window, it crowds out higher function. All you want to do is run away from "The Thing."

We were now basically one giant, drunken Conga line where the wall met the ceiling on the side away from the zombies. I had a boot in my face and a head on my calves, did I ever mention I was claustrophobic? The feeling of being constricted had such a hold of me in normal life I actually wore baggy clothes. A tight t-shirt could well up feelings of anxiety; how the fuck I made it in the womb for nine months is something I don't want to even think about. I was warring within myself to just sit still; I needed to move, make more room. I'd once, okay maybe a few times, punched the living shit out of opposing football players when I'd been at the bottom of a pile and they'd moved, in what my mind, I considered too slowly in getting the fuck up. Guys who knew me got off as fast as they could. The pressure, the difficulty to catch a breath—it was all panic-inducing, so besides the very real threat of the zombies, I had to deal with my inner demons.

Because of our location on the wall, the rollover itself had affected us minimally. Us humans moved maybe a foot total, and were relatively in control. It was the other stuff I was worried about, the flying housewares that inflicted the most damage. I almost blacked out as a cast iron pan clipped the side of my skull; a kitchen chair leg pegged me in the ribcage.

Glassware shattered all around us like glass hand grenades. There were outright cries and muffled screams as furniture hit the others. I could see nothing at all, but I imagine it looked like swirling stars in a cartoon maelstrom. Blood was free flowing from my head, and I knew the others had not come through unscathed, as I could smell their iron-rich leakings. I wished I couldn't, but I could.

The wall we were now calling a floor, had suffered some serious structural damage from the fall; it had buckled along the entire length of it. The fog must have lifted somewhat as there was now some light coming in the windows along what was now our ceiling. It allowed me to see a whole bunch of jagged edges where, when this thing flipped again, we would be flayed as if we were being keelhauled. If you don't know what that lovely act of sea-justice was, it was the practice of torture which involved a man being fastened to two ropes and dragged underneath a barnacle-encrusted ship bottom then raised up the far side. It was very effective. If the sailor didn't drown, the action would usually induce severe injuries, sometimes the loss of limbs would occur, or even decapitation. Odds were, we wouldn't suffer those types of drastic bodily harm, but major blood vessels are frighteningly close to the surface. One could easily be severed on the aluminum shards that were sticking up like stalagmites, and, while bleeding out might be better than being keelhauled, dying was dying.

We did not have time to pick our way through the obstacle course as we were once again tossed over, now onto the roof, like I feared. The injuries were becoming more pronounced; I'd hoped what I heard was the snapping of some furniture, but it sounded suspiciously like bone. Plus, the blood loss was greater, and if I was smelling it, how long would it be until the zombies did as well? We were now a rolling brick. The roof suffered much more damage due to the weakening of the wall, so much so, it collapsed in nearly a foot, causing many spontaneous screams. They likely feared being crushed like a scrapped Ford, but the odds of that were low. This thing would disintegrate long before that became a problem. I had a deep gash ripped open across my abdomen, and my ass, of all places—and that one hurt more than anything else I had suffered so far.

By the time we rolled onto the third side, the initial wall just fell away; it was gone. We'd left it behind like the garbage it was. I think it was BT's head bouncing off mine that made me black out for a moment. When I opened my eyes a few seconds later there were the moans and groans of those around me mixed with the sounds of thousands of zombies, though they were moving away from us. We'd somehow made it, or so it seemed. I sat up, my head doing spirals, and wanting to crash back down to a place where gravity wouldn't affect it. I fought against it, struggling to gain my bearings and sit up. There were those that needed help, I just wasn't sure if I was up to the task of giving any just yet.

It was a good thing Ryan was passed out, because there was a good chance he'd be screaming like a banshee. His leg had somehow become entangled in a cabinet and had snapped his ankle, which was hanging at a grotesque angle compared to the rest of him. No one had come through unscathed, but he was the only one that had become lamed.

"You alright?" I checked on Nicole and Wesley, how she'd kept him from crying out the entire time I wasn't sure until I saw his binkie. The power or at least comfort that can come from sucking on that little rubber device. That's the wonder of breasts though, even fake ones have the ability to calm us down. I realize women rule the world, even if it's mostly in the background. The only reason I can see for their not just taking over the world is because they know it sucks to be up front; sorry for the double-entendre.

"Get them out of here," Sanders said to me. "Winters, Biddie, and myself will watch your withdrawal."

"The boy's ankle. I should set it, sir." Biddeford said.

"No time. We have to allow them time to get somewhere safer; you can do it then," the major replied.

The zombies were about a hundred feet away, closing their circle. On what, we did not know. Right now we didn't have the resources to find out or challenge them outright; we had lost this position, and sooner rather than later, Ryan was going to wake up and realize he was in a fuckload of pain. Tommy hoisted the teenager up. I took Wesley from my daughter; she had a limp, said her hip was hurting. Gary looked a bit like any of Mike Tyson's opponents when he was in his prime–like he'd been banged in the head one too many times. Travis was up ahead a bit, closer to the herd. If he was scared, he was doing an admirable job of hiding it. Meredith was helping her uncle walk a straight line. I had my head on a swivel, looking for threats; stragglers, one of them to notice they'd passed the buffet table. Sanders and his men had not yet pulled back to our location. I was feeling we were mighty vulnerable, considering everyone was disoriented or broken and we only had one person with the ability to fire effectively at the moment.

"Travis, stay closer to us," I hush yelled. I know it sounds weird, but we've all done it. Maybe at a movie theater, when your kid is misbehaving and you want him to realize he's in trouble without ruining the movie-going experience for everyone else–the most common hush-whisper is, ironically, "Be quiet." We were a block over when automatic gunfire opened up.

"Shit. We gotta move," I said, but sometimes you realize you could not have said more superfluous words if you said water was wet or sex was great. There really was no need to verbalize these things, as they were universal truths. Thankfully, no one said, "Duh." I cradled Wesley and then moved over to get a shoulder propped up under Gary. He was starting to shake off the effects of his most-likely concussion-inducing headbang, but not fast enough.

"Pick a house!" I told Travis. This time there was no hush to it. Then, what I'd hoped was the unthinkable, so unthinkable that it hadn't even occurred to me to do it, happened right in front of us. Travis brought his rifle up to his shoulder and began to fire.

"Ri'm r'okay," Gary said. I didn't think slurred speech after a head injury was a great sign, but I could only deal with one calamity at a time. Never been much of a multitasker.

Walking wounded versus the walking dead; perhaps we could start our own fight game franchise. The deaders were pouring out all around us. They must have been left behind by their faster brethren. They were ambling and shambling and Travis was in danger of being cut off from the rest of us as he sought out something, anything where we could once again seek shelter. I handed the baby back to Nicole and grabbed Gary's heavier hunting rifle; it was of the wooden stock, as opposed to my composite. We had a fair number of zombies locked on to us. It was my hope to not draw more as I first made sure the rifle was on "safe" before I began to use the buttstock as my skull crusher.

We've all, at one point or another, seen the movies and TV shows that depict crushing a skull as something not much more difficult than busting open an overripe melon, thus the term "melonhead." I can assure you that is not the case. These were not half-rotted people rising from shallow graves after having been worm eaten for a decade. For the most part, these had been vibrant, healthy people with nice, thick skulls before the virus took over. No matter what you believed, it was not something you could do with your hands; even with a tool it was a jarringly difficult business. Knowing this, I used all the force available to me as I drove that heavy wooden stock into the forehead of the zombie nearest me. It was enough power that I drove the top part of his head a good three or four inches back into his brain. The end of the rifle emerged coated in a gooey black mass of brain and skull bits.

I had to step up to the next one, who seemed all too willing to accept his penance. His arms stretched out to meet me, though I was most definitely not his Lord and Savior. Or maybe I was the Savior part; who knew if any humanity remained in those human shells? Perhaps that small piece left was begging for a quick and merciful ending. There have been times when I'll admit I thought I'd seen a glimpse of relief in a battered head. Anyway, I thought I was getting some serious licks in until BT started up. He was quite literally taking the top halves of skulls clean off; looked like a bunch of yarmulkes spinning up into the air after a particularly heavy gust. Travis had fought his way to a porch, some fifty feet to our left. It wasn't a mobile home, so that was something. He'd got the memo we were doing our best to make this a somewhat quiet affair—although, cracking a head sounded a lot like smacking a two by four with a power hammer. It was fairly loud in its own right. Even with Ryan in his arms, Tommy was a death-dealing machine. His one-arm rifle thrusting was equally or more effective than my two-armed lunges.

The zombies were congealing on our location. Normally I would use the word "converging," but they were a slimy paste-coated sea of disgustingness. Tommy was kicking out and shattering knees and legs, incapacitating the ones getting too close. I nearly lost my grip and fell into a zombie as my hand slipped in the gore the rifle was coated in. It was a thrown shoulder from BT that kept me from going under.

I let out a "thanks," and he nodded to me. My sister and her son got to the porch first and were busy beating back the zombies that were trying to get them over the handrails. Maybe these were the early generation zombies, but they'd had their processing software updated. They saw where we were trying to go and were not only trying to get at us, but also trying to cut us off from that haven. Time for smashing skulls was diminishing rapidly, but the rub of it was we couldn't shoot either, because a bad shot or one that sailed clear through would come entirely too close to my son, sister, and nephew. Damned if you do, dead if you don't. How do you reconcile that?

"Get in the house!" I yelled to them. "We need to find somewhere else!"

"Mike, there is nowhere else!" BT was straining.

He was right. We were twenty feet from this one; the next nearest was a hundred or the moon, same distance, relatively speaking.

"Get in and make sure the back door is open!" I yelled to them. I heard a door slamming shut and was thankful that, at least, they were safe. Now I had to hope there was another door. The zombies were heaviest to our front. I jammed Gary's rifle back into his hands and had to spend an extra second or two to make sure he had the wits to hold on to it. "Sorry," I told him as his hands were immersed in goo better left undefined.

I got my rifle into position and began to make a hole. The noise couldn't be helped, and if we didn't make it, who was going to give a shit if we made the cacophony or not. Plus, Ryan had taken this opportunity to let us all know what he thought of being jostled around on Tommy's back. He was crying out from the pain and I had to think shock would be settling in soon enough. I caught a quick glance as Tommy was doing his martial arts routine, Ryan's ankle was flapping sickeningly across his broad chest, the boy's eyes were rolling around in his skull like loose marbles on a wooden floor. I was willing him to pass out again; for some reason he just wouldn't. BT and I were the only one's firing, trying to keep everyone except Tommy in the middle of our very incomplete circle.

BT almost immediately reverted back to clubbing the zombies.

"I'm out," was all I needed to hear to know why. A window opened up to our side, Travis poked his head and rifle out and was doing his best to make us some room. My sister was on the top floor, she nearly pelted Travis with a rung from a handy rope-style fire-escape ladder—you know, the kind you're only willing to risk your life climbing if your life is in peril. Kind of weird when you stop and think about it; out of the frying pan and into the fire type scenario. Well, it sure wasn't like we weren't in danger, so, ladder it was. The ladder passed by the first floor window, giving one a view of the living room as they scaled upward or hastily downward, as the case may be.

"Toward the house!" I yelled

BT was still trying to make it around to the other side where we didn't even know if there was an opening. Jesse had joined his mother, but he was firing down into the heads of zombies. We had the tiniest of openings; Nicole and Wesley pressed through and to the ladder. If I harbored any question that my waif of a daughter could drag her injured leg and a baby up a flimsy, swaying ladder, it disappeared as I watched her scale that thing like a monkey up a banana tree. Never doubt the resolve of a woman protecting her baby. She had a brief moment halfway up where the ladder moved off the house at an awkward angle; she was holding on by the tips of her fingers. My sister reached out and grabbed an arm, pulling her close. Jesse was holding on to his mother, who had not quite thought out the distances involved and almost pitched out herself. I wasn't sure how we were going to get Gary up because he still looked like counting to ten might be a little beyond his capabilities. I think the only reason he hadn't dropped the rifle yet was that it was now basically glued to his hands. His coordination would have got him pulled over for a suspected DUI; if you couldn't walk a straight line, there was no way you could drive one.

Tommy took care of that. He jumped up onto the ladder and basically forced Travis to take Ryan through the window. Then he wrapped an arm underneath Gary's left armpit and heaved him up. I didn't think the ladder was designed for two adult males at the same time, but if it couldn't hold those two then BT was in a lot of trouble. Gary wasn't complete dead weight, but close to it. He tried valiantly to get his feet on the individual steps but was having a monumentally difficult time. Looked like he was trying to thread a needle with silk during a gale. Tommy just kept grunting and heaving until he was within the reach of help up top.

"You next, BT!" I know he wanted to argue, but I still had

bullets. Not many, but he didn't need to know that. He was halfway up when the well went dry. I thought about hopping on the ladder behind him, but the rope above him, bearing all the weight, looked like it was stretched as thin as it could get.

"Dad, come on!" Travis urged through his window. It was a ground floor window, but the way the house sat on the landscaping, it was still a couple of feet above my outstretched hands. Jumping up was the only way to get to it. I looked like your prototypical middle-aged white man jumping; meaning, I launched not at all. Of course, I'm planning to blame that on the knee-capped zombie that had grabbed my calf and ankle. My chin bounced off the side of the house. I was somewhat happy that it was aluminum siding, as it gave a little, but it was still a hard-enough knock that I'd split my lip, I'm thinking busted my nose, and I was going to have a wallop of a knot on my forehead. And then, just to put a cherry on top, I slid the rest of the way down, grinding the side of my face against the concrete foundation. Going to have a serious case of raspberries. Rifle shots exploded all around me as those in the house began clearing out the riff-raff that had gathered around me waiting to do their version of a pig pile—or a pig-out pile might be a better name.

The zombie that had crushed my dreams of pulling an Air Jordan was headless, yet I still had to pry his cold dead hands from me. Must have been a die-hard NRA member.

"Talbot, get your ass in the house!" BT shouted. He made it sound like I was twelve and was out playing touch football after the street lights came on, but the girl next door was still out and I was in no mood to leave her behind to wash up and do my damn homework. Even in the dire straits I found myself in, I very much thought of flipping him a bird. Survival won out as I propped myself up against the house and began to scramble; there was no way I could get a running leap now. Travis was reaching down and we locked hands-the kid was strong, no doubt about it, as the death grip he had on my wrist did not break, but I didn't think he had the leverage to pull me through. Bullets were whizzing by me, dangerously close; I mean, closer than they ever had from the enemy during a firefight. Knowing it was coming from loved ones didn't make it much less frightening. An inch one way or the other and I was done for.

Travis and I were in an agonizing equilibrium, I was basically stuck about a foot off the ground. I jerked on his leverage in an attempt to pull myself up. I used enough force that I broke free from him, yet I missed the fucking sill by a good six inches. Thank God for BT. That massive arm shot out, and he not only halted my downward trajectory, he yanked me through like I was on a springboard. I had enough upward flight that I slammed the top of my head on the window casing. Hurt like fucking hell. I shouted out about it, but how do you fault a man that just saved your life…again?

"You alright?" BT was flipping me over and looking around my body. "Shit," he said as he manhandled me.

"Hey. I usually like a good meal first. Unhand me, sir!" was all I could think to say through my heavy exhalations.

"You bit?" Travis was concerned, now looking with BT.

I finally flipped over onto my ass. BT had turned the bottom of my jeans so I could see the hole one of the zombies had torn through the thick denim, it was rimmed in a heavy coating of blood. I pulled the jeans hurriedly past my knee and felt around.

"Is it mine?" I asked in desperation.

"You're good, you're good." BT let out a sigh.

I sat up and let my head sag. I'd fucking dodged another one. Seemed like these days I was dodging one and moving right into another. But for now, we could stop, at least for a moment. Gary had draped himself over a couch and was already asleep. At some point, those that had been upstairs had come down.

I stood, my legs surprisingly supporting my weight. "Travis, sis, can you get Gary up? If he has a concussion I don't think he should be asleep, and get whatever ammo we have left divvied up. BT, you think we can set an ankle?"

"Not really my level of expertise, but I'll give it a go."

"We need some splints, fabric of some sort, and tape, if we can find it."

"Uncle, we have zombies on the porch in both the front and the back," Jess said. His warning was punctuated one second later as they began to break out the glass. Wouldn't be long before the press of bodies burst through the locks.

"Alright, Gary and Ryan will have to wait. You know the drill, heavy shit to block the doors."

BT was a one-man forklift, taking a full china cabinet right off its hutch and crashing it into the back door. The sound of arms breaking was both satisfying and sickening. Travis and I were mostly right behind him, stutter-stepping the heavy ass hutch to back up the other piece. Tommy and Lyndsey were sliding, carrying the living room couch (sans Gary, whom they had gently put on the floor), toward the more stout front door, though this would yield just as easily as the back if pressed. In five minutes we had every stick of furniture piled up and braced. Without a bulker to fudge things up, we were in pretty good shape. Thought that right up until we heard a loud thud on the floor above us. Then another.

"What the fuck?" I asked, just now noticing that my rifle was propped up against the wall on the far side of the room. I didn't yet know why I needed it, but the thought that I did was running increasingly rampant through my head. I grabbed my rifle and ran to the bottom of the staircase only to realize that the enemy was not only at the gates, but had waltzed right through them. A zombie was at the top of the stairs looking down at me. Before I could get a shot off the bastard moved to the side and out of my view. I was readying to launch up after him when BT's hand clamped down on my shoulder.

"It's a trap."

"Okay, Admiral Ackbar," I said, trying to shoulder off his grip; would have had an easier time unwelding steel. Is that a thing? Doesn't matter; It was impossible.

"That a Star Wars thing? You gonna pull a nerd reference on me right now?"

"Shit, when you say it like that…"

"Dad!" Travis yelled out from near the window I had come in from.

"How the fuck did we miss that?" I didn't dare leave my post on the stairs. I could see a line of zombies climbing the damned fire-escape ladder. Occasionally one would fall, even take a couple of his buddies with him, but otherwise, they were having surprisingly good luck making it up. Much better than Gary, in fact, who had just suffered a head injury. I was looking from the window to the staircase and back; it was one of the interludes between that nearly got me brained. I ducked just as a heavy metal lamp crashed into the wall behind me. The zombie that had tossed it looked genuinely pissed off that he had missed. I gave him two shots to the chest to help him get over it. He absorbed the blows and let out a hellish shriek. I wanted to believe it was his lungs releasing the pent-up air, but nope–he'd really screamed in pain and anger. This was confirmed as a few of his buddies rounded the corner and he moved aside as they rushed the stairs. The problem was that they weren't overly interested in the stair part so much as they were in getting to me. They flat out jumped. Fortunately, a low hanging ceiling about midway down the flight of stairs stopped them from crashing right into me. Seemed they weren't quite as smart as they thought they were.

As it was, I found myself back-peddling until I hit the wall not three feet behind me. This was one of the most sphincter-clenching moments I have ever had in my entire life. It was just so unexpected; caught me completely off-guard. Fired three wild shots into the clusterfuck of zombies scrambling over each other in their haste to get to me. If not for their in-fighting it would have been a lot closer. Travis was picking off climbers, BT had helped me up as my sister was dealing with the three, coming head-first down the stairs, looking like some version of a zombie centipede. If you thought the movie with the similar title was gross, it had nothing on this. They were looking at me and chewing on each other as a poor substitute for what they were trying to get. It was my sister that put an end to the nightmare; she went all commando and put a well-aimed burst into their heads.

"Th..thank you," I said when I was able to get coherent words from my misfiring head past my voice box. I was talking to both my sister and her new boyfriend; that thought was both steadying and destabilizing.

"What do we do now?" BT asked as we all looked up the stairs.

"We need to get that ladder down or they're just going to keep coming in until they overwhelm us. "Travis shoot the rope!" I shouted across the room.

He turned to look at me, there was some doubt in that gaze; to be fair, it did sound like a sharpshooter request. Three shots later he told me the thing was moving too much to hit it.

"Fuck this," BT said as he ran toward the kitchen. He'd grabbed a butcher knife from one of the drawers.

"Be careful," my sister shouted out. She looked like she was going to fret and that in itself was weird because my sister never looked like she was going to fret; I wondered if she ever fretted over me.

One of the zombies, having caught wind of what BT had planned had parked his face right where BT wanted to cut. A head is a much easier target than a swaying rope. Travis ended that blockade quick enough, giving BT the time he needed to reach out, pull the ladder toward him and saw through one of the nylon ropes. Either that shit was stronger than it looked or the knife was just a glorified butter spreader, but it took him much longer than it should have. And before he could finish, it was jerked violently from his hands, and the knife he'd been holding spun wildly to the ground below.

"Fuck!" he shouted as he pulled his finger in and began to suck on it. My sister rushed to his aid. "It's alright, baby," he told her. "Just got tangled up in the line. He looked over at me sheepishly after having said those words.

I said nothing, just produced a small smile. It would be weird for a while, sure, but I could think of no better man I would love to call an in-law. He hammed it up a bit for her but otherwise, I think he was going to make it. Despite the activity around us, I couldn't help thinking there was potential here for a whole new world of shit I could give him. A loud twang from behind him cut through my thoughts as new weight on the ladder finally snapped the fibers he'd cut. One problem down. We'd stopped the supply line, now we just needed to take care of what had already been delivered. The wood was cracking from the back door as the zombies exerted more force. We needed to retake the house post-haste; I just wasn't so sure about going upstairs. The zombies weren't in a rush to come down, meaning they were either going to wait for the cover of darkness or for our stupid asses to challenge their superior position. There was no way we could risk waiting for them to come out and play; we were going to need to force the issue at some point. But we still had some wounded we needed to take care of in the event this went sideways. So far, they'd come up a ladder, hidden, and come to another's aid; this represented advancement, but the fact that they had the ability to use a weapon was truly concerning. Sure, it was just a thrown lamp, but even that was miles beyond anything they had done previously. How long until they swung a bat? Wielded a knife? Would only be a matter of time then until they picked up a gun and pulled a trigger. Yeah, then it was going to get real shitty, real quick, like an exploding septic tank truck in a hundred degree heat, shitty.

Gary was pretty groggy as Travis and Tommy propped him up against a wall. I was keeping an eye on the staircase. This time I had my rifle up, completely at the ready if any of them showed, even for a second. BT and my sister were tending to Ryan's ankle. Every time they even breathed on it, he stirred in pain. Would the zombies come running if they heard him scream out? I had to think they would; it would be like ringing a cowboy dinner triangle for them.

"Muffle his voice," I said softly. "Before you set that."

"You want me to put a gag on him?" my sister asked as if I'd told her to pretend this was a Civil War injury and just cut off the broken part with a dull saw.

"He's right," BT said, and yeah, because he said it she was fine with it. I get how these things work. Whichever way got them to quiet him before he began to incite the natives was fine with me.

I've seen some gruesome things–long before the zombie invasion–but that kid's ankle bent at a ninety-degree angle to the rest of his leg, was queasing up my insides. Maybe it was because of his age or the unnatural aspect of it; maybe because in most battles you don't get to just stare at an injury. Whatever it was, I was hoping they would fix it quickly and I could stop spending my time looking over at it like an accident gawker. I have no idea what it is about human nature that urges us to look. Perhaps it is something we need to witness as a deterrent to us, a warning not to make that person's mistakes. Or maybe it's our better nature coming forward, exercising empathy, reminding that it could be us next time. But then again, maybe it is a chance for us to revel in our superiority over that person's misfortune, strengthening our position in a pack. And I would imagine there are even some that enjoy seeing or even inflicting someone else's pain; those are the ones you need to keep an eye out for.

The house became unnaturally quiet just as they moved the ankle into position. Could even hear the bones scraping together, which is as unpleasant as it sounds. I was somewhat happy Gary was out of it because he would have been getting sick about now. How did I know this? Because I wanted to, and his stomach was much weaker than mine. They wrapped his lower leg in a sheet, placed two makeshift splints into position, and then duct taped his ankle and lower leg. My sister was pale, sweating, and a little shaky when they finished the job. I gave her a quick thumbs up. She didn't even think twice;

pretty sure it was an automatic response when she flipped me off.

"It's going to be dark soon, Mr. T." Tommy had come up next to me. I could see that Travis wanted to join us, but every time Gary was left alone, he slumped over. I think he needed a CAT scan in the worst way, but even if we somehow were able to perform one and found out the worst, then what? Modern medicine had its faults, that's for sure. When doctors are said to practice medicine, one needs only to look at the verb in that sentence. They didn't completely know what they were doing. Sure, they were working at it and getting better, but they were far from perfect; so much can go wrong with a person. But man, oh man, that was way better than it was now. Now, fairly regular, routine injuries could cost you your life. If Gary's brain swelled too much, there wasn't a single one of us there that would be able to successfully drill a hole in his skull to relieve the pressure, even if someone had the balls to try it. Or, if Ryan's bone had nicked an artery and he was bleeding internally, none of us would be able to go in and sew up the damaged blood vessel. We had rudimentary knowledge at best; nothing that would stave off the Reaper if he was even somewhat persistent. Pretty soon, as antibiotics aged and became ineffectual, something as mundane as strep throat or an infected cut could be fatal. It was an uphill battle we found ourselves in, each day bringing new ways to hasten our demise.

"Mr. T?"

"Sorry. How many do you think are up there?" I asked.

"Hard to say, fewer than fifty though."

"Why do you say that?"

"Because any more than that wouldn't fit."

"I appreciate the logical approach, but don't like the answer it yielded."

"Me neither," he replied. "You ready?" he asked.

"No. BT, we're going up."

"Hold up—I'll grab my rifle," he said.

"No, you stay and watch our retreat. It'll be too tight up

there for three to fight effectively and move around. You'll take up the whole hallway by your damn self–wedge us in too tight. Tommy and I will be stuck against the walls, trying to talk out the sides of our mouths."

"Shut up, Mike," he said, coming over. "I'll watch your backs. Don't be heroes."

"Probably too late for that, at least in my case," I told him.

"At least you've held on to your humility. Be safe, man," he said as Tommy took the lead. I was on the step behind him. Tommy was being extraordinarily careful, which translated to fear for me. In any kind of fight, armed or not, Tommy was a life-ending machine. That he was hesitant made things fairly scary. Okay, "fairly" wasn't adequate. Really, my palms were sweating, my heart was trying to hammer its way out of my chest, and I could barely swallow because my mouth was so dry that I should have posted red warnings about the fire-danger level. We were as quiet as two people climbing stairs could be, which was still much too loud, at least, for someone expecting it. Our clothes rustled, our equipment shifted, and no matter where we stepped on a tread there was the groaning of the wood under pressure. Each creak made me wince.

So sure, a slumbering homeowner in the dead of night most likely wouldn't hear our approach, but the fucking zombies waiting in the wings sure would. On hindsight, maybe it would have been better to just rush up the stairs, maybe catch a couple by surprise, and not give the deep doubt that was forming in my gut a place to settle. I'd like to say that the zombies, fearing our imminent arrival, had jumped from the same window they entered. That wasn't the case. When Tommy got to the top step he poked his head around the corner and he froze like we were playing a rousing game of freeze tag, and he wanted to win something fierce. Here was that urge to see again; wanting to know what had done that to him, I went around him to peek. The scene provoked one of those times when the mind races around, looking in all the dark corners of your logic, trying to make sense of the images being sent to your brain plate. The human mind can't abide leaving unsolved a mystery or unclassified an anomaly, hence our insatiable lust for knowledge at the expense of all other things.

There was a zombie in the middle of the hallway, in and of itself, not all that strange, considering the circumstances we found ourselves in, right? But that he was seated in a chair with his back to us, yeah, that was fucking weird. You want to know what it did though? Gawking at it cost us a few precious seconds as the three closed doors on that floor opened up and zombies flooded out. Tommy, in his haste to get his rifle up, about pushed me back into the wall. I'm not saying that he merely made me hit the wall, I'm saying I fucking almost became one with the drywall from the force. He was firing before I could recover. The house was small; therefore, the hallway was short. We'd already lost our position by the time they showed themselves.

"Down, Mr. T, now!"

I didn't even get a shot off as I found myself launching down the stairs, careful to not knock myself out on the low overhang. Travis and BT were waiting off to the side as we made our hasty retreat. The zombies did not follow. This was one of those things where I was angry either way. If a few of them had come, we could have extinguished some of the bastards. That they didn't, spoke volumes to their intelligence.

"What's going on?" BT asked, his rifle at the ready. He never took his eyes off the top of the stairs.

"They were waiting for us; laid a trap," I told him. "Shit, maybe you are Admiral Ackbar."

"I like reading suspense novels, Talbot. Not big on the whole zombie genre, though. I used to like reading about stuff I thought could actually happen in real life, made it scarier, you know what I mean?"

I nodded and said, "yeah."

"But that doesn't mean I didn't read one or two of them. They were always mindless brain-eating machines; they didn't lay traps, they didn't climb ladders. It was always the buxom blonde tripping over her own feet that got everybody into trouble. What the fuck is going on here?"

I couldn't really think of anything to say. We all knew they were getting smarter, but our lives depended on the answers none of us had. "I wish I had a grenade," was all I could think to tell him.

"They know how to throw shit now, or have you forgotten already?"

I'd forgotten already. Yeah, that would have sucked to have my thrown offering come back to greet me.

"Flamethrower, then?"

"Inside a stick-built house?"

"Don't be a dream-crusher, man," I told him.

"They're going to wait for the dead of night and then they're going to storm down those stairs," BT said. He was right, though they might not attempt it tonight, maybe not even tomorrow night. For all I knew they were thinking to catch us truly off-guard. We'd be exhausted soon enough, waiting, anticipating. Whoever had guard duty might nod off and well, we knew where that was going.

"Found this in the basement," Tommy said. He had a coil of thick, yellow rope, a fistful of nails, and a hammer.

"And?" I asked, wondering what he meant to do with it.

"Just cover me," he said, going halfway up the stairs. He started sinking nails halfway into studs then bending them upwards. He was on the fourth or fifth nail when a zombie quickly poked its head around the corner, I guess to see what was going on. I fired a shot, taking a chunk out of the wall but I don't think I hit him, he'd moved entirely too fast. Tommy then started crisscrossing the rope around the nails until he had what looked like a spider web in the middle of the stairwell.

"It won't stop them but it will delay them," he said as we both went back down.

I couldn't help but think it was also going to keep us from going up if we needed to, though right now, that was a closed avenue anyway. I was feeling way more trapped than I figured the zombies were; their enemies, or their food, was effectually surrounded. The backdoor groaned as the zombies launched another attack on it. Once they broke through, and they would, my guess was they would begin to pull our blockade out into the yard so we could not use it again.

"What kind of shittery is this?" I asked. We were holed up with not much more than some old condiments to see us through. Not sure how far one could get on a shot of ketchup every day. Then to make matters even better, it was like the zombies, after hearing my question, decided to raise the stakes, add a little *more* shittery into the equation, I suppose. They started stomping on the upstairs floor. Started out soft enough, but as more and more of them joined in we watched the light fixtures sway, then plaster dust and dead bugs rained down on us. It was enough noise to keep Gary awake and to awaken a screaming, crying, Ryan, who was in some terrible pain. At first, we wondered if it was their version of a tribal dance, something to get them amped up for a battle, that they would be rushing down the stairs as fast as they could to overpower us. After ten minutes, that was beginning to seem unlikely; after a half an hour, we knew it for what it was. They were going to drive us into exhaustion.

There was no reason not to think they couldn't keep the stomping up for days. We wouldn't be able to sleep, then all of a sudden, they would stop and we wouldn't even be able to help ourselves as we just passed out. Yeah, we'd eventually wake up, but it would be to the screams of each other getting our faces torn off. After an hour of it I was ready to give going outside a shot. I'm not sure if I have ever related this story before in a previous journal, but when I was still living in the townhouse at Little Turtle, we had a young neighbor for a while that was very much into club music. Which, for those of you that are unfamiliar with this genre, is basically just loud beats that can go on forever so you can enjoy your Ecstasy as you grind against your partner in a fit of psychedelic passion on the dance floor for hours on end. For some reason this assho...I mean, young kid, liked to turn this shit...I mean, music, on at around ten o'clock every night, you know, which is fine–he has a right to listen to whatever the fuck he wants to, even if it sucks. What's not cool, though, is when you have five-foot tall speakers with bass cones the size of dinner plates pushing the low, thumping sound waves through everyone else's house, causing dishes on the counter to vibrate and move from the shock waves.

For two days straight, I bit my tongue and dealt with it in a stewing anger, especially since he had somewhat of the decency to shut it off at midnight, thinking that everybody else maybe went to bed at the same time he did. I did not. When the third night rolled around and he started it up again, I didn't wait two minutes before I beat the shit out of his door trying to gain his attention. Had to wait for a lull in the action before he heard my assault, and like I said, club mixes go on for a good long while. He lowered it to about half, which meant my fillings didn't move around in my head. The fourth night, I showed up on his doorstep with a rifle in my hands. I didn't threaten him in any way. I just explained that lack of sleep tends to make me do irrational things and I left it at that. Never heard his shitty...I mean club music again. Where am I going with this? Oh yeah. A loud, rhythmic bass-pounding sound can quickly unravel the nerves, fray the edges, induce anger, and produce massive amounts of anxiety. I wondered if I could once again silence the offending party with a threat.

Maybe I could. I grabbed Gary's rifle and stomped into the kitchen, which was below the bedroom, where it seemed that most of the sound was coming from. I raised the rifle straight up. There was the fleeting hint of concern at just how smart of a move this was right before I pulled the trigger. I had to turn my head as plaster and wood bits sprinkled my head. I adjusted my aim and took two more shots.

"What the fuck are you doing, Mike?" BT asked over the jarring noise I was making in concert to the zombies. Black goo began to leak from the holes. I'd hit a target, though it had not persuaded the Lords of the Dead Dance to stop.

I took another two shots, heard a definite thump as a body dropped onto the floor. More brackish fluid leaked down the hole. I reloaded the rifle and took three more shots, primarily because it felt good. At least one more zombie fell to the ground, maybe not dead, but severely wounded, that was for sure.

"I can do this all fucking night long!" I shouted up.

Did they understand me? Maybe not the words, but the action and timing were crystal clear. It appeared that they did not wish to diminish their numbers too greatly before they launched their attack. With my threat verbalized and demonstrated, they ceased their psychological sound torture.

"No way," BT whispered after a minute of silence.

"Fuck, I hope so," I told him. "Not sure how much more of that I could have taken. Tommy, what's the basement like?" I asked, but in a whisper. If the zombies could somehow understand me, there was no reason I could think of to let them in on our plans.

"Two windows that maybe Nicole could fit out of. No outside doors, no crawl spaces or other hiding areas. The door leading down to the basement is a hollow core, and there is no effective way to barricade it because it opens outward into the kitchen, not towards the basement."

"A couple of months ago a door handle would have been beyond them," I said. I pointed around at our group. "Sick, terrified, wounded, exhausted. Can't attack, can't leave, can't stay, that about sum up our situation?" I asked everyone.

We were at most forty-eight hours from big trouble. Already my stomach was collapsing in on itself, but the thirst; that was beginning to become a real problem. I could feel my throat getting dryer by the minute. Soon our brain function would diminish as we lacked the lubricant to keep it working efficiently. Dying of thirst held absolutely no appeal.

"Dad." Travis had come up to me, I was sitting back

against a wall, catching a few uneasy minutes of sleep, or at least trying to–wasn't going so good.

"What's up?" I asked, trying to put on as brave a face as I could as I sat up straighter. It was difficult to look past the black bags under his eyes and the sallow complexion he was getting from not being properly hydrated.

"There's a stack of pallets downstairs and some tools," he said. I'm not sure if he was expecting me to put it all together; I didn't. I could blame it on the lack of water, but he'd given me woefully little to go on.

"I'm listening." I sat up more as he did so. What he was proposing closed in on preposterous and I was in love with it. When I rolled it out to the rest of the group they looked much more skeptical than I had.

"There's a couple of things you've overlooked," BT said. "First off, pallets are roughly forty pounds each, give or take. You're talking somewhere in the neighborhood of four hundred or five hundred pounds when this thing is done. Throw in Ryan, who will also need to be carried, and we're close to six hundred pounds. That's still doable, between Tommy and myself we could get that done, but we'd be completely useless for anything else."

"What about me?" I asked indignantly.

"You mean why are you completely useless?"

"No. I could help carry it."

"You'd be carrying Ryan or did you already forget?"

"Oh, you bawbag!"

"Bawbag?" BT asked.

"Scottish swear word, I think."

"Really? Not enough English ones to go around? What's it mean?" He asked.

"Could mean trolley for all I know."

"Then we're dealing with the width of the door," Tommy went on staving off my tangent.

That was a blow I'd never even considered.

"We'd have three feet," Tommy said. "It's slim, but it

could be done."

BT had weighed and voiced his objections and now they seemed overly optimistic. "Are you seriously thinking we can make it out of here in a long, thin, heavy wooden tank with the press of a thousand zombies on us?" he asked the boy. "Even at three pallets length, we're talking twelve feet. That gives each of us about a foot; we'll be half-stepping our way out of here, and it's not like the zombies are just going to leave us be when we get out. We would be a shuffling crate of cookies."

I just looked at him, then I looked at him some more, then I kept looking.

"What, man! You're freaking me out. Of course I'm in. We haven't done any crazy ass cracker shit in a while."

"That's the spirit," I told him as I moved in to clap his shoulder.

"You touch me and I'll break your gallbladder."

"That possible?" I asked Tommy.

"You want to try and find out?" he asked me back.

CHAPTER NINE
MIKE JOURNAL ENTRY 9

NOT SURE IF the homeowner was a pallet hoarder, but we pulled up thirty-two pallets from the basement. Some of them were no good, either rotted out or the space between the wood was too wide, allowing the zombies easy access to the food inside. But when it was all done, we had a giant rectangular box with no bottom. It was four pallets long, by one and a half high and a little under three feet wide, so that we could squeeze out the door. We had cross beams inside to keep it from being crushed and handholds to heft the box that was just north of six hundred pounds, by our reckoning. This was going to be like sneaking out of camp under a canoe.

"Looks like a giant fucking coffin," BT said as he stepped away from it.

"It could be," I answered.

"Oh, that's so fucking helpful, makes me feel all gooey inside. Jerk." He walked away.

"That going to be tall enough?" Meredith asked.

"For us normal humans, it'll be fine, that one over there is going to have a serious crick in his neck when we get out," I said to her. The plan was to head out the next morning; we'd try to get a little sleep and go at first light. Not like the cover of night would have worked in our favor, anyway. Let's face it, to humans, everything seems better in the light of day. How many nights have you personally lain awake and worried and fretted over something only to realize the next morning it wasn't that big a deal? So, yeah, that was the plan. Seemed the zombies had something else in mind. They heard us working and maybe on some level they realized we were either getting ready to leave or were building a new house where they couldn't come, and they didn't like that. Or they, like us, were just plain hungry. It was Meredith's turn to guard the stairs and she sounded the alarm when the first snarls of a caught-up zombie awoke her from a slumber. Got to admit, at that point, I was pretty happy about Tommy's snare.

She gave us a short, surprised, frightened, yelp followed by an extra loud gunshot. Anyone who had not been awakened by her exclaim certainly was after the report. The house was dark; not underground dark, but Meredith was only five feet away and I could just make her out.

"Mer?" I called out after the echo stopped.

"Fine Unc. Zombie in the trap." She was standing now, rifle at the ready. I could hear his groans and the twisting of rope as he moved around, trying to push his way through. I put a bullet where I figured his head was. The brief illumination told me this was no rogue zombie heading down to the fridge to grab a snack while the others slept. They were coming and the rope looked stretched to its capability. Ultimately, it was the nails that betrayed us; I knew hemp wouldn't let me down.

"Travis, over here! BT, Tommy, start clearing the back door! Sis, start rounding everyone else up," I shouted as I fired.

How in the fuck we were going to pull off the timing of this, I had no clue. In near pitch darkness, we needed to keep the upstairs zombies from coming down, then, as the back door was cleared, we needed to keep the outside zombies from coming in, and invariably, they would all meet up on this main floor. Which meant we had to get under the protective barrier of what we were affectionately calling the Palletonion Tank, before they could get at us. Either the gunfire or a message from above had the outside zombies stirred up because they were pressing the attack.

"Mike, we're a couch and an end table away from the zombies, you need to make a break for it!" BT shouted. I blasted the rest of my magazine into the horde in an attempt to log jam them.

"Mer, Travis, go for the tank." I was just going to cover the door when there was the twang of nails popping free. Thuds of heads, arms and bodies hitting stairs as they fell, tumbled and slid down followed me as I took over at the back door. I tapped BT's shoulder–he needed to get with Tommy and get that thing tilted over, so everyone could get in.

"Hurry, Mike, they're coming." This from my sister who was near the back of the contraption.

The back door was a frenetic bundle of activity. The zombies, feeling that the end of us was near, doubled their attack. The lock had given out and they were actually assisting me in moving the couch backward, though it really wasn't what I wanted. We needed to have that thing completely out of the way or it would trap us in the kitchen. I was pulling and they were pushing. We made short work of it, but I was in danger of becoming the meat in a zombie sandwich as they rushed at me from either side.

"Coming under!"

Tommy understood and placed his feet as wide as possible while also giving me a couple more inches of headroom. This either worked or I ended up on an ESPN compilation of the worst slide attempts. Most of the time those base runners were merely tagged out of the game; this time I would be tagged and bagged out of life. Yeah, rather dramatic, but still the truth. I took three steps before I launched headfirst. My step-off foot slipped a little on the linoleum, but I still felt confident about my trajectory and speed. I was half right; speed was up to snuff, but I was coming in high and to the left of my target. Clipped my ear as my head went under, which hurts unreasonably bad;

my shoulder took the brunt of the beating and took damn near all of my momentum. I was chest deep under the contraption. I could hear the groans of those holding it up as I rocked the boat. It was a groggy Gary that reached down and yanked me all the way in just as zombies bounced into the sides. No easy feat, considering he had Ryan on him, riding piggyback.

"Thank you, brother," I said as I stood. "Everyone in?" I got confirmation of that comforting fact, at least we were all in the scrap-pine mobile coffin. I grabbed my handholds in an attempt to ease BT and Tommy's burden. The zombies might be smarter, but they hadn't yet figured out this new twist, like covering a cat treat with a cup. They were scouring the main floor for the food they just absolutely knew was there. The ones streaming in had even fewer clues but that didn't stop them; they could smell us and forcing them back out so we could leave was going to be the hard part. It was like we had thrown open the doors at Walmart and dived behind a crate of cheese puffs on Black Friday when there were only five, sixty-inch televisions for two hundred and fifty bucks. Let the games begin.

"TV's are gone, motherfuckers!" I shouted as I strained to push the shoppers out.

"What the fuck are you talking about?" BT was able to grit out.

We were all too busy straining against the tide to talk anymore. It was like fighting a rip current, no matter how hard we paddled, we made little to no headway and, in fact, seemed to be going backward.

"Stop. Everyone stop. We let them flood in until the point of saturation." I said.

There were moans and groans as we set the box down and even the zombies got in on it, making sounds, I mean. We stayed quiet. There were curious zombies, but I think for the most part they really didn't know what to think. None were making any concerted effort to get in at us. That would change when that chair sitting motherfucker made his way down here, yeah, that one would know what was up. Maybe he'd get close enough I could point a pistol out through a small opening and liberate him from his oversized britches. It took a good hour until the house reached an equilibrium; no zombies were trying to get in or out. We had some in front of us, though I was pretty sure we would be able to push them out of the way easy enough.

"Ready?" I whispered. We lifted the tank up, that got the natives interested, either the movement or the ability to smell us a little better, as we exposed our legs. We smacked into the first of them, he seemed slightly surprised, but even more oblivious. He did not do much of anything as we forced him along, like maybe he thought it was normal to have walls push you around, or who knows? Maybe he thought he was the one hitting us. The second zombie we encountered was compliant as well. In fact, they all seemed to go with the flow, it was just that we were racking up the numbers as we walked into ever more congested areas and soon we would not have the momentum or strength to push our way through.

There were a few brief moments when it appeared the belly of the beast might be a tad too big to make it out the door. BT's front cleared with an inch to spare but that amount was rapidly diminishing as we got to my holding point. We didn't have a T-square, alright? Maybe with some speed built up we could have shaved wood off the box and the doorframe but as it was, we were wedged tight.

"Come on!" BT urged through gritted teeth.

He was trying to force us through, but I wasn't certain that was the best idea. Maybe I'd get through, but if the crate got progressively wider as it went, we were going to be stuck even worse, unable to go either way. Tommy must have realized that too, because not only had he stopped but was actively pulling backward. The premium wood we'd used was beginning to protest the undue stresses it was being exposed to.

"Stop. Both of you stop," I said just loud enough to be heard over the creaks of the box. The zombies were becoming increasingly curious about our little hideaway and the reason why had crossed the room. The brains of the outfit had come to investigate and he saw right through our ploy. You can generally pull good and bad out of any situation, and this one was no exception. There were nuances to his groans that could imply speech, or communication of some sort, because immediately, all the zombies in the room began to slowly turn our way. Their gauzed over eyes flared illumination of understanding that their sustenance was hiding right there in front of them. We could hear the collective "Aha!" That was the bad, yeah, definitely the bad. The good was that the mad rush to get at us pushed us through the opening like a champagne cork coming loose. Of course, we headed right back into bad. BT had not been prepared to get pushed out quite so quickly and misjudged the first step. He spilled down the stairs; the front end of the tank nosedived. BT rolled clear, but barely. The front end missed crushing his head by the slimmest of margins.

Should have had a glimmer of good here to offset the bad. We didn't. BT's only avenue of escape was to jump up on top of the tank. The thing had been arm-achingly heavy when he was on the inside helping heave it; with him on top, it might as well have been anchored to the ground. I wanted to yell at him to get the fuck off, but where was he going to go? I had my head back, cords on my neck pulsing out, teeth clamped tight in a grimace, and my arms burned as I did my damndest to get that thing up off the ground. I don't know who was up front attempting to pick up the slack, but we were slightly winning the war on gravity. Had the stupid box an inch or two above the ground. If we so much as ran into a rock it would halt what glacial pace we were making. Maybe a decent portion of the zombies still weren't sure about the moving block, but the delicious entrée being presented on top? Yeah, they were all about that. Suddenly we had become a dessert cart. In addition to trying to hold the thing up and keep moving, we were being jostled like seafarers in a hurricane. With so many zombies closing in, BT was forced to stand up. His arms were out like he was surfing, only with almost zero forward momentum, it was like balancing on a board in a slow river during a hippo stampede. I was still waiting for the good to emerge from this enormous, steaming pile of corn-crusted shit we had stepped in.

What we needed was a high-pressure water hose to clean off all our footwear and clear the sludge away; we got a lead hose, as luck would have it. The good had finally cropped up in the form of a large SUV and a machine gun-firing passenger. Sanders was driving and was backing up toward us. The rear end of the truck was taking damage as he just mowed over zombies like a combine to corn. He cut a path right to us.

"The latch is broken!" BT said as he reached down and tried to open it up.

"Break the glass!" Sanders yelled over the roar of the rifle.

I'd not been expecting the big man to go all PCP-crazed on the heavy glass but he did, rearing back and punching through like he had a hammer wrapped in his hand. I was figuring he was going to pull back a bloodied and mangled tangle of flesh and bone, but apparently, he'd done this before; he had a small scrape on his left-hand pinkie finger, could have been a hangnail for all the trouble it was causing. By now we'd let the box down, the trick was how were we going to get out from under it and into the back of the SUV, seems BT had the cure for that. Got to admit when I picked him as a friend I definitely got the better end of the exchange. He also recognized our dilemma and grabbed the pallet in front of him. At first, I didn't figure there was any way he could pull it loose from the nails; when I started to hear the high-pitched squeal and squelch as metal was yanked loose, I finally began to figure out what he was doing and that it could work and I moved to help him, placing my back against the pallet and pushing up in concert to his movements. We had two of the three inches of the nail exposed.

"BT stop!" I had to shout to get his attention.

"What Talbot!" He wasn't having any of it.

"We're about loose, you want to go hurtling into the zombies again?"

He eased up, realizing I was right. He peeled the top off like a Tupperware lid and tossed it like a huge square frisbee with nails in it onto a couple of zombies; it crushed the skull of one unsuspecting zee, got to figure one doesn't expect to be done in by flying pallets. I started handing him people as fast as I could reach out and grab them, he was tossing them into the back of the SUV like one might sacks of potatoes. The zombies were pressing in on the far side of our people-shipper, and we were pinned against the car up front. The jaws of the vice were closing in, beginning to crush us. The wood creaked and complained at first but this quickly gave way to cracking and splintering. Without that fifth side to brace our construction, we were just a tea-crate in a damned trash compactor. Finally, I could say I knew exactly what Luke's team had felt like on the Death Star, but there was no droid we could call to shut it down.

"We're it, Mr. T," Tommy said as he assisted me up. BT shoved me over and in; I pitched forward and Travis then yanked me the rest of the way through. "Go, BT!" I heard Tommy shout as one side of the tank finally caved in. Tommy's exit had just been pinched shut. BT had lost all balance with the collapse; he was hanging half in the bed and holding onto the crumbling tank, still reaching for Tommy. I had grabbed ahold of his belt and was tugging him through, he had been rocking with the tank and was in danger of falling out into the throng. Travis and I both struggled to pull him back.

"Tommy's stuck!" he cried out. The cracking sounds of the pallet box breaking were directly competing against the sounds of bullets being fired, and in some cases the wood was winning. Tommy's livable space inside was shrinking rapidly. In direct contrast to the rest of us watching, he seemed serene; he was waiting for an opportunity, a split-second window, which was coming at him at breakneck speed. Once the wood structure finally gave out, he was all action, moving with a speed that defied the senses. He launched through the back window like he'd been shot from one of those spring-loaded circus cannons. I'd pay to see them used to send the clowns into a wall embedded with spikes. Comparatively, Tommy had a soft landing, at the expense of the rest of us, that is.

"GO!" I shouted to Sanders who needed no further prompting. "Glad to see you guys," I told him. We were crammed into the car but it was worlds better than our previous ride; just feeling movement under us was space-age. Unlike the Flintstones, we didn't need to carry this one—sure could go for a rack of those Brontosaurus ribs right about now. Sorry, *brachio*saurus ribs.

Sanders told us we were racing back to the safe house and that, yes, everyone there was safe. Words couldn't even begin to explain the relief I had. BT clapped me on the shoulder, a big smile on his face.

"After what we just went through you're already smiling?" I asked him.

"This?" he asked, pointing to his face. "Oh hell no. This is what fear, anxiety and a heaping helping of relief looks like— and maybe some gas."

"Not packed in like this; don't do it," Travis begged.

"Well, for you and your aunt, I'll refrain."

"Consummate gentleman," I said. "Hey Sanders, not to minimize your awesome and timely rescue, but I figure finding us wasn't all that difficult. What I want to know is how did you get away from the initial zombies?"

Sanders looked over to Biddeford; there was a knowing exchange, though neither said anything.

"Why aren't they saying anything?" BT asked me in a stage whisper. I shook my head, I didn't know why either. When we got to the house, their methods were painfully obvious. Deneaux, that sallow, smoke-sucking succubus was on the porch, head slightly back as she plumed poisonous fumes like a volcano on the verge of erupting.

I couldn't get out of the car fast enough—had to push my way past two bodies in an effort to do so. Sanders was already out, doing his best to keep me from getting my weapon into the ready position. Biddeford helped his Major as I was about losing my shit in an effort to kill her.

"Let me go! I am going to rip her charcoal corrupted lungs right from her body!" I shouted.

BT was out now as well, indecisive on whether to help Sanders or me.

"Hello, Michael. What's with the theatrics?" she asked.

"Theatrics? You crazy bitch. You threatened to withhold help if…" I faltered. Sanders and his team didn't know about my condition, and I didn't think this was the time or the place, even if such a time or place existed, to reveal that.

"What Michael, what exactly did I hold out help for?" She had a twinkle in her eyes as she rested against the porch support column.

I changed tactics immediately. "Knox had her. No way he just let her go, she was too valuable. If she's here that means he knows we're here. We need to get rid of her, dispose of the body. The three Bs for sure!" I was hopped up.

"Three Bs?" BT asked.

"Behead, burn, and bury. Then, and only then, will we be sure that monster is dead."

"Monster? Which one of us is actually closer to that distinction?" She lit another smoke.

"What is she talking about?" Sanders asked looking at me.

"Nothing, forget it," I said as I shrugged him off. I brushed by him, though he stayed apace as I approached the house, fearful I might take a swing at Deneaux as I went past, and he was right to do so. At first, I hadn't wanted anything to do with her, but the closer I got and the smugger that pucker on her face got, the more I wanted to rip her throat out or something equally as disgusting and painful and damn the consequences. She nonchalantly tapped her ashes on the porch as I stomped past. When I walked into the house, Kylie was in the kitchen coming out with some water bottles.

"She's downstairs," she said when she saw me. "Her mother may have had a stroke."

All thoughts of Deneaux were flushed down the toilet. I had Kylie point me where I needed to go and I raced to get there. Tracy looked up when she saw me coming; tears streaked her face. Kylie made it sound like there was doubt about the prognosis; there wasn't. Half of Carol's face was slack, her mouth pulled down into a perpetual sneer. Tracy continually wiped away at the spittle that formed there.

"Oh, Mike," she sobbed as she got up to hug me. "I'm so glad you're back." She rested her head on my chest. "Mom isn't weathering this so well."

That was an optimistic viewpoint. She was the grey of forming storm clouds. Her skin looked ashen, her breathing, thready at best.

"How long?" I asked.

"She fell yesterday. I don't know if striking her head caused it, or the fall happened because of it."

Didn't matter much. She'd needed a real hospital hours ago for any attempt to mitigate the damage. Now? I doubted a recovery of any substantiation was possible. Moving her was out of the question; she would never survive on the road. Staying here wasn't the best-case scenario either; there were still thousands upon thousands of zombies a few miles from here.

"I'm sorry to interrupt," Biddeford said from the bottom of the stairs. "I was going to be a medic, once upon a time." We looked at him. "I know Kylie was down here earlier do you mind if I take a look?"

I looked to Tracy, she nodded.

He spent a few moments checking her pulse, shining a light into her eyes, reflexes, that kind of thing. I took Tracy upstairs so she could get a drink of water and maybe a couple of hours rest.

"I'll watch her, won't leave her side," I told her, and I meant it.

"How's she holding up?" BT asked before I went back downstairs.

"Tracy's a wreck and Carol is worse," I said honestly.

"You want me to kill Deneaux?" He wasn't kidding.

"No, wait for me. I want in on it."

"Fair enough," he said.

Biddeford was waiting for me when I came back down.

"I talked it over with Kylie, it's not good. We were hoping it was a mini-stroke or a warning stroke, as they call them, but looks like she had a full-blown hemorrhagic stroke. Maybe, *maybe* if she'd had it in a fully staffed hospital that deals with these things, she'd get a fair amount of her strength and faculties back after some serious rehab. But now…" He left it there. Really what more could he say?

"Thank you," I told him before he went back up. I walked over to sit in the chair Tracy had been in. I reached out and grabbed Carol's hand. Like I'd sent an electrical current into her, she gripped my hand tight, her right eye opened wide, the left lid drooped more than halfway down giving her a simultaneously sleepy, surprised look. She tugged gently on my hand, meaning she wanted me to come closer.

Her words slurred to the point of non-recognition; in honor of her, I will not write down how she said it, but rather what I interrupted it as. "How bad?"

I cried. I couldn't even manage one fucking consoling word; I cried. My world, the entire world, was crashing down on me. Loss is a part of life; they go hand in hand, but how much can one person be expected to burden? I once read a comforting poster that said God does not give us more than he knows we can handle. Right now, I wanted to burn that poster because I definitely could not take anymore. I'd been riding an edge for a good long while now, and every loss cuts me that much deeper. I'm not in danger of falling into the abyss, no, my real danger is that I'm going to be completely cut in half.

"That bad?" She attempted a smile.

"Oh, mom," I told her. "I remember the look you gave me when Tracy brought me to meet you. Guarded, but hopeful, I guess. Then I made a complete ass out of myself and instead of you rejecting me outright, you said you found it endearing that I was trying so hard."

"You're a good son." I don't know if she meant to add the in-law part or not, but just that sentence took most of her energy to finally get out. "Good father," she added.

"I heard horror stories from my siblings, from those I worked with, friends, about mother-in-laws. I never once got that vibe from you. We talked football–sure you were a Broncos fan–but I never held that against you."

She cough-laughed.

"We drank together; I loved when you came with us and the kids up to the mountains for vacation, never thought it was a burden. And the kids." I cried again. They were going to be devastated.

"I'll be alright." She squeezed my hand tight. "I miss Everett," she said, referring to her husband. She smiled again and closed her eyes. My head was bowed, tears falling freely from my eyes. I didn't even hear the kids come down. Nicole was leading the way; by the time she got over to me her eyes were also free-flowing. Travis and Justin were holding back a little, and it was obvious. I'd grown up old school, that a man never shows weakness, doesn't cry, all of that shit, and right now I regretted that they were doing their best to suppress those natural feelings of loss and remorse. Right now, I was hoping to lead by example. Even if I wanted to try and hide it, which I didn't, it couldn't be held. It wasn't long until they joined in. After another ten minutes, I was flushed out. I don't think I could have squeezed one more drop of water from me and my splitting headache let me know that I was on the way to complete dehydration. I needed a minute to collect myself.

"One of you stay with her, I'll be right back." Nicole nodded. I needed fresh air and didn't even think about it as I headed for the front door–I walked into a wall of smoke. Deneaux had not moved from her spot since we'd come back. She was in danger of being buried alive from the volume of cigarette butts she'd deposited around her. Looked like she was trying to recreate the Great Wall of China one used filter at a time.

She said nothing, though I could feel her eyes on me. Was expecting something cynical or crass. Odds were, she could tell I was near to snapping and she didn't want to be the recipient. I headed down the end of the walkway and sat on the curb, stretched my legs out onto the roadway. I let the sun shine on me for a while as I dried out my sinuses.

"What do you want?" I said, when I realized she had moved behind me. Would have been hard to miss the stale smell that emanated from her clothing. Well, that, and she was casting a shadow onto the road.

"I was never in league with Knox."

"Speaking of which, how are you here? You a spy now?"

"Oh heavens no. I keyed in a self-destruct code into the module when it was time to update the password."

I turned to look at her; not sure why. I've said it before. She was entirely too adept at lying for me to ever pick up any sort of visual clue or ever trust a damn thing she said. "Seems to me he would have killed you for that."

"I set a timer for eight hours later. He shot the man that was using it at the time; figured it was his fault."

"And when he had no more use for you, he just let you go? Doesn't much seem like him."

"I convinced him to give me a chance. He dropped me close to the zombie front lines."

"You couldn't have just been killed and saved us all the trouble?"

"I'm your friend, Michael. One of the best you have."

I snorted; it was involuntary. Her words caused a gust of wind to push past my diaphragm and through my throat and nose.

"No. You killed one of my best friends, that I remember. Then you threatened the safety of my family if I didn't capitulate and make you a vampire."

She took a heavy drag on her cigarette, maybe making sure she collected her thoughts, realizing that I still might kill her just to be done with it. "I was merely testing you, seeing what you would say. I had plenty of time to take care of those that were threatening them."

"You're shitting me, right? This is pretty thin even for you, Deneaux. Your lies are usually much more protected than that. What? Thinking on the fly, are you? Don't you remember? I was on the other side of that radio conversation. I heard the lust in your words, that perfect timing of your ultimatum. You weren't faking. What if I'd said no? Would you have packed up your rifle and gone to California like you wanted to?"

She finished her cigarette before she sat down next to me.

"Fine. I wanted to be immortal. Who wouldn't?"

"I could think of one," I said. "I'm sitting here right now wondering not just if I should kill you, but how. Nothing drawn out and painful like you deserve, but just stand up, walk behind you, grab your head and snap that neck of yours. Can't imagine it would be that difficult." I shifted because the concrete curb was hurting my ass—Deneaux actually flinched. Probably thinking I had decided to do just that. I'll admit it, her discomfort gave me satisfaction.

"I would have helped them no matter what. I don't know why I find myself so drawn to the Talbot clan—I don't. I've thought about it a lot. Why we were both in that God-forsaken townhome community together, how we've survived over all others. Most of all why, after the two times I have attempted to separate from you, we are always drawn close again. There's a reason; I'm certain of it. If I could take back the wrongs I have committed against you, I would."

"That's the truth?" I wasn't looking at her; what was the point?

"Possibly the most truthful thing I have said in many years."

"Yet my family was captured."

"Not sure what I have to do to prove my loyalty, Michael." She loosened the belt that held up her pants and began to pull up on her shirt.

"What the hell are you doing?" Before I could finish that sentence, she had revealed a blue and blackened area that traveled up from her thigh to the top of her ribcage.

"Holy shit," I said, looking at the discolored mass of misery she had. "What the hell does that prove? We've all been injured."

She sighed. "I killed three of the degenerates that were going to do harm to your family before one of them had snuck up on my location. This is the result of a kick to the side. He cracked two of my ribs." She then grabbed my hand and made me reluctantly touch a goose egg on the top of her head. "That is where he brought the stock of his rifle down. My understanding, while I was out cold, was that Knox had come on the scene, and instead of killing us all, thought better of it and was going to use us to flush you out. I could not prevent their capture, but I am completely convinced I saved them. If not for my actions, well, your wife's virtue may not be intact, much less her face."

Even if I had witnessed the event myself, I would always harbor doubt for anything Deneaux said. Yet there was evidence...but evidence isn't fact. Had she manipulated the evidence to appear to corroborate her story, or had it really happened that way? No way to be sure. "I...I don't know what to say. If that's how it happened, then, thank you."

She nodded. She had to understand that what she said was always going to be colored by distrust in my eyes, but I think she was satisfied with my qualified gratitude.

We sat in silence for the duration of three cigarettes. "How's Carol?" she finally asked.

"Please don't take the caring too far. It makes you seem

like you are no longer portraying your character in earnest."

"Fine. I'm sure you know why I'm asking. I did not want to come across as unsympathetic, but we will not be able to stay here much longer. The zombies or Knox or both will be back soon."

"Ah, there's Deneaux! So, you want to know if she's going to die soon or what, so we can get going. I don't know the answer to that. My guess is she's never leaving this place."

"And what about those of us that can?"

"Don't." I stood up. "I'm well aware of the risks and dangers of staying here. I don't need you whispering in my ear about it, about how surviving is paramount, about how I have to be vigilant with the rest of my family. I'm well aware. We've already come to common ground that we're both survivors. I will take whatever steps are necessary to ensure that for me and mine; don't push me on this one." I went back into the house, BT was standing in the doorway. "By the way," I said over my shoulder, "feel free to go it alone if that doesn't suit you."

"Can I kill her now?" he asked.

"Have at it." He seemed pretty confused as I walked past and back downstairs.

CHAPTER TEN
MIKE JOURNAL ENTRY 10

SANDERS CAME DOWNSTAIRS to pay his respects and then motioned for me to come to the other side of the room. "Biddie says the zombies have pulled back and we have an opportunity to get the rest of your people. We're gearing up, wanted to know if you wanted to come."

"Let me get my stuff. Nothing I can do here except be in the way." I downed three bottles of water in record time. As I loaded some magazines, I could feel it sloshing around in my belly. It did little to quell the hunger, but the thirst was sated. Sanders, Biddeford, Winters, and BT were all on the porch when I got there.

"You can sit this one out," I said to my friend.

"I'll sit this one out when you do," he said.

"Thanks, man."

We were cautious as we headed out but made great time; didn't encounter the slightest bit of resistance. Looking back, it was *too* good. The world wasn't built for "too good" anymore. In regular life, I was a fairly optimistic man, but I had a pessimistic streak as well; call it skeptical, I guess. I don't know if that was normal or not; I never asked anyone. But I was always on edge, slightly fearful when good things happened in life because things have to balance-out, right? For every good, there has to be bad, doesn't there? Yin and yang and all that shit? I mean how much does it suck to always be looking up, unable to enjoy the scenery because you're wondering when that other shoe was going to drop?

Biddeford was point, not more than twenty-five feet ahead. He raised a fist in the air for us to stop as he approached the house where we'd left Trip. I could see blood on the porch and the front door had been ripped from its hinges; the frame a jagged mess of splinters.

"Bulkers," BT said softly.

My heart was thumping. My first instinct was to rush in. Sanders saw me out of the corner of his eye as I crept up and put his arm out gently.

"Let him do his job, Talbot," he said.

Biddeford went up the steps slowly, tactically, rifle pressed against his shoulder. He was peering through his red dot scope, legs bent. He was swallowed up in the darkness of the foyer of what I was now convinced was a death trap. He came out five minutes later, though it felt like two hours. He was alone; he shook his head from side to side. Whatever hope I had been clinging to was ripped free from me. My head sagged.

"Fuck," was all I could mutter.

"Talbot, BT, I don't know if you're going to want to see this or not," Biddeford said as Sanders and Winters went toward the house.

I had to. It was my way of paying some respect of a sort. The inside of the house was destroyed, furniture splintered, windows broken, carpet torn up; the floors were soaked in blood. Dozens of zombies had been killed—bodies were strewn everywhere. The fighting had been intense—something I would not think the people who had taken temporary residence here could have ever mustered. Blood streaked the walls and dripped from the ceiling. The front door looked bad, but the safe room door was just gone, the wall around it having been pressed in from the attack. The house already looked like a horror show; the safe room appeared to be something straight from hell. Expended brass casings, blood, zombie heads and unidentifiable body parts. I dared not look under the dead for fear of what I would find. The world began to close in on me, my peripheral vision narrowed as my brain was overwhelmed. BT caught me before I could fall onto the mass. He dragged me out of the house with me doing the minimum to help.

He said nothing as he gently helped me sit on the lawn.

"How's he doing?" Sanders asked. He had come out a few minutes later.

"I'm…well, I'm not 'fine.' Don't think I'll ever be fine again, but not going to pass out, if that's what you mean." I was physically ill. If I could have vomited up every distasteful thing I had ever witnessed, I would have done so—even if it cost me my life.

"I'm not sure how to say this, so I'm just going to do it," Sanders said. "They're not all dead. Because of the well…carnage…and it's impossible to say who, but Biddeford is confident some of them may have made it out."

I turned away. A long, thick, ropy column of puke-water shot forth from my mouth. My stomach, my throat, my head were ablaze. And fuck the other shoe dropping, a steel toe boot hit me square in the face. I had just laid back as Travis and Tommy came running up.

"Grandma's getting worse," he said in a rush.

Getting back to the safe house was a blur. For safety reasons, I had pulled my consciousness as far back into myself as I could. It's a technique useful for just letting my body function to get me from point A to point B.

Carol died later that same night. It was as peaceful a passing as I'd seen in a good long while, not that this made it better, not at all, just different. Well, maybe a little better; we'd been prepared, and her family was with her. There was a small park, two streets over; dug as deep a hole as we could before gently placing her in the ground. More guns were there than any ceremony for a slain officer, though we didn't fire a salute. The zombies had decided to not crash the funeral, must have heard there wasn't a buffet. Tracy was a fucking mess; the kids little better. I'd like to say I picked up the slack this time because if it seems like I'm the one that stands firm, it's only with Tracy's support that I do so. In that absence, I think I did alright. There was a lot of heavy lifting to be done, and though I wasn't up for the task, auto-pilot kicked in. I went through the motions; that was the best I could come up with. Thankfully, the zombies, for some unforeseen reason, were gone for the night, though we couldn't hold that as any sort of guarantee.

BT and I had spent most of the next day looking for any sign of Trip or any occupants that had survived the slaughter box of a bunker. Nothing. No sign of them anywhere. Even just an ill-placed snack cake wrapper and I would have lobbied to stay and look for them longer. We had to assume that they had either got away, as unlikely as that seemed, and were waiting at a rallying point or, well, you know, been dragged down at a different spot. In terms of a fighting force, the people in that bunker were ill-prepared and would not have stood much of a chance, hell, that's why we left them in the bunker. Yet there was ample evidence that they had fought with an unbridled fury. I had left them there to die, and Trip's look...he had known. Why hadn't he said something? I'd killed them. My decisions had killed them; I was convinced of it. I had placed my brother's kids in there. Ron's entire family had been reduced to Meredith. A sob escaped my lips as I thought on how close I had been to putting Nicole and my grandson in that room. But I didn't. Had I known all along? Had I sacrificed some to save others? I looked at the muzzle of my rifle, wondered for a moment what lead might taste like.

"Whatever the fuck is going on in that head of yours drop it. I'm telling you to just drop it," BT said.

"Easier said than done, brother."

He uncharacteristically hugged me roughly. "We'll make it through this." He held me at arm's length like a little kid. "Let me hear you say it. Talbot—say it." He prodded my silence. "We'll stay like this forever if we have to. Your wife, your sister, they'll miss us both greatly, I'm sure, but I'm not moving until you say it."

Tears streamed down my face. "We'll make it through," I finally told him.

He hugged me tight again. "Damn right we will." I could feel his hot tears trail down my neck.

Carol's death was crushing. That, coupled with the potential loss of seven more, I began to continually question my decision to leave Ron's. I couldn't help it. We would have been surrounded, but we still would have been entrenched. One thing I had learned in the Marines: it is infinitely better to hold a great defensive position than spread out looking for something better. I knew that, and I had failed my platoon.

"What do you think, Mike?" BT asked as we watched the sun begin its descent. We'd got as close to the zombie line as we dared.

"We go back. I'll talk to Tracy, but I think tomorrow we should leave."

"How did this get so fucked up?" He asked. "We were doing alright and then it just kind of all went to shit. I can't stand Trip but I would have never wanted this for him." He was close to tears. We were all riding that particular train and it didn't appear to have any stops in the foreseeable future. I was so defeated, I hadn't looked up from my feet the entire walk back. If it wasn't for BT, I would have walked into multiple obstacles. Travis gave a small wave from an upstairs window as we approached. Nobody asked if we'd seen anything, I telegraphed the answer in my mannerisms.

Tracy merely nodded. Her red-rimmed eyes met mine when I suggested we leave in the morning. The only surprise we had was that Winters and Kylie's sister, Brooke, wanted to come with us. Even as I welcomed Winters' expertise, I dreaded the thought of adding any more responsibility to my shoulders. I had failed in that aspect; maybe I was just carrying too much. I had done everything I knew how to do to ensure the safety of those around me and had come up wanting.

Deneaux was outside early that morning–surprisingly, she was without a cigarette. There was a nip in the air I found refreshing; it woke me up immediately and let me know I was still alive.

"Michael," she said, a plume of cool air coming from her mouth.

"No cigarette?"

She stink-eyed me. "You might find this strange, but…I'm thinking of quitting."

I thought she was screwing with me. It was more likely Trip would give up weed than Deneaux would her smokes. "You're serious?" I asked after a moment.

"One can't normally live forever," she said. "The more I thought about having you bite me, the more I thought about my own mortality."

"I'm not sure I'm up for another existential moment with you."

"Too bad. Perhaps you might have learned a thing or two."

"I do have a question; it's been bothering me for a while and since you were with Knox…"

"I was not *with* Knox," she corrected me.

"Yeah, you said that. Highly uncharacteristic of him to let you go."

"He let you go, did he not?"

She had me there.

"He is truly interested in watching what others will do in a given situation. It's similar to reality television for him. Will they rise or fall to any given obstacle; will they ally or betray; who will emerge on top, that sort of thing. He was a psychiatrist before this happened, if you can believe that. He is very much into studying the human condition. How do you think a madman was able to start his own army?" She asked.

I'd read that shrinks were among some of the most troubled people on the planet; I can't imagine how they couldn't be, listening to other fucked up people's lives eight hours a day, five days a week. I would think you'd take on more psychoses than you could prescribe away. None of that mattered; unless we could outwit him with his own ego.

"Look, Deneaux. I want to know how he has been keeping tabs on us. If he had his own access to a satellite device, he would not have needed ours...or you, for that matter," I said.

"You do not know? Really? You are not thinking this through. He has helicopters; does he not?"

I feel like I would have noticed a chopper up on the sky, or at least heard it. But a plane flying high enough? Could have easily missed that. Wasn't much reason to look up these days; the enemy was on the ground. Looking up only gave them more of an opportunity to get at you.

"Planes. He has planes," I finally said.

"Two Cessna Skylarks and a Lear, I believe."

"The zombies?" I asked.

"What of the beasts?" she asked.

"Does he control them?"

"Humph," she half-cackled. "I doubt it. He is no Eliza. Speak of the devil...have you considered that it is possibly Tomas that draws them to you?" She arched an eyebrow.

"Don't. I fucking knew it. Don't even try and place wedges where none need to be. If I imagined I had a dangerous adversary in my ranks, it would be you. In any case, I wouldn't look to you for an alliance."

She shrugged and reached for a lighter she no longer carried. "I am merely citing the fact that Eliza was a vampire and she had control over zombies. Does it not make sense that her brother would have the same influence? Or you yourself, for that matter? I'm not suggesting it is even a conscious effort on either of your parts, but rather you ping off their sonar like a nuclear sub with fangs."

"You always make me feel my best." I walked away from her to help the others as we packed some provisions into the large SUVs we had rounded up.

"Just because you don't like it doesn't mean it's not true," she said to my back. I did the only thing afforded to me; I flipped her off.

We said our goodbyes and I thanked Sanders, his wife, and Biddeford profusely for their help.

"If you change your mind, you know where we're going," I told Sanders. I hoped I wouldn't have to repeat that speech ever again–just meant we were leaving more good people behind.

We had driven for about four hundred miles. I'd never been on a quieter jaunt in my entire life, even when I was alone. There was no music, no talking, thankfully minimal crying. When an occasional cough came, it was startling to the senses, sending a jolt of adrenaline through the system. I found myself periodically looking up for some sign of Knox's aerial reconnaissance; never saw them, if he was still out there. The sun was beginning its downward trend and I could barely keep my eyes open from the lack of outside stimulus. I would imagine this was a lot like what deprivation chambers felt like; wouldn't doubt if I began to hallucinate, or at least get road hypnotized. Seemed like the right place to do it as we rolled into Gettysburg. The place was deserted–like, I'm talking nuclear reactor melt-down deserted. No people, no zombies, no animals, no nothing. It was eerier than it had a right to be. Although, maybe all those Civil War soldiers were finally getting the peace and quiet they had so brutally earned all those years ago, free from the battle scavengers, then the war re-enactors, and finally, the legions of tourists that came to have their photos taken at the gravesite of the worst loss of life on American soil. Well, I mean, up until very recently, that is.

Looked like we had our pick of places to spend the night. I settled on the Inn at Cemetery Hill; wasn't as keen on the name as I was the building itself. It was a solid brick mansion that had been converted into an inn. At the moment, it did not appear that we would need to actively defend it; it looked stout enough that if it came to it, I did not think bulkers would be able to break through the walls. I watched as everyone got out of the cars, heads bowed, shoulders sagging, we were the defeated but not the dead, not quite yet.

"Winters, you help me do a quick check inside?" I asked. He nodded.

"BT, you keep an eye on the outside?"

"Yeah, I've got it," he said.

Twenty-five minutes later, Winters and I came out. The inn was as empty as the rest of the town. Well, not really. I was carrying a case of Moosehead beer on my shoulder. I cracked the box open and tossed a beer to Winters and BT. Justin and Travis came up just as I was popping the top off one for myself. There wasn't anyone, save the little kids that didn't grab one. I sat down on one of the many benches that were on the large, wraparound porch.

"Can't believe you found a case of beer in there," BT said as he sat down on the bench next to mine.

"Not just one," I said, tipping my beer to him. "I don't know what convention they were about to have come into town, but the bar is stocked and so is the holding room and the kitchen. There's a ton of stuff. The meat and anything else in the walk-in freezer is bad, but they have shelves and shelves of canned goods. I'm going to talk to Tracy and everyone else, but I'm going to advocate that we stay here for a while."

"You sure, Mike?"

"I think we need this. You saw this town; there's nothing for days. I don't know why that is," I said, briefly looking skyward for the shoe. I shrugged it off in favor of another beer. "Maybe we're finally catching a break. A minute to recharge and regroup—get our minds screwed back on."

"Well, at least the rest of us can. Yours was barely on before this shit started. I would imagine your threads are all rusted out by now, maybe even stripped. Never be able to seat it right. It's probably just sitting up there hanging by one twist. Stiff breeze would knock it down."

"You done?"

"You serious…about staying, I mean?"

"I am, buddy."

"How much booze did you say there was?"

"More than we could drink in a good long while."

"And you haven't considered the as of yet unseen reason why this is a ghost town?" he asked.

"Of course, but, and I can't believe I'm going to say this and I don't even know if it's believable, but what if no one is here, including the zombies, because this place is so damn haunted?"

"Like Amityville Horror haunted or Casper haunted?"

"Don't know, maybe both?"

"Part of me loves the idea of staying here for a little while…but I gotta say I'm not looking forward to finding out why everything is pristine."

"That's the spirit," I said.

"Did you mean the pun?"

"Pun?" I smiled.

CHAPTER ELEVEN.
MIKE JOURNAL ENTRY 11

ONE DAY TURNED to two, then a week, then a month, finally we were pushing two months in one place. No Knox, no zombies, no vampires, and more importantly, no fucking death. That first week I did a steady diet of beer and Vodka and maybe a giant can or two of beans. Not a great mix, and truth be told, I can't stand beans. Weird what you want to eat when you're fucked up. If we weren't all so busy healing, it would have been a damn near perfect vacation. Room service was a little spotty, though. I spent a lot of time wandering around the battlefields. Strange sensation being there. Could just about feel the ghosts of the dead soldiers swirling about as you walked among fields. It didn't help that more times than not there would be a thin mist coating the entire place like they were congregating. I wondered if other places around the world had the same phenomenon; did the beaches in Normandy feel this way? Waterloo, Stalingrad? So many lives lost, their bodies on the ground before most even realized they'd passed over–that had to do something to a soul, didn't it? Can't imagine how much it would suck being confused that you were actually dead, seeing your own face in the dirt…I could see how one could just remain stuck in easily one of the worst times in your life. Still, though, I found solace among those poor, tortured men. Felt that I had a connection. I'd seen people fall; the shock. And maybe I wasn't completely dead, but parts of me were. We shared that kinship.

"Weird place, isn't it?" BT asked as he came up alongside me. He was holding out a new bottle of vodka.

"It is, and didn't you hear me this morning? I said I wasn't drinking ever again."

"I figured you meant until noon. Then the clock resets."

"My insides are begging me to stop."

"Who you going to listen to? That weak-ass stomach of yours or the man with the hootch?" He was still holding the bottle out.

"Is this peer pressure? Because if I go back to the Inn today shittied again, I want to be able to tell Tracy I was forced."

"Call it whatever you want." He pulled the bottle in, spun off the top, and took a chug that made it look like he was drinking water. "Ah…smooth," he said in a gravelly voice, as he wiped the sleeve of his free arm across his mouth.

"Yeah, sounds it. This the bottom shelf shit?" I choked out after taking a particularly burning shot. That the bottle was made of plastic should have been my first clue.

"Don't be a candy ass." He took the bottle back and another swig. "Whoo!" he yelled. "If that doesn't make you feel like a man I don't know what does."

"Sex. Yeah, sex makes me feel like a man. Oh. And peeing standing up. That's a pretty big one, too."

We sat on a felled oak; killed half the bottle as we watched the sun climb up the sky.

"I've been here before," BT said after a while. "Linda wanted to see it. Didn't hold much appeal for me then, but…"

"So, you came."

"Of course I did. Lot different back then. More of a tourist trap vibe to it. There were stands that sold food and Chinese-made replicas. Hundreds of people were out here walking around taking thousands of pictures. There was still this strange undercurrent, a feeling that we were intruding on something private, but nothing like it is now. I think if we had a few of Trip's stores we'd be able to watch a battle. That's how close we are to the veil here. I...." He paused. His eyes filled with tears, though they had not fallen yet. "I can't believe I'm going to say this, but I miss that crazy stoner. I miss them all, your brother, Mad Jack, your father, the kids."

I think he would have run through the entire list, but I wasn't up for that. I was doing my best to rebuild the shattered parts of me, I wasn't ready to think on them all just yet, especially on my way to another drunk. I cut him off abruptly and he looked at me knowingly.

"Sorry," he said. "This was a good place to stop. I didn't think so at first. I was worried I wouldn't be able to stop thinking about Linda. But I feel differently now; we're healing up a bit. Putting band-aids on the gaping wounds, maybe throwing a stitch on them to keep them closed. I even have a scab or two."

I agreed, though I didn't say anything. Typical guy. I figured my silence was an affirmation of his words, and like a typical guy, he understood that. Women are wonderful creatures, far superior to men in a countless number of ways. This isn't one of them. More can be said within the silence two men make than the five thousand words two women speak.

"I've got to tell you something, Mike, but I don't know how you're going to feel about it." He paused. I again said nothing, waiting to hear his words. "Your sister..."

"I've already heard about it, man. You've got dibs," I told him.

"No, man. Hear me out. I love her."

Now I turned. I don't know what I thought he was going to say, maybe something like she was a wildcat, and no brother ever wanted to hear those words, but I knew this was different.

"Really, man?" I asked.

"I do, man."

"You realize that's the same woman that tried to cave my skull in with frozen pita bread when I was, like, ten."

"If anything, man, that makes me love her more."

"I'll drink to that," I told him as I took a swig. We were facing toward the Inn and we saw Tracy coming, from a long way off. She had her arms crossed in front of her to ward off the chill in the air, which always seemed to be about ten degrees cooler whenever you stepped onto the battlefield. I had thoughts of hiding the bottle, but that would only piss her off. I reeked of booze and you didn't need to be a cop to realize I shouldn't be operating heavy machinery.

She sat down next to me and grabbed it from my hands; took a longer drag on it than I'd ever seen her drink anything.

I held up the bottle. "Damn, woman! You planning on leaving any for us?"

"This is a strange place," she said, looking out over the grass. "A lot of peace to be found here, considering the events that took place. You think that's why it's so peaceful? Like maybe all the bad that could ever happen here, already has?"

"Shit, that's deep," BT said. "Like maybe this is hallowed ground," he added.

"You tell him?" Tracy asked once again taking the bottle from my hands.

"Just did."

"And?" she asked after she finished drinking.

"If you have kids are they going to be Talbots or Tynes?" I asked.

"Why would I burden them like that?" He smiled. "Anyway, I've got to figure my genes would completely wipe out anything Talbot related."

"Too much information," I told him.

"BT, do you mind if Mike and I have a few minutes?"

"Not at all. Right now, I'm surprisingly ready for a nap." He got up and rubbed his ass. As he started to walk away, he turned. "Your sister is a lot saner than you."

"Yeah, that's what you think. She's just luring you in close so when she springs the crazy-trap there's nowhere for you to go. I'd get out while you still can."

"Fuck you, Mike." He walked away.

I called after him. "And no matter what you think about your over-sized genes, those kids will have Talbot in them and then you get to have mini little berserkers running around. Going to fuck up everything you think you know about kids."

Tracy nodded in agreement. "He's telling the truth, I wish I had been warned."

"Hey." I turned.

We watched as BT crested a small rise and then disappeared.

"How are you doing?" she asked in all seriousness.

"Me? I could ask that about you."

"I'm better. It will be a long process, but I'm better. It's you, Mike, that I'm worried about. You take all of these deaths so personally. Wait, that's not the right word. We all take them personally; these are family and friends so close as to be indistinguishable from each other. What I meant to say is that you take personal responsibility for them. Like, whether we live or die is on you; our lives are your burdens. Maybe you're the de facto leader; we do turn to you when we're in trouble because somehow that crazy, beautiful mind of yours excels in crisis situations." She reached out and held my hand. "But the things that are happening? The people that are dying, those that get hurt; that is not your fault, Michael, and I won't sit around and watch as you beat yourself up about it. The world is a not a good place right now, well, that's an understatement. But the truth is it has always been a little fucked up; always had some less than desirable qualities, basically since the dawn of man. And even before, I'm sure there were asshole dinosaurs as well."

"The Raptors. Yeah, they were the dicks of the dino-world."

"Exactly. Are the stego-slaughters your fault too?"

"So, you're saying that none of this is my fault because raptors were tearing into the flesh of slower prey millions of years ago?"

"Yes. That's exactly what I'm saying. How much of this crap have you had?" She was shaking a three-quarter empty bottle in front of her face. "Listen, you...you dunderhead."

"You make that up?"

"Maybe. And it sounds fitting. Stop. Just stop blaming yourself. Bad things, horrible things are going to happen to people, have always happened to people. It is inevitable, and it is not because of you. Do you understand?"

"So, wait. I'm confused; am I the raptor or not?"

"I think of you more as the caveman with the big hard club. Just shut up and come back to the Inn with me; I thought maybe we could take a nap together."

"I'm not really all that tired."

"Oh my God. When did you get so thick!?"

It dawned on me where she was going with this but I relished the idea of her having to explain it.

"I want you to come and lay with me," she said slowly, raising her eyebrows and enunciating like she was talking to someone who might not have a complete grasp of his faculties. Well, I guess that was the definition of dunderhead.

"Say it," I replied.

"Say it?"

"You heard me."

She looked around, clearly embarrassed.

"They don't care." I was referring to the soldiers.

"I'm not going to."

"Tell me how much you want my pelvic thrust, my buttering of your biscuits, a good old baking of the potato."

"What the hell are you talking about?"

"Come on...a little lust and thrust, bump and grind, icing the cookie." I winked at her.

"You keep going on like that and you're going to be playing solo." She bent low and stood up slowly, making sure I got a good view.

"Not coming until you say it," I smiled.

I waited, she waited. "Fine. I want to get to know you in

the biblical sense." She rolled her eyes as she said it. I didn't move. "Fry the bacon? Grease the pan? Scramble some eggs?"

"Oooh, you dirty girl! I can't believe you kiss your kids with that mouth. Not sure if I want to have sex now or go and eat." I grabbed her and twirled her around. My head and stomach did not thank me for that considering the booze I had circulating throughout my body. Our little horizontal dancing had to wait for a few hours while I slept it off, but it was worth it. As humans, we don't have it all figured out. But lovemaking, true, tender, lovemaking is damn near a reboot on all that ails you.

I was staring up at the ceiling, a sheen of sweat covering my entire body, about as close to bliss as I had been in a while.

"You want to leave," I said. The thought seemingly randomly entered my head; I never figured out how she did that.

"This wasn't some ploy to break it to you, if that's what you mean, but yes. I love it here, I do, but we're no better here than we were at Ron's, isolated and alone. I want to give our kids some chance at normalcy, or at least a re-enacted version of it." She had turned on her side and was rubbing a hand on my chest.

"This place…it's somehow…it's like an oasis in a desert of death. We found this refuge, and we've taken it. But this place itself was a massive killing ground. Makes you think."

"I honestly think we could spend the rest of our lives here unbothered," she said.

They were nice words to hear; I didn't believe them. Oh, I wanted to, but even I'm not that delusional.

"But this," she stroked my hair. "This thing that you and I have, this marriage of mind, soul," she began.

"And body," I finished, pulling her close.

"I want the kids to be able to have that too."

"Mood killer."

"Put that thing away. I'm trying to talk to you."

"Not entirely my fault—look where your hand is."

A little bell went off in my head as we launched into round two.

THE NEXT MORNING, we all got together and talked about it. I couldn't help but notice how much less room we needed now. I was thankful this wasn't a normal meeting spot where I'd have to see all of the empty chairs that would never again be filled up. By the end of the discussion, it was more or less unanimous that we would head out in a couple of days. There was little in the way of dissent, but some were more reluctant to go than others. I mean how could there not be a desire to stay in the relative safety of our new location? After running so hard that we thought our lungs were going to burst, we'd finally been able to stop, to decompress, to catch our breaths and maybe even work some on our morale. Hell, we'd just had canned peaches.

"I'm going to miss this place," BT said. Everyone else had left, most to prepare for the next leg of the journey.

"Me too," I told him. "You think maybe there's the same type of haven at the Battle for Little Bighorn?"

"Maybe, but not for you white people," he said.

I just ignored him. "I mean, so much death maybe keeping a little peace around it?"

"Could be," he said, picking up where I was going. "Pretty much just plains and rolling hills there, I think. Might not be the most comfortable place to set up camp; for sure there won't be a Southern manor house."

"I was just thinking it might be a safe stop along the way."

"You think the world will ever be back to normal?" he asked, completely out of the blue.

"I can barely remember what 'normal' was like. I guess someday, right?"

"You really believe that?" he asked back.

I guess he didn't catch the upward lilt of my words when I answered him with a question. "I want to think it will, BT, you know, or why bother? The real question is, will we ever be back to normal."

"I'm not so worried about us; not sure anyone could ever come back from this. Not fully, I mean. Just too much damage done. We can live *normal* lives." He stressed normal. "Not sure we'll ever completely feel it, though."

"Where you going with this, man? I'm trying to push that from my mind."

"And see, that's the thing. You'll forever carry this around like a heavy suit of armor. No, my hope is we can pass a normal life, or at least a peaceful one, to those that come after us. For our legacy to be able to do great things, unencumbered by the disasters we brought on ourselves."

I was pondering his thoughts when it hit me like a ripped foul ball down the third base line. "No fucking way!" I stood up, pointing a finger at him.

"What the hell are you talking about?" He was looking around with an alarmed expression on his face.

"I can't believe this." I was scratching the back of my head with both hands as I walked across the room away from him.

"Not many people can figure out what's going on in that head of yours, Mike, even with instructions. You want to explain it to me? I left my lunatic to lucid dictionary in my other pants."

"That's what I'm talking about! Maybe you should have kept it in your pants!" I was smiling, maybe there was a veiled threat, but yeah, smiling.

"There's still no dictionary!" He was getting mad.

"Use the first three letters. That's what you should have kept there."

"What the fuck? ABC?" I shook my head and pointed at him. "What the fuck is a d-i-c? Oh, a dick. Yeah. That's what you're being."

"My sister's pregnant, isn't she?"

He reeled back a step like I had throat punched him with the words. "I...I don't even know what you're talking about."

"I'd give you the birds and bees, but we're talking about my sister and, you know, just ewww."

"There's nothing ewww about it!" That step he'd taken backward turned into two forward, and now he was pointing a finger at me.

I was still smiling. "I think the BT doth protest too much."

His finger came down and his head bowed slightly. "I told her I wouldn't say anything. She's going to kill me."

"I don't think my sister is a hundred and ten pounds, what the fuck are you worried about?"

"You seriously did not just say that. Any chance Tracy could beat you in an arm wrestle?"

"Fuck, no."

"Boxing match?"

"I doubt it, but she does have a mean right hook."

"Okay, so, physically, you probably have her, right?"

"Safe to say," I answered in as masculine a way as I could, knowing exactly where we were headed.

"Yet, I've seen you cower from that woman."

"Cower seems like a little much," I said.

"Want me to get her in here and we'll discuss it?"

"Fuck, no."

"You're going to keep your trap shut about this."

"I am?" I asked. "You looked like you had something else to tell me earlier on that log."

"I was drunk, man. I'm fine now and just because your sister can kick my ass, doesn't mean I can't kick yours."

"That's a reasonable assumption," I told him.

"Assumption? That leaves room for doubt."

"Don't worry, man, I won't tell anyone."

"Not even your wife. I'm serious, because you know the first person she'll go to when she finds out."

"Fine, fine, man. Stop posting up on me. I get nervous with your chest in my face. You flex one of those pecs and I'll get a black eye or a broken nose. And for what it's worth, man, I'm thrilled. I know it's a weird guy thing and we don't generally say it to one another. But I love you, man. I do. So much so, I will take only half the normal dowry for my sister. I'd like two goats and a llama."

"Yeah, I love you too, for some unknown reason. And just one goat."

"You can't negotiate a dowry. Two goats or nothing."

"What are you talking about, Mike?" Tracy had come in.

"What did you hear?" BT was doing his best to not look guilty, he was only marginally successful.

"Goats, something about goats." Tracy was looking from me to BT. "Spill it." She wasn't looking at either of us as she waited for an answer.

BT had sweat on his forehead.

"Mike?" Tracy now had me in her crosshairs.

"It's not mine to say," I told her, hoping some childhood honor thing would give me enough of a shield from her.

She sighed and refocused on BT. He was holding firm, though I think he would have cracked soon.

"Is this about Lyndsey's pregnancy?" she asked.

BT looked accusingly at me like he wanted to thump me on the head.

"Wait, man. When the hell did you see me leave this conversation to tell her?"

He was thinking back along the timeline, seeing if there was a way to blame me.

"I'm surprised the two of you know how to put your pants on in the morning. She's been sick every morning for the last week, and I've personally caught her twice with huge cans of green beans eating them as fast as she can get them into her mouth." We just looked at her. "Good lord. Last time I checked, none of the Talbots are all that big on greens. She's absolutely craving them."

"Don't say anything," BT pleaded.

"Of course, But there are pre-natal vitamins we're going to

need to get." She looked at me.

Drug stores and hospitals were bad places to go. Not so hard to believe the number of previously straight people that wanted to chemically check-out during the z-poc. Add into that, the shops were every druggie and junkie's nirvana. Every other group was concerned about band aids, penicillin, and Tylenol...and condoms, the thought occurred. Anyway, the vast majority of times, you could not find anything in there, not even baby aspirin. Compound the likelihood that you weren't going to find anything with the fact that these places were usually ground zero for zombies and the aforementioned druggies, and you had a recipe just waiting to brew disaster.

"I think I have an idea," I said.

"Oh, this ought to be good." BT folded his arms.

"Alright. We all know how shitty hospitals and drug stores can be."

They nodded at my words.

"What if we find some doctor offices? We rifle through the patient records until we find some pregnant patients. It'll list if they've been prescribed the vitamins and then we go to their house."

"It has some salient points." BT said, "but you're presuming that the woman no longer needs her meds."

"It sucks, man, but the reality is that most people don't need much of anything anymore," I said. "We wait until tomorrow. We'll get going early."

It was a little while later; I had been reading a book, of all things. I didn't think I'd ever have enough time for that luxury again. The light was beginning to fail, and I was giving myself a headache straining to see the print on the page. I decided at this point that maybe some outside air would keep away the spike that was about pierce my head. Tommy was on the front porch; he was standing, had a far-off look in his eyes.

"Hey, kid," I said.

He barely acknowledged my presence, if at all. I was heading out to climb a knoll on the far side of the field. I found peace there. Though the thick, swirling mist that was rolling in should have been a deterrent, it wasn't. The only ghosts that were going to hurt me would be the ones of my own creation. The mist eddied around me as I walked to meet it. Its cooling effect chilled me as it rushed past to hide the Inn from me. It should have been eerie, but it wasn't, not then, at least. I kept walking; the mist was getting thicker with each step, thicker than I'd seen it before. It got to the point where I could have been walking amongst the clouds; I could not see my feet touching ground. Right there I started thinking about how bad it would be if the zombies decided to attack. I'd get virtually no warning. This mist was as bad as being in a pitch-dark room, only everything was white instead of black.

"I've been waiting for you," the disembodied voice said. Didn't think it was a Civil War soldier as it was definitely female, and not only female, but it spoke with a European accent.

"Payne." I gripped my rifle tight and brought it halfway up, though there was nothing I could aim at.

"You contain so much power, yet you will not allow yourself to fully realize it. Instead you foolishly rely on others and the crude weapons they create, hoping to keep the monsters at bay."

"What do you want?" I asked, doing my best to find the direction the voice was coming from; it was impossible due to the diffusion the ground cloud was causing.

There was a laugh that carried with it no warmth. It sounded like the sigh of someone long dead, which, in hindsight was a very accurate description.

"At first it was merely curiosity…." She trailed off. I felt a stinging sensation on my left side; I looked down to realize I had been stabbed, just enough to let me know it had happened, to draw first blood, but nothing dangerous yet.

I was in trouble. I felt very much like the mouse this cat was toying with. Three more strikes—so lightning fast I did not even register the pain of the first one until the blade had been removed the third time. As much as I wanted to shoot blindly or to lash out, throwing wild punches, swinging my arms back and forth in a vain attempt to hit the nearly invisible entity that was haunting me, I did not. A part of me knew that to do so would only encourage her, that she would absolutely realize how vulnerable I was. And fuck if I wanted to give her that satisfaction.

"What is it now?" I asked breathlessly, referring to her opening statement, hoping that if she talked, she would be less likely to attack.

Like any woman, though, she was able to multi-task. I was struck a fifth time, a gash appearing along the right side of my face. "Oh well. Curiosity has yielded to revenge. I thought perhaps I had outgrown that particular emotion, that I had changed sufficiently enough that I would not be driven by my baser, former, human instincts. But I was wrong. Poor, sweet, damaged Sophia, I did not love her. I do not think me capable of real love, but I did care for her in a way only a vampire can care for another of its kind. She deserves some measure of remittance, does she not?"

"Take me, have your measure!"

That laughter returned; it chilled far more than the mist. I turned slowly, as it was seemingly all around me.

"You believe yourself worthy of that measure?"

Wisely or not, I said nothing.

"Tomas would be a start to the payment I feel due, but that does not include the damage done to my Charity. Should I hold you accountable for these things, though you had little or no part in them?"

"I am willing to accept my responsibility and all of theirs." I was trying to strike a deal with one that did not appear open to negotiations.

"I could have had any of you at any time. You are not nearly as vigilant as you believe yourselves to be."

She needed to be stopped, I knew where this was going. Seemed vampires liked to hold grudges; she wanted to take vengeance from everything she imagined done to her on those around me. And that I could not allow. I undid the buckle that held my rifle up in its tactical position. I stood up straight, closed my eyes and took in a deep breath. I didn't even know if I could produce a flicker, but it was nigh time to fight fire with fire, if possible. Payne came in again, this wound a little deeper than the others as if she was aware of what I was attempting and didn't like it. That was good for me, to a point. It meant she was concerned, but there was no doubt she could finish me off long before I became a viable threat. Now I could sense her movements within the mist that hid her. I lashed out, mostly missing, but there was some satisfaction to the punch that glanced off the side of her head.

"Ah, there it is!" I could sense she was smiling. "You feel it, don't you? The ancient power, it courses through your veins like an untamed beast, yet you dare to chain it. As if you could!" She came in again, I moved enough to miss the thrust of her blade. There was an "oomph" as I put a foot in her midsection, sending her on her way.

"Leave, Payne. Take what remains of Charity and the zombies and leave. Forget you ever stepped foot in the New World."

"The zombies?" She paused. "What do you believe I have to do with those filthy, living dead things?"

"You don't control them?" I asked.

"I would rather return to the well from which I originated than sully myself with those hideous creatures." Then she laughed. "You don't know, do you? For all your power, you don't!"

"What are you talking about?" I asked, partly because I wanted to know what she knew, but more importantly, this kept her from stabbing me.

"I don't know all, Michael, but someone in your group does. And on some level, you know that as well."

"Mr. T!" Tommy shouted. It sounded like he was approaching, but this fog was making it difficult to tell.

"If you yell out to him, I will kill you and then him. I have no love for the one that betrayed his own sister."

"Now you lie. You don't care. You yourself said vampires are incapable of love; why avenge a death for someone that means nothing?"

"It is not that I cared for Eliza, but a betrayer of one's kind must be taught a lesson. You should heed the words that you and I have spoken, Michael. If you somehow survive me, they may very well revisit you."

"I don't know what are you talking about. I've made no betrayal."

The mist began to recede, giving me more sight-lines. It rolled out like the tide, thankfully, taking Payne with it. When I felt she had gone, I wiped the blood from my face and lifted my shirt to see the five wounds she had given me. I was thinking about what she had said; if vampires were incapable of love, but betrayal and avenging fit in very nicely with their mindsets, Tommy could indeed be dangerous.

"Mr. T! Are you alright?" Tommy asked as he ran toward me.

"You knew, didn't you?" He had a confused look on his face. "You knew she was out here." I let my shirt drop down and picked up my rifle. Adrenaline had been keeping the pain away, but now the cuts throbbed, like anything created by a sharp blade is wont to do.

"I thought she might be," he confessed, "but I wasn't sure."

"A heads-up when I walked by you would have been appreciated."

"When did you walk by me?" he asked. I could not detect any sort of deception in his voice. He must have been focused on something pretty big to have missed me and our greeting.

"The zombies, are they your doing?"

"What?"

"You heard me."

"What did she say?"

"Are you afraid she told me something you don't want me

to know?"

"What are you talking about, Mr.T?" I felt like my own tactics were being used against me.

BT was at a full sprint coming my way, Travis and Justin hot on his heels. Would have been hard not to spot Tommy and I squared off, at least, I was.

"What's going on here?" BT asked breathlessly.

"Ask him. I've got some wounds that need tending." I walked off but not before I caught a shrug from Tommy.

"Dad?" Travis asked.

"I'm alright. Get everyone inside, we have company coming and not the kind we want to entertain."

"Zombies!" Gary yelled from his perch on the roof.

"Son of a bitch," I said under my breath as I turned around. Two lone zombies stood far out in the field looking our way. Scouts. Then a few more marched up; this continued for another half an hour, until there were zombies as far as the eye could see. It looked like we were going to have our own battle here, though I didn't think there would ever be enough people left to come on a pilgrimage and look for trinkets left over. In fact, there might never be anyone to record it. How many massive battles through time must have been waged that were never retold? There was no reason whatsoever to believe the ancient civilizations that had risen and fallen before recorded history were without their own bloody conflicts. The moment Flunt stumbled onto the much more spacious cave of Vart, there was war. It was pretty coincidental that moments after Payne's departure, an army of zombies showed. Just because she denied her involvement didn't make it true.

"That's interesting," Deneaux said smugly as she flicked a make-believe ash off of the straw she was not smoking. She was looking over the field, as were we all. "What are they waiting for, you suppose?" she asked.

"Probably their boss to make her safe departure."

"Or his," she said softly. She looked about to ask another question; I was not in the mood and went inside. Tracy was there, she had Wesley in her arms.

"I think I need some help." I was suddenly feeling light-headed. I fumbled with the buckle to my rifle and harness, I took them off and then peeled my shirt off.

"My god!" Tracy exclaimed. I hadn't thought any of the wounds too vicious, that was until I looked at the dark red lines radiating out from them.

"Bitch poisoned me." I sat. I was getting weaker by the moment. By now, most of the inhabitants of the Inn had come into the main room.

"They're not moving." Justin had run into the room but stopped talking when he saw me.

"Justin, get me the strongest proof liquor you can find and a towel!" Tracy ordered. She helped me lie down and placed a pillow under my head. "Travis get Tommy!"

I wanted to tell her I didn't want him here but my throat was beginning to close up, to the point where breathing was going to be difficult soon. I shook my head. It was a three-way tie as Travis, Justin, and Tommy came to skidding halts in the room.

Tommy's cool touch brushed my forehead. "He has a fever." He traced one of the wounds before saying anything. "Vervain." I thought he was speaking a Latin swear. "It's an herb often used to ward off or even kill vampires; it has varying effects depending on how it is introduced into the system."

"Do something!" Tracy beseeched as the lines marched upwards towards my heart.

"There is very little we can do; this fight is his own."

"How long?" BT asked, thinking about my recovery and now the very real threat of a zombie invasion.

"I don't suggest moving him. We need to set-up an IV, get some fluids in him, get him upstairs and into a bed, make him comfortable."

My body felt like I was being stung by a hive of angry hornets. Not an inch of me didn't feel on fire. The fever was intense; at times I thought I might burst into flames from the heat of it. I drifted in and out of consciousness, sometimes waking to the fevered pitch of a battle being waged, to screams and commands of those around me. A good amount of the time, I was dead, or dead to this world anyway. I traveled the highways and byways of Dreamland, Coma Town, Out Of Itsville.

"You yet live?" Payne whispered. She appeared before me in a long, flowing blue dress; it had a high, white trim collar and her bodice cinched tight showing her more than ample bust and narrow waist. There was hardly an inch of her exposed, yet the presumption of what was underneath those clothes could stir many a loincloth. "It is painful is it not? The vervain, I mean. I had to be careful even collecting it. I poisoned you with enough of it to drop you where you stood; perhaps I have underestimated your will."

Charity came up alongside Payne. She wore a white dress with tassels that looked more in tune with something a flapper from the roaring twenties would wear. Her body was no less perfect than Payne's, though she liked to put much more of it on display; times change.

"Are you shocked to see my sweet Charity? Alas, this is the only place we can still communicate. The bullet has left her physical body in a state of disrepair; here, though, she is still free to roam."

"He is weakened, and he is in our territory, Payne. Stop toying with him. Kill him now and end the threat."

"Are you so sure, sweet sister?"

"What are you talking about?" Charity asked.

"Are you so sure this is our territory and our territory alone? He is here, that speaks volumes."

I was a fan of Payne's cautious approach because if they attacked, I wasn't sure I could do much except cheer them on in the hopes they would finish me fast.

"Look, even now he finds a way to defend himself." Payne looked amused, I watched incredulously as a sword formed in my hand. The pommel was a deep golden color and the blade shone bright as the morning sun. I still said nothing; I was afraid my voice would betray me, a quiver in tone could be all that Charity needed to force the issue.

"If he is so powerful, why is he in need of a weapon?" Charity sneered.

"Do you not recognize the blade?" Payne asked. "That is Dawn Setter, the blade blessed by the…"

"I know the blade!" Charity snapped. "It has bitten deep of our kind. He has no right to wield it!"

"Do not upset yourself, little one. We will strike some other time," Payne said.

That was all I needed to hear to get my indecisive ass into gear. I refused to be hunted. I'd thought about saying something dramatic like: "We end this here!" in some authoritative Viking-type voice, but why? I was already at a disadvantage; a quick, unexpected strike might be the only thing that turned the tide. Tough to not telegraph your moves when the very weapon you are swinging takes up half the room and shines as bright as the morning sun and all. But I was up and I'd halved the distance; Payne was already on the move, separating from Charity, getting to my sword-less side. Charity was a little slower on the uptake, but she still had plenty of time to avoid my charge. My swing missed her by a foot, maybe more.

"You are as clumsy as an oaf in a realm you should be as graceful as quicksilver."

"Shit," I muttered when I watched Payne rise up into the air, she hovered ten feet above my head. It got no better when Charity did the same.

Didn't need to read the Art of War to see where this was going, they now had air superiority, the old high-ground. Odds were pretty good they were going to attack. I did not have the luxury to wait and react; acting without direction was now my default mode, maybe always was my default mode in whatever realm I found myself in. I swung that blade up and around, Payne had to veer abruptly to avoid being struck.

"Still think I'm oafish?" I asked when she stared angrily down at me. Now how's that for superior war-brains? Egg on one opponent with your back to another, and women, no less. Charity hit me with an impact that looked and felt like a charging Rhino slamming into a Safari Jeep. My back was jarred and my neck whipped, causing my brain to rattle around in its housing. I knew in my head, that as soon as I hit the ground, Charity had me. She would rip into my neck like a jaguar would a deer. Then a funny thing happened. Well, not so much funny as fantastical, magical, bordering on the miraculous. I was wondering how hard dream-ground was, just as my face was about to be blasted into it, when, there was…nothing. No concrete, no asphalt, no hard-packed earth, no grassy surface, just…nothing. I spun completely around. Charity had, at some point in my revolution, been thrown from me. I didn't think about the hows or the whys; I didn't think about reacting. I just did. She was looking up at me, and I swung that sword, striking her in the shoulder. The blade bit deeply; it came to a rest just above her breast. The scream she let loose was savage; it ripped at my ears. Her eyes glowed a bright red as her fangs elongated. Her right hand reached over and grabbed the sword; she cried out even harder as she touched it.

As loud as Charity's cries were, they were nothing to the primal war-scream Payne let loose as she attacked. For someone incapable of love, she sure was pissed. She hit me hard enough I had to reset my teeth. I was wrenched away from Charity; my grip sufficiently tight that I took the sword with me, which made a particularly horrific squelching sound as it was removed and amplified her screams. My mind was far too addled to once again alter the ground; this time I skidded along it face first for nearly twenty feet. When I righted myself, Payne and Charity were gone. Exhausted didn't even begin to explain my sorry state. The sword dissolved into nothingness; my arms felt as if they were made from stone. I sat down, convinced that I now found myself in an atmosphere of heavy gravity, and I was very much in danger of being melded to the ground by the extreme pressure. I lay down, as this was the only position that allowed any form of comfort or end to the vertigo that threatened to spin me off my feet. Right now, Wesley could have beat me to death with a rattle and there wouldn't have been a thing I could do about it.

I awoke sometime later to the smell of cordite and smoke, a scent I was all too familiar with: spent gunpowder. I craned my neck around. I was in bed; Tracy was at the window, leaning out and firing. I sat up, expecting my head to be swimming in a sea of misery. Surprisingly, I felt great. I know right?! What does that say about you that on any given morning you expect to wake up feeling like shit, and then are genuinely surprised when you don't? Still, we take the good surprises with the bad; my wife was shooting at something while I lay there. I tossed the covers to the side and stood, stretched, gave the normal ball-scratch, and walked over to give Tracy a kiss as if this was part of our regular routine. I wrapped my arm around her waist and put my head on her shoulder, careful not to disrupt her aim. I looked out the window. In terms of a battle, this one was nearly finished. Zombie bodies were strewn all over the lawn and parking lot; she was busy picking off those lucky few who appeared to be moving away.

"You're awake!" she said, happily enough.

"Everyone alright?" I asked, dreading anything but one answer.

"Everyone is fine." Something made her look over her shoulder at me. She frowned. "Michael, you realize you're not clothed, right?"

"Oh, motherfucking hell, Talbot!" BT yelled from the doorway. He held an ammo can-clad hand in front of his face. "Have you no fucking modesty? Shit, it's not even that! We're in the middle of a damn zombie battle and you aren't going to be able to do much with that weapon."

"Fucking ouch, man. That just hurts." I made sure I was

facing him in full frontal mode.

"Fucking deviant." He put the ammunition down and walked away.

"Well, it seems my weapon worked well on him." I had my hands on my hips and sent him off with a pelvic power thrust.

"No, you did not just do that." Tracy had placed a cupped hand over her eyes. I got dressed, but only because it seemed the right thing to do in this particular situation. By the time I was done and had grabbed my rifle it was all over except the cheering. I would have to time more battles like this one—good strategy.

"This was a strange attack." Tracy turned to me as I raised my rifle out the window; there wasn't a target worth wasting a bullet on.

CHAPTER TWELVE
THE BATTLE FOR CEMETERY HILL

AFTER WEEKS OF peace, the zombies had followed Mike and the others up to the Inn. BT had Travis and Justin lock all the bottom floor shutters, and then they had barricaded the front door in expectation of an attack that had yet to launch. The zombies had mustered fifty feet from the entrance.

"What are they doing?" Gary asked, peeking from one of the windows.

"If they had candles, I would almost say it was a vigil," Tiffany said.

"For who? Why would they do that?"

"I didn't *say* it was a vigil; I said it looks like one," she replied.

Winters and BT were standing by a small conference table discussing how they should proceed.

"Anything?" BT asked Gary.

"Nothing. They're just standing there," Gary said.

"They're waiting for the night or for some, what do you call them? Bulkers?" Winters posed.

"Possible," BT said, "but they're not usually shy or cautious in regards to attacking. They pretty much go balls out once they've got a target."

"Let's give them something to think about before they do,

then," Winters said.

"I'm all for killing zombies," Tommy said, still visibly shaken up by Mike's accusations. "But if we start firing, that might spur them into action."

"You're saying we wait? Wait for what?" Winters asked. "For them to get more reinforcements? For the dark? For the earth to split open and swallow them up? They're zombies. Doesn't matter what it looks like; they're here to kill us. They're not pondering if they should kill and eat us; they're just pondering when."

"Sorry, Tommy. I'm with Winters on this one," BT said. "How's Mike?" he asked as he saw Tracy come down the stairs.

"Resting, but far from comfortable. Tommy, I'd like it if you were up there; it seems the vervain poisoning has stopped spreading, but I can't tell...the discoloration doesn't look so great." She looked tired and extremely worried.

Tommy went upstairs; Justin followed, Avalyn in his arms.

"They've stopped?" Tracy asked, referring to the zombies. BT nodded.

"There a reason why we haven't started firing yet?" She cocked her head at them and frowned.

"None that I can think of," BT replied.

Deneaux came down the stairs, a half-chewed straw in her mouth. "I want a cigarette so badly I would walk out there and pull one off a zombie and strike my match across his face. That being said, I just might. I would prefer it was dead, but I could take my chances...how about we kill a few so I can look over some corpses?"

The waiting was over; retreats were rare and reinforcements seemed a more likely outcome. The word was given and a few minutes later there was at least one rifle in every second-floor window.

"Fire!" BT shouted from the middle room, making sure he was heard throughout the Inn. Gunfire erupted, zombies fell in droves, heads exploded, chests ripped open, arms and legs blown off, yet still, the horde did not shift. After five solid minutes of wrecking their front lines, BT called a cease-fire. Except for the zombies that had been obliterated, none of the others had budged. They did not look at the dead at their feet, they did not look to the Inn where the ferocious and barbaric shots had come from. The nothingness, the absence, was disturbing in its own right. BT now had to weigh options; how many rounds did they expend on an enemy that did not seem interested in the conflict? Thanks to Sanders, they had replenished their stock and then some, but he wouldn't pour water out in the desert merely because he had plenty to drink.

BT turned as he heard Michael cry out in pain. A moment later, Travis ran past the room to check on his father; Tracy was with her husband–she would call out if help was needed.

"They're coming!" Winters shouted. BT whipped his head back around.

"Just coincidence," he whispered as he pulled the trigger. By the time they stopped advancing, the shooters were firing nearly straight down. Then, inexplicably, they began to pull away again. BT watched as they made a slow, apathetic retreat, making sure this was not some kind of ruse. He wanted to check on Michael; he used the excuse of an ammo check to do so. He wasn't sure why he needed subterfuge, or even what he was looking for, but when he saw the man up and about and in good spirits, his suspicion of a correlation was confirmed. There was a connection between his most trusted friend and the strange behavior of the zombies. But what kind of connection? What did any of this mean? For, surely there was a relationship, right? The zombies had come when Payne showed; what if Michael somehow defined their purpose? They had stood outside in vigil while he was sick; they had advanced when he had cried out, whether in pain or for help. Then they had pulled back...realizing what? That he was alright?

CHAPTER THIRTEEN
MICHAEL JOURNAL ENTRY 13

I GOT DRESSED, went out to the porch, and watched as the last of the zombies receded–tough to call it a retreat; not something they generally do.

"Feeling better, Mr. T?" Tommy asked. He seemed so sincere, I felt guilty that I had accused him of trying to kill me.

"I saw Payne and Charity, and no, it wasn't a hallucination. I was traveling in the astral realms."

"And?" he asked.

"Charity is wounded on this plain and Payne gave me an…indication that she may never heal. But she was all tigress in there, until I wounded her."

"What does she want?"

"Pretty sure it's to kill all of us. Isn't that generally what vampires want?"

"Not all vampires," he replied.

BT came out onto the porch. "Happy to see you with some common decency," he said, referring to my pants.

"Don't act all coy and shit. You liked what you saw–kinda scared you," I goaded.

"Fine. Since you opened this conversation up in that manner I'm bringing out the big guns," he replied.

"Don't, man–don't do it," I said.

"The only Talbot I want to see naked is your sister."

Tommy snorted at that. I may have turned a slight green. "You been hanging with my wife?" I asked. "She teach you to 'bring a tank to a thumb wrestle?'"

"Ain't got time for your games. I'd like to talk to you," BT said, and he looked serious.

I looked over to Tommy, who got the message and walked back into the Inn.

BT laid it on me—what he'd witnessed. I had nothing I could add. If I somehow had a measure of control over the zombies, sure, I'd use it to wipe them out. But I certainly wasn't aware of anything big. In a pinch, I could maybe direct three or four to do my bidding, simple stuff, but that oily, disgusting feeling I got by linking with them was not something I relished doing, and I had avoided it altogether for a good, long time now. I'd rather lick the seat of an ill-tended gas station toilet, and we all know that just wasn't going to happen—if you needed a conclusive image to follow my sentiments.

"Is it a subconscious thing?" he asked, reaching. "Maybe you don't even know you're doing it?"

"It doesn't work like that, BT. There's all this concentration, focus, reaching out. It'd be like trying to fly a plane subconsciously."

"What the fuck is going on then?"

"I'm worried about Tommy," I said. If I couldn't say it to him, then I couldn't say it period.

"In what way? Is he in danger?"

"No...I'm more worried about the danger to us."

"From the kid? Really?"

"Just a feeling, couple of small things. He left me hanging there for a minute."

"I can tell you this. While you were out, he swore up and down he didn't know she was out there, for sure. And he was even more vehement that he had not seen you pass. And, I believed him. I have a pretty good instinct when someone is lying, or even half-truthing."

"My understanding is psychopaths have no tells; that a lie does nothing to them physiology-wise."

"You saying that kid is a psychopath? He's been with us since the beginning. You don't think someone would have noticed?"

"I don't know what I'm saying, ok? But first off, he's not a kid. He also had an extended stay with his sister not all that long ago. And there's no denying *she was* a psychopath."

"Mike. Think about what you're saying. That kid, okay, man, vampire, whatever, has saved all of us, multiple times. If he wanted us harmed or dead he could have achieved that just by some inaction on his part. He would not need to do anything overt, and no one would even question him on it."

"You're right," I finally said. "You're right. It's me, man. The accumulated stress of all of this–I'm starting to see shadows in the corners of brightly lit rooms. As much as we all needed this break, a way to heal and decompress…maybe it's a sign that we should get moving again."

"Yeah, it's a scary thing when we give you too much time to think."

I couldn't even deny his words. He'd meant them as a joke, but there was a fair measure of truth to them. Idle hands might be the devil's workshop, but an idle mind can be the birth of hell itself.

Even with the threat of Payne around and the strange zombie invasion, we had still found solace at that place, a measure of peace we had not had since the beginning. Two days later we packed up. We had enough food to make the trek by horse-drawn cart if need be and enough ammunition to fight off a city-sized horde. The only thing lacking could be the one thing we'd always had in excess. Hope. It took an immeasurable toll every time we lost someone. Death is a finality; you can never recoup the loss. There will always be something unique about that individual, their wit, charm, the way they smiled or the way they made you smile, hell, even their silence when others spoke. Those people aren't just gone; when they go they take something from you as well, something tangible, it can never be replaced. That's why they say you "miss" them; there's something missing now besides another body. How many holes can you have in your heart before you begin to bleed out? It seemed to be a question we were all reluctantly and rapidly facing, searching for that number. But this was no Tootsie Pop with a gooey chocolatey center we wanted to get at.

BT and I headed out the next morning to Doctor Mary Jane Bones. If I'd made that name up, you wouldn't even believe me. She wasn't the closest obstetrician, not by a couple of miles. But come on, I had to. Like, I was compelled. It was an upscale medical building, couple of plastic surgeons shared the place as well. It was in remarkably good shape, but there wasn't going to be many people coming to get a nose job or to check on why the missus couldn't get pregnant during a z-poc. There were no zombies, no people, and no vampires, perfect trifecta.

"Door is locked," BT said, pulling on it.

"Well, I guess they're closed. Maybe we should just go then," I said.

"Is it hard being that much of an ass? I meant I was going to have to bust the window. Be prepared for some noise."

He grabbed a decorative flower pot full of dirt and some weeds, thing had to have been a hundred pounds. He hefted it up onto his shoulder and heaved it a good ten feet. The resultant noise and shock wave was felt three counties over.

"Holy fuck, man! Maybe you should have just shot it," I said to him. "Anything within a mile is going to come and check on it."

"Sorry," he said rather sheepishly. "I didn't think it was going to be that loud."

"Yeah, who's the ass now?"

"Still you, always you," he said.

We cautiously went in; nothing looked out of place, or

better yet smelled bad. On the initial hallway were three doors. I went into the first one, Dr. H. Tuckman.

"This is a plastic surgeon's office," BT said, following me in.

I walked past the reception area and to the records room right behind. I pulled open a drawer and started flipping through some files.

"Talbot, what the fuck are you doing? Oh! Wow…" he said, getting closer when I handed him some before and after photos.

This guy is like an artist," I said as we looked at some of his handiwork. For a solid five minutes, I kept handing off photos to BT.

He dropped his stack and grabbed my shoulder. "Come on. We've wasted enough time."

"Wasted? Admiring art is no waste of time."

"Not like this is the Louvre, and I'm sure your wife would be thrilled to hear about why this trip took so long."

"I'll miss you, patient 5642," I said as I put her file back.

Dr. Mary Jane's office was a bright blend of pinks and baby blues. She had an entire wall devoted to photos of all the children she had helped bring into the world. I couldn't help but wonder how many of them might still be alive.

"So many," I said, walking past the pictures.

BT had found the file room and was scouring files.

"Mike. Come on, man, there's got to be thousands of files here. I'm going to need help."

BT had a growing stack by his feet of women that were not viable candidates; each of them had already had their child or were conclusively incapable, as the case may be. I grabbed my first file and had just flipped it open when I looked across the room.

"Done," I said.

"Really? You open one fucking file and we're done?" He grabbed it from my hands quickly. "What the hell are you talking about? She had her kid ten years ago," he said as he read the sheet.

I was walking to a cabinet that said "samples" on it.

"Mike, I looked at the damn booby pictures—the least you can do is help me with this."

"When did you get so narrow-focused? Oh, I know what it is—you still have too much blood running around in your little man."

"What? What the hell are you talking about? And me and you were standing entirely too close for me to be comfortable getting a…well, you know what I mean."

"I wonder what my sister would say if she knew you got tumescent looking at other women's breasts?"

"Tumescent? You talk like a third grader most of the time and then you throw a word like that out. What the hell is wrong with you? No, I wasn't *tumescent*, you sick bastard. Let's just find a house we can go to and get some damn vitamins!"

He was getting angry. "It's okay, my stiffened friend! It's a natural reaction. Men are very visually stimulated. Did your dad not have 'the talk' with you? We can go over the basics, if that helps."

"I did not have a hard-on!" he roared. "I want to get the fucking vitamins and go!"

"*Fucking vitamins*? That a code word for Viagra? I mean, because, that's a whole other set of problems. You seem young for that kind of issue, but all that anger could be blocking your chi. Don't worry. Breathing techniques, maybe a little yoga could clear that all up."

He flexed for a fraction of a second. Probably best I wasn't standing behind him, I could be eating my words about now.

"I have to think the world would be a better place if I just spun your head off. The. Prenatal. Vitamins," he said slowly and succinctly, hoping I wouldn't find a way to distort his words. "I just want the prenatal vitamins," he sighed.

"Done," I said stuffing a pile of them into the backpack I had with me.

"Huh…what?" he asked as I walked by. "You have got to

be kidding me? Why couldn't you have just said something?"

"It's a two-foot by two-foot clear display case that has six-inch letters that say 'Pre-Natal Vitamin Samples.' Should I have done some hand flourishes around it like Vanna White?"

"You could have tried, but she's much prettier than you."

"Can we go now, or did you want to grab some souvenirs from Tuckman's?"

I didn't need to turn around to realize he was flipping me off; I could feel the wind whip past my ear from the way he forced his finger into the upright position. We were back at the Inn in under two hours, might be a record for us. I didn't want to say it was *too easy* because that implied that we were being set up for something right around the corner. I wouldn't have minded in the least if all of our runs, hell, if half our runs went that smoothly. It was rare to have complete success, and even rarer to not have to fight or avoid serious danger.

"Any problems?" my sister asked when we came back.

"You should have used a thicker loaf of bread," BT said.

"What?" Lyndsey was completely lost.

I smiled. "I'm thinking he wished you had smacked me harder or with something bigger when you hit me with the frozen pita bread."

"Was he giving you shit?" Lyndsey asked BT.

"Your brother is a childish, mean, little man," BT said, hugging my sister. Her back was to me, so not only was he freely flipping double eagles, but he was also sticking his tongue out.

"Oh...look at you making friends!" Tracy said to me as she came into the room. BT did his best to hide his gestures; it was about as effective as a kid with chocolate streaks down his face denying he'd eaten the cookies before dinner.

CHAPTER FOURTEEN
MIKE JOURNAL ENTRY 14

"ON THE ROAD again…" Gary sang out from the back seat in a key I wasn't even sure was measured on the musical scale.

"Does he realize how bad he sounds?" Tracy murmured from the passenger seat. She was doing her best to not show Gary she was plugging her ears.

"All the possessions we've lost, and he somehow holds on to a Walkman." I had my window rolled down, hoping the seventy miles per hour air rushing in would drown out my brother's crooning. It didn't. If anything, it made the sound twirl around the car and directly into my right ear.

We all had our own unique ways of dealing with the problems this life was handing us. Mine generally involved an extra heaping of sarcasm steeped in large doses of alcohol. Gary liked to sing. It was the only time he was truly happy, the only time he could push his demons away, or at the very minimum, temporarily scare them off. The road was surprisingly clear of monsters and people, not debris–there was plenty of that. I couldn't imagine that it would be much longer than ten to twenty years before car travel would no longer be possible, not to say with the way things were going we'd still have cars. We were already coming across stores of gas that were gumming up; wouldn't be too much longer before we had no fuel. Sure, we could shift to diesel, but that would only buy us another year, max. Even if we used some sort of hybrid fuel or electric car, the rubber in the tires was only going to be good for so long before dry rot set in. Once you added the breakdown of roads no longer being maintained, we were facing the end of America's love affair with the automobile. In reality, we had maybe a year or two more of driving wherever we went; our kids would never drive. I almost choked up at that thought.

I understood that civilization was already on the ropes, but that would be one big nail in the coffin. Not just because some of my fondest memories centered around road trips and backseat romantic encounters, either. Without rapid transportation or a means to communicate, great swaths of the country would become isolated. Wouldn't doubt it if we started to revert back to the Old West. That was, of course, if people made it that long. Mad Jack had scoured the country looking for settlements and the only one of note was Etna Station. I know there were pockets like ours, family groups banding together, fighting for our humanity, but tied off from all others they would inevitably begin to choke and die off. I hated to admit it because for most of my life I had tried to put as much distance as I could between myself and the rest of humanity, but we needed each other if we wanted to survive, if we wanted to come out the other side.

Deneaux pulled up alongside me. "You should take these two." She was referring to BT and Lyndsey. "I've seen teenagers less handsy."

"Not going to happen, and you've given me less of a reason to do so." I rolled up my window and pulled ahead. We were making decent time and as we rolled from Indiana into Illinois, I could not help but think back on Camp Custer and the destruction that had been wrought there. Was I even now racing ahead to a new base, ready to insert a new virus into the community? Would I be considered this age's Typhoid Mary? I mean, if you got down to the brass tacks of it, we had one vampire following us, there were two vampires in our midst, two people who maybe didn't have the zombie virus in them anymore but had definitely been exposed, and a baby delivered from a zombie. That was a lot of potentially disruptive variables brought into a community that I'm sure had a very delicate ecosystem. I wondered if it was morally necessary to warn them about us.

"I'm worried about what our presence could potentially mean for Etna," I said, finally putting words to my fears.

Typical Tracy, she immediately picked up on what I was thinking. "Custer wasn't your fault, Mike. You can't blame what happened there because of you or us. Eliza brought that storm to them."

"But I lead her there. If not for me, there's a chance that place would still be thriving. How many people lost their lives that day? How many countless others who never had a chance to find that sanctuary? We knew she was following us. Just like Payne is now. I can't bring another wolf into the hen house. I won't allow it."

"What are you saying?"

"We need to stop her, to kill her before we get there, or at least I have to. There's no other choice."

"How? How are you going to do that? She told you herself, she can strike whenever she wants to. We have no idea where she's at or from what direction she'll come."

"She said that, but she's a predator. She's wary. She's not going to attack when we're at our strongest, she's going to wait. She'll stalk, maybe pick off some of our weak," I said, and my thoughts immediately went to Ryan, who was just barely walking now. "She'll strike when she knows her odds of success are at their highest." An idea began to percolate in my head. I had to trust Tommy; I would need him in on this one hundred percent. Well, I'd need all of us, actually. How we were going to pull it off with the threat of her watching would be the tricky part, but I was thinking I had the perfect spot to set up an ambush. We could be rid of that threat, at least. There was still

Knox, but he was human and insane, the devil we knew. And he wasn't insane enough to attack a well-armed base. He didn't have that kind of numbers, and if I could persuade the command at Etna Station to strike him first, he never would.

THAT NIGHT WE talked.

"I don't know," BT said. "That's a pretty big detour and we don't know if she'll even come out of hiding."

"He's right, though," Tommy said. "What if she pulls something like my sister did? If we can make her believe her success will be quick, thorough, and relatively safely done, she might not be able to help herself."

"Seems like getting to Etna Station would be enough to stop her–if it's something she wants to do without risking herself."

"Double-edged sword," I said to BT. "If she knows where we're going, she might get desperate, strike us soon, before we can get to that relative safe haven."

"You're overestimating her. She can't know all that. Tracy?" He pleaded his case to the person who was the best by far at reeling me back when I began to dangle my feet over the edge.

"The large man has merit," Deneaux said.

"Don't remember asking you," I said. She shrugged as she reached into her pocket for the ghost of cigarettes past. "Well. Looks like you're on the same side as Deneaux; that should tell you something," I said to BT.

"Don't attack him," Lyndsey said.

"Sis, I'm not attacking him. You weren't there. All those people–they never stood a chance. One pissed-off vampire was able to do that."

"She had an army," BT said. "Eliza was a whole shitload

smarter than Payne. She knew her limitations and her strengths. She raised an army of the living and the dead to help her do her bidding. I'm sorry, man, but I don't see Payne being able to pull this off."

"You saw the zombie horde at Cemetery Hill; you can't deny that," I said.

"About that…." He paused looking around the room and lowered his voice. "If they were controlled by her, they were certainly acting strangely. There was enough of them—we would have had a hard time defending the fort. She had us right then if she wanted."

"What do you mean if? Look. Maybe no one is controlling them. Maybe they are just evolving." I said.

"I realize you do not wish to hear from me, Michael, but it is December," Mrs. Deneaux said.

"What's your point? If you're hoping I'll remember to put you on my gift list, you're tooting the wrong horn."

"Eloquent, as always," she said. "My point is, so far we have had an incredible run of luck with the weather being so mild. We are talking about making a pass through the Rockies; what do you propose we do if we should get snowed in by a blizzard?"

"Don't worry. If I go all Alferd Packer, I'm eating him first." I thumbed at BT.

"Gee. Thanks, man," BT said.

"Who's Alferd Packer?" Meredith asked.

"Colorado pioneer that ate his traveling companions when they got stuck in the mountains," Jess told her.

"Oh gross," she said, gagging.

"There are no plows, Michael. It's December. There is most certainly snow on the roads through the Rockies."

I knew she was right, which made me want to dig my heels in even more.

"Wait…wait," BT said. "I've seen that look before. If you're dead set on this shit, ok, bad choice of words—I know a better place, and we don't have to go so far out of our way."

"Now you're agreeing with him?" Lyndsey asked.

"You know this man, right? He's going to do it anyway; aren't you." The last part was not a question.

"She has to be stopped. I can plead ignorance about what Eliza was going to do, that's fair enough, but it does little to ease my nightmares. I should have known, and knowing that now, how could I ever live with myself if I thought there was even a small chance Payne could do the same thing?"

"Goddammit. I hate when he's right," BT said.

"Perhaps we swing up to Washington State and drop off those that cannot fight," Deneaux said. "Do not look at me that way, Michael. I fully intend on seeing this through. I would think it would ease your mind somewhat if only soldiers were involved in this."

"Soldiers? What are we talking about?" Winters had come into the room.

Quiet didn't even begin to convey the noiseless vacuum it had become in there.

"Real smooth; that's not too suspicious. I already have an inkling of what's going on, even if I think maybe all of you have lost your minds and this is some sort of collective hallucination."

"What is it you think you know, my dear?" Deneaux asked.

"That Mike had a run in with what he is saying was a vampire at Gettysburg, and that you've had run-ins with vampires before. Sounds like something out of a tv show, and I'm sorry; I respect what you've all gone through and what you've survived, but I think that maybe the stress is beginning to take its toll."

I sighed. "Tommy?" I looked over at the boy.

"You sure, Mr. T?"

"He doesn't believe us and I don't want him thinking we're all about to crack."

"Sure about—" That was all Winters could get out before Tommy covered the distance of the room, appearing before Winters, teeth elongated, eyes red.

"What the fuck?" He stumbled backwards, tripping and knocking over a chair which he then stayed behind. He was looking from the floor up at Tommy then to the rest of us. "What the fuck is he? This some sort of trick?" He was scrambling to get back up, holding his chair like a reluctant circus lion tamer.

"I'm a vampire," Tommy said, extending his hand to help the man up, even as his fangs receded.

"Bullshit." Winters said, but refused to reach out to Tommy.

"Do we look like we're doing parlor tricks, Winters? That we have nothing better to do than scare each other? There's enough scary shit out there that I would hope we would be able to refrain from dangling fake spiders. Especially with all the guns around," I said.

BT had gone over to help Winters up. The Marine shrugged him off. "Are...are you all vampires? Did you lure me and Brooke here just so, you know...you could..."

"Eat you?" I said.

"We're not all vampires," BT said, ignoring me and attempting to placate Winters, who looked like he was going to bolt from the room. "If we were all vampires and were evil, don't you think we would have just taken you all back in New Hampshire?"

Winters thought on that, but having everything you think you know turned on its ear, again, takes a minute to go through. "Vampires aren't real," he said.

"Yes. Neither are zombies," Deneaux cackled. "Oh God, I would skin baby animals for a cigarette," she sighed.

"I figured that would be something you just did for fun," BT replied quickly.

We fist bumped that one.

"Are any others of you vampires?" he asked.

I thought my heart was going to drop out. No one said anything, but invariably gazes shifted around, some looking at walls, the ceiling, all finally heading in my direction.

"You too?" he asked, picking up on my discomfort.

"Half," I finally answered. "Enough to be burdened, but not so much that I can't push the reality of it away."

Tommy had pulled away and was back at his original spot across the room. Winters realized this wasn't some huge conspiracy and that if we'd wanted him dead, he would be a hundred times by now.

"What were you talking about before I came in?" Winters asked more like his normal self, though still suspicious.

Well, I guess you're in. Going to need your help, anyway," I said. "We're trying to set up a trap for the vampire that is following us before we get to Washington State." I laid out everything we had so far; he offered some suggestions as he moved past what he had just learned about his new group. I don't know if he'd ever feel safe around us again, and I wondered how this would affect us at Etna Station. If and when he rejoined a unit, I had to think the odds were pretty good he'd give us up, maybe not even on purpose, just talking, as soldiers often do.

It was later that night when I went over to see him; he didn't seem surprised about it. In fact, it seemed he even knew what I was there for because he spoke first.

"I love the Marine Corps," he said. I wasn't sure how that fit into the general discussion, but I let him speak. I also was thankful for all the Corps had done for me, for the swift kick in the ass that had righted my sinking ship. I loved the Marine Corps even more now, now that I was no longer active; the Marines we'd met had been nothing but honorable, courageous men; many, like Winters, had gone to bat for us even though we were strangers. And I will always love what they had done for our country, I let him continue.

"Next week, if you can believe it, my regular enlistment is up."

I was going to tell him I didn't think anyone would consider him a deserter at this point he was without a unit and, on the road with civvies; although, he had been with Sanders.

"The major is, was, like a father to me, and I would have re-upped just to make him proud. But with Brooke depending on me, I want something different. I would like to try and have a family, a home; not go traipsing all over the world like I've seen the major do. It might be a pipe dream, but I would like to shoot for a normal life–if such a thing even exists anymore."

"Or ever did," I added. I had no idea where he was going with this.

"True." He smiled. "What I'm trying to say is that, if they find out I was in the Marines and have experience in demolition, there's a very good chance that whatever military people are there are going to want me to stay in." He looked directly at me. "What kind of life are you hoping for there?"

Then it dawned on me. "The same. The very same as you. I want my kids to have a chance, to live, love, and grow. I don't want to keep fighting the rest of my life. Your secret is safe with me."

"And you mean no one there harm?" he asked. I guess it was a fair question.

"I do not," I told him sincerely.

"Then your secret is safe with me, sir."

"Then we're even. And you might want to drop the sir, that's a dead giveaway you were a soldier. And quit shaving."

CHAPTER FIFTEEN
MIKE JOURNAL ENTRY 15

I DON'T KNOW why the fates had eased up on us as we traveled closer to our destination. I could not get the feeling out of my head that they were storing everything up for one final blowback. The next day and a half were wholly unremarkable, which, in itself, made them extremely remarkable. It seemed we had hit the sweet spot for all things fiend but they were on vacation, taking some time from all their monster duties.

"The Pacific Ocean. We've almost made it," I said to Tracy as we looked upon the sparkling jewel. I wanted to shout in joyful triumph, but we hadn't quite won. Maybe there were two outs in our game seven of the World Series and we were up by a run, but that didn't mean it was a done deal. I'd been a Red Sox fan long enough to know that. I'd celebrate. I'd celebrate hard when we made it to the other side. To do so early was foolhardy, it tempted fate, spurred the enemy on, and made any defeat that much more crushing. If you think you've already won, you let your guard down. You allow room for disaster, and opportunists will use that to their advantage. It is much more difficult to rebound, to re-obtain what you assumed was yours–it's like that smug receiver that believes he has caught the winning touchdown. He looks, for a fraction of a second at the camera, takes his eyes off the prize just long enough to then see the ball glance off his fingertips and out of bounds. Lots of mixed sports references here, but games are extremely applicable to life. We were first and goal to our goal, but that was still a Hail Mary from safe at home, or a touchdown.

We stood at the scenic pull out as a group, taking it all in, in silence, each of us lost in thought. Then Henry took a shit. There we were, peering into the endless horizon, trying to figure out what was going to happen, what could happen. Then Henry took center stage, dropped his haunches and let loose something looked like he'd been building since Iowa. Laughter, sweet laughter rang out from nearly all of us. Henry, after taking care of business, turned to admire his creation then scraped the earth a few times with his hind legs in a vain attempt to hide it.

"Going to need a backhoe to bury that, buddy," I said to him as I crouched down. He came over and got his obligatory head scratch. "Well, I guess that's his way of getting us moving." The breeze was coming off the ocean and bringing with it Henry's odiferous offering.

"Getting late. Do we maybe wait?" BT asked. He was nervous, we all were. Confrontations were one thing, you dealt with them as they came, but forcing one was more difficult.

I was almost of a mind to stall. Find a picturesque place on the beach and enjoy what could be our last night on the planet. I would have, too, if not for Riley. While we were all facing west, and taking in the incredible sunset view, she was facing east, looking towards a small mountain ridge. The fur on her nape was sticking up; she wasn't growling, exactly, but something in her, something instinctual, had her hackles raised. I had a good idea of what it was and that was confirmed when Tommy turned as well, a questioning look on his face. We locked glances for a moment, and in that millisecond, we knew. She was out there, maybe watching remotely, or just maybe close enough to be of concern. I didn't say anything; I wanted our exit to be as normal as could be. The less she knew we knew, the better; I didn't want to give her any reason to be suspicious of our activities.

We were twenty miles from our objective, heading up the Oregon Coast Highway–easily one of the most beautiful roads I'd ever had the pleasure of being on. Would have loved to stop, snap ten thousand pictures, ooh and aah at every magnificent site, maybe get some fried clams–the strips, not the bellies. That's just gross. But we weren't tourists, we were refugees, and it was sanctuary we sought. We wanted to lay our own trap, and not of the tourist type.

"Traffic's getting thicker," Tracy said.

Honestly, I hadn't even noticed it. I was checking my six constantly, making sure our small convoy wasn't being followed and that everyone was on course. And when I wasn't looking in the rearview mirror, I was looking past Tracy to the rolling hills to our right, wondering when she was going to show herself. I could feel her now; she wanted me to feel her. She wanted me to be afraid, and in that, she was succeeding. Like a cold, black eel, she swam through the neurons of my mind, infecting everything in her path with her desire for revenge.

"Earth to Talbot." Tracy was about to flick me on the side of the head but I'd turned at the last moment and she nearly poked me in the eye.

"Huh?"

"Cars. There's more of them on the road. Maybe if you actually looked ahead you could see them."

She was right, about the cars I mean, well, and the need to look forward more I guess, too. Just twenty miles ago it was rare to see anything; occasionally there would be a vehicle on the side of the road as if it had broken down and was now long forgotten. Now both sides of the two-lane highway had cars. I was dodging continuously and traveling was slower. From what I could see up ahead, it was only getting thicker. Deneaux flashed her lights to signify she wanted me to stop. She pulled up alongside.

"This could be problematic," she said, referring to the cars. It wasn't snow, but it might as well be. Inaccessible was inaccessible, any way you looked at it. "Must have been some sort of evacuation route. Whatever struck here, it was quick," she said.

"And how would you know that?" Might have been a hint of peevish in there, only because we were making our bed and I really wanted to lie in it, but now we might have to deal with a serious case of bed bugs before we could get between the sheets. Well, that and it was Deneaux, our not-that-necessary evil.

She didn't say anything for a moment, then pursed her lips. "You haven't noticed? He hasn't noticed?" she asked again looking past me and to Tracy.

"I don't think so," she replied.

"What did we miss?"

Deneaux pointed to the car slightly ahead and to my left. There was a zombie peering through the rear windshield. When it had been human he had been around eight-years old. What was left of his parents looked to be scattered all over the dashboard, and I would imagine, strewn throughout the entire car.

"Lately, more cars than not have had zombies in them," she said.

"What? Why?" I was now looking around. There were ten cars visible. Seven of them had movement inside; safe to say it wasn't of the human variety. I turned the car off and got out; the percentages stayed fairly consistent as I checked more and more. "How can this be?" I asked anyone willing to venture an answer.

"I believe Portland was one of the first places on the West Coast to receive flu shots," Deneaux said. "When it hit, perhaps they were evacuating."

"How do you know that?" I asked her.

Like I said, Deneaux is as smooth as butter when it comes

to concealing the truth, so I don't know if I absolutely believed her, but she gave a valid response.

"There was an article in the Denver Post in regards to it. I was very upset that Denver had not received theirs yet," she replied.

"Here, though? Why would they evacuate Oregon by one-o-one? No one uses coastal roads if they're trying to get anywhere fast," BT said.

"I don't know. None of this makes sense. We've talked about this before; none of us got a warning about the zombies. One second, I'm taking a shower during a typical work night and the next there's zombies. What did these people know?"

"Uncle," Meredith said, "most of these cars have blue stickers on the front windshield." She was looking around but careful not to move quickly or get too close. The zombies would be thrown into a fever pitch if any of us did. They would slap their hands and heads against the windows in desperate bids to get to us; once you've seen it you don't need a replay.

"Military identification. They're coming from a base somewhere." I found a car with a small kid zombie; I didn't feel like he'd be able to bust through the safety glass. "Coast Guard," I said once I was able to read the print on the sticker. Another read "National Guard." Made sense. From what we knew, the military had been the first to get the tainted shots. Also made sense they'd be the first trying to protect their families and get away from the spread of the infection.

"Stay the course?" BT asked.

We weren't committed, not yet, but Payne was out there and it would be foolish to believe she wasn't planning on striking soon. That she had let down her guard enough that we could "see" her made that painfully obvious; I wondered if she'd known about this hundred-mile pile-up.

"I don't see any reason not to." I said the words, but in my heart, I wondered if perhaps we were heading into Payne's trap and not the other way around. I'll always wonder if I should have spoken up, should have said something. Would they have listened? Or would I have been vetoed? We were tired of running and Payne needed to be dealt with. This was our chance to be rid of her, to finally put the worst of this damned war behind us. Even I wasn't naïve enough to believe that would be the ultimate outcome, but hope has a way of spreading its flowery tendrils over the nastiest of situations, even if it is mostly for ornamentation.

We were five miles from the Arch Cape tunnel, according to the signs. I wasn't thrilled that most of these were riddled with bullet holes. I don't really have a problem with a street sign being shot, it happens. Idiots, for some reason, get a kick out of it. Not my particular flavor of Kool-Aid, but whatever. Just that with zombies everywhere, why would you unnecessarily do anything to attract them? By now, we were traveling at a blistering twenty miles per hour, picking our way through the thickening traffic. Even the breakdown lanes were becoming more congested as those that had fled had desperately driven the shoulders and even farther off the road where possible.

Have you ever found yourself on a juice diet sometime in your life, for whatever reason? Maybe shed a few pounds before a big day, or just trying to eat a little more healthy? A nice raspberry smoothie in place of an oh-so-delicious quarter pounder with cheese and an extra large fry? So, you grab the blender that hasn't been used for anything but Margaritas since you got it, (no matter what you told yourself the reasons for buying it were.) Now, finally, it will serve that purpose. So, you cut up some bananas, toss in a basket of fresh strawberries and raspberries along with a helping of milk and some ice cubes. If you're going to have a liquid lunch, you're going to make it as close to a milkshake as humanly possible. You blend that thing into a thick, rich smoothie frappe, pour it into a nice, tall glass. Then you lament when you look back at the blender and the amount of clean-up it is going to require. The sides are coated in congealing clumps of red, unidentifiable bits of brown and black stand out among the debris, and this is all coated with a thick white layer which, if left alone for too long, will mold a sickly greenish color.

Right now, you're staring at this journal wondering "where in the hell is this man going with this. Smack dab in the middle of a zombie invasion and this idiot is talking about shakes." Stay with me–I'm about to get there. You see, the insides of a lot of the cars we were passing looked a lot like those healthy frappes. Like, instead of a gearshift, the car had a huge twirling blade inside of it and it made a puree out of everything living or dead in that vehicle. Though the brown and black strawberry seeds were more likely eyeballs or pieces of livers and intestines. I don't know what horror show happened on this highway, but these cars were fucked up. Maybe one occupant was able to get a shot off, splattering the brains of a loved one all over the interior, or the more likely scenario–a hungry zombie with little-to-no table manners. Or it was even possible that the dead trapped in the cars had exploded as a result of the gases bodies released and the greenhouse effect the car would have on those corpses. Too much information? Try driving past it.

Whatever the reason, it was happening more and more and no matter how much I tried to ignore it, avoid it, unsee it, even, I could not. Every once in a while, the nightmare would get just a little more vivid; a hand would smear against the detritus trying to clear away the gunk to watch the living pass. Once I even saw an incredibly long tongue try to lick its way through like it was tasting a corpsicle. Had to admit, I was happy Gary had switched rides. I was barely holding on; I could only imagine the strangled sounds his stomach and throat would be making. Those that weren't driving were doing everything in their power to scope out their laps or check out the patterns in their skin from their clasped hands.

"Can't drive any faster, Mike?" Tracy asked, never looking up as she did so. I didn't answer because I was afraid what would come out if I opened my mouth. It was a blessing when we finally got to the mouth of the tunnel; it was dark inside and made seeing the cars that much more difficult. According to BT, he had thought it had a slight bend in it, which I happily confirmed, as I could not see the light from the other side. This would work to our advantage. The jam was as thick as it could get. The only slice of luck that we'd had was that someone with a plow had done his best to slam his way through; cars had been pushed over and onto each other, as he or she tried to get past. Like a slow-moving needle, we threaded through the narrow opening afforded us.

We weren't more than twenty feet in when the temperature and the lighting plummeted. Not the first misgivings, but definitely the deepest hit me just then. The sun was setting, and when it did, well we all knew what that meant– the blackness was going to be absolute. The pile-up of cars had finally disappeared about three quarters through the tunnel. It was clear to us all, as we looked out the far side at what had caused it to begin with.

"Military blockade," BT said.

"Why would they do this?" Winters asked.

"In a vain attempt to stop the spread, of course," Deneaux replied. We had gotten out and were all standing there in more or less a line, looking at the opening. The pull was strong to forgo this crazy plan and make a straight line up the coast and on to Etna Station. I wanted to check the Humvees up ahead for some heavy machine guns, but fun would have to wait, plus, that would defeat the purpose of what we were trying to accomplish.

"I'm going to set the charges," Winters said as he peeled away from the group.

"This looked way better on paper," BT said when we were alone.

We got the kids and the animals all locked up in one of the cars as we took our places. The idea was to fake a crash; the small explosion Winters was going to set off would hopefully convince Payne that we had crashed, and when no one came out the other side, she would be forced to investigate. When she was in range, we would kill her, just like that, quick and easy. Although now that we were here, it seemed anything but. First, a fatal crash seemed unlikely given the traffic. What if she didn't bite? What if she waited a week? A month before checking it out? What if the stupid tunnel collapsed from a magnitude eight earthquake? What if it collapsed from Winters' charge? I could do the bad outcomes game all day long and still maybe never come across what was really going to go wrong.

"Fire in the hole." Winters made sure we heard it, but not loud enough that it would reach either end. This was our cue to find cover and cover our ears. Even then, I thought the resultant explosion was going to shred my eardrums. The tunnel, the ground, the cars around us vibrated from the concussive forces, a few ceiling tiles shook loose and smashed against the ground and cars. The destructive noise was even scarier than the initial explosion because we had not been expecting it.

"Should we light a fire?" BT asked. I thought about it; would certainly lend authenticity to our crash site.

"No. As much as I'd like to chase away the dark and the chill, it'll screw up our vision."

"Not to speak the obvious, Mike, but we're not going to be able to see anything anyway."

"Are you already forgetting about the NVGs that came with Winters?"

"I hate those things, man. Make everything look that ghostly green shit like we're in a horror movie."

"I'm not sure what pleasure cruise you've been riding, big man, but we are in a horror movie and I for one don't want to be the brother that goes down the basement by himself."

BT laughed.

"What the hell is funny about any of this?" I asked in all seriousness.

"Just trying to picture you with a 'fro is all."

"I could pull it off." I said.

"No man, not at all, but it is funny."

"You want the night vision goggles or what?" I asked handing out a pair.

"Naw. We only have the three and Winters isn't giving his up. You keep them so you can keep an eye out on Deneaux," he said.

It truly sucked always having to keep one eye on a member of the group and there had been serious debate about giving her a set of the coveted goggles. But no matter the arguments against, it always circled back to her incredible marksmanship skills. Not a one of us could touch her. Now the problem was would she stand and fight or tactically withdraw as the situation dictated. It wouldn't be the first time; that was obviously the flip side.

"You just tell me when to hit the flares." Winters had set up a string of flares, five on each side, spaced out roughly ten feet apart. The hope was we pulled Payne in close, BT lit up the tunnel putting her in the spotlight, and we blew her into whatever realm she belonged. We got into the best positions we could. Winters was facing the south entrance, Deneaux the north, and I was constantly turning back and forth like a weather vane in a fickle wind.

The dark was a cruel and crushing enemy, but a necessary ally. Not sure how the cookie crumbles on that. By increments, we lost all of our ambient lighting. By the time we switched over to the goggles, it was impossible to see your own hand. You want to know what sense picks up the slack and distorts everything incredibly? Hearing. It feels the need to make everything it senses become a monster in the dark. Maybe not quite so relevant when there were fewer monsters in the world, but right now one had to assume everything one heard was a monster. Car suspensions squeaked as zombies shifted around inside their prisons, trying to find ways out. There was the skittering of rodents and other small animals as they scavenged for food, no longer able to rely on the droppings of the most wasteful beings on the planet. Fuck them. Now they had to work at it like the rest of us. Got to imagine rats were pretty pissed off, no longer able to subsidize their existence with potato chips and corndog crust.

Bird calls entered in from either side; by the time they reached us, they had become how I figured the prehistoric world sounded. In the dark it was hard not to imagine them as fifteen-foot pteranodons. There was a cacophony of noise, but no Payne. She was conspicuously absent. With the goggles on, our sight took on the alien green ghostly landscape that BT disliked. Don't get me wrong, these devices are an incredible invention, but they are not without their drawbacks. First off is that color. The human brain is used to dealing with vivid and varied colors. When the landscape suddenly becomes that drab, eerie green, the brain, in its ever-determined desire to make sense of whatever input it receives, will resort to creating shadows and hallucinations, specters where none exist. If you are vigilant, you can overcome this flaw, but the bigger one is the complete lack of peripheral vision, and that's physical. A primary human defense is to spot threats from the side; the goggles are essentially blinders, creating the constant need to swivel your head, which is a diverting and a time-consuming venture.

"Anything?" BT asked for at least the fifth time in the last ten minutes. I'd answered him civilly enough the first couple of times, then I had to bite back on what I wanted to say. "Yeah, man. They're all coming–I'm just trying to see how close they can get before I sound the alarm." I had to remember he was sitting in the complete dark, and I've got to tell you, that does something to time, or our perception of it, anyway. Seconds become minutes, minutes become hours, well, you get the picture.

"Nothing man," I whispered. The tunnel had been as black as Eliza's soul for two hours; my eyes and my skull were beginning to fatigue from the goggles, and that was far from the worst of it. I kept looking up to the far right corner where information on what the goggles were receiving was displayed, along with the life of the batteries. I was sitting comfortably at half, but where would I be in another hour or two? Three hours from now, when Payne was sure to show, they would be completely drained. How many of us could she kill in that complete darkness before we were even aware she was among us?

"I'll be right back," I said to BT.

"You're shitting me, right? You're really going to leave me in the dark?"

"Just got to talk to Winters for a second."

"Make him come over here."

"I'll be right back, man."

"I hate you," he hissed as I started to move. "Wait. Sorry. Just in case anything happens I don't want those to be my last words. I loathe you. Yeah, that has more oomph behind it."

Winters turned as he heard me approaching.

"How you doing?" I asked.

"Feel the building of an enormous headache coming on."

"Yeah, I think I've beaten you to that punch. How's your battery?"

"Little under half," he replied, knowing where I was going with this.

"We should maybe do this in shifts," I said.

"I don't like that; there are too many blind spots for one person to pick up."

"They're all going to be blind spots if we don't."

He mulled that one for a moment. "Half hour shifts then?" he asked.

"Sounds good."

"I'll take the first. Rest your eyes." He said as he readjusted his position to be able to more easily see down the tunnel in both directions.

I then found Deneaux and told her my concern as well.

"You sure? She could cover the distance before any one of us could scope out the entire tunnel."

"Not sure what choices we have. We're going to have to

hope we're not that unlucky."

"Michael, I realize you rely heavily on luck in your life. I am not sure how smart it is to bank everyone else's on it."

"If the well runs dry, there will be no one left to be concerned about it." I wasn't trying to be flippant, I was trying to ignore her words. To acknowledge them was to potentially imbue them with a potent curse or make them somehow true. Words can bring power to thoughts and ideas, one should be careful not to give negative ones any more of a hold over us than they already had.

"I'm coming back," I whispered to BT. I could see him doing his best to pierce the darkness with his eyes. Of course, he was not succeeding by straining, and I didn't want to receive a friendly fire punch to the head.

"What the hell, man? You go out for a sandwich and a show or something?"

"I've been gone for five minutes."

"Really?" he asked. He sounded and looked so sincere I had to believe that was how he felt. "What's up?" he asked, knowing full well I wouldn't have left a post without having a good reason.

"We're running out of battery time."

"Shit. How long?"

"Couple of hours at the most. Talked to Winters and Deneaux; we're going to do shifts."

"Can't say I like how vulnerable that is going to leave us."

"I know, brother. Don't know what else to do."

"We could leave this tunnel," he replied.

"Thought of that, but I can feel it in my bones, BT. She is going to strike tonight. The tunnel keeps her somewhat limited to where she can come from; we won't be afforded the same advantage outside."

"Advantage? Fighting in the dark is somehow an advantage to you? Is there anything you won't say?"

"Not much and it's not the dark that's the advantage it's the set-up, odds are she can see pretty good in this and she thinks we won't be able to," I told him as I shut down my goggles.

BT sighed at my words.

"Wow, this sucks," I said. I tried to peer through the darkness with the exact results you would expect.

"You think?" he asked sarcastically.

Could occasionally hear someone moving around, the murmurings of a baby or two; luckily Ben-Ben was keeping his bacon-loving self quiet. Of us all, he had me the most worried. That thought released some hold I'd kept on my claustrophobia. Suddenly I was doing my best to mentally push against the walls of the tunnel, they had begun to constrict around us. The more I struggled to keep control of the space around me, the harder my heart thumped. It was getting to the point where each beat physically hurt. I was just reaching up to turn the goggles back on when I heard the scrape of metal on metal.

"What was that?" BT asked.

"Shh," I said quietly. I powered up my goggles and waited an interminable amount of time while they booted up. Couldn't have been more than fifteen seconds—seemed like a fucking eon. And in that time frame, I heard two more pops and squeals. Then I recognized the sound. It was car doors being opened, and too far away to be our people doing it.

"That what I think it is?" BT asked.

"What do you think it is?" I asked.

"Car doors opening."

"Yeah, that's what I thought, too."

"How are the zombies opening their doors just now after all the time they've been trapped?"

"Oh, I don't think it's zombies opening the doors," I said when I caught a black flash of something moving quickly through the vehicles.

"I hate her."

"Nice to see that anger directed at someone else besides me."

"Don't worry," BT said, "I have enough to go around."

"Crap," I said as I peered through the goggles.

"What is it, Mike? You usually don't give two shits when I utter my dislike for you."

"She's opened the zoo, man. Zombies are coming."

"Contact," Winters said from his side. "Zombies, couple dozen."

"Same," I told him.

"She's going to know we're playing possum the moment we start firing on those zombies, Mike. She's testing us," BT said.

"Winters, pull back to me. Get everyone in with you," I said. I reached around and tapped those nearby and guided them to my spot. "Payne is here," I told them. "She's letting loose the zombies to see if we will betray our location and plan. Right now, we have to hope it's because she doesn't know if we're alive or not."

"Yeah, but dad, there are zombies coming and none of us can see anything." This from Travis; he was putting on a brave face but there was a noticeable tremor in his voice. Could not fault him that. Being in a battle was stressful enough; being in a battle where you couldn't see your enemy? Far, far worse.

"How close you planning on letting them get?" Tracy asked.

"Too fucking close," I told her.

"I don't like what that implies, Mike. What the exact-fuck does that mean?" BT asked, looking for clarification.

"I don't know, I don't know. Payne is going to want to confirm our deaths, that I know. The question is, will she wait until the zombies finish eating us to come and take a gander."

"That's too close," BT said.

"Yeah, I'm getting that. I'm just hoping Payne brings her happy ass in with the zees."

"If she doesn't?" Tracy asked.

"Then we kill the zombies and get the hell out of here."

"She won't fall for another trap," my wife said.

"Doesn't really seem like she fell for this one," BT said.

"Not so sure about that. She's here, isn't she?" I replied.

"Yeah, with her own army," BT replied.

"Twenty-five yards." Winters was keeping an eye on the northern side of the tunnel.

"Fifty yards." I was doing my best to judge the distance. Depth perception was difficult at best with the goggles.

"Any sign of Payne?" Tommy asked.

"No," I said, tight-lipped. I had another shitty idea and I was wondering if I should play it. "I think we should go out to meet her."

"You can't do that! How will you get by the zombies?" Tracy asked.

"We stay up against the wall; there are no zombies there," I said.

"Who would go?" BT asked.

"Tommy and myself."

"So, you're going to leave us all alone back here with one set of NVGs and zombies coming in from both sides? You realize we'll be firing straight past you, I mean, hopefully, and not into you."

"We'll stay pinned to the wall while we can, but this is a chance we have to take. She's close. We have to strike while we can. Maybe it would be for the best if you all got back in the cars. Winters, do we have enough time for you to get them all back in a car?"

"Just."

"Alright, let's do this, then. Deneaux, I need the goggles." She handed them over reluctantly. "You ready, Tommy?"

"I'd rather be eating a Pop-Tart," he replied.

"I've seen some of the flavors you dig up; this is safer."

"If you say so, but that eggplant filled, hollandaise sauce-glazed one was out of this world."

"If you say so," I said, repeating his words.

No matter how slowly and cautiously the group moved to get into the cars, I could still hear the groan of metal as the doors were being opened; I could only hope that the sound of the moaning and shuffling zombies was sufficiently loud enough to drown it out. My back was getting damp from the wet weeping through the cracks in the concrete wall. I'm sure it didn't help that I was sweating from the stress of what we were attempting to do. Tommy was leading the way, moving a lot quicker than I was comfortable with. The zombies, for the most part, were like thrown arrows, meaning they were only going in the direction Payne threw them, or in this case, shown. Though now and again, some would turn our way as we approached, like a particularly delicious-smelling hamburger being paraded around a bunch of poor college students. Tommy put his hand out and hit me in the shoulder, halting my progress. He pointed to a place up ahead of us; zombies were coming straight our way, being funneled by a camper that had collided with a small pickup.

Our only option was to get up on the SUV in front of us. Once atop it, we would be like dual surfers above a sea of shit, which just barely beats being duel swimmers in the sea of shit. The hood pinged loudly as I jumped onto it, but that had nothing on the sound the roof made as Tommy climbed up. Sounded like a Tibetan monk smacking the hell out of a gong. If anything was ever going to scream "Dinner!" to the zees, that was it. As I looked up at Tommy to see what the hell he could have done to make that kind of noise, I swear I saw Payne move quickly past in the shadows behind him. No doubt she'd heard it as well; could only hope she thought it was a minivan banging into the back of a band bus. Tommy reached over and helped me up. The zombies were indeed curious about what was causing all the racket. I felt a hand smack against my calf; jagged fingernails sought purchase in the thick leather of my boots. I stood up to keep less of me in reach; it worked in that respect, but with so many zombies crowding around they were making the car rock. I was only using the surfing bit as an analogy–I didn't think it was going to come true.

"I can smell your fear." Payne's voice drifted over to us like an ill wind. Tommy tapped me on the shoulder and pointed. I didn't see much of anything, though he was emphatic. "I cannot believe you would make it quite this easy for me." With the zombies and the acoustics of the tunnel it was difficult for me to locate her. Tommy had brought his rifle to his shoulder.

"You have a better angle," he whispered.

I wanted to tell him: "better angle at what?" but it was all I could do to keep my feet under me as the zombies pitched our boat around like orcas tossing a seal.

"Keep me steady," I told him as I brought my rifle up. He lowered his weapon and did as I asked. "Safe to assume she knows we're here."

"I'd say so," he answered.

With my forward right hand, I pushed a button that illuminated my green laser. It cut through the fog and unsettled dust and just for the tiniest of moments, it illuminated silver off the eye of what I figured was Payne. I didn't even bother waiting for a return message from my brain to confirm what I had seen; I pulled the trigger the exact moment the green twinkled silver. The resultant flare from my muzzle temporarily blinded me to the results of the bullet I sent outwards. I didn't see a prone body or a blood spray on the far wall, no scream nor wail; there was nothing to give me any hint of success or failure. Well, there was a fair measure of failure as I had completely blown our cover. Zombies that had passed us by were coming back; that was good for our loved ones, bad for us.

"The camper!" Tommy shouted as zombies began to press in from all around.

"Sounds like a wonderful idea, it's just that the camper's ten feet away," I told him. He backed up as far as the roof of the SUV would allow, took two running steps and leaped. His trailing foot caught a zombie flush in the face, busting out a row of teeth, but it didn't slow him down as he crash-landed into the camper ladder. He quickly climbed up and on to the much higher roof.

"Now you, Mr. T!" He had got down onto his stomach and had his arms outstretched.

My jump, in comparison to Tommy's near graceful one, was a comedy of errors. I backed up like he did, and that's where all similarities stopped. Instead of two steps, I went for three, giving the zombies around me just enough time to grab at the bottom of my pants; one succeeded. It was not a momentum-stopping grab, and it surely cost him most of the fingernails on his right hand, but it was just enough to make my flight for life come up a tad short. I was in the air, knowing full well I was not going to make it. Didn't keep me from stretching my arms out in a desperate attempt to fly to that chrome-plated ladder. So, when my fingers grazed against the middle rungs, I almost wanted to cry out in disbelief at my good fortune. I was finally able to grab hold of the second rung from the bottom–I pulled my body over the closest zombies and started scrambling up.

That's when I heard POP, POP, POP in quick succession. Noises everywhere, didn't think too much of it, until the ladder began yawing backward. It was pulling free of its moorings. My guess is it wasn't designed to withstand the stresses of two full-grown men jumping from distance onto it. I don't know why I always forget about Tommy's inhuman strength; he reached out and grabbed the ladder before I could spill back into the throng. He stood and lifted the thing with me on it straight up into the air, even going so far as to let a zombie hitch a ride for part of the way. I kicked out repeatedly with my left foot until the monster's face was a disfigured, bleeding mess of broken bone and damaged flesh. I'd crushed the right side of his face sufficiently enough that his eyeball was dislodged and hanging loose. His nose was not just lying flat but was now embedded in his face. My boot had completely ripped his top lip off, and still the thing hung in there. I figure that's what happens when you've been living on a diet rich in floor-fries from a car you could not escape. If you had a meal this close you'd be reluctant to let go, as well. Tommy reached out and grabbed me while simultaneously dropping the ladder. It, along with the zombie I had chewed up with my boot, fell back into the crowd.

"Did you get her?" he asked.

"No idea. I feel like I had to have hit her, but I have no way of knowing for sure."

The camper began to rock as the zombies started closing in on it. The back and forth was not as pronounced as it had been on the SUV, but it would only take one wrong placement of a foot or leaning the wrong way to send either of us over the edge. Four shots rang out from the direction we had come from, but no screams, which I took as a good sign. Unless the gunman had been silenced, that would be a bad sign. While I was looking back to the cars, Tommy had got down and was looking at the vent cover atop the camper, he'd ripped it clear from its hinges; it had not gone quietly into the night. It had protested loudly with a heavy cracking sound as he shattered the plastic cover and frame.

"No zombies inside," he said after removing his head from the opening.

"You want to go through there? Will we even fit?"

"If this engine starts, we can drive it back, grab everyone, and get out of here."

"What about Payne?" I asked.

"If she's dead, we're rid of her. If she's not, she'll find us."

"What the hell, Tommy? That's like telling your kid 'Yep, the monster's under your bed—might be dead or it might eat your face; we'll see come morning.' Should we at least wait until tomorrow, first light? Maybe we can find a body or something?"

"I suppose we could ask the zombies to move away so we could check," he said. "If she's out there, she's going to be angry. I say we don't give her enough time to regroup and strike while we're separated."

I couldn't argue with that. "You should go in first," I said.

"It's because you're afraid of getting stuck, isn't it?" he asked. I could only shrug in answer. I don't tend to keep my anxieties secret. He wriggled a little bit, but otherwise got in easily enough. I dropped in after him. I was not a fan of the dozen zombies peering in at us from the front of the camper, although, creepy as it was, odds were, they could not see us.

"Will it start?" I asked. Tommy hadn't made it to the front console yet. He turned to look back, his expression asking if I was serious.

"We're about to find out. You might want to take the goggles off." The seat cushion let out a squelch of air. I heard the jingle of keys, then the wonderful, telltale dinging of a battery that still had some juice left. There was a moment where I heard nothing else, then there was the grinding of the starter as it fired off and got the engine running. The headlights were muted but only because the zombies were crowding the light out. I peered around, trying to catch any trace of Payne; I saw nothing but more zombies.

When I was confident as I could be that Payne was no longer in the building, I got up beside Tommy, not yet comfortable enough to sit in the passenger seat. I had my rifle ready and cracked the passenger side window, but I was also prepared to shoot through the windshield if the need arose. We were moving at a pace slow enough that we were pushing the zombies ahead of us out of the way. Every once in a while, one didn't get the memo to not play in the street and we would subsequently run over it with a resounding crunchy squish, but for the most part, we were like an ice-busting barge in the Arctic, clearing a path.

"How's the gas?"

"Three-quarters of a tank."

Took us close to fifteen minutes to get back to our cars.

"Everyone alright?" I asked through the window.

BT gave a thumbs up. "Payne?" he asked.

"Got a shot off…but I don't know. She wouldn't tell me if she was dead or not."

"Just like a vampire to be a cryptic bitch."

"Tommy is going to clear a path for us out with this behemoth. You all just stay in tight behind us," I said.

We had to use the camper as a battering ram to get through the military blockade; it had been my hope we'd be able to confiscate the much larger and more comfortable vehicle for our own purposes, but Tommy had done some front-end damage. We were leaking coolant and from the sound of it, the fan blade was smacking up against the radiator or possibly the engine block. Either way, it was badly damaged, though it had served its purpose well enough. He got it up to twenty miles per hour for a couple of miles; it sounded like an infant with a wooden spoon beating on a variety of pots and pans from the cupboard. By the time he stopped, we had a geyser issuing forth from the front end. But we'd put distance between us and the zombies, the roadway was clear, and there was no sign of Payne. I can't say I thought she was dead, but it sure was a beautiful day and I *wanted* to believe that.

"What now, Mike?" Tracy asked.

I looked over each and every one of us still standing; even the indefatigable Deneaux looked done. We were so far past being on our last legs, we were writhing around on the ground. I could not, and I would not, delay it any longer. Etna Station was our destination. History can judge if I'd made a mistake; but I was certain of my decision at the time. You cannot fault me for my actions as I looked upon my kids, my wife, my friends, and family. They were scared, tired, and I would not watch another of them die in this fucking apocalypse. I was drawing a line in the sand. Sure, it was going to be crossed many times before this was over, but right there and then the symbolism of that drawn line gave me hope and purpose.

Not sure what type of technology they had at Etna, but we were twenty miles south of our destination when we found ourselves staring down the barrels of a very well-coordinated ambush.

"Do not fire upon us!" came through a megaphone. "These are fifty cal cannons, you will all be dead before the repercussion of your first round is finished. All of you that can, step out of your vehicles, hands held high, no weapons of any sort!"

BT looked over at me from the car he was in. "Your call," he said.

"We're coming out!" I yelled, placing my empty hands out the window first. "Don't shoot, we're coming out!" I was the first to stand outside the car and was immediately followed by the rest.

They had all of us sitting on the curb with our hands zip-tied behind our backs except for the babies, and they let Nicole loose so she could care for them. Henry had to stay in the car because he was not digging how I was being treated. I appreciated the hell out of that, I did, but I didn't want a soldier inadvertently hurting my dog because of his loyalty.

"My name is Gunnery Sergeant Tajima. I am part of the intercept group for Etna Station. Heard of it?"

"We have," I said.

"And what's your reason for coming here?" he asked.

I figured this wasn't the time to tell him it was to take over the base and become lord of all I surveyed. "Sanctuary. We've been on our own for so long, I...we just want to have some sense of normalcy. A place where our kids have a chance."

"What's your name?" he asked.

"Michael Talbot."

"You the leader here?"

"More of an honorary thing," I replied.

"You're married?" he asked, picking up my tone quickly. I nodded.

"I can't guarantee that you'll get to stay; there's a vetting process. And even if you pass that, we're not a big enough facility to open up to everyone that's left. We need people with skills. Engineers, doctors, teachers."

"You might as well cut us loose, then, Gunnery Sergeant.

Save everyone the trouble." I sighed.

"Michael, perhaps you should tell the man about your other talents before you discount us all so quickly," Deneaux said

"What are you doing?" I fairly hissed, afraid of what the crone was about to reveal.

"Michael is…" she started.

"Deneaux!" I shouted.

"A former Marine with more combat under his belt than I am willing to bet any of the men under your command, Gunnery Sergeant. Of course, it is imperative to welcome the intellectuals in, but is it also not important that those very same people are protected?"

"What are you doing, Deneaux?" I asked.

"Do you want in, Michael, or do you not? It would appear they do not have much need for pothole repairmen."

She was right; she was absolutely right. But if my hands were free I think I would have shot her and her smug, self-important self. Well maybe not shot, throat punched would be much more satisfying.

"How many of you can fight?" he asked.

Except for the babies, every one of us nodded that we could, including Deneaux, which surprised the hell out of me, as I figured she was going to try and pull the Senator card. She probably still would once they brought us to the base, or in case the Gunnery Sergeant wasn't looking for any new, old recruits.

"Most of you don't look like my traditional troops, but the woman is right. We always need more soldiers," Tajima said.

My head bowed of its own volition. I had brought my family here with the hopes that we could be done fighting. Turned out that was their resident criteria.

The Master Sergeant must have seen my resignation. "It's not like that, Talbot. If you're allowed to stay, only a few of you would need to join up. The rest would be allowed to pursue some other useful field, like those aforementioned ones."

"He doesn't do well with authority," BT said.

"Yeah, you're one to talk," I said to him.

"Only your authority," he responded.

"Let's go," Tajima said. "Even if it all goes bad, worst case scenario we cut you loose and you'll get a meal and some new clothes out of this."

"And our weapons?" I asked.

"You'll get those back."

They placed us all into the back of a large, troop transport truck. The ride was uncomfortable, compounded by the fact that our hands were restrained behind us. Safe to say that BT, Tommy, and myself could have worked our way out of the zip ties easily enough, but we didn't. That didn't stop Deneaux, though.

"Treating me like a common criminal," she said as she brought her hands to the front and rubbed her wrists.

"Yeah, there is nothing common about your criminal activities," I told her. I smiled but she sneered at me.

We were separated from the rest of the camp, and brought into a holding area, where, true to his word, we were given a hot meal, a place to clean up and some new clothes. Had been there for about three days sleeping on cots without much contact from them, before the interviews began. Thought for sure I'd be one of the first to get questioned; ended up being the last.

I was brought to the main building, up two flights of ornate steps, down a hallway and finally to a large oak-paneled office. "Ah, Lieutenant Talbot, a pleasure to meet you. I am Colonel Bennington." A grizzled, gray-haired man in full uniform rolled out from behind his desk. He maneuvered his wheelchair so he could shake my hand.

"Lieutenant? I think you have me confused with someone else," I told him.

"No, I do not. I very rarely get confused. I pulled your service records. Seems you've had some trouble both in the civilian and military worlds, but your tour of duty was exemplary. Your group speaks most highly of you, to a person. Everyone says they owe their lives to you. I need that kind of leadership here."

"But?" I asked looking around warily.

"You have a large group, Talbot. Our resources are already stretched thin. We need medical personnel; your daughter has stated that would be something she would like to achieve, along with your niece. Your wife expressed that she would teach, as did your sister. These are all things that will greatly aid our development here, but it will take time until any of them are up to speed and contributing."

"So, to pay their dues, you need me in your army? Is that where this is going?" I asked.

"You and a few others from your group, yes."

"And if I were to say no?"

"Don't let pride impede what you have traveled across the country to obtain. We have all made necessary sacrifices for the greater good."

"You have no idea, Colonel, the amount of sacrifice we all have endured."

"I do not doubt it. You haven't been here long enough to realize what we are trying to accomplish. Is that a fair enough statement?"

I nodded.

"You'll see soon enough, come, join us. Help us to get there. Maybe someday soon we will be able to just accept all people regardless of skills or previous occupation."

"Well, since I'm an officer now, does that mean I can drink at the OC?"

"If we had one, you most assuredly would be welcome." I shook the Colonel's hand. "Gunnery Sergeant Tajima has your uniform. He'll brief you on where and when you need to report for duty."

"I am way too old for this shit," I muttered as I walked out of the Colonel's office.

EPILOGUE ONE

SPENT THE NEXT three months of my life going through officer boot camp. When they realized I could fight and shoot, I was promoted from a butter bar 2nd lieutenant to a silver bar 1st lieutenant. In that time, Tracy had picked up a history teaching gig, and Nicole was taking her first rounds of exams to become a nurse. She eventually wanted to be a doctor, but it was imperative for her to begin contributing quickly. Travis was allowed to finish his traditional schooling. We were all, in one way or another, beginning to assimilate into this new world we had struggled to place ourselves in. When I was done with my training, I was allowed to requisition personnel for my squad. I snagged Sergeant Tynes, who ended up being entirely too surly for anyone else. Sergeant Winters asked to be on my team, as did Tommy and Gary. My chosen, along with seven other men and women made up my squad; we were part of the Fifty-Second, Marine Corps Exploratory Brigade.

My squad's basic mission was to discover and retrieve assets for the camp. This could include, but was not limited to, food, supplies, weaponry, or people. I wasn't keen on the regimentation of military life, but it was hard to deny the benefits my family was deriving. Travis was dating a girl; Nicole was starting at the hospital next week. Tracy had received four apples as her second-grade students' favorite teacher. My sister, her baby boy, Ryan, Justin, all of them were in school and had secondary chores like tending gardens, watching pre-schoolers. We had a mission; we were working toward building a strong, vibrant community that could thrive after the end of the world, and we could feel it. I had hopes that my grandson would grow up in a world devoid of zombies. Another added benefit of being here was I saw less and less of Deneaux; she appeared to be working her own magic in setting herself up. Last I had heard, she was being added to the Civilian Board that dealt with, well you get it. Maybe not the absolute power she was striving for, but certainly a stepping stone in the right direction.

The average Joe here wanted to believe that the people ran the show, but Etna was a militarily-run organization from top to bottom. The board was only created as a sort of liaison. Sure, citizens had input, but at the end of the day, nothing here existed without the iron fist of the military keeping all of the monsters, human and zombie alike, outside the gates. Normally, I would not be alright with that as the status quo, but for the time being, I understood the necessity of it.

I think because of this, when I did run into Deneaux I felt like I always got a heavy dose of thinly veiled contempt wrapped in a heavy cloak of passive aggression. I also think she only pretended to hide it that well to irritate me even more. She just couldn't stand that in the hierarchy of things, I was many rungs above her station. Honestly, I didn't give a shit. As long as she stayed away from me and mine, she could feel however she wanted. Although I knew that was a bad stance to take when dealing with Deneaux. It's never wise to turn one's back on a pit viper. But at the moment, I felt I had bigger things to worry about.

"AH, LIEUTENANT TALBOT. Good to see you," Colonel Bennington said.

"You as well, sir," I told him.

"I heard your training went well. You ready for your first mission?"

"I am, sir. I never thought I'd be in a rush to leave the relative safety of camp, but now I'm beginning to get a little stir crazy."

"Well, this ought to stretch your legs a bit. Sending your team to Idaho."

"Idaho, sir?"

"Missile silo 272, as a matter of fact."

"Please tell me I'm not retrieving a nuke, sir. Sergeant Tynes will kill me."

"No, nothing like that. Somehow a group of molecular biologists found their way into the defunct silo and were able to get the communications up. We picked the signal up yesterday. You and your team will parachute within ten clicks of the silo, report back your findings, and secure the scientists. Then we'll arrange for helo extraction."

"Sounds easy enough. Anything else I should know?"

"Well, I would imagine keep an eye out for zombies."

I laughed. "Yes, sir."

EPILOGUE TWO
OR TALBOTSODE 1

OKAY, I FEEL like I may have related this story before or possibly I'm dealing with the Mandela Effect, either way here goes, either for the first time or not. Did I ever tell you about that time I almost died? Isn't that a rich line? I mean, this entire set of journals revolves around me almost dying. Somehow, I've avoided that tenacious bastard, but eventually I'll pick the right door and he'll be standing there, like in *Let's Make a Deal*, or I could just cheat, like I'm sure they did. I used to wonder if maybe Bob from Spokane never really had a chance as he picked door number three, like, maybe all the prizes were on wheels and they just slid the pallet with the forty-seven cans of spicy spam to whichever door he chose, and the new car and home entertainment center to the others. So, yeah, I was playing the shell game with the dark one, and someday he'd figure out there was actually no ball underneath because I had palmed it. Until then, he can go fuck himself. I mean, really, what other choice did I have?

Let me get back to where I was going with this. I was out in Colorado, and Dennis had come up to visit from Colorado Springs. Not entirely sure why; maybe he knew I was going to try to kill myself and wanted to prevent it, though I almost took him with me. Interest peaked yet? Not as salacious as it sounds, but much more terrifying. I know, I know—stop telling you and let it unfold. So, I'd had my Jeep for a couple of years. I'd taken her off-road more than a few times, plus I had some experience with another Jeep I owned once upon a time. I wasn't a novice, but I also wasn't a seasoned veteran. Just enough bravado, stupidity, and booze as to be dangerous. Really, though, isn't that how most craptastic things start? Plenty of cringe-worthy videos on Youtube start with the line, "Hold my beer." So, we're heading out from Denver to the mountains, to Waldorf Pass. Almost sounds like there would be a resort up there. There isn't.

After about an hour and a half of normal driving and three beers, (I was pacing myself) we get to the actual trailhead. The first three miles were fairly easy. Sure, there's a lot of tossing around and some avoidance of bigger boulders and ruts, but for the most part, it is a tree-lined route, beautiful in its own right but for a couple of switchbacks—not overly dangerous. Of course, by now we were officially off-road, and I wasn't terribly worried about a police cruiser pulling up behind me, maybe a forest ranger, but we were talking the Rocky Mountains; that's a lot of terrain to cover.

"Beer me!" I shouted to Dennis over the music playing much too loudly. I'd had to turn it up to mask the squelching of the styrofoam cooler we had brought with us. You know that high pitched squeal from hell I'm talking about. Now pretend that loose lidded cooler was weighted with ice and beer and locked into a paint shaker, because that's what a Jeep feels like on uneven terrain, and that son of a bitch was letting us know exactly how it felt in the most disruptive and aggravating way possible. I was enjoying nature in the only way men know how, with a burgeoning buzz. It's almost like we feel that we've so tamed the beast of Nature that we can flaunt our arrogance at it. We got up to the top of the first summit, used to be an old silver mine, I believe. There are the ghosts of two structures long since succumbed to the elements.

It was an incredibly beautiful day. Blue skies for miles. We were looking down over an expansive green field replete with wildflowers and the occasional elk, and just to make it that much more picturesque, there was a deep blue stream cutting a wide ribbon straight through the middle. I'd brought the family up here before; the kids loved the silver slag piles–they are loaded with pyrite, or fool's gold. We had enough of it at our house we could have opened our own gift shop. I mean, if people wanted to pay for that kind of thing. I wonder if you know where I'm going with this; if you've read enough of my journals it should be fairly obvious. Beautiful day, check. Beautiful scenery, check. Drunk? Pull out the rifles, check.

Had a little Marlin .22 caliber with me. We plinked at some cans and other targets, because obviously beer and guns go well together. At this point in my life, one has to wonder how I had not received multiple Darwin award mentions; maybe I had, just they'd never invited me to the ceremony. We'd shot off a hundred rounds or so, chewed through some jerky, and drank a few more beers when Dennis pointed to some other trails that led off from the plateau we found ourselves on.

I'd looked upon those trails many times before with my kids and wife. The one to the right looked terrifying, had to be a forty-five-degree angle straight up the side of the mountain. My Jeep was a beast, but I'd done nothing aftermarket to beef her up, and that particular trail looked out of my depth of range, even with beer goggles, which, even as I write this, I'm clapping myself on the back for getting that one right. If I stalled out or maybe she just didn't have enough torque, or who knows? I run over a big enough rock with enough speed it lifts my front end just enough to fuck up my center of gravity, and we're flipping end over end down the side of a mountain. Roll bars are designed to deal with that exact scenario, but just because they're there doesn't mean you want to test them out. Ever want to use a flotation device on an airplane? Fuck no you didn't. Or a gas mask during a chemical attack? Again, no. They're designed to potentially keep you safe, but if whatever shit-fest you find yourself in has gone down, who wants to have to rely on them?

The other trail, to the left, we couldn't see much of. The trailhead, as it curved around the base of the mountain, was slightly steeper than the trail that brought us up, and the rocks a little more pronounced, but with the level of liquor I had imbibed, it was more of a challenge than a dare. Not sure of the distinction, but it seems relevant. A challenge you place on yourself; it's yours to conquer. A dare comes from elsewhere, meaning your pride is at stake. Never had gone up this particular trail with the kids, first off because it took an hour and a half to get to the mountains then another hour and a half to get to the mine, so once you start doing the math and realize I still have to go back home, and well, there is a time-dilation event that happens with kids in any vehicle; all trips stretch on indeterminably. Six regular hours in a car, is somewhere near twenty-four with kids. Weird fucking phenomenon, but that doesn't make it any less true. Secondly, when I was sober, there was a small, rarely-listened to voice in the back of my head, that said it was mostly untraveled because it was a more technical trail. But I'd drowned out that little fucker after the sixth beer, he couldn't do much except scream under the fluid, and by that time you can't distinguish words.

"Let's do it," I said as I got back into the Jeep.

Dennis grabbed a couple more beers from the cooler and off we went. Started off easy enough, kind of like the introductory screens to a video game, learning the basics, nothing overly challenging. That changed abruptly the farther up the side of the mountain we went. The trail continually got thinner, from something a large Ford truck might be comfortable with to a trail a goat might feel a wee bit claustrophobic on. Had a steep rock mountain to my right and a sheer drop off to my left. I'm not exaggerating when I say that I was hanging half a tire off the edge. My liquid courage was rapidly vacating and I was stuck with my white-knuckled hands at ten and two doing my utmost to not look out my driver side window.

Dennis had yet to pick up on the precariousness of our situation until I navigated the first switch back and his happy ass got to be in the hot seat. I mean, we were both screwed if I went over, but when you can actually look out your window into space like you are on an open-air biplane about to do a barrel roll, well, let me tell you, that begins to pucker the old poop shooter. For a while, he could do nothing but stare out that window. Then he was all eyes front, holding on to the "fuck me" bar that is right above the glove box. It's basically there to keep you from shaking back and forth and smacking your head into the window or as something to make you feel better when you're about to wet your pants.

"You should move over," he squeaked out without looking over at me. Or maybe he did, lord knows I wasn't going to swivel my head to see if he had.

"Nowhere to go, brother."

"Maybe back?"

"No place to turn around. You want me to back down this thing?"

"On second thought…I'd get you a beer, but I'm petrified, Talbot."

"What makes you think I could spare a hand to grab it?"

"I can appreciate that."

And as if this weren't screwed up enough, want to know what happens in the mountains a lot in the afternoon? Crazy ass storms, that's what happens. There was a range of peaks off to our right and the sky over them had turned a steely dark tone; a wall of thick clouds releasing torrents of rain was coming our way.

"What the fuck is that, Talbot?" Dennis asked.

"Trouble," was all I could manage.

"What do we do? What do we do?" he repeated it quickly like maybe the answer would miraculously come to me the second time around.

I did the only thing I could. I kept moving up. There had

to be a way out of this, or we'd be seeing multiple wrecks down at the bottom of the chasm; of course, we couldn't see the bottom of the chasm. We watched in fascination as the curtain of rain marched toward us. It was just starting up the side of our mountain when I finally came to a widening in the road. When I say "widening," I mean a slight bulge. In the narrowest way possible, I did an eighteen point turn around, getting us headed back to sanctuary. By this time, the first fat droplets began to hit the windshield and I prudently decided to stay put in the relative safety the bump out afforded us. The droplets became a steady rain, and then a monsoon beat down. We weren't moving, and my wipers were on fast but could not keep up. Driving was out of the question. Want to know what we could see before the buildup of water on the window made it impossible to look out? Sure, you do. Our trail home was eroding. The deluge so vicious it was taking dirt and rock with it. Maybe it was attempting to show us our own, upcoming fate.

"That's probably not good," I said aloud as I pointed it out.

"How attached to this Jeep are you?" he asked. He wanted to walk out; I understood the sentiment, but we were pretty deep in the clutches of the Rocky Mountains and it would be many long hours in inclement weather attempting to break loose of her hold.

We held on until the rain stopped and the sun came back. The weather was acting like nothing at all had happened, but we'd witnessed her little tirade and wouldn't soon forget it. Dennis got out and I scooted over the gear shift to exit out his side as mine was up against the mountainside. We walked down the path a little; the ground wasn't too bad but I swear an inch or two had been shaved off of our precarious perch.

"Bud, if you want to wait behind the Jeep, that's cool. I'm going to give it a go," I said, looking at Dennis and to the next front rolling in.

"Seriously, Talbot?"

"How many choices you think we have?"

"Hypothermia doesn't sound all that bad when I'm looking at that cliff," he answered honestly.

"It's going to be in the thirties tonight. Might snow. We have long sleeve shirts on against the elements. It'll be a lot quicker this way."

"Really man? That's your fucking reasoning? Our deaths will be quicker?"

"My death will be; you'll be behind the Jeep, remember? You can hike out and, if you don't freeze to death, you can tell my wife where I ended up. Maybe we should hide the empties though, she'll be pissed if she thinks I was drinking."

"They'll do a toxicology report on you."

"Shit, what do you think we'd blow right now?"

"Definitely over the legal limit."

"How do you know that?"

"Because I'm drunk enough I'm going to get in the Jeep with you, and I can't imagine doing that fucking stone-cold sober or anywhere near it. Plus, man, if you die, I'm dying."

I got in and buckled up. Dennis followed behind, shut the door, and immediately grabbed the fuck me bar.

"Buckle up for safety," I told him.

"Will it make a difference?" he asked as he grabbed the belt.

"Doubt it," I answered as he clicked in.

"The next time you want to invite me to go four wheeling, don't."

"Roger that." I started the Jeep and began to creep forward. I had such a tight grip on the steering wheel the friction between my hand and the rubber covering was squelching. The next storm was barreling down on us; it was safe to say that at the two miles per hour I was traveling we weren't going to outpace it, but we could ill afford to be on the road as another inch was shaved off our path. As it was, three quarters of my driver's side tire was now hovering in space. No doubt we were on the verge of defying some laws of gravity or quantum physics, we just weren't smart enough to know that.

Another switchback and I was attempting to hug Dennis' side so much that my side view mirror was scraping up against the mountainside. At first, it was startling and I was somewhat upset at what I was doing to it, then I realized as long as I was still hearing that sound it meant we were still on the trail. The rain was trailing us this time, heavy droplets smacked on top of the plastic roof; it was loud enough to be hail. It swept over the front windshield, hood, and then onto the path where it started its relentless beating.

"Fuck, Talbot. This isn't how I wanted to go out."

"Who the fuck does," was what I answered without ever turning to him. I don't even think I was blinking, too afraid of what I might miss in that fraction of a second as my eyelid came down.

The squall was much smaller, but what it lacked in size it made up for in tenacity. It passed over us pretty quickly, but was taking chunks from the roadway. I watched as a pie-shaped wedge about a foot long dropped off the edge to settle some thousand feet below.

"We're not going to make it." Dennis was looking at the same thing I was. Like he was precognizant, the Jeep jolted and dipped down on my side. The edge was crumbling—we were going to go over. I did the only thing I could. I gunned it. At first, nothing, as I believe the wheels on my side weren't even touching ground. Then suddenly we lurched forward. Not sure if you've ever had the pleasure of driving a Jeep or riding in one, but even on the newest of roads it's somewhat like being in a washing machine with an unbalanced load, if that gives you a fair idea of what my vision looked like as we bounced and bounded over rocks and uneven terrain. We shouldn't have made it, plain and simple. The trail was maybe for mountain-biking; in any case, it wasn't wide enough. We were bouncing around like a super ball with a chunk out of it and I was going much too fast for the conditions. Tough to say which of us was paler when we got to the bottom—yeah, we got to the bottom. Dennis' hands were shaking as he handed me a beer. I popped the top off that thing, took a huge swig, and then started laughing my ass off. Dennis at first wanted nothing to do with it, but eventually, he joined in on the fun. We didn't say much on the ride home, both of us had just faced our mortality head on and were dealing with what we'd seen.

He gave me a hug when I dropped him off at his car and then flipped me off as he drove away. That very next week, I did something I hadn't done in ages: I bought the Sunday newspaper. No idea why. But on, like, page seven, there was a small article about two men that had died up on Waldorf pass; their cherry red Jeep had rolled from the top to crash land into an outcropping of rocks the size of a herd of elephants. I think on that sometimes. Had death felt cheated the day Dennis and I escaped? Had I somehow doomed those two men who died a few days after us? Like, maybe at the last minute I switched doors with them. Sometimes, things happen; they cannot be explained by you or any wiser source. Maybe those things are better left unsolved; the mysteries of life, its unpredictability, is what makes it all worth doing.

About The Author

Visit Mark at www.marktufo.com

Zombie Fallout trailer

https://youtu.be/FUQEUWy-v5o

For the most current updates join Mark Tufo's newsletter

http://www.marktufo.com/contact.html

Also By Mark Tufo

Zombie Fallout Series book 1 currently free

Lycan Fallout Series

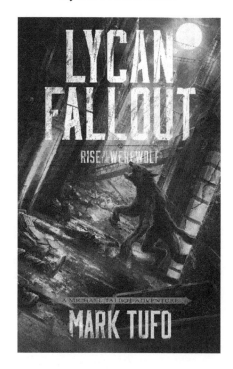

Indian Hill Series

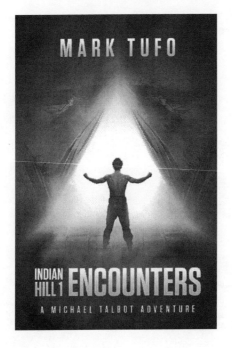

The Book Of Riley Series

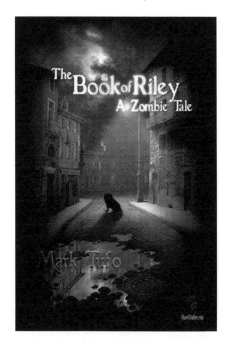

Also By Devil Dog Press

www.devildogpress.com

Burkheart Witch Saga By Christine Sutton

All That Remain By Travis Tufo

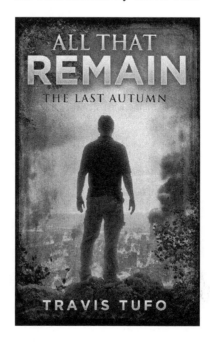

Nemesis by Suzanne Madron

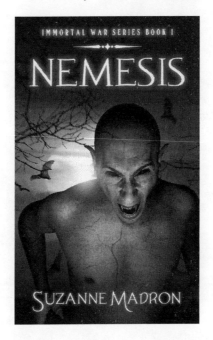

Prey By Tim Majka

Thank you for reading Zombie Fallout 11: Etna Station.. Gaining exposure as an independent author relies mostly on word-of-mouth; please consider leaving a review wherever you purchased this story.